Where the Light Plays

by C. Fonseca

Dedication

Jane. Thank you for all the countless hours you sacrificed so I could pursue my dream. With you beside me, my life is the perfect romance novel.

Acknowledgements

They say the road to a published novel is long and winding. Astrid Ohletz and the fantastic team at Ylva Publishing have made my journey so much easier. Astrid, thank you for your patience, nurturing, and support. Special thanks to my sensational editor, Jove Belle, aka *superwoman*; to project manager, Gill McKnight; and to my copy editor, CK King. I couldn't have got here without you.

There are many people who helped me along the way with this book. My friends Marlies, Paula, Carole, Kathryn, Fiona, Meryl, and Deb—I am incredibly grateful for your feedback and encouragement. Paula, I remember fondly the time spent with your family. Their example of growing, cooking, and sharing nutritious and simple food was inspirational.

To my family—I love you all. Thanks for your good humour and gentle nudges when I needed it.

I extend my sincere gratitude to my online lesfic family—to Salem West and the Rainbow Reader for re-establishing my love of reading and writing after a ten-year absence from fiction. You started me on my journey; watch this space…

Also to L.T. Smith and RJ Samuel for their messages and friendship. Linda, thank you so much for taking the time in your busy life to read that very rough first draft.

Thank you, reader for taking a chance on me. I hope you have as much fun reading this novel as I had writing it.

To Jane and Pia, for all your love and cuddles, I am forever grateful. Jane, your perseverance and unflagging optimism during the countless read-throughs was phenomenal. You really do deserve that gold star.

I am fortunate to have a home on the beautiful southern coastline of Victoria, Australia. I live and breathe this landscape everyday; it keeps me sane and provided a perfect backdrop for my first novel.

Chapter 1

Andi Rey meandered along the windswept beach and inhaled the sharp, salty air as the boom of breaking waves echoed in her ears. A gentle breeze ruffled Andi's dark-blonde hair and swept it into her eyes. She pushed it away instinctively. The tide was on its way out, exposing new treasures and leaving ripple patterns in its wake. Andi nudged her red Converse boot into the pale, golden sand to reveal tiny sparkling seashells. Plump balls of cottony-red seaweed blew across the water's edge, and newly created blue-green rock pools glistened with washed orange and brown pebbles. Ripples and reflections. This was nature's own magical canvas.

The beach was almost deserted, but Andi didn't feel the loneliness she'd experienced while living in Melbourne. In the city, she'd felt suffocated, hemmed in by thousands of people. She lifted her face and listened to the roar of the incoming tide, inhaling the fresh, clear air. Inspired by wide-open spaces and the beauty of her surroundings by the ocean, she had the latitude and breathing space she required; anything was possible.

Seagulls glided and swooped over the wave tops, shrieking as they followed shoals of fish. She marvelled at the tube-shaped spinning clouds; their movement cast ghostly shadows along the towering ochre cliffs that skirted the beach. Located between Gull Rock and Rocky Point, where the creek enters the strait through undulating sand dunes, Hakea, Andi's home, was renowned for its surf. The booming swells steeped over the shallow reefs and produced outstanding waves that dropped into the powerful Southern Ocean.

She picked up a smooth piece of sea-foam glass, rolled it through her fingers, and tucked it into her jacket pocket. As an artist working towards her first solo exhibition, she was experimenting with finely ground glass and sand mixed with acrylic paint. She used it to enhance the texture and increase the vibrancy of colours.

There were fewer tourists around than usual. The cooler-than-average temperatures and higher-than-average rainfall resulted in a slower start to spring and fewer visitors to Hakea.

A sudden gust of wind blew briny mist across the beach. Andi pulled the hood of her rain jacket around her damp hair and jogged towards the stairs.

As the rain started to fall in heavy droplets, she bounded up the wooden steps and reached the well-trodden path at the top of the cliff in record time. She dropped her hands to her knees and slowed her breathing. The rituals of running the steps, walking the beach, and surfing kept Andi healthy and connected to her surroundings. These activities provided structure to her otherwise free-flowing existence.

She jogged towards home along the shale track through lush ground layers of coastal grasses and wildflowers. Gold dust wattle trees dripped with clusters of bright-yellow balls, the abundant flowers that attracted flocks of yellow-tailed black cockatoo and crimson rosella to this coastal mosaic.

As she approached the popular wooden viewing platform that overlooked Gull Rock, she noticed a pair of shapely legs, clad in formfitting trousers, teetering unsteadily over the guardrail. She stared, wide eyed, momentarily mesmerised by the perplexing vision before her. It took far too long for Andi to register that the top half of the woman dangled over the cliff.

What the? The guardrail protected viewers from a ninety-metre drop onto the rocky foreshore and pounding waves. If she didn't take immediate action, the woman could fall and be injured. Or worse.

She ran towards her and grabbed the woman's calves firmly just above her two black leather ankle boots.

"Arrah…crikey, what the hell are you doing?" the woman yelled as Andi pulled her to safety. Andi didn't release her until her feet rested safely on the wooden deck. Before she could respond, the woman continued her rant. "Get away with you. What on earth did you do that for?" the woman cried out, her singsong Irish accent mimicking the shriek of the silver gull circling above.

Andi stepped back, letting her hands fall to her sides. Why was this woman so angry with her? She wasn't the one leaning over a safety rail trying to get herself killed. Was it too much to hope for a simple thank-you for saving this ridiculous woman's life? She swallowed the heated words that threatened to escape from her mouth and looked directly into fiery, dark-blue eyes.

Andi averted her gaze when she realised she was still staring into the eyes of a stranger. The woman was elegantly dressed and wore plaid wool trousers, but who wears *plaid* wool trousers to the beach?

"I was *this* close." The woman held up her hand centimetres from Andi's face, her finger and thumb almost touching each other. "My lens cap… I nearly had it… I was *this* close!" she repeated. Her voice was lilting and sweet, almost lyrical despite her angry words. She drew her graceful body to full height and leaned towards Andi menacingly. She was tall, undeniably beautiful, and *furious.*

Before Caitlin Quinn had time to stop her, the woman discarded her rain jacket and tossed it casually onto the ground. In one sweeping movement, she launched herself effortlessly over the barrier with the agility of a deer and disappeared into the void. It was startling to witness, even though she knew there was a ledge on the other side of the railing where her lens cap lay.

Why the hell did she go and do that? It was just a silly lens cap. Okay, she did make a fuss about the situation but really didn't expect the other woman to leap over the barrier after it. Caitlin wiped her hands on her trousers. Her clothes were wet and clung to her skin uncomfortably. She retrieved her camera from where she'd placed it under the bench on the platform, removed her jacket, and used the garment to protect it. Her white linen shirt soaked through in moments and was embarrassingly translucent. Tiny rivulets of water trickled along her neckline and down her back.

She moved towards the wooden handrail and sighed with relief when a hand came into view, clutching the lens cap. Caitlin blinked in disbelief as the woman swiftly leapt back over the barrier to land a few centimetres away from her.

Through the drizzle, a few persistent rays of sunlight hit the woman's short, wavy, dark-blonde hair. She wore a sodden, red T-shirt that hugged her subtle curves. Her loose fitting cargo pants sat low enough on her hips to show a hint of tanned, smooth skin along her midriff. She stood three or four centimetres shorter than Caitlin and grinned triumphantly as she presented her with the lens cap.

Caitlin's anger dissolved. It was impossible to hold on to it when standing face to face with this attractive woman and her irresistible smile. She allowed herself a moment to stare, and why wouldn't she? Caitlin wouldn't be alive if she didn't notice her agile, graceful figure and natural beauty.

A sudden flash of lightning and a rumble of thunder caught Caitlin by surprise. She looked up at the threatening sky with alarm, before she accepted the runaway lens cap from the woman's outstretched hand.

The woman stared at her. "You're not exactly dressed for what's coming. The rain will most likely get heavier." She spoke confidently as she angled her head towards the sky laden with heavy clouds. "Maybe you should take your lens cap and get under cover ASAP…and I hope your camera kit is waterproof."

Caitlin breathed a sigh of relief; she'd thought the woman was going to tell her to shove it.

Instead, she pulled her discarded raincoat over her wet clothes, dismissed Caitlin with a wave, and raced away along the pathway.

"Hey wait," Caitlin called. "I didn't thank you…What is your name?"

Rain pelted down on her; the huge drops forced Caitlin to clutch the camera gear and run to her car.

"I'm Andi. And you're welcome," she yelled from a distance.

"Thank you, Andi," she replied, but Andi was already gone. Caitlin hit the key fob, hastily opened the door, and fell into the plush leather seat of the BMW Roadster.

She grabbed a towel from the back seat and quickly wrapped it around her wet, tangled hair. She pulled the cold, drenched shirt away from her body as she turned the ignition and brought the engine to life with a low-pitched purr. She revved the car and pulled out onto the side road.

Her stereo came to life in the middle of London Grammar's latest release, and Caitlin hummed along with the smoky voice of the lead vocalist. The weather had caught her by surprise, and she hoped the rain wouldn't spoil her entire weekend. On the positive side, the woman, Andi, was just as unexpected but also thoroughly appealing.

Five minutes later, Caitlin slipped her Roadster into the garage, gathered her belongings from the rear seat, and walked towards the house as the timber garage door automatically closed behind her.

Her clothes were saturated and unpleasantly clammy in places. She needed a hot shower and a cold drink. Or should that be the other way around?

The encounter on the viewing platform was still on her mind. Andi had delivered the weather report as though she was a local. She was cute in her delivery, cheeky, and possibly excitable.

A shower would relax Caitlin's muscles, help her escape a fleeting dash of loneliness, and chase away the memory of those chocolate-brown eyes that flashed in sheer exasperation.

Caitlin was accustomed to rain. Spring on the Victorian coast was milder than at home in Cork. South-West Ireland experienced plenty of rain, averaging one hundred and fifty days annually—and there was the fog. She pictured the way the fog, moody and romantic, would lift over a patch of woodland as she crossed the River Lee and made her way from her apartment to the arts campus of University College. Caitlin grew nostalgic for her parents' house, situated near the dramatic and picturesque university grounds where it overlooked the river. Patrick, her English professor father, loved to quote Jerome K. Jerome, and he often did.

"But who wants to be foretold the weather? It is bad enough when it comes, without our having the misery of knowing about it beforehand."

Caitlin thought it wise to reserve her judgment on the mildness of this coastal climate. After all, she had yet to experience an Australian summer and all of this region's other weather extremes. She wasn't looking forward to facing the peak of the summer heat.

She climbed the stairs, unlocked the door, and punched in the alarm code as she stepped inside. Her eyes were drawn towards the floor-to-ceiling windows that enhanced the remarkable view from the cliff-top house. From this elevation, it was impossible not to notice the stunning outlook. No matter how many times she saw it, the rolling dunes and sweeping expanse of ocean took her breath away.

She kicked off her boots and peeled away her rain-soaked clothes as she walked into the luxury, ground floor bathroom.

Caitlin made it a point to exercise regularly. She ran at least three times a week and practiced yoga daily. She looked forward to running along the beach to improve her stride and was adamant about taking advantage of the pure sea air whenever she spent time at her grandaunt's house. Her grandaunt Isabella had named the property Kinsale, after her birthplace in Ireland.

Next April, Caitlin would be thirty-nine years old. Not quite forty, but not far off it. Thanks to a combination of exercise, a healthy diet, and good genes, she was in fine shape. Caitlin intended to stay that way.

The cascading double shower, built to cantilever over the cliff edge, was the perfect place to indulge herself. The 180-degree view was spectacular and one of her favourite features of the house.

Caitlin stood under the massaging jets, and the water soothed her restless spirit. She thought about Andi and grinned. Andi? Bambi? She's certainly as nimble and light footed as a deer. Caitlin hoped she wasn't offended by her outburst, because if she were a local, it would be nice to see her again. The way Andi stared at her with those passionate eyes made Caitlin wonder if she had a hot-blooded temperament to match. *She's attractive and fiery. Definitely cute.*

It was dinnertime when Caitlin finished her shower and pulled on her favourite pair of faded jeans and a sage-green, ribbed T-shirt. The sea air always made her hungry. A glass of red usually went down nicely too.

On her way from Melbourne to the coast, she'd abandoned the idea of buying fresh fruit and vegetables at the Queen Victoria Market, trying to avoid the heavy afternoon traffic. Shopping for provisions would have to wait until tomorrow. It was her fourth visit to Kinsale, and she looked forward to preparing simple meals from the fresh seafood and locally grown produce. But not tonight. Tonight, she was weary from her hectic week and the two-hour drive from Melbourne. Birdie's, the only café in Hakea, would provide a light meal, a glass of Pinot, and the possibility of some local distraction.

The sound of clinking glasses and laughter greeted Caitlin as she stepped into the café. She waved to the chef, Birdie, who dispensed drinks from behind the main bar. Birdie waved back and nodded in welcome as Caitlin made her way to one of the small tables by the window.

"I'll have a glass of Jack Rabbit pinot noir, the salmon with roasted fennel, and a spinach salad, please." Caitlin thanked the server as he moved away. She scanned the room, drawn towards the chatter coming from a group standing at the bar.

Andi?

There she was, the woman Caitlin had met earlier. She leaned against the bar with her thumbs casually tucked in the loops of her black cargo pants. As if she sensed Caitlin's presence, she turned. Their gazes met across the room, and Andi grinned shyly in recognition. She lowered her eyes, absent-mindedly pushing a lock of hair from her face.

Caitlin watched as Birdie handed Andi a glass of red wine and a schooner of pale ale.

"Two glasses? Who's the wine for, Birdie?" Andi asked.

Birdie replied, "Would you be a darling and deliver the wine to the table by the window?"

Andi took a quick gulp of the amber ale before she strode across the room. As she looked directly at Caitlin, she fumbled and nearly spilled the wine.

That was a close call. Luckily it didn't land in her lap. Caitlin was relieved she wasn't wearing the wine, but she enjoyed the flush that crept across Andi's face.

Andi placed the glass down gently and stood at the table. Her hand trembled as she circled the icy rim of the beer glass with her index finger. Caitlin wondered if *she* was making Andi nervous.

"Hi."

"Hello again, and thank you. It is Andi, isn't it? I'm Caitlin." She casually picked up her wine glass, lifted it to her lips, and let her gaze roam over Andi's body. "I didn't expect to see you again so soon. Do you work here?"

"Kath-leen?" asked Andi.

"That is the correct pronunciation, but you can call me Cait-lin; everyone I've met in Australia does."

"Nice to meet you, Caitlin."

Andi shifted her weight from one foot to the other, her canvas shoes squeaking against the wooden floorboards. She placed her drink on the table and wiped her hands along the front of her trousers. "I do live here, and I've been known to assist Birdie from time to time but not generally, no." She smiled shyly. "I'm not on staff."

Caitlin grinned. "So I'm just lucky, then?"

Andi looked relieved when the waiter delivered Caitlin's meal and said, "Can I bring you anything else now? Condiments?"

She shook her head. As the waiter stepped away, he winked at Andi, and Caitlin wondered about the significance of his gesture.

"Maybe you'd consider joining me? I'd like to thank you for saving my lens..." Her voice trailed off as Andi turned towards the door. A woman had just stepped inside the café.

"Sorry, I can't tonight. I'm actually waiting for a friend, and here she is." Andi gestured towards the woman who shook out her raincoat and pulled off her speckled beanie to reveal a head of short, brown hair.

"So much for our sunny spring weekend," the newcomer said, as she looked around the room and briefly focused on Caitlin before her gaze finally settled on Andi.

Caitlin could tell by the way she smiled affectionately at Andi that she was a special friend.

Birdie called out, "Doc, it's good to see you... It's been ages. Too busy playing doctor and saving lives, eh?"

She turned towards Birdie. "Of course, but more like working double shifts and being too darn tired to move when I get time off. Now," she placed her hands on the bar, "I could use a Scotch, single malt, straight up, and some of your excellent food." She moved to Andi's side, grabbed her around the waist, pulled her into a crushing embrace, and lifted her off the ground.

Caitlin watched as Andi wriggled and moved her feet in the air.

"Ellie, put me down," Andi cried out. Caitlin observed the exchange and contemplated the nature of their friendship.

"Is that any way to greet me?" The woman returned Andi to the floor. "Are you ready for dinner? I'm starving."

Andi's friend peered over Andi's shoulder and stared at Caitlin curiously.

Andi spun around and looked at Caitlin, one hand clutching Ellie's arm. "I should introduce you. This is Ellie. Ellie, this is Caitlin. I met Caitlin today on the platform above Gull Rock."

Caitlin held out her hand. "Nice to meet you, Ellie."

"Likewise, nice to meet you too." Ellie smiled charmingly and took Caitlin's hand.

She glanced at Andi and then back to Ellie and wondered if this was Andi's girlfriend. Disappointing as it was, she supposed it was inevitable that Andi would have a girlfriend.

"Tim has my order already," Andi said to Ellie. "Seeing as you're starving, why don't you tell him what you'd like, and I'll be with you soon?"

Ellie shrugged casually and headed towards the bar.

When Andi turned her attention back to her, Caitlin raised her glass and said, "I won't keep you, and it was nice to see you again. Thank you for saving me this afternoon."

"No problem. Enjoy your dinner."

"Since you're from around here, we may run into each other again," Caitlin said. Her gaze followed Andi as she made her way across the room and sat at a table for two. She thought it would be grand to know Andi, even if she was not available for further exploration. A woman, especially one as attractive as Andi, would have been perfect to help her wile away the evening hours here in Hakea.

Andi waited patiently for Ellie as she chatted to Jim and Dave at the bar. They were tradesmen, local plumbers, who spent all their spare time surfing. Dave swept his shaggy, bleached-blonde hair off his forehead as he made some statement about Aussie rules football and speculated about their team's chances of making the finals later this month.

After she finished her conversation, Ellie approached her with a mischievous grin on her face. She had lost even more weight, and her hazel eyes looked tired with dark shadows beneath them. Probably a result of too much work and not enough play. All the same, she looked striking in denim jeans and a black turtleneck sweater, and Andi hoped that time away from the hospital over the next two days would help Ellie relax and get the rest she obviously needed.

"Why are you looking at me like that?" Ellie smiled as she leaned over to brush her lips across Andi's cheek.

"Since when have you been interested in football?" Andi asked.

Ellie pulled her chair closer and grinned. "Who do you think she barracks for?" She inclined her head towards Caitlin.

"Don't be ridiculous. She's Irish," said Andi with a smirk.

Ellie raised an eyebrow. "You know what I mean. Does she play on *our* team?"

Andi blushed.

"Well, who is she?" Ellie asked as she ran her hand through her hair. "Come on, spill it… and please start at the beginning."

Andi sighed. "Not much to tell you. I met her this afternoon on the platform at Gull Rock. I don't know much more than that, sorry." Andi leaned across the table and lowered her voice. "She's interesting, don't you think?" She pretended to survey the room as an excuse to glance across at the intriguing woman.

Ellie's gaze followed Andi's, and she gave Caitlin a quick once-over. "Very, with those long legs and lovely wavy strands of dark hair. She's gorgeous. Big blue eyes, *very* nice body, *and* an Irish accent… Is that what you're asking about?"

"Ellie, you're staring." She agreed. Caitlin was gorgeous, but it was easy to get caught up in the whirlpool of attraction when someone was so far out of reach. And Caitlin was clearly out of Andi's league. Dream on.

Ellie placed her hand over Andi's and gave her a comforting squeeze. "Pity, I think she's leaving. We should have invited her over to our table for a drink. What do you think, Andi? Shall we?"

They both watched as Caitlin stepped out the door.

"Too late Ellie. She's gone."

Chapter 2

Andi woke to spring sunshine filtering through the slatted blinds. She rubbed the sleep from her eyes and flattened the pillow with her fist so she had a better view of Ellie, who was burrowed snugly under the covers, sound asleep. Andi smiled and reached over to gently trace Ellie's cheek with her finger, careful not to wake her. She looked so content and peaceful.

Something tickled the back of Andi's knees, and she placed her hand on warm, silky fur. She lifted back the sheet to see Koda curled up, and at the touch of her hand, the cat purred loudly.

"Good morning, Koda," she whispered. Koda gave her finger a friendly bite. "Ouch!" Andi pulled her hand back and rolled out of bed. Koda settled next to Ellie and nestled in along the curve of her hip.

Andi reached for her clothes, dressed quietly, and made her way through her studio and into the living room.

Half an hour later, Ellie appeared at the doorway. Andi peered over the newspaper from where she sat on the sofa and smiled as Ellie pulled her long, white T-shirt down over her legs. Her feet looked snug in Andi's worn, woollen Ugg boots.

"Hmm…just what I need. There's nothing better than the smell of freshly brewed coffee," Ellie murmured.

"Good morning, sunshine. Sleep well?" Andi held out her empty mug and gestured towards the kitchen. "Coffee's on. I'm ready for a refill."

Ellie rolled her eyes. "What did your last slave die of?" She filled two mugs from the drip coffee maker. "I slept so well, I may even join you on your run this morning." She placed the steaming beverages on the side table and elbowed Andi. "Shove over," she said as she sat down and stretched her long frame beside her. "Yum, this is good."

"Yeah, thanks to you." Andi would have never bought a coffee machine as expensive as this one for herself. It had been Ellie's present to Andi just a few weeks ago, on her thirtieth birthday. It was easy to use, made great coffee, and was beautifully designed. Andi loved things that were beautifully put together.

"Are you up for the seven k run along the cliff-top? I'd like to check the swell down at the point. The rain and onshore wind has kept me out of the surf for ages," Andi said.

"I could easily crawl back into bed and sleep for the rest of the day, but yep, I'm up for it. Just let the caffeine work its magic." Ellie laid her head back against the sofa and sighed as she hugged her coffee mug against her chest.

Andi folded the newspaper and placed it on the table. "I'm glad you could make it this weekend. I've missed you." She gave Ellie a concerned look. "You're exhausted. Are you still working those ridiculously long hours? You were asleep five minutes after your head hit the pillow last night."

Ellie rubbed her eyes. "These are the joys of surgical residency. I've missed you too, but it will get better. I'm nearly through the worst of it now." She raised her eyebrows and playfully prodded Andi with her toe. "Tell me more about Ms. sultry, seductive Ireland. She did ask you to have dinner with her, didn't she? She's not shy."

"I guess. She was just thanking me for saving her life," Andi said. "Look, I don't even know where she's staying, and I'll probably never see her again."

"Aww...Didn't she slip you her phone number? What is her story, I wonder? Hey, maybe she dropped in on a paraglider. Or rode in on her white horse."

Andi bent down to run her hand over Koda's soft tummy. The playful Burmese cat sat pressed against her leg and nudged her lovingly. "Or maybe she's a traveller just passing through or has a husband, children, girlfriend. Look, the possibilities are endless."

Ellie placed an arm around her shoulder, and Andi shifted into her embrace. Ellie asked, "How long's it been. Andi? Over a year since Martha went back to Germany? Don't you think it's time to get back out there? Start dating again."

She rested her head against Ellie's shoulder. "I think about it sometimes, I do. It's not like I *haven't* dated since Martha left, but there's been no one special."

Ellie smirked. "Let's see. First there was your weekend with the Hawaiian pro surfer. That was a *wipeout*, wasn't it? Then your fling with Freya, the Danish backpacker. An international smorgasbord."

Andi scowled. "Anyway, I've been trying to work on my exhibition and build some financial security. You know how it is. Things just get in the way."

"I understand all about financial security, but a girl's got to have some fun. And that woman looks like a *lot* of fun."

"More like a lot of trouble," said Andi as she bounced up from the sofa. "Come on, let's get a move on. Are you running in a T-shirt and my Ugg boots or slipping into some track pants?" She grabbed Ellie by the arm and pulled her to her feet. "Let's get out there and see if you've improved your running times."

"Just go easy on me; remember, I don't get a chance to run as often as you do. Especially on the sand in the fresh air by the sea."

"Excuses, excuses." Andi laughed and headed out the front door. "I'll wait for you out in the sunshine, *sunshine*. Don't be long."

It was so good that Ellie had finally taken time out from work. Andi had hardly seen her over the last few months. She knew that Ellie was dedicated and loved her work, but lately, when they had spoken on the phone, she'd sounded so tired. Andi hoped that their time together this weekend would give her friend the respite she needed.

Caitlin steered the blue Roadster along the winding road towards Aireys Inlet. With the rooftop down, she revelled in the warm morning sun as it danced against her skin. The day had warmed considerably to a comfortable twenty degrees. After yesterday's rain, the air was fresh, and everything appeared lush and pure. She looked forward to visiting Black-Tern, the art gallery Isabella had told her about that showcased the works of established and emerging artists from this region.

The fresh smell of eucalyptus trees and a hint of ocean air filled her senses. As the road zigzagged out of the ironbark forest, with its sparse understorey of wattles and shrubs, Caitlin caught sight of the stark, white tower and the red cap of Split Point Lighthouse against the clear azure sky. She was far away from home, but the sight of the lighthouse was a comfort. It stood like a beacon, a symbol of strength and a safe harbour. She intended to photograph it later in the day.

Caitlin had her day all planned out. After she'd visited the gallery, she would treat herself to a late lunch at one of the nearby restaurants and then take a walk along the beach. She'd done her research and knew the short track to Eagle Rock Marine Sanctuary would give her the best views west, towards the wide beaches of Fairhaven and Lorne.

Caitlin pulled into the empty car park; she appeared to be the only visitor. She entered the foyer and had little chance to take in the environment before an elegant woman, who Caitlin guessed to be in her midsixties, appeared by her side. The woman had the imperious look of an art gallery curator. Caitlin knew it well.

"Welcome to Black-Tern. I'm Cynthia." With an enthusiastic smile, she handed Caitlin a catalogue. "Have a look around and let me know if I can help you at all."

"I'll be fine, Cynthia. I'm looking forward to exploring, and I'm in no hurry." She accepted the catalogue. "I'll take my time and come back to you if I need more information."

"Oh, you're Irish, aren't you?" she stated the obvious and tilted her head quizzically.

Caitlin nodded. "Hmm…that I am."

"Are you holidaying in Australia?" Cynthia asked.

"I'm currently working in Melbourne, but I like to spend time here on the coast when I can."

"In that case, I'm so glad you found the gallery, and I hope you enjoy our collection."

Caitlin moved towards the front room. The space was filled with a mixture of small seascapes in oil and acrylic, print works of flora and fauna, some mixed media, and a few framed black and white photographs of Split Point Lighthouse. She ran her fingers gently over the small carvings of echidnas, wombats, and lizards made of ironwood. Caitlin frowned and pushed her hair from her eyes. Nearly everything she'd seen so far was aimed at the tourist market. Quaint and well executed, they nevertheless lacked the complexity and cutting-edge freshness that she looked for when visiting an art gallery.

As she turned back towards the entrance, a luminous glow drew Caitlin towards an open doorway. "Wow," she exclaimed. She walked into an intimate space that displayed only four works of art. "Now, this is more like it—the good stuff."

Three landscapes that focused on the environment graced the left wall. But it was the radiance and luminosity from one sizeable painting on the opposite wall that really captured Caitlin's attention.

"You have a good eye."

Taken by surprise, Caitlin turned around and blinked. Out of nowhere Cynthia had reappeared.

"Simply magical, isn't it?"

"It is," Caitlin agreed and turned back to move closer to the painting. A sweeping receding tide, wet sand, ochre cliffs, and a majestically undulating sea drew her into a seascape reflecting intensity and passion. It looked as though the broad textured strokes were produced through direct use of a palette knife. Whoever had done this knew what he, or she, was doing.

"It is one of my favourites of *this* particular artist's work. The painting is part of my own collection," Cynthia commented.

Caitlin dragged her gaze away from the canvas. "Who is the artist?" She glanced through the catalogue.

"Andréa Rey. We have shown a number of her smaller works over the last few years. Andréa did take a hiatus for over twelve months before producing this particular piece. I am impressed by the quality of her work."

When she found the details of the painting in the catalogue, Caitlin's skin tingled. What luck, Andréa's studio was in Hakea. "It says here she's based in Hakea. Do you think it would it be okay for me to visit? Looks like it worked, whatever she did during her break."

"She does live close by; I'll be happy to give you her email address." Cynthia moved towards the front desk, and Caitlin followed. "Perhaps you can arrange a visit. Andréa is truly a delightful woman; I'm sure she wouldn't mind." She handed Caitlin a business card on which she had handwritten Andréa's email address. "Do you know Hakea?"

Caitlin nodded. "Fortunately, I'm staying there at a friend's house." She didn't feel inclined to tell Cynthia that she was Isabella's grandniece, because she wanted to avoid the inevitable interrogation. Her aunt was too well known for a local not to be curious about her.

"You're in luck, then."

"If you don't mind, I will go back and take another look at the painting. Thank you so much for giving me Andréa's email address."

"You're welcome. You may be interested to know she is currently working on her first solo exhibition. I can't wait to see the direction she's taking," Cynthia said and then added, "If you're looking for a place to eat this afternoon, Demetrio's at the lighthouse has an utterly marvellous lunch menu."

"Thank you so much." Caitlin smiled. "Sounds wonderful, I may just do that." She turned and walked back towards the painting that had both soothed her and sparked pleasure.

The risotto of local seafood cooked with arborio rice, white wine, and dill, finished with mascarpone, was absolutely delicious. Caitlin licked her lips in appreciation. Cynthia had been right about the views from the restaurant and Demetrio's menu. The risotto was cooked to perfection. She sat back, took a sip of her espresso, and relished the smooth, rich Marocchino with a sprinkling of cacao and milk foam.

Caitlin reached into her pocket to extract the business card with Andréa's email address. She was intrigued by the artist's work, and now that Caitlin knew Andréa lived in Hakea, she was keen to meet her. She picked up her iPhone, added the address into her contacts list, and tapped out an email. So, who is she? There was only one way to find out.

To: a.rey@gmail.com
Subject: Come To Light

Hi Andréa,
I just visited the Black-Tern Gallery, where I had the pleasure of seeing your painting, Come to Light. Cynthia, the manager, mentioned it might be possible to visit your studio? I'm in Hakea for the next few days, and if it's convenient, I am interested to view more of your work.
Yours sincerely,
C. Quinn

P.S. Your painting has brought A. Rey of light into my day.

Half an hour later, Caitlin descended the narrow steps from the lighthouse to the beach below. She wandered along the sand, shoes in one hand and camera around her neck, simply taking pleasure in the rolling surf and spectacular views of the Otway Ranges. Her phone vibrated, alerting her to incoming email.

To: cquinn@bella.org
Subject: Come To Light

Thank you for your interest. If you are in the area tomorrow, I currently have a small number of paintings at the studio and will be happy for you to view them. A ray of light?
Thank you. I hope you won't be disappointed.
A.Rey

P.S. Studio A. Rey. Follow the road to the end of Surfview Court, at the start of the reserve. Any time after midday.

Caitlin returned her phone to her pocket. With a new burst of energy, she lifted her camera to her eye. Using the razor-sharp lens, she set about taking photographs of the coastal landscape. She captured some interesting rock formations and, from a changed perspective, took several shots of the lighthouse set against the horizon.

She recalled the absolute radiance and force of Andréa's painting. There was something about it that made her feel less solitary and heightened Caitlin's awareness of her surroundings. Cynthia mentioned Andréa had a tendency to be a bit reclusive, but she hadn't hesitated to invite her to the studio. Caitlin was curious, and her visit tomorrow would be a sure way to find out more about the mysterious artist.

Chapter 3

Caitlin glanced at her watch and was surprised that her walk along the pathway from Kinsale to Andréa's studio had taken less than twenty-five minutes. The path was a scenic route that traversed the cliff from one end of the town to the other, with fantastic views of the ocean.

She entered through a garden filled with native flowering shrubs and a scattering of sculptural, black-trunked *xanthorrhoea* grass trees. Caitlin approached the studio under a canopy of graceful hanging branches, soft green leaves, and clusters of feathery flowers. She brushed past the foliage, and the air filled with the sweet smell of lemon and lime. She inhaled deeply to enjoy the perfume. The fragrance was tangy and intoxicating.

The exterior of the studio was modest but striking. Caitlin wasn't surprised to see solar panels on the blue-grey, sloping roof. They were a feature on nearly every house in Hakea.

A small, beige cat wearing a bright-red collar and tag greeted Caitlin at the top of the timber stairs. The cat stared suspiciously and slinked towards her with slow, graceful movements.

"Hello, little one. Aren't you beautiful…are you a Burmese? I think you are." She bent down to stroke the cat, and it closed its eyes and rubbed its head against Caitlin's wrist.

Before she reached the brass bell, the door swung open. Caitlin stared with a mixture of surprise and disbelief.

"Andi?"

The puzzled look on Andi's face soon gave way to a broad grin. Time stood still as they gazed at one another, and when Andi blinked, her intense brown eyes fleetingly disappeared behind long lashes.

"C. Quinn?"

Caitlin returned Andi's smile. "It is I, Caitlin Quinn. Well, this is serendipitous." It really was. Caitlin had envisioned the reclusive artist Cynthia had spoken about to be many things. She had pictured an eccentric, antisocial, spectacled woman with wild hair. Wrong, wrong, wrong. Andréa Rey was gorgeous.

"It is unexpected, isn't it?" Andi asked. "Please, come in. I see you've already met Koda. Just watch out. If she likes you, you'll have beige hair all over those dark trousers." Andi ran her hand through her hair as she stood aside to welcome Caitlin into the studio. They both stepped inside, followed closely by the friendly little feline.

"She is beautiful, and a bit of fur doesn't bother me. Thank you so much for letting me visit today," Caitlin said as she took in her surroundings. Visiting an artist's studio allowed a glimpse into their private world, and she certainly was curious about *this* artist's private world. Andi appeared to have a quiet strength. A body that was strong, yet fluid in movement. As Caitlin stepped closer to her, electricity seemed to spark through her own body.

Andi grinned shyly. "That's cool. I haven't had any visitors at the studio for a while. I was pleased to receive your email and surprised to see you again."

A happy surprise, she hoped. "Cynthia explained that you're recently back at work after taking some time off. Is this your home too?" she asked as she looked around the large room that included a comfortable lounge area and a doorway leading to a small kitchen. The high roof space, ceiling fans, and natural light filtering through diffused, overhead skylight panels created a perfect space for painting.

"Yes, this is my studio and my home."

Caitlin couldn't help but admire Andi's bohemian attire—paint-splattered jeans and a polka dotted T-shirt. She was sexy. Caitlin averted her gaze; she had been staring. "You've created a fantastic working environment here." She smiled warmly at Andi. "It really is nice to see you again, and bizarre, don't you think?"

"It's totally random," Andi said. "So, would you like to look around now?"

They stood before the rough-hewn planks that formed Andi's workbench. It was covered with splashes of paint and, like a canvas, told its own story. Two stainless steel trolleys held art supplies, multiple pots of acrylic paint, boxes of brushes, rollers, and palette knives of all sizes. On the top of the bench lay a large rectangular painting.

"Work in progress," explained Andi.

Caitlin looked at the painting. The unfinished work appeared to consist of urgent gestural strokes that conveyed the energy and movement of the sea, of shifting light, and of blurred skies.

Andi slowly traced one finger over the canvas surface. "I love the water. But when it's like this, big and turbulent, the moody sea and the sky is ever changing. I'm in awe, and it terrifies me." She looked directly at Caitlin. "This is a piece for my exhibition next December." Her voice had an enticing rhythm, a mix of calm and fierce energy. She spoke with such passion, and Caitlin wondered if that intensity was only reserved for her art.

"And the exhibition would be where?"

"At the Watershed in Geelong, a private gallery that exhibits mainly artists from this region. It's on the old pier, and the harbour is an excellent backdrop. Do you know Geelong at all?"

Caitlin shook her head. On her visits to Kinsale, Caitlin took the ring road that diverted around Geelong. It was the second largest city in Victoria, located on the shores of Port Phillip Bay, but she hadn't yet taken the time to explore.

"The waterfront is worth visiting. Lots of good restaurants and cafés, the art deco pool is fun for a dip in summer," Andi said.

Caitlin hovered over Andi's shoulder to examine the painting. She felt unusually tongue-tied. It was unsettling being in close proximity to Andi. Her sun-streaked hair was just long enough to brush the base of her neck. With her finely muscled shoulders just a few centimetres away, Caitlin inhaled her subtle fragrance of citrus and sandalwood. She breathed out slowly, reminded herself she was here to look at the artworks, and placed a serious look on her face.

"The painting at Black-Tern is breathtaking. I'm curious—would you tell me what inspired you to paint *Come to Light*?" That seascape was a combination of intense light and raw emotion, and it exuded the same visceral physicality and energy as Andi's unfinished work.

Andi turned, and Caitlin stepped back to wait for an answer. Andi leaned up against the workbench with her arms folded tightly across her chest. "My

inspiration? I don't know if it was any *one* thing." She pushed her hands into her pockets. "I went through a bit of a slump, and I couldn't paint for a while. At the time, I was so disconnected that I was only just managing to keep up with my design work."

Caitlin tilted her head to one side. What had caused Andi's separation from something she was clearly so passionate about? "What changed?" she asked softly.

"After months of no motivation and wandering around aimlessly, I started reconnecting with the landscape, especially the sea. And it suddenly became important to create something tangible and familiar. I pulled out a large canvas and thought, 'This is it.'"

Caitlin nodded. The painting reflected the absorption and scattering of light. "That's why you called it *Come to Light*. It was you emerging from your fog?"

Andi hesitated. "Yes, that was the turning point. I was lucky Cynthia appreciated my shift in style, especially since I hadn't shown her anything new for over a year."

Caitlin recalled that Cynthia displayed quite a proprietary attitude to the painting. "She must really love it, because she immediately told me it was not for sale." Smiling, she added, "I am really looking forward to seeing more of your work."

Andi grinned and lowered her eyes self-consciously.

Caitlin watched, amused, as Andi shifted from one leg to the other, her gaze fixed down at her bare feet. She looked vulnerable, a little uncertain, which made her even more intriguing. Passion seemed to simmer below the surface. Caitlin moved back to the art trolley. She needed to change her focus again.

"I see you are mixing your own pigments," she said. Many jars of dry powders, mediums, additives, and fillers such as mica, quartz, and ground glass were arranged on the art trolley.

Sixteenth century Renaissance pigments and painting techniques had fascinated Caitlin during her research sojourn in Venice. "Are you using glass in your paintings as a reflective medium, like the paintings of the old masters?"

Andi glanced at Caitlin curiously. "I've been experimenting with ground glass, mixing it in with raw pigment. It alters the shade and luminosity. Making my own paint allows me to get the precise hue and shade I need." She gestured towards the canvas on her workbench. "I can't always do it, but I did for this painting."

"It must give you a much finer degree of control and exactness."

"That's it exactly. Of course, mixing my own paint is much more affordable. Art materials can be so expensive."

"How do you manage? This piece is large. It takes a lot of paint to cover a canvas this size, and the finishes are costly too." Caitlin hoped that her question wasn't too personal.

Andi moved away from her art bench. Hands in her pockets, she appeared deep in thought. "I manage." She shrugged. "When I lived in Melbourne, I worked for a small graphic design company. They do a lot of work for businesses on the Surf Coast—surfboard manufacturers, clothing designers, and sports travel. When I moved to Hakea, I continued to work with them on projects from home. It gives me flexibility and earns me enough money to pursue this." She spread her arms wide to encompass her studio.

"It must be fantastic to live and work in a purpose-built space," Caitlin said.

"It definitely has its advantages. I love the feeling of stepping over the threshold each morning from my living space into my own creative space." Andi pointed to the various areas of her home. "A small galley kitchen is on the right. My bedroom and bathroom are on the left, and the storeroom and laundry are off the back deck. I don't need much more," she concluded. "I spend a lot of time outdoors, surfing and walking. I don't usually run off at the mouth like this. Please, excuse me." Andi spun around on one foot. "Can I get you a coffee or tea? Then, if you'd like, I can show you some of the paintings in the storeroom."

"You look like a surfer girl," Caitlin said. The words escaped before she could stop them. "I would love a cup of tea." Andi did look like a surfer girl, with her hair all tousled and kissed by the sun and her golden skin visible below the hem of her T-shirt. Caitlin cleared her throat and met Andi's shy but amused look.

"Okay, I'll get the tea. Make yourself comfortable, and I'll be back in a minute."

Caitlin wondered what drove her creativity. She looked forward to learning more about the artist and the woman who seemed so refreshingly natural and connected to her surroundings.

Filtered sunlight filled the entire space with even natural light. The room was divided into three functional areas. On one side, a rectangular table held a large iMac, A3 printer, assorted notebooks, and colour swatches. Caitlin glanced up at the high-angled roof and floor-to-ceiling windows; they made the area seem much larger than it actually was.

To the left of the entrance, tucked into a corner, were a small log burner, a half-wall library, and a reading nook. It looked really cosy.

Caitlin sat down at one end of an orange sofa. Andi's home was stylish and eclectic and felt homely and comfortable. The afternoon's visit had taken an altogether more interesting turn the moment she'd discovered Andréa Rey's identity.

Andi poured tea from a red and white spotted teapot into two matching cups. "If you had signed your email as Caitlin, I may have guessed who you were," she said. "But C. Quinn? That gave me no clue at all."

Caitlin laughed. "I am sorry. That was my mistake. When I sent the email from my iPhone, I must have removed the digital signature with my full name."

"Well, that explains it. Are you a *quin*?"

Caitlin smirked as she accepted the cup from Andi. "No, there's only one of me. I'm not a twin, nor a triplet, or a quadruplet. I am, in fact, an only child. "

Andi looked over at Caitlin. "And you have a sense of humour too."

Caitlin raised her eyebrows. She hoped to convey that she was enjoying their easy banter. "I try. This is grand. Thank you for the tea."

Andi settled herself into a chair across from Caitlin, her tanned legs tucked up under herself and one arm draped over the back of the chair. "No worries."

"Have you lived here long?"

"I found this half-acre block of land just over four years ago. I loved it straight away, because it borders the reserve. The green belt runs through Hakea down to the beach, where the creek ends."

"You are so close to the surf beach. That would be a huge advantage for a surfer girl," Caitlin teased. It was good to see Andi relax and be comfortable with her.

"Yes, it was perfect for the lifestyle I wanted. Before I changed my mind, I used my savings and bought it. Then I lived in a caravan on site for the first six months while the studio was being built."

"Was it designed by an architect? It seems perfectly laid out to suit your needs."

"I knew what I wanted, so I drew up the plans." Andi shrugged her shoulders like it was no special achievement.

Caitlin leaned back into the sofa and allowed herself to admire Andi, who had placed her hands gracefully in her lap. She had beautiful, expressive artist's hands. Strong and slender. Just the thought of those hands on her sent a shudder of longing through her body.

As Andi held her gaze for a fleeting moment, Caitlin wondered if she could read her thoughts.

"My brother, Luc, was the builder. His company specialises in eco-friendly builds, so it was a no-brainer."

"Does your brother live in Hakea too?"

"No, Luc and the rest of my family live in country Victoria, near Ballarat. Have you heard of a small town called Navigators?" Caitlin shook her head, and Andi continued, "It's not far from an extinct volcano called Mt. Buninyong. The area is known for its rich volcanic soil; it's perfect for vegetable and fruit growing." Her eyes twinkled. "Am I sounding like a travel brochure?"

"That's good. I want to learn all I can. Navigators, that's an interesting name."

"I think it has something to do with the rail link from Melbourne to Ballarat."

"I'll add it to my growing list. It sounds like another place to visit."

Andi stood with the teapot poised over Caitlin's empty cup. "Top up?"

Caitlin nodded and waited for Andi to settle back into her chair. For a few minutes they sat quietly and listened to the occasional shrieking of birds, while Koda scuffled across the timber floor in pursuit of a soft toy.

"She's pretty cute. Is she still a kitten?" Caitlin asked, as Koda leapt onto the back of the sofa, almost causing her to spill her tea.

Koda slinked over and purred as she headbutted Caitlin's shoulder.

"She's four years old, very energetic, but she'll always be my baby," Andi said, looking affectionately at the beige ball of fluff.

Oh yes, there was no doubt that Andréa Rey could be a very attractive, enticing diversion while Caitlin was in Hakea.

Chapter 4

Andi took particular care in the way she dressed for dinner. The dark-grey tunic top over a pale-lilac shirt, combined with black renegade pants, looked sharp yet felt comfortable. She glanced at her reflection in the mirror. Satisfied with her outfit, Andi rearranged her hair and shook out the loose, untidy strands. Tonight, her hair was a perfect expression of her inner feelings—messy.

"Why does she make me so nervous?" she muttered. She had chosen her clothes because she wanted to feel confident—not because she wanted to impress.

Earlier that afternoon, Caitlin had studied her paintings, unhurriedly examining the ten completed works to be included in the exhibition. Andi had left Caitlin in the storeroom to explore the preliminary line drawings and works on paper. She'd returned to her desk and worked at her computer while she waited for Caitlin.

Andi played with an illustration—the new logo for a surfboard manufacturer in Hakea. The company made wooden boards to order and wanted the logo to exude "colour and groove." She'd used a cedar surfboard herself and had experienced the special connection and joy of riding a handcrafted board. She wanted to create an artistic motif that would speak for itself.

Andi felt a hand on her shoulder; she jumped and swung around in her chair.

"Far out!" she cried.

Caitlin's hand remained in place for several seconds, before she trailed it across Andi's bare shoulder and down her arm. "I'm so sorry. Did I scare you?"

"I didn't hear you come back inside," Andi whispered and withdrew from her touch. Caitlin moved to the sofa, and Andi followed to sit in the chair across from her. Caitlin leaned across the coffee table to take Andi's hands, and her forefinger moved slowly over Andi's knuckles. Andi could barely breathe. What was she doing?

"I think your use of colour and style are unique. I can't wait to see more as you work towards your exhibition in December." Caitlin's sincere words eased her tension.

Andi had accepted Caitlin's last-minute invitation to dinner without hesitation. As most of their afternoon together had been spent talking about her art, tonight she wanted to discover a little more about the enigmatic and captivating Irish woman.

At six forty five, she took a deep breath to calm her jittery nerves as she pulled on her white canvas boots. She added a simple emerald and silver wire necklace, tucked a slim wallet into her back pocket, grabbed her phone, and headed out the door. It wasn't a date, but dinner with Caitlin Quinn was probably the closest thing to one in a long while.

Andi arrived at Birdie's Café just after seven fifteen. The handful of patrons were residents. She made her way to her favourite table by the window, thankful that the hordes of weekend visitors had already left the coast and returned to the city. It was Birdie's night off, but Andi was confident that no matter which chef was on duty tonight, the food would be excellent. She swirled the wine in her glass, brought it slowly to her lips, and waited for Caitlin.

A sleek, blue BMW Roadster pulled into the car park. The broad tyres skidded on the loose gravel, the headlights dimmed, and the engine purred to a stop. *Nice car.*

The driver's door opened, and one elegant leg appeared, followed by another. Andi moved closer to the window to get a better view. She held her breath.

The soft, diffused lighting in the car park illuminated Caitlin's face.

"Oh my God," Andi murmured.

Caitlin entered the café and smiled directly at Andi. Her eyes sparkled mischievously, and her dark hair gleamed, cascading in wavy tendrils to just above her shoulders.

Dressed in fitting jeans that sat low on her waist, and a magenta V-neck sweater that revealed a hint of pale skin, she was lovely. Andi tried hard not to stare, but she couldn't stop the biggest grin from spreading across her face.

"Hi," Andi whispered. She could barely speak.

"Hi," Caitlin replied, as she lowered herself gracefully into a chair. "I hope I'm not late? My grandaunt called just as I stepped out the door with a bit of news from home. She had loads to say. I am sorry." She took a deep breath. Andi was captivated by the way her blue eyes shone behind her thick black lashes.

Andi smiled. She was doing that a lot. "I did wonder if you'd stood me up."

"As if." She winked, and her hand closed lightly over Andi's shirtsleeve. "You look amazing. This colour is beautiful on you." Andi blushed. The Irish accent was a sweet lilt, music to Andi's ears.

Caitlin withdrew her hand as Tim, the waiter, approached their table. Andi accepted the menu with a nod of thanks.

Tim looked professional, smart in his black and whites, a significant change from the casual jeans and T-shirts worn by Birdie's staff during the breakfast and lunch service.

"Good evening, ladies, may I show you the wine list?"

Caitlin angled her head towards Andi. "What are you drinking?" Without waiting for an answer, she lifted the glass from Andi's hand, and for a fleeting moment, their fingers touched. Caitlin tilted the glass, and the wine rolled to the edges; she raised the glass to her lips. "Ripe and plummy, that's very nice. I'll have the same, please."

"Good choice. A glass of Farr Rising Pinot Noir for you, coming up straight away."

"We're here for dinner… Why not bring us the bottle?" she said as she brought Andi's glass to her lips again.

"Certainly. Please check the menu; our specials for tonight are on the blackboard here." He pointed to his left. "I'll return shortly to take your order."

Andi retrieved her glass and held it to her mouth, enjoying the hint of honey where Caitlin's lips had brushed it just seconds ago. Caitlin smiled as though they were sharing a secret—co-conspirators. Her lips curled up at the corners, and she gazed at Andi until Andi had to look away. It was too intense.

Now that they were together in an intimate environment, Andi allowed herself to appreciate how gorgeous Caitlin was. She was funny and witty too.

Andi didn't know Caitlin at all, but when she looked into her eyes, she felt as if she were on her surfboard, facing a dauntingly powerful wave. Spending time with Caitlin was equal parts exhilarating and terrifying.

After a second glass of wine, Andi began to mellow.

"It's all part of the Great Ocean Road," Andi explained when Caitlin asked her about the township of Lorne and the Otway Ranges. "Have you visited Bells Beach?"

"Not yet. I've heard of it though, and I passed a sign on my way to Aireys Inlet yesterday," Caitlin said.

"Hakea transforms when the surf comp is on. The place is abuzz with surfers from all over the world. You can walk along the path, all the way from Hakea to where they hold the competition, in thirty minutes. The women's pro competition is scorching."

"That must be hard on the eyes." Caitlin smirked and raised her eyebrows.

Andi's gaydar bleeped with such intensity, she wanted to stuff her fingers in her ears so she couldn't hear it. She tapped on the linen tablecloth and told herself to calm down. She was out of touch and just imagining the attraction signals. That was it; she was delusional.

"Point Addis is a great place to go bush walking and swimming in the summer, and there are loads of places around here for you to discover." Andi changed the subject, and the curious look Caitlin gave her made it clear that she knew it was deliberate.

Before long, their meals arrived. Caitlin had selected the seared tuna with black sesame, fresh peas, and grilled fennel, while Andi chose a simple pan-fried barramundi with steamed broad beans and lime-olive salt.

"We're really lucky to have this café here in Hakea," said Andi. "Not only is the food great, but Birdie also tries to source all her produce from regional suppliers."

"The food is of a high standard and very enjoyable," agreed Caitlin as she sampled her tuna. "This is perfectly cooked." She dabbed at her lips with a napkin. "You're a fountain of local knowledge. I'll come to you in the future if I need information about the area."

Caitlin's foot came into contact with hers under the table and Andi swallowed. "Are you teasing me?" Andi asked.

Caitlin grinned. "You think?" She placed her cutlery on her plate and gave a satisfied sigh. "The quality of the food here is as good as, if not better than, in much more expensive restaurants in the city."

Their main course plates were cleared away, and Caitlin topped up Andi's glass but didn't refill her own. Instead, she drained a large glass of water. She was obviously pacing herself, and Andi knew she should do the same. But the wine should calm her nerves. Why wasn't it working?

"If you don't mind me asking, what brings you to our little speck of a town?" Andi tugged at her shirt collar. Was it getting hotter in here?

"You're blushing." Caitlin lowered her voice to almost a whisper as she leaned across the table. "You're adorable when you do. No, I don't mind you asking. After all, you shared quite a lot about yourself this afternoon." Caitlin's blue eyes shimmered in the candlelight. "My aunt…actually, grandaunt, has a property here in Hakea, on the point."

Phew, she'd changed the subject. "Rocky Point?"

Caitlin elegantly arched one eyebrow. "Yes, that is right, Rocky Point."

"There are only a handful of properties at the point. I often run past those houses. Which one is your aunt's house?"

"My grandaunt. Kinsale."

"Wow. The house on the cliff? Oh, that must have stunning views."

"That is the one. It does have fantastic views of the ocean and the coastline."

Andi shifted around in her chair. Caitlin's steady gaze made her fidget. "Are you living at Kinsale? I haven't seen you around here before." She would have noticed her for sure.

"I try and spend as much time as I can here, but my grandaunt, Isabella, lives in Melbourne, and that is the base for my current work," she replied.

"Okay, I see. So what do you do in Melbourne?"

Caitlin glanced away and raised her arm to get Tim's attention.

As Andi waited for an answer, the waiter arrived at their table.

"May I show you the menu? Maybe interest you in some coffee or an after-dinner drink?"

Caitlin checked the menu and looked questioningly at Andi.

"I'd love a coffee, thanks. Long black, decaf."

"Regular coffee for me." Caitlin handed back the menu. "Espresso, thanks."

"So. What is it you do in Melbourne?" Andi repeated.

Caitlin hesitated. "I'm an art historian researching and cataloguing a private family collection," she said.

"Art historian?" Well, that made sense. "Sounds like a cool job. Can I ask what family… the collection you are cataloguing, I mean?"

Seconds ticked by. "That would be my family. Well, not directly, but yes, my family. The collection belongs to Isabella."

Andi stared. "Really? Your grandaunt has her own art collection?" She moved in closer and chuckled. "You *are* well connected."

Caitlin laughed. "It's a long story, but Isabella and her partner started their collection over forty years ago and assembled a varied assortment of artworks. Not just paintings and drawings, but also original artist's sketches and sculpture."

Andi nodded and waited for her to continue.

"I've been in awe of Isabella all my life. I'm very lucky to have her and this opportunity. It has given me a chance to spend time in Australia." Caitlin looked even more alluring with the slight blush, and her eyes lowered. "So I can't complain. I get to escape the cold winter in Ireland, spend time exploring Melbourne and this beautiful coast, involve myself in a project I love, and make new friends."

"A chance too good to pass up," Andi agreed. "Is the collection open to the public?"

Tim placed their coffees on the table, refilled the water glasses, and left.

"There is a small gallery that is open by appointment, but we are working on a much larger space and a new storage facility. If all goes well, it will be open to the public early next year."

"What is your role?" Although she and Caitlin moved in very different circles, they did have shared interests.

"My time is divided among research, inventory, and archiving, as well as cataloguing the collection. But at the moment, because we are working on renovating the main exhibition space, I work with architects, designers, tradespeople, and lighting specialists."

"Sounds like you have a very busy and exciting time ahead," said Andi. "I suppose you won't get to the coast very often."

Caitlin sipped her coffee and licked her lips. "Since I arrived in Melbourne, four months ago, I've been flat to the boards—initiating the project, establishing procedures, and working with new staff. Now I have a little more time for myself.

I've visited Melbourne twice in my life, but this is the first opportunity I've had to explore the city, and I'd like to see more of Victoria."

"There's a great deal to see," said Andi. "How long are you staying in Australia? Will you have a chance to do much travel?"

"Hmm…it depends on a number of things. That's a hard question to answer."

The café door opened, and a light gust of wind caused the glossy tendrils of Caitlin's hair to flutter and brush against her cheek. Andi was captivated as Caitlin pulled her hair back from her face.

"Sorry, I'm not deliberately avoiding your question. It depends on a few variables—how long it takes to finish my work and if we encounter any complications." She drained the last of her coffee. "Maybe twelve months."

Andi tried not to show her disappointment. "What about your family? Are they in Ireland? Do you have a job to go back to?" She was asking a lot of freaking questions. What was this, the Spanish Inquisition?

Caitlin looked relaxed. If she thought Andi was asking too many questions, she didn't show it. "My parents live and work in Cork and have very active careers of their own." She looked up to the ceiling as if thanking the heavens. "As far as my job goes, I'm on sabbatical. The university has allowed me twelve months leave, and my research will benefit its standing in international art studies."

"You certainly seem to have it all sorted." Andi looked around the café and was surprised to see that apart from their table, the room was now empty of patrons. Tim was the only person behind the counter, restocking the bar, trying to look busy.

"The time seems to have got away from us." Caitlin sighed wistfully. "It's after eleven. I think we should take pity on our waiter and let him go home."

Andi rose from the table to settle the bill, but Caitlin stood and gently touched Andi's arm. "This is my shout." Andi started to object, but Caitlin insisted. "It's the least I can do after you shared your art and trusted me in your studio today." Caitlin walked towards the bar, and then turned back with a grin. "Anyway, I owe you for saving my lens cap."

"This will definitely make us even."

Did she mean twelve months from now, or twelve months in total? She'd already been here four months, so maybe she had only eight months more in Australia.

There was that telltale pull of attraction, and it wasn't just Andi's imagination; Caitlin definitely showed some interest. Andi grimaced. There was no way she could do it. She did not want a casual affair with another temporary resident.

A few minutes later, Caitlin returned to the table and handed her a business card. "These are my details." She turned the card over to reveal a mobile number neatly printed on the back. "And my private contact." She reached into her leather satchel for her iPhone. "So, can I have your phone number?"

Andi hesitated. *Should she?* "Okay…Yep, 0-4-0-5 11223."

"0405 11223," Caitlin repeated and tapped the numbers into her contacts list. "Sorted."

Andi held the door open for Caitlin, and Tim waved goodbye.

"Good night ladies," he called. He looked relieved to see them go.

Caitlin followed Andi outside into the car park. The night was clear and bracing. Andi jogged on the spot as Caitlin pushed the key fob to unlock the Roadster.

"Where did you park?" Caitlin peered into the shadows.

"Oh, I walked over, so I'll say goodnight. Thanks for a great evening."

"You walked?"

Andi shrugged. "Yep." She shoved her hands deep into her pockets and rocked back and forth on her heels.

Caitlin walked around and pulled the passenger side door open. "Hop in, I'll run you home. It's nearly midnight." She leaned on the doorframe and casually tapped her fingers on the hood, waiting.

"I'll be fine, Caitlin. I do this all the time." It was late to be walking home alone, but the danger seemed infinitesimal compared to being alone in a car with Caitlin.

Caitlin cleared her throat and didn't move. Andi conceded. She walked to the car, lowered herself into the passenger seat, and murmured, "Yeah, it is dark. I could trip over an echidna."

Caitlin closed the door, drew the seatbelt across her shoulder, and started the engine. "Did you say something about an echidna?"

Andi shook her head, closed her eyes, and leaned against the backrest.

Sitting in the BMW, with only the stick shift between them, Caitlin wanted to lean across the narrow space and kiss her—but she resisted. Andi's eyes were closed, and she'd seemed to withdraw.

It was a short, silent drive, and it wasn't long before Caitlin stopped the car and unbuckled her seatbelt. She turned to Andi. "I enjoyed spending time with you." She placed her hand gently on Andi's arm but removed it just as quickly when Andi flinched. "And visiting your studio."

Andi opened her eyes and reached for the door handle. "I did too. It was really good to meet you, Caitlin. I hope we… I mean, it would be nice to see you again."

Caitlin gently trailed her lips across Andi's cheek to stop her hesitant words. "I would like to see you again too," she said.

Andi tilted her head and leaned slightly towards her. Caitlin moved her arm along the back of Andi's shoulder, but Andi moaned, opened the door, and stepped quickly out of the car. She reached the front steps in a few long strides.

"Andi, wait," Caitlin cried out, exasperated, and clambered out of the car. She caught up to her at the top of the stairs, placed her hands gently around her waist, and turned her around.

She rested her forehead against Andi's. "Hey, I'm sorry if I did something to make you feel uncomfortable," she said. She pulled back slightly and looked into Andi's soulful brown eyes. "I like you."

"You didn't. I like you too," Andi said softly, and she rested one hand on Caitlin's hip.

Caitlin caressed Andi's cheek and then lightly traced the curve of her jaw with her finger. They moved closer until their mouths brushed delicately against each other, and Andi's hands circled her waist.

Andi's muscles seemed to relax as Caitlin melted into their embrace. Her senses were aroused, and the warmth that radiated off Andi's body enveloped her.

Caitlin pulled her closer as she gently moved her tongue over Andi's lips. Their kiss deepened, and she tightened her arms around Andi. "I've been staring at your beautiful mouth all night, and I've so wanted to do this."

Andi's body went rigid, and she pushed Caitlin aside firmly. The jolt of separation left her breathless, and Caitlin stared helplessly into Andi's eyes. The hesitation in those dark eyes was impossible to ignore, so with regret, she backed away.

"Goodnight, Caitlin. Thanks again for dinner." Her words were barely audible.

"Andi," she groaned and struggled to keep her distance. "Goodnight. I'll be heading back to Melbourne in the morning." Andi nodded. "You have my number. I hope to be back in Hakea next weekend. Maybe I'll see you then?"

"I'd like that," Andi said, as she stepped up onto the veranda.

"Good, I'd like that too." Caitlin turned around, walked down the stairs, climbed into the car, and drove towards Kinsale.

She waited for the electronic gates to open. The sky above was crystal clear. Thousands of stars glistened, and the moon cast a peaceful glow across the glassy ocean.

She touched her fingers to her mouth, recalling the heat and the incredible softness of Andi's sweet lips. Was she too forward? Possibly. But she had wanted to kiss Andi several times that day. Earlier in the studio, as she spoke about her art with such vitality and passion. At dinner, her brown eyes sparkled in the candlelight, emotions dancing close to the surface. She'd tried in the car and would have definitely kissed her if Andi hadn't made such a hasty exit. Finally, on the stairs, she'd felt an unmistakable pull and was drawn to Andi's expressive, sensuous mouth; she *had* kissed her, and for a few wonderful moments, Andi had kissed her back.

Caitlin parked the car in the garage and made her way to the house. She threw herself into a chair close to a window and gazed out over the water. There was no point going to bed; she was too restless to sleep.

Normally, Caitlin was good at picking up the signs. How did she get it wrong? But there were no fixed rules about attraction or reaction. Either Andi was not interested, or she was involved with someone already. That someone could be Ellie, the attractive woman she'd seen with her at the café a few days ago. And what about the two wetsuits hanging over her studio balcony? It made sense. But for a fleeting moment, Andi had kissed her, and that was going to be hard to forget.

Chapter 5

"Izzy, I know she'll want to talk to you too. Why don't we have supper together and then telephone Ma?" Caitlin asked.

Kim stepped into Caitlin's office, clutching a folder, and Caitlin motioned for her to be seated.

"If we try after nine thirty tonight, it will be just after midday in Cork, and Da will be home for lunch." She finished her conversation with Isabella and returned the phone to her desk. She greeted her colleague. "Kim, it is good to see you."

Caitlin reached across the desk and accepted the bulging folder. On Mondays, it was customary for Kim and Caitlin to plan their week and head off problems before they surfaced.

"You too. Feels like it's been forever," Kim said.

"It has been a long day." Caitlin sighed. She was delighted to finally catch up with the estate's registrar, Kim Jones, who had attempted to meet with Caitlin on several occasions that day with no success.

Since her early morning drive back from Hakea, Caitlin had been locked in several meetings. First with the accountant, then with the designer working on the new storage area, followed by an appointment with the secretary of Women in Arts. After nearly a full day of spreadsheets, projection concepts, and budgets, Caitlin was very glad to see Kim's friendly face.

"Caitie, how was your weekend? Did you get up to any mischief down the coast?" She wriggled her eyebrows. "Rub shoulders with any of those bronzed, Aussie surfer girls at Hakea Beach?"

Though Caitlin was now accustomed to Kim's familiar manner of speech and her sometimes colourful Aussie slang, she was still getting used to the disarming Australian casualness and humour.

"I had a very relaxing weekend, thank you Kim. There's nothing better than a bit of sunshine and fresh air to restore the energy." Caitlin stretched her arms over her head. "I visited the Black-Tern Gallery at Aireys Inlet, did some running along the beach, and discovered an artist's studio in Hakea."

Kim looked at Caitlin with interest. "I haven't been down that way for ages. I must take my Sharon there for a weekend soon." She chuckled. "You can keep the beach running to yourself, though. I prefer to get my exercise in more pleasurable ways, thank you very much."

"Ah-ha, I'm sure you do."

"Met a local artist? You've got my attention, Caitie. Male or female?"

"A young, modern expressionist named Andi Rey. Her paintings have such an energetic style. Spirited, intense, and vibrant. She's working on her first solo exhibition opening in December."

"Real talent, eh?" She smirked. "Andi Rey? That's a catchy name. Must have something going for her if you were impressed."

"I am looking forward to finding out exactly that." Caitlin sat upright; it was time to get back to work. "So, did you manage to get through Storeroom B since I saw you last? Maxwell Designs left some drawings for the proposed new storage area." Caitlin reached for the yellow folder sitting at the top of the pile on her desk. "Maybe you'll have time to look at them by early next week?"

"Of course, no problem at all." Kim took the folder and tucked it under her arm. "I could take it home with me tonight if you want it earlier?"

"No, there's no need. I'm sure Sharon wants your full attention when you are home."

"Oh, Caitie, there's plenty of me to go around." She looked at her watch. "Okay, I'd better hop to it. I'm about to place an order for acid-free tissue. Is there anything else we need?"

"Nothing off the top of my head." Caitlin checked her list. "Was there enough tissue to interleave all the Rickson prints? Some of the older tissues are discoloured and starting to curl. I'd like to replace them as soon as possible."

Isabella's collection of early twentieth-century landscapes by Australian painter Will Rickson was one of the best privately owned collections in the country. Caitlin loved the Rickson landscapes and knew they were the jewels in Isabella's collection.

"All taken care of Caitie. Consider it done." Kim assured her. After fourteen years as a collection manager at Museum Victoria, Kim had made a brave decision to return to university and complete her studies in Australian art history. For the last twelve months, her job involved cataloguing and looking after Isabella's collection. She was Caitlin's invaluable right-hand-woman.

Kim had been a bit miffed when Caitlin first arrived. After all, until then, the collection had been her responsibility. Now, after working together for a few months, they had developed a mutual respect and genuine fondness for each other. Kim's work ethic and eagerness to include Caitlin in social gatherings had proven to Caitlin that she had been accepted.

"Are you heading home?" Caitlin asked, as she glanced at her iPhone.

"As soon as we finish here. I may take the missus for a bite to eat at the new Vietnamese in High Street. I've heard they do a fabulous seafood laksa," she said and rubbed circles against her stomach.

Caitlin shut down her MacBook and stood to tidy the papers on her desk. "Lucky you. Off you go then, Jonesy." She pointed to the door. "Give my best wishes to the missus."

"I will do that. You look like you could use an early night yourself," she observed.

"I've just a couple of things to finish here. A hot bath, dinner with Isabella, and then I'm curling up in bed with a good book."

"Sounds fabulous." Kim exited the room, then peeked her blonde head around the doorway and said, "Mind you, pity it's only a good book you're curling up with and not something a little warmer." She chuckled mischievously and scampered out the door.

After Kim had departed, Caitlin completed a few more tasks and milled around her office. She wondered what Andi was doing. Hopefully, she was in her studio painting. Impulsively, she scrolled through her contacts and tapped out a quick message.

Thinking about you. Hope you've had a great day. Caitlin x

She didn't write "thinking about that kiss," although she would have liked to. After several minutes, she heard the *buzz* and checked her mobile. New text.

Thank you. I did.

Caitlin sighed. At least Andi had replied. She shut the door to her office and took the concealed spiral staircase that led up to her second-floor apartment. She loved that her stylish private space enjoyed views of the rose garden and landscaped grounds below. The large three-storey Federation mansion was set in a beautiful English-styled garden. The apartment had a spacious main bedroom and bathroom, a guest bedroom and ensuite, an open-plan sitting room, plus a dining area and kitchen. Isabella's architect had assured that Caitlin would never want for comfort.

An hour later, Caitlin made her way through the main house. It was a stately but magical building. Caitlin would never forget her first visit to Maggie and Isabella's home. The heavy, wooden front door had seemed enormous. She'd looked in awe at the sweeping staircase with its intricate carvings. The ceilings were so high, and the house had made her feel tiny.

Isabella's estate was in the leafy suburb of Kew, the house built in 1899 for businessman, Robert James Hegetty and his wife. On their passing, the entire estate was left to their only daughter, Captain Margaret Hegetty.

In Korea in 1951, the twenty-seven-year-old army captain and twenty-two-year-old Red Cross nurse, Isabella O'Riorden, were introduced at a party hosted by the British Commonwealth General Hospital in Seoul.

Their relationship began in late 1952, and the estate became their home. They'd lived together until five years ago when Maggie died in the arms of her long-time lover.

Caitlin tapped lightly on the door and walked straight into Isabella's home. The cottage was tucked behind the main house, near the extensive rose garden. Once Maggie's painting studio, it had been transformed into a self-contained home for Isabella and many of her personal treasures.

"Hello, my darling girl. It's so very lovely to see you," Isabella greeted. "You must have left Kinsale quite early. I believe Marion spotted you on her way in this morning."

"It's always wonderful to see you looking so well, Isabella." Caitlin hugged her grandaunt and enjoyed the softness of her fine merino jumper and warm embrace. "I did leave early to avoid the rush hour, and I'm happy to report it was a pleasant drive and stress-free journey."

Isabella hovered near the small, rosewood bar cabinet. "I'm pouring myself a wee drop of Paddy's whiskey. Caitlin, will you join me?"

She nodded. Her fingers wandered over the group of ornate frames on the carved, highly polished sideboard. Isabella's collection included photographs of Caitlin and her parents, at various stages of her life, from childhood to the present day.

The cottage was filled with colourful trinkets and treasures from Isabella and Maggie's life of travel, adventure, and passion. Caitlin's heart swelled at the memories of their encouragement and support through the years. Her grandaunts were the grandmothers she had never known.

"Sit yourself down, darling." Isabella handed her a crystal tumbler containing a generous splash of amber-gold liquid. "Let's take a look at you. Ah… That sea air has given you a touch of colour. My girl, you have a sparkle in your eyes and a spring in your step." Isabella sat down beside Caitlin on the comfortably worn Chesterfield sofa. As always, her back was upright, and she sat with her legs slightly crossed at the ankles. "Even with these old eyes of mine, I can see the weekend away did you the world of good." She lovingly patted Caitlin's knee. "I think you will have to do this more often. Take a bit of time for yourself and enjoy Kinsale."

Caitlin savoured the whiskey's toffee and butterscotch smokiness. "Well, maybe I will if I can persuade you to join me next time?" Caitlin asked.

"Oh? And what would you be doing with your old grandaunt getting in the way? Time for you to start making some happy memories of your own," she said. "Come on, tell me what you got up to, my girl. I'm an old woman who loves to hear a good story."

"You do, don't you?" Caitlin nudged Isabella gently. "I love being at Kinsale, I mean how could I not? The house is absolutely amazing. The views are stunning from every corner of the place. Even the shower. Although, I don't know what your architect was thinking when she planned that one." She laughed.

Isabella clinked their tumblers together. "Cheers to Margaret, God bless her. The cantilevered shower was entirely her idea. She always said because I made her give up that tin can in the sky she loved to fly around in, the glass shower with a view to infinity was the next best thing."

Caitlin nodded in agreement. "Cheers, indeed. I'm so glad I had an opportunity to fly with her that one time in Ireland." She raised her glass. "To Maggie and the infinity shower and all of us who now have the pleasure of enjoying it."

Isabella squeezed Caitlin's knee. "What else did you get up to?"

"I did a bit of exploring around Hakea, and I went for a drive to Aireys Inlet."

"Ahh… Did you go to the Black-Tern Gallery?" She rubbed her brow. "Now, who runs it? Her name's on the tip of my tongue, I'm sure it begins with C. Is it Cathryn?"

"Cynthia, her name is Cynthia."

"Yes, I do remember now. What did you think of the gallery? I haven't been there for many years."

Caitlin nestled back into the sofa, her long legs crossed at the knee. "It's in a good location to attract day trippers. A lot of the work is aimed at the tourist market, but it is good to see that Cynthia supports some talented artists. There was one particular piece that stood out from the others."

"Oh? Tell me more." Isabella's eyes lit up with interest. "Was it a painting?"

"Yes, it was. To be honest, once I saw *it*, I didn't spend a lot of time looking at the rest." She closed her eyes to recall the artwork. As she thought of Andi, heat spread through her body like the slow, mellow burn of the spicy whiskey. "It was a seascape on the wall, all by itself. I was instantly captured by its energy. The work was certainly different from the rest, and thanks to Cynthia, I obtained the artist's details. Unfortunately, the painting was not for sale."

"The Black-Tern, and particularly Cynthia, has been very good in supporting artists in that area," said Isabella. "I can tell by your expression that you're on to something. So you say the artist's studio is in Hakea?"

Caitlin remembered Andi's deep brown eyes and the way they simmered as she spoke. "I have to draw, and I have to paint. It is like breathing for me," she'd said. Caitlin sighed, recalling the warmth of Andi's body and the sensation of her strong arms circling her waist.

"Caitlin?"

"Oh, I am sorry. Yes, she does live in Hakea."

"Is there something you're not telling me?"

Caitlin smiled. Isabella knew her well. "I don't know if I can explain it. Andi's work has a profound quality that seems to go beyond what the eye sees. I would call her primary style modern expressionism. The paintings I saw were acrylic, sometimes with a hint of charcoal. But it's more than that. It is as if she paints with light that seems to shift in front of you. In the painting on display at the gallery, Andi used a method incorporating acrylic pigment with crushed glass." She shrugged. "Yes, I know this isn't like me. I'm rambling." Caitlin narrowed her eyes. She hoped she'd communicated how she had felt about Andi's painting.

Isabella nodded. "Would she be following some of the Italian masters during the Renaissance period?"

"Yes, that's what she's doing. Andi allowed me to visit her studio. Her attention to detail, composition, and brushwork is exceptional. The particles of glass in some of the paintings act like a prism. The colour seems to be intensified, and light is reflected, bringing everything to life. I'd love you to see her work, Isabella."

"I would like to meet the artist. Who is this Andi?" she asked. "Does she have a background in Renaissance studies? Tintoretto, Vermeer?"

Caitlin laughed. It was incredible. "That's just it, Izzy, I don't think so… not formally anyway. From what I know, Andréa Rey completed her bachelor of visual arts at Ballarat University and has a diploma in graphic design. I don't think she's had the opportunity to study overseas. She's young and developing her own style."

"Sounds as if this young woman made an impression, Caitlin."

"I would like to learn more about her art process." She placed the glass gently down on the table beside her.

"Just her art process?" Isabella asked. Her wise, old eyes twinkled with delight.

"Oh, she's a bewitching mix. Golden, shiny, intense…shy." She shook her head. "Can't hide much from you, can I?"

Isabella drained her glass and rose from the sofa. "Dangerous?" Her tone was serious, but Caitlin knew from her smile that she was teasing. "I'm sure this won't be the last I hear of young Andi. Come on, now. I think we should eat. Marion knew you would be here for dinner and has made one of your favourites. She would be very upset if we let the potato and cheddar tart turn to charcoal." Isabella wrinkled her nose. "Could you please collect the green salad from the refrigerator?"

"Sounds like a grand idea. I'm starving. She is such a darling, your Marion."

Chapter 6

Andi ran along the beach. The sand was firm, still free of footprints, and the tide had ebbed, leaving the clean beach hard but forgiving enough to protect her knees. She paused to gather her breath and looked at the stark expanse of vertical rock above her, the interplay of light and shadow, rich tones, and subtle hues. Inspiration.

She balanced her foot on a boulder and re-tied her shoelaces.

Since meeting Caitlin Quinn, she'd altered her route and now ran to the end of the beach, up the winding track, and along the gravel path. Her new course took her past the cliff-top house. Andi knew there was little chance that Caitlin would be there, but she found herself drawn to Kinsale. Of course, she told herself the longer route gave her a better workout. Sure.

Just after moving to Hakea, she'd asked the locals about the distinctive, contemporary styled home with its curved stone walls. Most speculated that the owners were a business family from Melbourne. Others thought Kinsale, with its wide iron gate and silvery-grey nameplate, belonged to a reclusive artist who rarely used the property. If she and Caitlin became friends, she would find out more about the iconic house and its owner.

Andi groaned, picked up her pace, and ran faster. Would Caitlin return to Hakea this weekend? She enjoyed Caitlin's company. How could she not? She hadn't met anyone like her before. Caitlin had shown genuine interest in her work; she just seemed to get her.

It had been a tough year, and at times, Andi doubted her abilities as a painter. It was good to get positive feedback and encouragement from someone with a background in art history. Caitlin's enthusiasm had given her *that* buzz. She made Andi laugh and reminded her not to take herself too seriously. Of course, it didn't hurt that Caitlin was captivating and sexy. Andi's body had betrayed her when she'd responded to her kiss.

That kiss, Caitlin's luscious mouth. Ending their kiss had taken all of her resolve, but the danger signs flashed, warning her to proceed with caution. A passing affair with a traveller, especially a beautiful woman like Caitlin, would be trouble.

"Get a grip, Andi," she muttered.

This spring morning, the sea was a brilliant turquoise blue, and beyond the ochre cliffs, a few surfers were trying to make the most of a gentle swell. The smaller waves did not deter those who enjoyed being out on the water, no matter the conditions.

It was one of those magical mornings when the air was still and the light was delicate and diffused. Andi came to the beach most mornings to clear her head and organise her day.

She was the youngest of three children. By the time Andi arrived, her parents were occupied with their expanding business, and her two older siblings were at school.

When her mother was in the fields or the seed-cultivating house, four-year-old Andi, with the help of her imaginary friends, would pick out small pots of her favourite colourful plants. She would arrange the potted plants on the ground, according to their colours, to make pictures that would look like a mosaic from above. As a young adult, she discarded her imaginary friends, but concluded she was introspective by nature.

She adjusted the volume on her headphones and hit repeat on her playlist. Since Caitlin had kissed her—and she had kissed her back—her favourite tracks from Christina Perri's album had played over and over in her head. The lyrics and rhythms tapped into her emotional and physical awakening. Andi sighed. The morning sun warmed her face, and her skin glistened with perspiration. At the base of the stairs, she wiped the moisture from her forehead with the back of her hand before bounding up the steps and heading for home.

Ten minutes later, she kicked off her runners on her front porch and opened the door to a loudly meowing cat. "Sorry, Koda, sweetie… You must be hungry." She stroked her fur. "Come on, then. Time for breakfast. What have you been doing this morning? Lying in the sun?"

Koda followed Andi into the galley kitchen. She weaved through Andi's bare legs and stood patiently in front of the food bowl. Andi fed her and then grabbed a green smoothie for herself.

Her phone rang, and she read the number on the screen. "Hi Mum. Good morning."

"Good morning, Andréa, did I interrupt your work?"

"No, I'm just having breakfast."

"Hopefully a real breakfast, not one of those green drinks. I don't know how you can stomach that green slime," she said. Lina Rey spent her life cultivating and appreciating the very green things she was complaining about, and she firmly believed vegetables should crunch when eaten, not be sucked through a straw.

Andi pictured her mother with one hand on her hip and the other holding the telephone, shaking her head in disapproval.

"Yes, but it is quick and healthy."

"So is toast. A poached egg. A little cheese. Some coffee or milk."

"How are you? How is Dad?" Andi changed the subject. Her father would be out in the fields by now, checking his crops. Six days a week, he supervised the packing for the morning delivery of produce to the central depot, nearby restaurants, and grocers.

"Your father is busy, as usual. I'm good. Annalise and Mick are here already, arriving before the sun was even up," Lina said. There was so much more for Ana and Mick to do now that they managed the market garden.

"Dad is much more relaxed," Andi said.

Her mother chuckled. "Yes. And I'm back in the potting shed where I belong."

Andi smiled. "How are my nephew and niece?" She switched on her iMac and waited for it to boot.

"Manny, when he's not at school, helps his father with the deliveries. God help us, can you believe he has his licence already? He is in that car as much as possible."

"Oh, Mum…you worry too much. Manny is seventeen." If their grandmother could do anything about it, Manny and his younger sister Mia would never get behind the wheel. *Ever.*

"He is still on L plates and needs supervision," Lina reminded her. "Andréa, what have you been doing? How is the painting going for the exhibition? Do you have enough paid work at the moment?"

"Mmm." Andi agreed absently, as she skimmed her list of emails.

"Andréa, are you listening to me?"

Sprung. She hadn't been paying proper attention to her. Not that she would admit it.

"Of course, I'm listening, Mum. Things are coming to life around here. There's always a lot to do at this time of year. But I've just finished a project for Bailey Graphics. It was a big job, which means I'll get a nice cheque in the mail. My painting is going well. Daylight hours are longer, so I can work later."

"Money helps to pay the bills. What about matters of the heart, querida? Have you met anybody? Your family waits for you to bring a sweet girl home to meet us."

Lina didn't often interfere, but Andi knew she worried about her being lonely and away from her mother's watchful eye. She'd never trusted Martha and always thought Andi's ex-girlfriend had controlled her life and isolated her from friends and family.

"I have until the first week in December to finish the paintings for the exhibition. That doesn't include all the other things I need to do before the opening, and I have to finish a project designing the logo for a new surfboard company in town. Mum, I have enough to keep me occupied. No need for added distractions." It was true. She didn't need any more complications.

"Love and companionship are a necessity in life, Andréa," Lina said gently. Andi understood that her mother wanted her children to be successful with their careers, but more than that, she wanted all three of them to be happily settled in a relationship. She couldn't help but push; it was simply the way her mother was designed, and Andi took it as an expression of her mother's love.

Andi sighed. She didn't *always* like her mother nagging about her love life.

"Okay, okay. A mother can ask." She paused a moment, as if searching for a change of topic. "Make sure Luca fixes everything you need while he's there. Otherwise, he'll be out in the water for hours."

Her brother was her favourite surfing companion and was scheduled to visit in about a week. She would love it if they could spend all their time together on the ocean, but he had promised to finish building the air-conditioned storeroom. "I am excited about Luc's visit. We will both be out riding our boards if the conditions are right." Andi cherished any time spent on her surfboard in Luc's company.

"Do you need anything from home? I can send it with Luca." Her mother always insisted on calling her children by their proper baptismal names.

"A box of whatever's in season would be great. Maybe a jar of Ana's orange marmalade. I notice the grocers here are stocking more of our produce."

"Birdie is so wonderful. She always has her regular delivery, and now they've started to order punnets of microgreens as well. Yours is an easy request to fill. Maybe I'll have time to bake you a batch of *pastéis de nata*."

"Yum. I miss your cooking." Her mother's Portuguese custard tarts were the best. "Okay, Mum, I probably should get on with my work."

"Of course, of course."

"Talk again soon, love you. Love to Dad. Bye."

"I love you too, Andréa. Keep safe."

It was good to have her own space and an independent life, but Andi sometimes missed her family, especially her mother's cooking.

She looked out at the garden. The deck was protected from the wind, and although Koda had managed to find a sliver of sunlight in which to sleep, it was mostly shaded. The conditions were perfect for painting.

Andi set up a blank canvas and moved her art trolley, laden with materials, onto the deck.

She began a new painting, part of a series she'd been working on for the last three months.

Andi's work was always about her intuitive response. Eyes wide open, all senses engaged, feeling one with the landscape. She allowed the sea, clouds, and trees to fill her senses and gave herself permission to explore the sensuous nature of paint.

Her art process could be messy. She tapped into her emotion-based intuition and let it flow. She painted quickly. It was about observation, capturing on canvas the patterns of weather and light. Bold brushstrokes. Thick layers of acrylic. Her palette knife, large brush, roller, and paint were the tools she used to express herself.

Today, she used only palette knives, a technique that allowed her to work quickly. She'd previously prepared the canvas with a thick layer of chalky-white gesso and had allowed it to dry. The layer of gesso meant that the paint would not be absorbed into the canvas.

Andi scooped phthalo green onto a knife and spread it thinly. She lifted the knife high above the canvas with her left hand and dropped blobs of phthalo blue and leaf green and a touch of cadmium yellow. With her right hand, she controlled the surface, guiding the colours to merge into rhythmic patterns.

She wiped her hands on her already paint-spattered shirt and cargo shorts and stepped back to grab a larger palette knife. Andi applied primary yellow and sap green with circular motions to create leaf fronds. While the previous layer was still wet, she scraped lines of grey and titanium white across the canvas.

Satisfied with the lushness of colour and texture, Andi exhaled slowly and rotated tension from her shoulders. The painting was her representation of grass trees, and when it dried, the luminous pigments would continue to glow, even in the half light, brightening the whole work.

Ancient grass trees were one of Andi's favourite native plants. Their slow-growing, blackened trunks were encircled by a skirt of rough, grasslike leaves, topped by a long, spear-shaped flower. Even a mere one-metre trunk could be over two hundred years old.

Koda—curled up asleep in her basket under the workbench—opened one eye and yawned at a pair of magpies who caroled loudly.

"Now the painting is ready for the final stages," Andi told Koda and the magpies as she carried it inside. She placed it on the table, ready for the finishing glaze. Andi stretched her back and raised her arms above her head. She was tired but satisfied. It had been a productive day.

Chapter 7

Caitlin breathed a sigh of relief as she loaded the last of her things, including her computer, into the tiny boot of the Roadster. She couldn't wait to return to the seaside, back to Kinsale. She checked her phone again.

There were no new messages. She slammed the boot closed and rested her hands heavily on the trunk. Why wasn't Andi replying?

It was early Saturday afternoon, and she'd been working her arse off for two long weeks. She'd managed to rearrange her schedule in order to escape to the coast for a few days. Isabella was right. She needed a break.

Okay, she would still have to do some work online. She'd told Kim that she could be contacted anytime, via video chat or phone. She considered these were small concessions to make. If she got to spend time with Andi, it would be worth it.

Caitlin had been occupied in meetings with conservators, the architectural firm responsible for the historic preservation of the estate, and art storage specialists. They'd discussed ways to improve the estate's storage in order to house all of the collections at one location. They agreed that the new facility would be discreet and designed to architecturally compliment the estate.

The construction needed to happen as a matter of urgency. Caitlin was excited to bring all of the artworks together in one large, temperature-controlled facility.

She took the Eastern Freeway and drove past Melbourne's outer suburbs of new homes and light industry.

Caitlin punched the audio button on the Roadster's Bang & Olufsen stereo system, and music filled the car. When one of her favourite songs from university days started, she increased the volume. Caitlin hummed and recalled The Corrs concert she and Rachel had attended in Dublin ten years ago.

Rachel. Her only long-term relationship had died a slow death. With both of them struggling to establish their academic careers, they'd had little time or energy to balance the demands of work and their personal relationship. There had been no fighting, no jealousy. Just a slow end. They'd tried to remain friends, but before Caitlin left Ireland, even their dinner catch-ups had all but ceased.

At the end of their relationship, Caitlin threw herself into an even more hectic schedule. She'd worked gruelling, long hours until one day, a researcher with a fiery sex drive breezed into her dreary life and showed her what she was missing.

Neither woman was interested in a long-term relationship, and Laura left to pursue a job in New York four months later. Caitlin completed a year-long research post in Paris and enjoyed the occasional casual liaison. All mutual. All friendly. No strings. No expectations. Painless.

Since her arrival in Australia, she'd listened to Isabella talk about her love affair with Maggie and the rewarding life they'd shared together. It made Caitlin yearn for more from her own life. She was changing.

She glanced at the petrol gauge and was forced back to the practicalities of her journey. The Roadster needed juice. Ten minutes later, she pulled into the service lane, parked at a petrol pump, and momentarily rested her head on the steering wheel.

She didn't have the foggiest idea what she wanted or how to go about getting it. This level of introspection was entirely new to her.

Caitlin's phone beeped with an incoming text. She reached across the passenger seat for her jacket and grabbed the phone from the pocket. *Finally.*

Just got your message. Can't do dinner. Surfing near the reef, below the lookout. Around 5:30 pm. CU there?

Caitlin tapped out a return message.

LOL Surfing? Me? I'm about forty minutes away.

A minute later, Andi replied.

Perfect.

Andi's big brother was tall and broad shouldered. They shared the same dark-blonde hair colour and the same dark-brown eyes. His career as a builder kept him well muscled and fit, and his skin was deeply tanned from many hours spent working in the sun.

"It is good to see some sand in your hair instead of sawdust, Luc." Andi punched her brother's shoulder.

"Well, it's good to have time to have sand in my hair." He lay his longboard down and sat on the beach beside her. "It's been ages since I've had time to spend an afternoon surfing." He lifted his face, soaking in the sun's warmth. "Do you get to surf as much as you'd like when you're painting?"

"I do… Surfing the waves, being in the water, running, meditation. It's all essential to my process."

"Are you going all Zen on me?" He grinned, his eyes sparkling.

The afternoon was perfect. Plenty of sunshine, a gentle breeze, and rolling swells. Andi loved the chance to surf with her brother. He'd taught her when she was fourteen, on a wooden shortboard he'd handcrafted. A few years later, while still at school, she'd tagged along with Luc and his friends on their weekend trips to the coast.

They'd drive to the beach on a Friday night, and Andi would sleep in Luc's old VW Kombi, while he and his mates pitched a tent beside the van. Surfing with Luc was always an adventure. He'd inspired her fluid style and taught her that the ocean was a place to be one with nature and escape life's stresses.

"How's business?" she asked.

"You know, sustainability is popular, especially in country Victoria. Every man, woman, and galah wants an eco-friendly house." He shrugged his shoulders. "Even if they don't always know what that means. I'm getting a lot of interest in the eco pods." Luc leaned into Andi. "I'm glad I could help you out this week, kid. It may be a while before I get back here, because business is booming."

She was proud of her brother. He'd managed to establish a successful business, specialising in small, eco-friendly homes, holiday cabins, and beach houses. Her own home was one of Luc's first solo projects, and with her initial design, he'd crafted a home that was both comfortable and affordable. Andi loved the private sanctuary they had created together.

Luc glanced around. "I wouldn't mind being closer to the coast myself. You have a great lifestyle here, Andi. Everything except—" He held his finger to her lips as she started to protest. "Let me finish. Mum isn't the only one who worries about you. Goes with the territory, baby sis."

Andi rolled her eyes. "I know, but I'm doing okay. What about *you*?"

Luc stared out to the horizon. "I know what you're thinking." He paused. "It's been a long time since Susie died. Life is too short, and we both need to move on. Martha was not the right fit for you." He placed an arm around her shoulders. "You're just a young chick, but maybe there *is* hope for this cynical old chippie." He grinned.

"What? What are you saying, Luc? You've met someone?"

When Luc had lost his fiancée, Susie, in a car accident, he'd been a mess. For a long time, Andi and her family worried that he may never want to risk his heart again.

"Don't jump to any conclusions. It's early days yet." Smiling, he lifted his board and headed towards the surf.

"Hey, I want more information," she called after him.

"All in due time. But now, let's go catch us some waves." His laughter mixed with the screech of seagulls echoing along the beach.

Andi grabbed her board and chased after him. Thirty years old, and she was still playing catch-up.

Caitlin stood on the platform directly above Gull Rock, just after five thirty. She checked the waves all the way to Bells Beach in the west and used the long-range lens on her camera to scan the surfers out beyond the rock. It took a moment for her eyes to adjust, before she found the grace, style, and rhythm of Andi's unmistakable feminine form.

Damn. She was glorious.

She captured a few quick shots of Andi before descending the stairs to the beach just east of the lookout.

As her feet touched the sand, an eager puppy jumped excitedly around her legs, barking and yapping playfully. "Whoa." She patted the dog's head carefully. "You're a friendly girl. Who do you belong to?" The pup's ears were up, eyes bright, and tail wagging rapidly. The mottled black and white bundle of energy jumped and ran in circles around her.

Andi emerged from the water. "Zzzip, come!" she yelled.

Immediately, the small dog looked up and charged towards Andi.

"You made it." Andi smiled breathlessly and placed her board on the sand. She ran a hand through her hair, shaking the wet strands loose. "This naughty puppy, by the way, is Zip." The pup jumped around Andi excitedly, picked up a half-chewed tennis ball, and dropped it at Caitlin's feet. "Zip, this is Caitlin. Are you in the mood to play?"

Caitlin grabbed the ball and tossed it down the beach. "Are you talking to me?" she asked, shaking her drool-covered hand.

Andi laughed and held out her towel. "Here, I don't think you should wipe that on your linen pants."

Caitlin looked down at her white wide-leg trousers. She wiped her hands on the end of Andi's towel. "Straight from the office." She shrugged and gazed into Andi's eyes.

Beads of seawater clung to her naturally thick eyelashes and sparkled at the ends of her hair. In the sunlight, Andi's eyes were the colour of rich caramel, speckled with flecks of gold.

The neoprene wetsuit must have been designed specifically for her body, because it hugged her athletic form perfectly. Andi was liquid sunshine—healthy and glowing.

"You looked great out on the water." Caitlin's remark brought a faint flush to Andi's cheeks.

As Andi towel dried her hair, Zip ran back and forth, barking loudly, then raced towards the sea.

"She is full of energy."

"Manic actually, hence the name...Zip." Andi turned her back towards Caitlin.

"Speaking of zips, I don't suppose you could help me? I need to get out of this wetsuit while there's still water inside, or it will be impossible to peel off."

"Sure." Caitlin caressed the nape of Andi's neck with her fingertips, and a faint shiver rippled through Andi. She gently pulled open the Velcro fastening, lowering the zip to reveal a sweep of golden skin.

Caitlin moved back as Andi peeled the material down over her slender waist, then pulled it past her knees, and finally stepped out of the wetsuit.

Caitlin tilted her head to one side. "So, I definitely can't persuade you to have dinner with me tonight?" Her heart beat fast against her chest, and she couldn't take her eyes off Andi. She stood, still dripping from the surf, in an orange, one-piece swimsuit. Caitlin pressed her fingers into her thighs. What she really wanted was to pull Andi into her arms and erase the physical distance between them.

"I'm sorry. I can't, not tonight." Andi dragged on a chunky, white, oversized cardigan, and pulled it down over her thighs. "I was out of range for most of the morning, so I didn't get your messages until this afternoon. And here's the reason why."

A tall man approached them with a curious grin. He ran a towel over his unshaven face, before offering Caitlin his hand in greeting.

"Hi, I'm Luc…Andi's brother."

He was good-looking, olive-skinned with straight, strong eyebrows. Luc flashed a megawatt smile at her. He crossed his muscled arms and tilted his head to one side as his gaze travelled from Caitlin to his sister, then back to Caitlin. "And you are?"

"Nice to meet you Luc, I'm Caitlin."

Andi gathered the scattered items from the sand and turned to Caitlin. "This is my *big* brother. You've already met his blue heeler, Zip."

"Not from around here?" Luc asked, as he tossed his towel onto the sand.

"I'm living in Melbourne." Caitlin crouched down to play with Zip, who was rolling on her back. "Oh, you are an adorable pup."

"Caitlin is from Cork, Ireland. *Temporarily* working in Melbourne," said Andi.

Andi's emphasis on the word was not lost on Caitlin. "Wonderful to meet you. I do see the family resemblance." She smiled. The siblings were a very attractive pair.

"Yeah to some extent, but with my craggy, square face, I can't be compared to *this* beautiful creature." He nudged Andi.

"Sure, I definitely won't argue the fact." Caitlin threw the tennis ball down the beach. "Not at all." She smiled at Luc. Not having siblings herself, Caitlin enjoyed the interaction between brother and sister.

Andi rolled her eyes. "Caitlin wanted to have dinner, but I explained that unfortunately we've already made plans for tonight."

"Please, don't apologise. Maybe we can make it another night. I'll be in Hakea for a few days."

Luc picked up both surfboards with little effort and tucked one under each arm. "I'm sure Maddie and Tom wouldn't mind an extra guest. How about it, Caitlin? You could join us? Everyone around here is pretty easygoing," he said as they walked together towards the steps.

"That's very kind of you to offer. It's been a long week, and I think a quiet night in is just the thing for me. I'll put my feet up and watch a movie."

Disappointment flashed across Andi's face.

"Why don't you both come to Kinsale for dinner tomorrow night? I've had little chance to use the gourmet kitchen to make more than scrambled eggs for one," Caitlin said. "Indulge me, please." She stared at Andi. *Say yes.*

Andi glanced questioningly at Luc, who answered without hesitation. "That would be brilliant. What can we bring?"

"Just yourselves, but is there anything at all either of you can't eat?"

"No offal!" they said in unison, laughing.

"Not a chance," she assured them.

"Apart from that, we're not fussy at all. Surprise us," Andi added.

At the top of the stairs, Luc turned to Caitlin with a broad grin. "I'm really looking forward to experiencing your cooking tomorrow night and exploring the hillside house. With a builder's eye, of course." He winked at his sister. "See you at home, Andi."

Alone with Andi at last, Caitlin stepped towards her and gently lifted a wet strand of hair from her face. Andi's skin glowed in the early evening light.

Andi captured her hand, held it against her cheek and lowered her gaze. She licked her lips as Caitlin leaned forward and lightly kissed the tip of her nose. She just couldn't resist.

"It is good to see you. I'd be lying if I said you haven't crossed my mind many times over the last two weeks." Caitlin sighed.

Andi tugged at her hair and stared at the ground before lifting those dark, soulful eyes to gaze at Caitlin. "I've thought about you too, and it is nice to see you again." She hesitated, and Caitlin waited for her to continue. Finally, Andi said, "Enjoy your evening at home, Caitlin. I'll see you tomorrow."

"I will. And you will."

Caitlin stood for several minutes and watched Andi walk along the path till she was out of sight. Tomorrow evening couldn't come soon enough.

After a meal of steamed spinach and a single poached egg on toast, Caitlin sat at her desk, staring at spreadsheets.

For five years, Isabella and Caitlin had worked on a plan for the estate and the mansion's metamorphosis to a private art gallery. Bella Gallery.

Caitlin admired Isabella's generosity and dedication in sharing her art collection—and her home—with the public.

By coming to Australia, she had accepted the challenge, and it was now Caitlin's responsibility to facilitate their plan.

Using their new data collection system, she spent the evening checking the records Kim had updated during the week. After two hours at her desk, Caitlin was still distracted, and her thoughts kept returning to Andi. She was drawn to her. Her earthiness. Her wholesome intensity. Caitlin could not forget her supercalifragilistic body and captivating smile.

"I'm acting like I'm fifteen years old." She sighed at herself.

Right on cue, her phone beeped with an incoming text from Andi.

I hope UR relaxing. Recharging?

Caitlin replied.

Thank you. I am. Cx

That was a lie. How could she relax when all she could think about was Andi?

Caitlin closed her laptop and headed downstairs. She might as well spend more time thinking about Andi, wearing that formfitting orange swimsuit, in the comfort of her own bed. Alone.

Chapter 8

With the sound of the ocean waves as background music, Andi and Luc walked together along the cliff path. The spring evening was warm, and insects hummed, clicked, and chirped; it was an impressive chorus. The crisp, clean smell of coastal tea-tree filled the air.

"Let me just say before we get there—I think she's a bit of all right," Luc said.

"I could tell by the way you were checking her out." Andi punched his arm. "You weren't half-obvious." She kicked a stone along the path in frustration.

He raised his eyebrows. "I wasn't that obvious, was I? Wouldn't do *me* much good. Let me tell you, I think this long-legged Irish lass… She's smoking. Actually…she is gorgeous." He tapped Andi on the shoulder. "And I think she has her eye on you, little sister."

"Yes, that's right—get it all out *now*, before we get to Caitlin's house, so you don't embarrass yourself or me."

"You do like her, don't you?" he asked.

"Yeah, how could I not? But nothing is ever that simple is it? Look, it's complicated. Caitlin is not in Australia for long, and I just don't want to go down that road again."

"You're talking about Martha, aren't you? Just because you and Caitlin like each other, spend time together, it doesn't have to be—move in and live together, does it? What about having a bit of fun?"

"The exhibition is what matters at the moment, and I don't need to be distracted by anything." Andi tried to convince herself, but Caitlin was so distracting.

"I'd say go for it. Enjoy life, Andi."

The iron entrance gates loomed before them, and Andi turned to Luc. "Not another word from you on the subject. Please, behave." She pushed the intercom button on the stone pillar.

A silky voice came through the small speakers. "Welcome to Kinsale. Just follow the line of grass trees that curve to the front staircase. The front door is unlocked, and I'm in the kitchen."

Luc pointed to a tiny camera above the speaker. "Right you are." He prodded Andi.

He could act up now, but he'd better behave when they got inside, or Andi would make him suffer. A rubber spider in his wetsuit should do it.

They followed a series of low, discreetly lit wooden platforms that cut through the landscaped garden of native trees and low shrubs.

"Hot damn." Luc moved his hands along a low sandstone wall. He walked up the timber stairs to a door painted solid turquoise. "Some nice work here."

Andi stood at the front entrance. The playfully curved expanse of glass reflected the pinks and oranges of the setting sun. As requested, they entered the doorway and walked through to a spacious hallway.

Caitlin wiped her hands on a tea towel and walked towards them, casually sexy in faded denim jeans, white T-shirt, and bare feet. She was framed perfectly in the large picture window with the ocean and the glowing evening sky behind her.

As Caitlin drew her into an enveloping hug, Andi's body tensed, skittish and wary. She recalled the easy heat of their kiss and stepped out of Caitlin's embrace.

"You have an absolutely stunning home. Thanks for your invitation." Luc moved in and circled Caitlin's shoulder briefly. "Whatever you're cooking smells fantastic… I'm starving."

"That's what I like to hear." Caitlin's arm tightened around Andi's shoulder once again. She released her to lead them into the living room. "Please, have a seat. I am a little out of practice, but I hope my cooking satisfies your hunger." She grinned and placed her hand casually to the gentle curve of her hip. "Now, what can I offer you two to drink?"

Andi reached into her canvas satchel. "I know you said not to, but it's a local wine, and I think you'd like it," she said, handing Caitlin the bottle.

"Hay Shed Hill Chardonnay." Caitlin read out the label. "Perfect. The wine will go superbly with our first course." She placed the bottle on the white stone bench and handed Luc a corkscrew. "Make yourself at home. The dining alcove has stunning views of the water and the lights from the bay are magnificent tonight. I won't be long."

"Can I help?" Andi followed Caitlin into the kitchen.

The room was spacious with stark white walls and streamlined stone benchtops. The lack of dividing walls in the kitchen opened it up to the living room. Glass sliding doors, now closed to keep out the chill of the evening, revealed an outdoor deck.

Caitlin glided around the kitchen with the ease of a professional. She seasoned the bright white scallops with sea salt and pepper before dropping them into the hot pan sizzling with butter.

"Did you enjoy your evening out?" She looked amused as Andi peered over her shoulder inquisitively. "Careful, I wouldn't want hot butter to splash on your shirt." She flipped the scallops deftly. "You could grab the lemon watercress. Middle shelf, on the left." She pointed to the refrigerator with glass doors. "So, how was your night out?"

"It was fun. Maddie and Tom are old friends from Navigators. It was an early night. Just homemade Portuguese pizza and a catch-up."

Andi placed the container of watercress on the bench. She hooked her thumbs into the belt loops of her jeans and resisted the urge to reach out and swipe a morsel of seafood from the pan.

Caitlin served the scallops onto three white-china plates, drizzled brown butter over the dark, crusty, caramelised tops, and garnished with the watercress.

Rey Farm watercress. Andi was pleased that Caitlin was using their produce. Caitlin obviously hadn't made the connection, and for now, Andi was happy to leave it that way.

"Yummy that looks and smells amazing," Andi said.

Caitlin bumped the oven door shut with her knee and pointed to the loaf of garlic-infused bread and bowl of lemon wedges on the bench. "Would you grab those for me, Andi? I think we're ready to eat."

Andi slid into a chair across from Luc at the rectangular, Victorian, ash table. He winked conspiratorially and poured the wine. Delicious aromas filled the room, as Caitlin placed the food on the table.

Luc raised his glass in a toast. "This looks fantastic, and I'm sure it tastes incredible. Thank you, Caitlin." He clinked his glass against hers. "Here's to new friends."

Andi and Luc were easy guests to please. Their conversation drifted from Luc's work to the construction of Kinsale. He asked a lot of questions about the architect and the materials used. Luc was so interested in the build that Caitlin offered to show him the photographic record her grandaunts had kept.

Caitlin returned to the kitchen, leaving Andi and Luc to browse through the photographs while she prepared the main course—a crispy skin fillet of mulloway fish, green beans, and shaved fennel served with a light, citrus sauce. She'd selected local ingredients, taken pleasure in the preparation, and hoped she'd produced a satisfying meal to share with her new friends.

Andi and Luc were still leafing through the albums and Maggie's sketchbooks when Caitlin rejoined them. She carried in three plates of food, two plates balanced on her forearm.

"This is an amazing record," Luc said. "It would have been great to see them drill into these cliffs to lay the foundations." Luc picked up the albums and placed them at the other end of the table.

"I believe Maggie and Isabella were very particular that the house made as little impact on this environment as possible."

"I would love to look more carefully at some of Maggie's sketchbooks. Her drawings of the coastal plants and birds are so detailed," Andi said and looked up as Caitlin placed a steaming plate of food in front of her.

"Of course you can. I think there are some other sketchbooks of Maggie's you may appreciate. We'll have to arrange a time for you to come over and look through them, if you'd like?"

Andi nodded, and her face lit up with pleasure. "Yes, please, I'd like that very much."

Caitlin sat down at the table and lifted her glass. "Welcome to Kinsale. You two are the first guests I've entertained here. I hope we will do this again soon."

She sipped slowly on the crisp chardonnay and tried not to stare at how beautifully Andi's sleeveless swing top outlined her smooth, muscled biceps.

"Fantastic. I thought you wouldn't be able to top that first course, but you have," Luc complemented.

"Thanks, Luc. I'm told that the fish was caught near Lorne this morning, and all the ingredients are locally grown."

Andi smiled appreciatively. "Thank you for preparing this meal for us." Her eyes flashed a fiery copper in the candlelight. "It is scrummy."

"I love cooking. I'm glad you are enjoying my efforts." Caitlin held her gaze until Andi dipped her head and looked away.

Caitlin turned to Luc, who watched their exchange with a small smile on his face.

"So, Andi said you are the genius who built her home studio."

"Genius?" He laughed. "Well, yes…using Andi's initial drawing. She wanted a simple, functional space using low-impact materials. She was a hard taskmistress and pretty sure of what she wanted. Or should I say, what she didn't want."

"Very funny. I was really fortunate, actually. He took my plan and made it into something special," Andi said, sounding proud of her brother. "Because Luc did most of the work himself, I got much more for my money. Solar power, cross-vertical ventilation, natural lighting…even a planted, green roof strip."

"Very lucky," agreed Caitlin. Andi gathered food onto her fork. She seemed to hesitate, her hand paused near her mouth. As her gaze met Caitlin's, Andi licked her lips. Caitlin sighed and cleared her throat. She spent way too much time focusing on Andi's lips.

Caitlin turned to Luc. "So do you visit Hakea often?"

"I'm here finishing the air-controlled storeroom for Andi's paintings. We need to have the room ready before the heat arrives. It can reach temperatures up to forty-two degrees here in the summer."

Caitlin shook her head. "That is extreme. I'd like to take a look at the storeroom when you've finished, if I could?"

Andi and Luc nodded in unison.

"I enjoyed the ambience of your place, Andi," Caitlin continued. "It has such a light, natural feel. You have an amazing creative space."

Andi smiled, pushing her empty plate aside. "It's home."

The conversation continued smoothly, as they cleared the dishes away. Andi scraped and rinsed, while Caitlin stacked the dishwasher. Luc leaned against the kitchen bench and answered Caitlin's questions about his business based in their hometown, Navigators.

"Andi's done the sea change, but a lot of city folk are doing the tree change. That just means more work for me, so I'm not complaining." He laughed. "Sustainable housing is the new buzzword."

Caitlin ground the beans and switched on the coffee machine. The aroma of rich, fresh-ground coffee filled the air. "Make your way into the lounge, and I'll bring the coffee." She spun around to face her guests. "Oh, I didn't ask—would either of you prefer tea?"

"Coffee, please. It smells fantastic," said Andi. She led her brother back into the living room.

Caitlin joined them, carrying a serving tray laden with three tulip-shaped coffee cups and a matching bowl of sugar cubes she placed on the side table. She handed an espresso to Luc, who reclined in the red Jacobsen egg chair. She pushed the table closer to Andi and sat down beside her, legs tucked beneath her.

"This is nice, eh?" Luc said. He relaxed into the curved upholstered chair. "This place is kind of understated but plush, luxurious, and comfortable at the same time."

Andi looked around from her corner of the leather sofa. "I love this sandstone wall and oblong fireplace. It creates such a cosy atmosphere," she said.

"It is lovely. I wish Isabella would come here more. Do you visit your family often Andi?"

"Not enough," Luc complained. "Mum would love to see her more. Actually we would all like to see more of her, but—"

"Ah-ha," said Caitlin.

Andi ignored their jibe. "I haven't had as much time lately, but I try to get home at least once a month."

"Once a month? That seems perfectly reasonable."

"Uh-huh. This is really good coffee."

"Sensory Lab dark roast… It's my favourite in Melbourne."

Andi moaned. “It’s smoky, and I can taste caramel or toffee.” She ran her tongue along the rim of her cup and licked the créma from her top lip. As their gazes connected, Caitlin blinked and then looked away.

“I’m glad you like it.” She stroked Andi’s forearm, enjoying the gentle ripple of muscles. “Are you always so easily pleased?”

Luc bit into a square of dark, fudgy chocolate and sighed.

“I can’t accept praise for the chocolate brownie either. They’re from a little café in Collingwood named Tomboy. Pistachio and macadamia.”

Andi placed her empty coffee cup on the table and leaned back, fingers steepled to her lips. Caitlin traced her own mouth with her finger. She could easily lose herself in the softness of Andi’s lips.

“Caitlin might enjoy a trip to Lorne with you…”

She heard her name, and Caitlin refocused on the conversation. “What? Sorry, Luc, did you say something about Lorne?” she asked.

“Andi has to make a trip to Lorne day after tomorrow, and I thought you might want to tag along?”

“I’m sure Caitlin has better things to do than trail along after me.” Andi rolled her eyes. There was an irritated edge to her voice.

“I *would* actually enjoy a trip to Lorne.” Caitlin sipped her hot drink carefully, surprised by Andi’s quick response. “If you don’t mind the company?”

Andi hesitated. “I don’t mind. I’m just collecting a parcel, but if you want to come along, you can. Have you seen much of the Great Ocean Road?”

“No, I haven’t, apart from Aireys Inlet. It would give me a chance to discover a bit more about the area from someone who knows.” Smiling, she added, “Someday I’d like to drive all the way along to Port Campbell. I’ve heard it’s one of the most spectacular drives in Australia.”

Luc rubbed his chin, clearly hatching a plan. “Why don’t you two visit Sheoak Falls? I’m sure Caitlin would love the rainforest walk. The fern-lined valley is spectacular this time of year.”

“I’m keen. If you have time, we could have lunch in Lorne,” suggested Caitlin.

“You two seem to have this whole thing sewn up.” Andi shrugged. “Okay, I’m game.”

She didn’t sound too enthusiastic, and Caitlin wondered if she was being too pushy, but it was Luc’s idea.

"Do you always let your big brother boss you around?"

"Oh, you don't know the half of it," Andi sighed. "When I was five, Luc and his band of cowboys tied me to the Hills Hoist and left me there till dinner time."

Luc spluttered. "Till dinner time…more like five minutes, tops."

"Hills Hoist? What on earth is that? Sounds painful."

"It's a whirligig clothesline invented by an Aussie," Luc explained.

She turned to Andi. "You poor wee thing. I can only imagine the teasing behaviour between siblings. You must have had a lot of fun growing up, hopefully with no lasting scars." Caitlin looked from Andi to Luc. "What's the age difference?"

"I'm thirty-eight, Ana is four years older than me, and baby Andi is thirty."

"Thirty? She *is* just a baby, indeed."

Andi watched Caitlin surreptitiously. She guessed Caitlin would be a few years older than her. Somewhere in her midthirties. Caitlin had a graceful body—finely muscled, lean, and strong. Feminine and alluring. A flawless complexion, naturally arched eyebrows, high cheekbones, and a secret smile that curved her full lips.

"How about you? Do you have brothers and sisters?" asked Luc.

"No, it's just me, no siblings. Although, there were always lots of extras milling around our home."

Caitlin appeared relaxed, her arm resting on the back of the sofa behind Andi. So close that heat radiated along her shoulders from the proximity.

"My father is an English literature professor at Cork University. When I was growing up, students would join us for lunch, especially on Sundays. There was never a dull moment. Mum and Dad still live in the same house on campus."

"They must miss you," Andi murmured.

"I hope they miss me a little," she said. "They lead busy lives of their own. I can't see either of them retiring for many years, and Mum's position as head librarian for the arts faculty keeps her on her toes. She's also involved with community groups and fundraisers on campus."

Andi was mesmerised by the way Caitlin twirled her fingers through her dark hair as she spoke.

"I've spent time travelling a bit…away from home, now and again. So, yes, I'm sure they miss me. And I miss them."

Luc stood, stretched his tall frame, and stifled a yawn with his hand. "Even the night view from here is amazing," he said.

They turned towards the window and looked out across the ocean. Lights twinkled like stars in the water, and the distant silhouette of a cargo ship moved slowly across the horizon.

"I think you fed us too well, Caitlin. I'm ready to turn in," he said.

Andi jumped to her feet. "I've really enjoyed tonight. Thank you so much. The meal was delicious, and I hope I can return the invitation soon…err… without poisoning you."

"Don't you like cooking?" Caitlin asked.

Luc smirked, shaking his head.

"I love good food. When it comes to cooking, I get by, but I do like to keep it simple."

"Simple can be good."

Andi walked into the hallway and sensed Caitlin's gaze on her as she followed.

At the front door, Luc gave Caitlin a quick, casual kiss on the cheek. Andi grabbed her bag and pulled on her jacket. She hesitated near the doorway.

Before she could escape, Caitlin put an arm around her shoulder and drew her close for a hug.

"I'll see you day after tomorrow, then. What time would you like to get away?"

Andi tensed, and Caitlin let go. As much as Andi wanted to be released, she couldn't deny how much she enjoyed the sensation as their bodies briefly pressed together.

"Should I pick you up?" Caitlin asked.

Andi shook her head and followed Luc towards the stairs. "I'll swing by here. Around ten? I think the Jeep would be best on the back roads…if we decide to explore."

"All settled, then. I'll see you at ten, if not before."

"Goodnight, Caitlin, thanks again." She waved, descended the stairs, and set off after Luc. She muttered to herself, "I'm such an idiot." What made her imagine that Luc would behave? He had set her up, and now her stomach was doing somersaults.

"So what aren't you telling me, Caitlin?" It was hopeless trying to hide anything from Kiera. They had shared a lot over the years and could read each other well.

Caitlin lounged on the king-sized bed, propped up on several pillows, with her iPhone on speaker. "I don't know what you're talking about."

"Well, you've talked about Isabella, waxed lyrical about the estate, the staff, and Melbourne. Let me see…the beach…the town…the house."

"Yes, that's true," said Caitlin. She pulled the pink, mohair throw over her legs. The green, gingham pajama shirt she wore wasn't quite long enough to cover them.

"I've known you too long, my friend," Kiera giggled. "What? You've been in Australia for over three months. We talk every week, and for the last two weeks, you haven't mentioned that art curator you were seeing—"

"You mean Erica. She's an art director, actually," Caitlin said. Kiera knew very well the difference between the two roles. As an art director of a large university gallery, Erica was the boss, overseeing the curators. "I've been busy working."

Kiera guffawed. "So? That's never stopped you before. Wasn't Erica *entertaining* enough for you?"

Caitlin laughed. "Kiera, please. Erica is a very intelligent and attractive woman. She's fun."

"I'm sure she is. And you're too busy for *fun*? Since your relationship with Rachel ended, you're the one who's enjoyed the perks of uncomplicated, disposable, no-strings-attached sex. Actually, let me quote you. 'It's as important as fresh air and exercise.' And then you said, 'It keeps the cogs turning.'"

"Oh, the arrangements have always been advantageous to both sides," Caitlin said. "Consenting adults. You know the expression." Had she really said that? Probably. "No one has ever complained. Have they?"

"Oh to be sure, to be sure." Kiera hummed into the phone annoyingly.

"You're such an arse, Kiera Brady."

"So tell me, Caitlin. You sound different. Is there something on your mind? Talk to me."

Caitlin knew she would never get Kiera off the phone if she didn't give her a little *something*. "I have been meeting some new people. I've made a new friend."

"Ah-ha, I knew it. *Friend*?"

"No, I mean yes. I do mean a friend. She's a young artist living here at Hakea."

"Spill it. I want to hear the rest, all of it," persisted Kiera. "What's her name?"

"Andi, her name is Andi. What else can I say? She's a breath of fresh air. Unadulterated. Angelic, yet so, so sexy." Caitlin moaned. Just thinking about Andi made her restless. "She's an enigma, and damn it, oh so young."

"You sound a wee bit smitten, Caitlin. Angelic and sexy? Every girl's dream. What's the problem?" Kiera asked. "What's young? Twenty? Twenty-five?"

"What do you take me for? Andi is thirty."

"Perfect age. So, where did you meet her? What have you done? When are you seeing her again?"

Caitlin rattled back her answers. "We met on the cliffs. Just talked. Day after tomorrow. Maybe we did kiss...once."

"How could you forget a detail like that?"

"Definitely. Not. Forgotten. It is nearly midnight here, and I have to get off the phone."

"Not so fast, Caitlin Quinn. Hair? Eyes? Nose? Mouth? Distinguishing features?"

"She has all of those." She smiled just thinking about her. How to describe Andi? "Picture golden skin. Rich, deep-chocolate eyes. Gracefully muscled, agile body."

"Sounds like you've found the quintessentially bronzed, Aussie, surfer-girl archetype. Which makes me wonder—why are you at home alone?"

"You and me both." Caitlin shifted her body, adjusting the pillows around her. "But she has me confused. One minute she kisses me. Next minute she's cool, cautious."

"Sending a few mixed signals?"

"Exactly. I don't think she has a girlfriend," Caitlin said. "Even her brother suggested we spend the day together."

"And?"

"I'll let you know how it goes. My head hurts thinking about it." Caitlin looked at the clock. "Why aren't you working?"

"I am. I'm in the office marking level-one papers." Kiera sighed. "I'll go, but promise you'll keep me in the know."

"I promise. Goodnight, Kiera."

"I miss you. Caitlin?"

"Yes, Kiera?"

"But surely love wouldn't get so much talked about if there were not something in it."

"It's definitely time for sleep when you quote Elizabeth Bowen to me. Goodnight, Kiera. I miss you too." Since their university days, Kiera had ended their phone conversations by testing Caitlin with quotes from literature. She had rarely got the better of Caitlin on this particular subject.

"Right again. Sweet dreams."

Caitlin climbed between the sheets, punched her pillow, tossed and turned, and felt very alone in the overly large bed.

She remembered how Andi's lips felt pressed against her own. She wanted to kiss her again. And more. She growled and punched her pillow again.

Chapter 9

Andi drove her Jeep down the paved driveway to the house, where Caitlin leaned casually against a pillar under the shade of the roof overhang. She looked ready for a day of adventure. As Andi stopped the car, Caitlin gave a small wave of her hand, picked up her daypack, and walked towards her. Andi smiled. Caitlin's clothes showed off her toned legs and shoulders. She looked incredibly good in a blue and white striped sleeveless shirt and charcoal-grey cargo shorts. There was no denying Andi was intrigued by Caitlin. If she was completely honest, she had to admit her attraction to her. But she was not going to explore that any further.

Andi adjusted the passenger seat fully back to make room for those wonderfully long legs.

Yeah right, definitely not going there, Andi reminded herself.

"Hi." Caitlin slipped gracefully into the passenger seat and pulled until the heavy door closed with a metallic clunk. She smiled radiantly and nodded to Andi. "You're very punctual," she said as she fastened her seat belt. "I checked the weather forecast. Cool, clear, and sunny." She trailed her finger slowly down Andi's bare arm. "You look fetching."

Andi trembled, and she forced herself to take a slow, steady breath before speaking. "Looks like you're all ready to go. It could get drizzly in the rainforest. Did you pack a jacket?"

Caitlin tapped her daypack. "Fully prepared. Rain jacket, camera, water, mosquito repellent, sunscreen, and trail bar." She pointed to her feet. "And my sturdy, lace-up Scarpa boots."

"What, no compass?"

"You mean you don't know where we're going?" Caitlin smirked and pinched Andi's forearm.

Andi turned the key in the ignition. "No driver abuse, *please,* Ms. Quinn." She put the Jeep in reverse with a noisy, grinding gear change and backed out of the driveway. "Sorry about that. Okay, we're off."

Andi took the road towards Bells Beach. She pointed at a group of kangaroos grazing in a distant grassy paddock. "I hoped we'd see the eastern greys today. They are quite shy and often keep behind the tree line. We're in luck."

"Wow, they're huge. We have wildlife practically on our doorstep."

"Mmm." Andi smiled at the excitement in Caitlin's voice.

"Excellent, what an exceptional start to our adventure," Caitlin said, and Andi shuddered as Caitlin's hand brushed against her leg.

They approached a tree-lined gully, where the rusty ironbark eucalyptus towered over tea-trees, scrubland, and groves of grass trees.

"This is stunning. It's lovely to see the grass trees in their natural environment. I'm starting to really appreciate the magic of the Victorian landscape. At first, it seemed so dry, compared to Ireland, but now I can see the details and the distinctiveness of this coast."

"We have such a diverse mix of vegetation. I try to capture those contrasting layers in my paintings. There's an intensity of colour here that continues to inspire and challenge me. I want people to experience colours through my eyes… the way I see things."

"You do. You represent the landscape in layers of emerging energy." Caitlin stared out the window; occasionally, she would lift her camera to shoot a quick photograph. Andi was aware when Caitlin's gaze settled on her.

"I love the way you use colour. Colours have the ability to make us feel and dream, in an indescribable way. It is true that the value of any medium exists in its ability to express what nothing else can."

Andi turned her head, astonished at Caitlin's perception. "I like that. *You* make me see my own paintings in a totally new light." She hadn't known her long, but Caitlin seemed to understand her. Andi sighed. Or was it just that Irish charm?

"Are you okay?" Caitlin asked.

"Yes, I'm good." Andi turned the car onto the Great Ocean Road. "We'll be in Lorne in half an hour, unless you and your camera have me stopping every five minutes. In that case, it could take us an hour, and it could be dangerous."

Caitlin gave her a bewildered look, but didn't respond.

Andi teased. "I'm not leaping off these steep hillsides to retrieve your lens cap."

Caitlin's eyes twinkled in amusement. "To be sure."

For the next twenty kilometres, they drove in silence. Caitlin seemed to be lost in the beauty of the surrounding landscape. The road wound along the cliff-tops, down onto the edge of pale gold sandy beaches, with views of the turquoise sea and crashing waves. It then rose towards a lookout, across river estuaries, and through lush rain forests. Caitlin reached for her camera and pleaded with Andi to pull over on the roadside.

Caitlin stood on the side of the road and brought the camera up to her eye to take a series of shots towards the coastal rock formations and the rolling green hills southwest towards Lorne.

"The smell of these trees is intoxicating." Caitlin took a deep breath. "Eucalyptus gums?"

"Yes, this area is known as the manna gum woodland, but closer to Lorne, we'll pass through the blue gum forests. The sweet, fresh smell of eucalyptus is incredible, especially after the recent rain."

As Caitlin stepped back from the railing, she lost her footing and stumbled. Andi reached out, automatically, to steady her. "Got you."

As she climbed back into the Jeep, Caitlin said, "These trees remind me of your big painting at the studio."

"*Filtered Through*?" asked Andi.

"That's the one. You've captured the subtleties of colour and light through those beautiful tall trunks."

Andi smiled and rolled down her window to enjoy the invigorating scent. "Inspiration for that came from a place not far from here. It was a misty autumn morning. I wanted to build an image with a series of translucent layers. One on top of the other, showing those flaxen tones when the sun is high and doesn't have the strength to cast many shadows—giving the whole of nature a lightness."

"The atmospheric effects are soft, yet powerful." Caitlin's hand rested briefly on Andi's arm. "Do you know the work of Will Rickson?" she asked.

"Yes, I do. I've seen his series on the Victorian ranges at the National Gallery. Unfortunately, I missed his retrospective exhibition in Canberra two years ago."

Andi steered the Jeep back onto the main road, towards Lorne.

"Well, next time you're in Melbourne, you might like to visit Isabella's home in Kew. She has a number of Rickson's paintings and some of his earlier sketches and drawings."

"Are you serious?"

Caitlin laughed—the joyful sound filled the car. "I am indeed. And it will give you a chance to meet Isabella, because I am positive she would love to meet you."

Andi absorbed this new revelation. There were many layers to Caitlin Quinn. Just like Vermeer's paintings; when subjected to X-ray photography, they'd revealed many translucent layers. Caitlin was full of surprises and subtleties.

What else would Andi discover, peeling back her layers?

Caitlin climbed out of the Jeep to stretch her legs. Andi had disappeared around the back of a small timber cottage. Parked at the top of a steep hill in Bay Street, from Caitlin's vantage point, the beauty of Lorne's pale, golden beaches and cerulean waters was clearly visible.

They had driven through the main street, lined with specialist shops and numerous cafés. Lorne had the charm of a fishing village, while it possessed its share of cosmopolitan chic.

So far, the day had been clear and warm with just a light, offshore breeze. Andi appeared relaxed, content to let the day unfold organically. Caitlin suggested they lunch at Big Blue, located near the pier at the end of town. She'd read that the Mediterranean-styled restaurant was casual and contemporary. Andi had agreed immediately. It may well turn out to be a perfect day.

When she'd accidentally stepped backwards at the lookout, her body pressing into Andi—Andi's hands had automatically encircled her waist, and she'd leaned into her shoulder. Her need to increase their physical contact was palpable, her attraction for Andi undeniable.

"I'm so sorry," Caitlin had apologised and turned in Andi's arms.

Andi's expression was soft, and she lowered her gaze before looking up to settle on Caitlin's face. Andi said, "No problem." She smiled, her beautiful lips parted slightly, and Caitlin yearned to kiss her. Andi's untamed spirit and sensitivity were a dangerous combination. She had been very hard to resist.

Andi bounded towards the Jeep, holding a small hessian-covered parcel. She opened the passenger door for Caitlin. Her eyes sparkled, full of intrigue.

"And what have you got there?" Caitlin asked, pointing to the small package.

"I'll show you later, but now, I'm famished. I can't wait to try the food at Big Blue."

"Okay, then. I'm patient. *Not!*" She laughed and reached for the parcel.

Andi swatted her hand away and moved the parcel into the back seat, out of reach. "It's a medium I've wanted to work with for a long time. The artist I just visited imports it from Afghanistan."

"Lapis lazuli?"

"How did you know that? Can't surprise you, can I?" Andi said. She looked a little disappointed.

"Ultramarine blue pigment comes from the lapis lazuli stone. It was used in cave paintings in Afghanistan, as far back as the sixth century." Caitlin rattled off the information. She wriggled her eyebrows for effect.

Andi grinned, and rolled her eyes. "You're such a smart alec."

Caitlin pointed an index finger at her own chest. "You are in the presence of an art historian," she said in jest. "And I love ultramarine blue. Like Frida Kahlo, I'd love a house painted exactly that colour." She laughed. "I can't wait to see how *you* use it."

Andi hummed and drove the car back down the hill, towards the sea and the pier. "You will have to wait for that. I'm actually not sure myself."

It had been Luc's idea that they spend the day together, and although Andi had scowled and dismissed her brother, she now seemed genuinely happy to be with Caitlin.

She didn't know where this would lead, but for now Caitlin enjoyed their connection.

What was their connection? She couldn't quite put her finger on it yet. Bad choice of words. At least she was sure of two things—Andi would be exciting;

she was complicated and passionate. But Andi would also challenge Caitlin; she couldn't be complacent.

"May I suggest the Remarkable Gibbston Pinot Gris? It is an elegant blend from New Zealand and will accompany your meal beautifully."

Caitlin nodded her approval.

Their waiter was a young, blonde Greek, who introduced himself as Kosta. He looked as if he'd be more at home on a surfboard than in the uniform black and whites he wore. Kosta filled their water glasses, collected the menus, and made his way towards the bar.

Andi and Caitlin were seated outside on the terrace, under a veranda extension that sheltered them from the afternoon sun. It allowed them an unrestricted view of the long, wooden pier, the bay, and the incoming waves.

"This is a beautiful spot, Andi," Caitlin said. She stretched her arm along the table towards Andi. "It's particularly lovely with you here."

Andi studied Caitlin and held her gaze for several seconds before she looked away.

Andi looked enticing in a fitting, short-sleeved, red T-shirt and faded blue jeans. She sat with her legs crossed at the ankles and had sensibly worn a pair of green Gore-Tex boots in preparation for their afternoon walk to Sheoak Falls. Her sleeveless down vest hung on the back of her chair.

"Can you tell me about where you are from?" asked Andi. She folded and unfolded her cloth napkin. "Tell me about Cork…"

"Of course. What would you be wanting to know?"

"About your hometown, where you grew up. About your job at the university. Anything." She smiled and caught her bottom lip between her beautiful white teeth. "You seem to know much more about me, and I'd like to know you better."

Their waiter placed two glasses of wine on the linen tablecloth. He hovered near Andi, unnecessarily rearranging the cutlery and clearing the extra place settings. His assiduous attention to detail went unnoticed by Andi.

After he finally left, Caitlin said, "I think our waiter has a bit of a crush on you." She inclined her head towards his retreating figure.

Andi glanced his way and shrugged, clearly not interested.

"So, have you ever been to Ireland?" Caitlin sidestepped Andi's request for information.

Andi shook her head. "The only time I ever travelled to Europe was to Portugal, when I was eight years old. My grandpa died, and we flew over for the funeral."

"I'm so sorry, Andi."

Andi sighed. "I would have loved to meet him. I have his name. I mean his name was Andrés. He was an artist too." Andi's eyes sparkled. "But that's another story, and you are telling me yours."

"Okay. But I would like to hear about your trip to Portugal on another occasion and about your grandparents," Caitlin said and tasted the wine. "Hmm, this is good. Well, where should I start? My father's parents were from Cork City. Grandfather William was a Protestant landowner and shipping merchant. My mother's family, on the other hand, came from the Dingle Peninsula, in County Kerry. The O'Riordens were hard working Irish Catholics—sheep farmers. Isabella is my mother's aunt. She was born and lived in County Kerry until she left home at twenty-one."

"You are from a mixed bunch," Andi said. "I've read about the Dingle Peninsula and the warm water from the Gulf Stream."

"That's right, it's on the edge of the Atlantic. Parts of the coastline here remind me of Dingle Bay. Except it's very, *very* green, and there are loads of sheep. But, like this area, full of friendly pubs, music, and tourists in summer."

"Just like Hakea?"

"Yes, a bit. The range of mountains on the peninsula is much higher than anything you have here. It dominates the landscape. Then, of course, we have the Blasket Islands that lie to the west. It's stunning, Andi. Maybe one day you will want to visit that part of the world?"

"It sounds incredible. I would love to see Ireland—one day."

"Then I am sure you will," said Caitlin. She enjoyed this version of Andi—enthusiastic and bubbly—and Caitlin hoped *she* was partly the reason why.

Their food arrived and smelled divine; her stomach rumbled.

"Can I get you another wine?" asked Kosta. Caitlin glanced towards Andi, who shook her head.

"As much as I'd like to, the combination of sun and the fact that we're hiking this afternoon makes it a no for me," Andi said. "Thank you. It is a lovely wine."

"Thanks, Kosta. This spread looks wonderful," Caitlin said, a little reminder that Andi wasn't the only one at the table.

"My pleasure. Please, enjoy and let me know if I can be of any help."

They had chosen a selection of mezze to share: freshly shucked oysters with cider and shallot vinaigrette; chargrilled calamari; spicy lamb bourek with mint yoghurt and salsa verde; and a salad of watercress and asparagus, with feta, hazelnut, and tarragon dressing.

Caitlin lifted the half shell to her mouth and slurped the succulent, salty oyster straight from the shell. She licked her lips. "Oh, this is exquisite." She did the same again, but instead of putting it in her own mouth, she held it in front of Andi's lips. "Here, try this." *Scrumptious and seductive, just like Andi*, Caitlin mused.

Andi leaned forward to delicately take the plump oyster into her mouth and swallowed it whole. She dabbed away the vinaigrette that threatened to drip onto her clothes. "Mmm…yum. It is delicious." She reached for her glass but would not meet Caitlin's gaze. "How did you get into art history?" Andi asked as she concentrated on the plate in front of her.

"When I was seven, Isabella gifted me an annual subscription to *The Great Masters of Art.* Mother and I would read about a different artist every week, and I would scour through the pictures over and again. That was the beginning… and the rest is history." Caitlin winked. "Okay, okay. I started out following my father's footsteps, studying English literature. However, it wasn't long before I realised I should have stuck with what I loved all along. I did my MA in art history majoring in Celtic and Renaissance studies. Soooo…then I did my Ph.D. in international arts."

"So I should address you as *Doctor* Quinn?" Andi asked cheekily as she pushed her plate away. "I've eaten too much." She patted her trim, toned midriff.

"You can address me any way you like." Caitlin smiled and raised an eyebrow flirtatiously. "But really, Caitlin will do."

"Seeing we didn't leave many scraps for the seagulls—I think we should go for that walk I promised you." Andi stood, gathered her belongings, and picked up the bill. "But I do want to hear more, just let me settle our bill."

Caitlin grabbed the paper from Andi's hand. "No, lunch here was my suggestion and meant as a thank-you for being my tour guide today."

When Caitlin returned, she scanned the terrace for Andi and spotted her with a casually dressed man. He was leaning towards her, unsteady on his feet. Hearing his voice raised, she walked towards them quickly.

"Just one drink? My friends and I would love you to join us," he said as he moved closer to Andi. "I'm Matt."

Andi backed away and smiled weakly. "Thank you, but we were just leaving."

"Oh, that's a shame. You *really* are gorgeous," he slurred. "And sweetheart, I feel so bad that you've been sitting here all alone," he said, lurching towards her again.

"Actually, she's not alone." Caitlin stepped beside Andi and draped her arm across her shoulders in a protective way.

"Hi." A relieved smile formed on Andi's face. "Are we ready to go?"

Caitlin turned towards Matt, who stood propped against the table.

"Definitely," she said.

"Okay love…no worries," he muttered. "What a waste." He walked away.

"Really? I don't think so." She shook her head and threaded an arm through Andi's. "How about that hike?"

Chapter 10

As they drove out of Lorne, through the beginnings of lush, green woodland, they left a light cloud of brown dust in their wake.

Andi pointed towards a steep, winding track that headed up through a stand of tall trees. "That's where we'll be climbing in a few minutes." She glanced at Caitlin. "It should take us an hour to the falls and then a little less on the way back. The track down may be a bit slippery after all the rain we've had."

"I'm up for it. Although I am glad to be wearing sturdy walking shoes."

As they pulled into a small parking area, Caitlin rolled up her window and pushed open the passenger door.

Andi breathed in and filled her lungs with the rich, sweet scent. The air was slightly damp, cool, and clear. She gathered her gear and secured the car as she explained the route they would take through the rainforest of myrtle beech and blackwood trees. She watched as Caitlin slipped on her daypack and tied her rain jacket around her waist.

They walked the first ten minutes in silence, through the understorey of low ferns and mosses. Soft, dappled light illuminated the forest floor. Andi smiled as she noticed Caitlin's camera around her neck. She always had it ready.

At this stage of the hike, Andi followed just behind Caitlin, allowing her to set the pace. The track was clearly marked and signposted. There was only one way to go.

It was so easy being around Caitlin, but it hadn't escaped Andi's attention just how often Caitlin initiated physical contact between them. It was in a friendly, easygoing manner. Nevertheless, her touch couldn't be underestimated, and it made Andi's heart race. Caitlin was not subtle in communicating her interest, and it would be so easy for Andi to let her guard down, to give in to the shared attraction.

Caitlin turned around and pointed the camera at Andi. *Click. Click.*

"What are you thinking?" she asked, and snapped more photographs. *Click. Click.*

Andi held her hands in front of her face. "Hey...you're supposed to be taking photos of nature," she protested. "You know, the trees, the ferns, the birds. I'm shy."

"And that makes you an even more appealing subject."

Andi studied Caitlin. How should she respond to a statement like that? "Come on, you should point your lens towards what lies ahead." She moved past Caitlin, to lead the way.

"I see what you mean. There's absolutely nothing wrong with the view from back here either," said Caitlin. She whistled softly as she followed.

The woman was exasperating.

As they approached the falls, they heard the thunderous sound of gushing water cascading over the rock shelf and into the stream below. They stared at their reflections as water poured down into the bracken-fringed pool. The fern gully was lush, blanketed by every shade of green blending into each other.

"Andi, this is so very beautiful. It is stunning," Caitlin said, standing amid the giant tree ferns. A fine mist surrounded them. "The condensation makes your hair seem much darker, glossy and soft."

Caitlin danced fingers over the nape of Andi's neck, letting them linger on her skin. Andi swayed into the touch. Caitlin had a disturbing effect on her equilibrium, making her light-headed with the barest hint of seduction.

She ducked away from Caitlin. "If you are game enough to cross the creek, I have something special to show you," she said, by way of changing the subject.

"I've done my share of walking around the Irish countryside. And crossed many a mountain and stream. Lead the way."

Impulsively, she captured Caitlin's hand within hers. "Let me help you," Andi said, even though she was the one who needed help.

They traversed the stream, making their way across the slippery stepping stones, and reached the other side without incident. Still holding her hand, Andi led Caitlin up a steep embankment and through a thick patch of ferns. The greenery cleared, and they stood on a rock platform overlooking a panoramic view of the coastline.

"Wow." Caitlin let go of her hand and reached for her camera. Andi sat on the rock platform, leaned back against a large boulder, and took in the view.

A loud screeching interrupted their silence. Caitlin jumped, and Andi doubled over with laughter as a large seedpod barely missed Caitlin and landed near her boots.

"What on earth is that racket? And what do you find so funny?" Caitlin asked. She checked the top of her head. "Have I got bird droppings in my hair?"

"Oh, you should see your face, and no, you haven't." She tried to suppress her giggles and pointed up into the tree. Straight above Caitlin, two large birds were feeding, cracking open the seeds and sending a rain of debris onto the ground. Their curved beaks and showy crests were visible through a break in the canopy.

"What are they? Parrots?" She pointed the camera upwards; her lens followed the screeching birds.

"Those noisy blighters are gang-gang cockatoos. The male is the one with the scarlet crest; the female has the dark-grey head."

"Gang-gang? They sound like a gang, gang." Caitlin looked through the long lens. "They do look very different from one another."

Andi glanced at her watch. "We have another six kilometres back to the car, but it is an easier walk. No more rivers to cross."

Caitlin quietly sang the lyrics to "Many Rivers to Cross," as she pulled on her backpack. Andi rolled her eyes, and Caitlin added, "Okay, so I can do my share of corny. Must be all the fresh air."

Caitlin seemed relaxed on the drive home, gazing contentedly out the window. Andi reflected on their day together. There wasn't much not to like. Caitlin was engaging, fun, and as her brother would say, too damn hot.

She thought about her relationship with Martha, the professional snowboarder, one year younger than herself. It had ended abruptly.

In Australia on a promotional exchange, she'd pursued Andi, and it wasn't long before they'd fallen into each other's arms and into bed. An unstoppable dynamo, with instinctual athleticism, Martha was fearless and competitive. Andi had been smitten.

Even though her mother blamed Martha for Andi's withdrawal after their breakup, Andi knew it hadn't all been Martha's fault. She'd made it clear that with her career and her family in Europe, she was only in the country temporarily. That she'd based herself in Australia with Andi for nearly two years was remarkable.

Andi had been caught up in a whirlwind. In the summer, they surfed and partied, and in winter, Martha taught Andi to snowboard in the Victorian and New Zealand snowfields. This left Andi little time to focus on her art or her family.

When Martha's two-year visa expired, she returned home to Germany, never suggesting that Andi accompany or even visit her. Their relationship had been fun, but as far as Martha was concerned, it was time to move on. She'd obviously done just that. It had taken Andi a little longer.

Martha and Caitlin were very different, although they did have one thing in common—they were both visitors to Australia.

Caitlin, like Martha, was likely to return home when her work ended.

If they were to be friends, Andi had to make her wishes clear. But the more time she spent in Caitlin's company, the harder it was to know just what she wanted.

Caitlin dozed in the midafternoon sunlight that shimmered through the windscreen. Her creamy, smooth skin was flushed from today's fresh air and exercise. Andi's fingers gripped the steering wheel as she fought the temptation to reach across and caress her cheek.

As if sensing Andi's gaze on her, Caitlin opened her eyes and blinked as they adjusted to the strong light. She stretched, stifling a yawn with her hand. She smiled sweetly.

"Decided to wake, did you?" Andi grinned.

"Are we there yet?" Caitlin said and pulled herself into an upright position. "You should have woken me."

"You looked so peaceful, I didn't have the heart to wake you. So I just ignored the snoring and the dribbling," Andi deadpanned as she concentrated on her driving.

Caitlin hurriedly checked her face in the mirror. "I do not snore. And I did not dribble."

"Gotcha. I'm only teasing. We're about fifteen minutes from your place. Go back to sleep, if you like."

Caitlin shook her head. "I'm wide awake now. I actually feel one hundred percent. The combination of sea air, exercise, great food, and good company is working its magic."

"You look fantastic," Andi spluttered. "I mean…you do look…very relaxed."

"Hmm, I am."

Fifteen minutes later, Andi got out of the Jeep and moved to the rear of the car. She helped Caitlin with the treasures she had claimed from their walk along Shelly Beach by the Lorne pier.

"What do you plan to do with all this?" Andi lifted out a large, gnarled piece of driftwood, blonde and smoothed from the ocean.

"Isabella has a great collection of exotic succulents and bromeliads. This will create an excellent home for several of the plants."

"Okay, sounds like a good idea." Andi smiled. They worked in silence, unloading a bag of seaweed and the collection of shells Caitlin had gathered. Andi brushed her sandy hands onto her jeans. "All right. It's a little after six now. Maybe I should go. I guess—"

Caitlin must have noticed her hesitation. She asked, "Why don't you come in for a while? I've had such a wonderful day, and I don't want it to end yet. I can offer you a cold drink or a cup of tea?"

"Maybe for a short time. Luc's at home, so I shouldn't be too long."

Andi followed Caitlin out of the garage and into the house.

"Make yourself comfortable. I'll be back in a minute. Should I find us a bottle of wine?"

Definitely no wine. Andi needed a clear head and a fully functioning brain. "Actually, if you don't mind, I could use a cup of tea…and the bathroom?"

Caitlin paused at the top of the stairs. "Of course. Do you remember where it is?"

Andi nodded.

Caitlin smiled and said, "Give me five minutes, I also need to freshen up. There are clean towels in the guest bathroom."

Andi was glad to have a few minutes alone to remind herself why Caitlin was a bad idea. The more time she spent with Caitlin, the harder it was to remember.

When Caitlin returned upstairs, she found Andi gazing out the window towards the ocean. It would have been easy to put her arms around her. Although, with Andi's distant look, maybe it wasn't the right time. She'd sensed Andi's withdrawal since their return. It had been such a wonderful day; maybe she was just tired?

"There you are," Caitlin said. Andi turned around as Caitlin approached.

"I've had a great day. I really enjoyed lunch and our bush walk to the falls," Andi said and turned back to gaze out the window. An awkward silence filled the room.

Caitlin poured hot water into the teapot and carried the tray into the living room. "I'll pour the tea, and maybe we can sit down and talk."

She settled into one of the two comfortable chairs by the bay window and patted the seat beside her. Andi moved slowly across the room and sat down, a strained look on her face. She gripped the teacup, her body in a tense, unnaturally upright position.

"This is one of my favourite places to sit in the afternoons. A great place to read, and the perfect place to think." Caitlin shifted in her chair to face Andi. "You seem distracted. Do you have something on your mind?"

Andi put the teacup down on the table beside her. She pushed her body back into the chair and rolled her shoulders. "I guess I'd like to clear up a couple of things." Andi hesitated, as if unsure how to proceed.

Caitlin remained silent and raised an eyebrow as if inviting her to continue.

"I may be mistaken, but I feel there's something going on here." Andi gestured loosely between them. "I can't…I mean, I don't…damn." She rubbed her hands on her jeans and then picked at a loose thread on her shirtsleeve and twirled it between her fingers.

"You know I like you, Andi."

Andi looked up to meet her gaze, her mouth curved slightly. "And I like you, Caitlin." The moment she said it, Andi looked as if she wanted to take the words back.

With a wry smile, Caitlin said, "Why do I feel like there's a *but*?"

Andi hesitated. She looked pensive. "The other night, Luc mentioned Martha…"

Caitlin tried to keep the disappointment out of her voice. "Is Martha your girlfriend?"

Andi shook her head. "Martha *was* my girlfriend until a year ago when she returned home to Germany."

"Oh, I'm so sorry, Andi. Do you still keep in touch with her?" she asked. Obviously Martha had caused Andi some hurt on her departure.

"No, I don't. Martha moved home and moved on." Andi stood up and paced in front of the window, her hands thrust deeply in her pockets. "I should have seen it coming, but when it happened, I couldn't get my act together." She stared, almost accusingly, at Caitlin. "She left, and I couldn't function for a while."

"I'm sorry you had to go through that. Breakups are never much fun, are they?" Caitlin wondered if Andi was still in love with her.

Andi shook her head, as if trying to erase an unpleasant memory. "Even before Martha left, I'd been so caught up in a world of partying and playing that I lost my connection with my surroundings. I couldn't paint. Things lost their sharpness. Colours were hazy…blurred." She stopped pacing and sat down on the couch. "I'm babbling."

"I'm so happy that you've been able to paint again and hopefully work through some of that stuff," Caitlin said carefully. When Andi didn't respond, Caitlin moved her chair closer and clasped her hands. "So tell me what you think is happening here?"

Andi unclasped their hands and stood to move away. "Nothing is happening, Caitlin. Nothing at all." She rocked back and forth on the balls of her feet—that distinctly Andi mannerism.

"You know, I would never intentionally hurt you. I've never lied to you. I told you I am here in Melbourne working on a project. I haven't made any solid decision yet about the future."

Andi looked down at her feet.

"Can't we just take things slowly?" Caitlin asked hopefully. "Get to know each other a bit more? You know I'm attracted to you. I thought you felt the same."

"It's not that… God, it's never been that," Andi stuttered. She seemed to be on the verge of tears.

Caitlin tried to put her arms around her, but Andi stepped back with her hands up in defence. "I can't. I just can't do this now."

"But you kissed me back," Caitlin said, frustration edging its way into her voice.

Andi picked up her bag and headed for the door.

"I'll ring you, Caitlin." She opened the door, letting in a blast of cold air. "Because if I stay—" Andi took off, and Caitlin heard her footsteps hammering down the stairway.

Caitlin stared at the empty doorway as the wheels of the Jeep spun on the gravel driveway. "*Fuck*. But if you stayed—*what*? I didn't handle that very well, did I? Damn it."

Andi parked in the carport and walked over to Luc, who was packing his gear into the builder's trailer attached to the rear of his Volkswagen camper. She really didn't want to talk about what had just happened, but Andi knew she couldn't put off the inevitable for long.

Luc finished securing a pair of ladder racks to the trailer. "You're home earlier than I expected. Actually, I wondered if I'd see you at all tonight." He winked. "How'd you go?"

She kicked the trailer tyre. "Really? What did you think was going to happen? I hardly know the woman, Luc."

"Whoa, you don't have to take it out on the poor tyre, Sis." He placed his hand on her shoulder. "So, how did it go? Really?"

"I'm sorry. I had a great day. Lunch at Big Blue was amazing, and our walk to the falls was great. I think Caitlin enjoyed the day too." Andi avoided his direct look. Her eyes stung with tears on the verge of spilling over. "Do you need help with this?" she asked, pointing to the toolbox.

"No thanks, it's sorted. I'm parched, though. In twenty minutes, Zip and I will be ready for a cold beer. Won't we, girl?" he said, patting the eager pup.

"Great idea, I could use a drink myself. I'm going to grab a quick shower and change, and then we can sit out here on the veranda. How about food? Are you hungry?"

"Starving. I'll ring Birdie's and order a couple of wood-fired pizzas while you shower. The usual for you?"

"Yes, that's fine," she said. She climbed up onto the porch and picked up Koda. "How's my girl? Glad to see me, are you?" she asked as Koda headbutted her and purred loudly. "Oh Koda, why do things have to be so complicated?"

Luc called after Andi, "Oh yeah, Koda must be starving too. She and Zip have been my furry assistants all day, sleeping under the work bench, playing in the sun, chasing butterflies."

Andi crooned to the Burmese cat, "Helping Uncle Luc, were you? What a good little cat. Come on, you can keep me company while I take a shower." Koda's rough tongue grazed her knuckle. "Okay, maybe not in the shower. I know you don't like the water."

Andi called out to Luc, "Make it a small vegetarian. I had a big lunch."

"No worries," he said, reaching for his phone. "You know me, I'll finish the leftovers."

Half an hour later, Luc and Andi sat on the veranda, enjoying a beer. Zip was under the table, and Koda sat perched on the end of the long wooden bench, waiting for Luc to share one of the prawns from his pizza marinara.

"Please don't feed her any garlic. She sleeps right near my head and licks my hair."

"Spoiled cat," he exclaimed affectionately and fed her another seafood morsel. "So, are you going to spill? What had you so upset when you got home?"

That was the million-dollar question. Why was she so upset? She wasn't sure herself, but Luc was perceptive, and she couldn't pretend. Although she didn't fully understand her own feelings, Andi was grateful for his concern and his company.

Andi frowned and pushed away the rest of her food. "I think I blew it," she said. "We had a great day together, but then I let my insecurities and fears take over. Now I don't even know if she'll want to be friends."

"What happened? You like her, don't you?" He raised his eyebrows. "She seems to like you too. She's kinda touchy-feely around you all the time. And she's hot!"

Andi gulped her beer and then pressed her forehead against the icy glass. "I have no argument about that," she agreed. "I mean, I'd like to live in the moment, listen to what my body and my feelings are telling me, but—"

"But? What's the problem, then?"

"I guess I'm not prepared for a fling. Caitlin has a job, a family, and a life in Ireland. Where will that leave me when she goes home?"

Luc raised his hands in disbelief. "What is it with you girls? You share a kiss—you have kissed, haven't you?" he joked. "And you already want to move in together and exchange rings?"

"Ah, my brother, the expert on lesbian behaviour." Andi couldn't help but smile. "I wouldn't go that far. And yes, we've kissed." She closed her eyes, remembering the silky softness of Caitlin's lips as she lightly nibbled Andi's bottom lip, before pressing their mouths together in a passionate kiss. The tip of her tongue swept gently…

Luc cleared his throat. "Eh. Earth to Andi." He grinned. "So you kissed, and if that look on your face tells me anything, it was some kiss." Luc finished off the last of Andi's pizza and wiped his hands in satisfaction. "Look, I know you've been burnt and you're scared, but don't you think you're jumping the gun a little? If you haven't even been on a real date or slept together, how do you know if the two of you are even compatible?"

Embarrassed, Andi shook her head. There was definitely chemistry and that initial jolt of electricity between them. Maybe she *should* consider giving it a go.

As if reading her mind, Luc said, "If you don't give it a chance, you'll never know. Where will any of us be tomorrow?" There was a hint of sadness in his voice, and Andi knew he was thinking about Susie. "So Caitlin may go back to Ireland…and then again, she may not. You may want to get to know her a little better, or you may not. Sometimes you do have to leap before you look."

"How did you get so wise?" She smiled, pulling Koda close for a cuddle.

"Who? You mean me, wise? Maybe I need to take some of my own advice."

"Your new greenie friend?"

Luc nodded, but didn't elaborate. He brought the conversation back to Andi. "Caitlin seems like a great lady. Take it slow, get to know her more… Who knows?" He stood, checked his watch, and headed inside. "How did it get so late? Now, I'm going to put the kettle on and make us a cuppa. Then I'm hitting the hay. I'd like to be on the road by midday, so I thought we could catch a few early waves."

"I'd like that. And Luc," she called out as she reached for her phone.

"Yeah Sis?"

"Thank you."

"Hey, what are big brothers for?"

Andi tapped out a text before she had second thoughts.

I'm so sorry I rushed off like an idiot. Can we talk? If you're still interested in being friends?

Two hours later, Andi had just about given up hope of hearing from Caitlin. Feeling miserable, she crawled into bed and snuggled close to Koda.

Startled by the sound of a late incoming text, she reached for the phone.

I am sorry I pushed you. Yes, let's talk. Returned to the city early. Work stuff. I'm still interested. Caitlin

Chapter 11

Isabella's garden, filled with colourful spring blooms, reminded Caitlin of Monet's painting—*Le Jardin de Monet à Giverny*. Brightly coloured patches of flowers. Informal yet balanced.

Through the window of her second-floor bedroom, Caitlin had a bird's eye view of her grandaunt surrounded by yellows, pinks, lilacs, vivid oranges, and reds. In her wide-brimmed straw hat and olive-green gardening gloves as she held her pruning shears, Isabella was indulging in her favourite pastime in the morning sunshine.

Isabella seemed most at peace here, at home in her garden, similar to Monet, who spent much of his later life in his beloved sanctuary at Giverny, France.

Caitlin turned away from the window. Following Andi's emotional outburst and abrupt departure yesterday evening, Caitlin had felt so wound up and unsettled that she'd returned to Melbourne. When she'd arrived late last night, Caitlin had been relieved to see Andi's text, and she'd replied immediately. She couldn't lie to herself. Of course she was disappointed that Andi was not prepared to have a casual relationship. At least Andi's text offered a chance of friendship, and that was a small relief.

Caitlin's instincts told her the attraction was mutual. Andi had said so in her own words, but she didn't want to explore the attraction. Caitlin had to respect her wishes. If things had gone to her plan, she would be getting to know Andréa Rey in that large, comfortable bed at Kinsale right now. Yet, here she was.

With a frustrated sigh, she grabbed her straw hat and made her way down to the garden to join Isabella.

"Top of the morning to you, my dear," Isabella greeted her with a radiant smile. "This is a surprise. I didn't expect you home so soon." She looked at Caitlin carefully and frowned.

"Morning, Isabella. What a beautiful morning to be out in the garden." Caitlin leaned down to kiss her cheek. "I needed to get back to confirm a few details about the loan for Edge Gallery. The opening is this Thursday, and you know how pedantic Erica Hunt can be."

Isabella smiled slyly and wriggled her slightly turned-up nose. "The huntress?"

Caitlin smirked. Isabella was not wrong to call Erica the huntress. Erica had pursued her from the moment they'd met.

Isabella chuckled. She handed Caitlin a dark red rose. "The perfume is heaven, and so is teasing you." Her gaze met Caitlin's. Isabella's eyes were deep blue, a physical characteristic they shared. "It would make me deliriously happy if you found your soulmate."

Caitlin looked at the perfect flower in her hand and sighed. She held it to her nose and enjoyed the heady perfume. Was there really such a thing as a perfect soulmate?

"Let's have a cup of tea. I have some of your favourite gingernut biscuits," Isabella said. She placed the secateurs onto the garden trolley and removed her gardening gloves. "We'll take our tea on the veranda; it's getting much too hot out here for me. I'm glad to see you're wearing a hat and protecting your beautiful complexion."

Caitlin held out her arm and helped Isabella onto the shady veranda.

She carried the laden tea tray and set it down on the small table. She sat across from Isabella, who had selected her favourite high-backed cane chair.

"Sitting here at this time of year reminds me very much of a tea party in colonial India." Isabella shook her head from side to side; she had a mischievous twinkle in her eyes. "Surrounded by flowering jasmine, palm fronds, and geraniums. On our holiday in 1956, Maggie and I were entertained by a very handsome young maharajah." Her wicked laugh echoed through the garden. "He was terribly *gay* of course. We had such a fabulous time that Maggie wanted to recreate part of his tea garden."

"I have memories of Maggie here; I loved watching her paint. It was my first trip to Australia, and I must have been about ten. It was the first time I visited my fairy godmothers Down Under."

"We had to keep a close eye on you even then." Isabella chuckled as she reached for a buttery ginger biscuit. "You were such a high-spirited young miss, always up to mischief."

"I can't recall that part." Caitlin smiled. "Shall I pour the tea?"

"Please."

They sat together companionably. The sun was high in the sky, and streams of light made patterns under the wide, spreading branches of the elm tree. Caitlin picked up the Belleek bone china teapot with its dainty, hand-painted shamrocks and poured the tea. She passed the delicate cup and saucer to Isabella. "I remember you serving tea to Ma, Da, and me in these beautiful cups all that time ago. I was really nervous and felt so awkward handling this precious china."

"Ah, but you always had an appreciation for beautiful things, Caitlin. Maggie brought the tea set from Ireland a long, long time ago. This set meant so much to her, and when she shared it with me, it felt like a wedding present."

"Oh, you are a hopeless romantic. Don't you worry about breakages?"

"In all these years, we've had only a few losses. The original set had thirty-four pieces, but we still have enough of them to enjoy. There are a lot of treasures in the house, Caitlin, and I trust you to take care of them." She pushed her cup towards Caitlin for a refill. "Now, help yourself to one of Marion's gingernuts before I eat them all, and tell me why you really came back early."

The cane chair squeaked as Caitlin shifted uncomfortably in her seat. She looked down into her teacup and then raised her head. Isabella was watching her intently.

"You don't have to read the tea leaves, darling. Has your melancholy got something to do with a particular young artist?"

Caitlin drummed her fingernails on the teacup. "I'd hoped to see her again, and I did. I invited Andi and her brother to Kinsale for dinner." Caitlin pushed her hands through her hair. "Then yesterday, Andi and I had lunch together at Big Blue in Lorne and spent the afternoon walking at Sheoak Falls."

"Sounds like you had a marvellous time. Which makes me all the more curious; why did you cut short your visit?"

Caitlin had thought Andi wanted the same thing, but she clearly didn't. Yesterday evening, when Andi had rejected Caitlin, her beautifully expressive eyes were close to tears. She'd caught her lip between her teeth and lowered her eyes.

What did she expect after two dinners and a day spent together? An affair? Why should Andi risk her emotions for physical pleasure? Caitlin's inner voice chastised her.

"I guess I want something I can't have," Caitlin said.

"Oh really? You'll have to tell me more. It's not like you to give up so quickly on something you want." Isabella's observation was correct, but Caitlin knew she might not have a choice this time.

"Andi is hesitant to take a step forward, and I don't know how I feel." She drew in a breath and exhaled slowly. Caitlin wanted to sleep with Andi. Dammit. But was she willing to offer more? "I usually know what I want. Casual has always worked for me."

"So Andréa…Andi, is not willing? You haven't known her very long, so that does seem reasonable," Isabella said.

Caitlin shook her head. "I suppose that is true."

"Casual has been your modus operandi for the last few years, hasn't it?"

"I moved around a lot after my relationship with Rachel ended. A year in Paris, three months in Italy, and then New York for almost a year. As I knew I wasn't staying, it was easier not to get too involved with anyone."

Isabella nodded and gently patted Caitlin's forearm. "But you did meet and spend…time with many different people over the years, I gather? Surely some of those women wanted more of a commitment from you?"

"Most of the time, no. It was mutually beneficial for both, or so I thought. A couple of times, it got a bit uncomfortable, and I knew it was time to move on. But I have kept in touch with a few women, and they've remained good friends."

"No strings attached?" asked Isabella in a gentle tone. "I've never really understood the term. Don't get me wrong, I can understand when you're in a good place with your career and social life, and all that's missing is sex—it may work. But for how long?"

Caitlin raised her eyebrows. "I guess it has worked for me. But I admit it's not ever like that—no strings. There is a difference between a hook-up and a casual relationship."

"What is the difference? How would you define a casual relationship?" Isabella asked.

"I like to think that in any relationship, even when it is casual, you share a friendship, fun, companionship—and respect."

"If Andi is saying she doesn't want a casual relationship, how do you feel about that?"

Caitlin stood up and leaned against the veranda post. She stared out into the garden. "I'm not sure, Isabella. I'm restless. Apart from the fact that Andi is beautiful and passionate about her art—she *speaks* to me." She turned to her grandaunt. "Even though we haven't known each other long, I must admit I am beginning to question what I do want. And…" She looked down at her feet.

"And?"

"Andi is young, she is only thirty."

Isabella laughed. "And you are thirty-eight—so what?"

"She was hurt, only a year ago, when her girlfriend went home to Germany and cut off all contact." Caitlin avoided the question about Andi's age. *Why did it matter?*

"Of course Andi is scared to take a risk. If you want to deepen your friendship, you'll have to be patient." She coaxed Caitlin back into the chair beside her. "If life was a script…we would know what came next, and we could plan accordingly. But my darling, it isn't scripted, and you know what? It wouldn't be half the adventure if it were. So…"

"So?" repeated Caitlin.

Isabella's face was calm and serene as she looked at Caitlin. "I have no doubt that you can attract all the company you want, but everything worth having takes patience. Here's the secret, Caitlin; *you* have to take the risk. You have to open your heart."

Caitlin laughed. "I'd prefer to be in the driver's seat when it comes to my emotions."

"Are you scared of feeling more than just a superficial physical attraction?" Isabella asked.

"It appears that I am." She stared at her hands. "Being here for a relatively short time, I don't want my life to be complicated. And I don't want to complicate Andi's life, either."

Isabella tossed her hands in the air. "Complicated, Caitlin. Isn't that what makes life richer? You're going to have to take one day at a time. Keep in contact.

Use all those twenty-first century, thingy-me what's-its. Texts, emails, video chat." She slapped her knee. "I have an excellent idea. In two weeks, the Women in Arts Foundation is having their annual fundraiser. We always support the event. Why don't you send young Andi a couple of tickets to the dance? Four hundred women, she might enjoy a night on the tiles."

Caitlin wasn't entirely sure if that was a good idea. Four hundred women… with Andi?

"Two weeks gives you time to get to know her a little better. It gives you a chance to practice *verbal* communication skills, for a change." Isabella grinned.

Two weeks—would Andi even accept her invitation?

Chapter 12

"The waves are huge today," Ellie called as she paddled out before duck-diving under the breakers.

Andi passed smoothly through the swell, surfaced, and yelled out over the booming surf, "Yep, we've been lucky so far, but the ocean will go flat now between sets. Do you want to sit around out here and wait for another?"

They had caught a couple of good sets earlier, when the waves had peaked at over four feet. Andi knew to avoid the rip current that could pull a less experienced surfer out to sea. They'd started the day with a seven kilometre run along the cliffs, and now, after two hours in the water, she was satisfied that her muscles had taken enough of a workout.

"Let's head in. I could use some lunch," Ellie replied.

Andi gave her the thumbs-up and approached the lineup just outside the breakers. She swung the nose of her board left to catch an oncoming wave. As it approached, she turned towards the beach, lay down flat, and started paddling. With practiced style, she pushed up with her arms and stood. Finding her balance on the shortboard, she caught the glassy wave and glided gently towards the shore.

Andi slowly peeled the sleeves of her Roxy springsuit to her elbows, one sleeve at a time. She turned to watch as Ellie followed her in, smoothly riding through the whitewash and manoeuvring her board onto the sand. She threw a towel towards her. "It's been too long, Ell. We haven't done this for ages." Andi peeled and rolled the sodden wetsuit down her torso, then pulled it over her hips and legs in one fluid motion. She stretched, enjoying the warmth of the early afternoon sun as it touched her skin.

Ellie leaned forward so Andi could help with her zip. She struggled to get out of her wetsuit. "I can't remember the last time I had the luxury of three days off consecutively. My schedule at the hospital for the last twelve months has been manic."

Andi punched Ellie playfully on the arm. "Aww, I am touched that you chose to spend them with me."

"Listen, you. I haven't heard from you for weeks, apart from a few hurried text messages. Come on, I think it's time to head to Birdie's so you can fill me in on what's been going on." Ellie grabbed her gear and walked towards the steps.

"I'm right behind you," Andi said. She picked up her surfboard and followed.

She'd first met Ellie at Saint Catherine's College in Ballarat when they were thirteen years old. They were best friends and so much more… They'd even made the local paper by being the first same-sex couple to attend their graduation ball.

"Move along, slow coach," Ellie called. "Why are you dawdling?"

Andi picked up her pace and jogged up the stairs.

They relaxed in the sun at their table on the deck. Ellie bit into her veggie burger and caught a slice of avocado with her lips as it slipped out of the toasted bun. "Oh, I've missed Birdie's cooking."

"I thought you were going to say you've missed…Birdie."

Ellie stuck her tongue out. "There you go again, just won't let me forget it, will you?" Andi enjoyed poking fun at Ellie about her minor misdemeanour at a party last summer when, after a couple of drinks, she'd propositioned the *very* straight chef.

"Ah-ha, whatever you say."

Ellie stole a handful of sweet potato fries from Andi's plate. "Let's not forget who we're here to talk about." Ellie's dark eyebrows frowned in concern. "So I get a text from you saying, 'I've blown it.' What does that mean? Since you've continued to be evasive on the phone, I'm here in person to find out what's going on." She caught Andi's wrist. "This is about Caitlin, isn't it?"

Andi shrugged. "I don't know what to do. She likes me and I like her, but I don't want to do fleeting or temporary. So I told her I'm not going there."

"You mean you told her you didn't want to see her again?" Ellie asked.

"No, I do want to see her again. As friends."

"Okay. But it's not because you're not attracted to her, right?"

"Uh-huh."

"Then why? Is it because she's passing through?" Ellie narrowed her eyes. "But doesn't Caitlin have a job in Melbourne?"

"Yes, but she is only here in Australia for another eight months, give or take. She has a position back home as a lecturer in art history at Cork University."

Ellie shook her head. "Okay, that is something. But a lot can happen in eight months."

"Yeah, a *lot* can happen—and then she goes back to Ireland." Andi lowered her eyes. "Ellie, I don't know if Caitlin is the kind of woman I can have only a physical relationship with." Andi looked up and shrugged. "It's not worth it."

Ellie reached for Andi's hand. "If you actually thought that, you wouldn't be wearing your sad hat. I've learned that life is totally unpredictable, and sometimes we have to take chances. Have you talked to her lately?"

Andi nodded. "I got an email this morning. It was friendly. She'd promised to send me some information for the exhibition, which she did."

"That's good, then, isn't it?"

"Yep, it is good. I'd like to keep in touch with her."

Ellie rolled her eyes. "Keep in touch? Are you really sure that's all you want?"

Andi leaned back in her chair and looked up at the vast blue sky. "She has a way of looking at me that makes me lose concentration—it's as though we're sharing a secret, except I don't know what it is. She has the most expressive eyes. They dance. And her eyebrows seem to have a life of their own. It's as though she's about to bubble over with laughter. And..."

"Okay Andi." Ellie spluttered, her body shaking with laughter. "I think you've answered my question." She leaned forward to tug Andi's hair.

"What question?" Andi asked.

"Hello, this is Andi's phone."

Caitlin was surprised to hear an unfamiliar voice. It was a woman's voice—husky, a little sleepy, and way too relaxed. She glanced at her watch. It was ten fifteen at night. Why was a woman who was not Andi answering Andi's phone?

After a pause, Caitlin asked in her most polite voice, "Hi, could I speak to Andi, please?" She hoped she sounded unfazed.

"Andi's in the shower. May I ask who's calling?"

"This is Caitlin. And I'm speaking to?" Caitlin realised she must sound supercilious—but who was this damn woman?

"Ahh…" The voice was annoyingly soft and languid. "This is Ellie. I'll just check if Andi's dressed." Long pause. "Oh! *No*, she's not." Ellie seemed to be trying to wind her up, and it worked.

Caitlin hesitated, irritated and trying not to show it. "Okay, no problem, I'll ring back at a more convenient time," she said, still in her most polite, sterile voice.

"Hang on, don't go…here she is. In her towel," Ellie said, a hint of mischief colouring her voice.

Caitlin heard Ellie murmur. "It's *her.*"

Seconds later, she was relieved to hear a familiar voice. "Hello. Caitlin?" Andi asked in an uncertain tone.

"Hi Andi, I'm sorry if I'm disturbing you. I seem to have caught you at an awkward time." She scowled as she heard Andi's half-suppressed giggle. "And you're fresh from the shower." She pictured Andi wrapped in the fluffy towel, ruffled hair, skin flushed from the hot water.

"No, you're not disturbing *anything.* It is just Ellie. I think you met briefly at Birdie's." The way Andi said it sounded more like a question than a statement.

Caitlin kept silent, waiting for Andi to continue.

Eventually, she did. "Ellie is visiting for a couple of days for some rest and relaxation."

"That's right. Ellie is a doctor in Melbourne, isn't she?" Caitlin was curious about where Ellie fit into Andi's life. Friend with benefits? Ex-girlfriend? How close were they? Pretty close, if she was staying at Andi's small house. With only one bedroom. And only one bed. They'd seemed pretty intimate that night at Birdie's.

"Yes, Ellie is a paediatrician at The Royal Children's Hospital." Andi lowered her voice. "We've been catching up, surfing…having a bit of fun."

Sitting on the sofa in her apartment, Caitlin visualised Andi twisting a short strand of hair between her fingers. With phone in one hand and MacBook balanced on her lap, Caitlin scrolled through the photographs she'd taken on their day at Sheoak Falls. She'd shot a lot of images. In some of the pictures, rays of light beamed through the rainforest. The filtered light, especially near the waterfall, had created almost surreal effects. But the photograph that captured her attention now was of Andi standing in front of the falls, gazing upward to the tree canopy.

She'd been so spellbound by Andi's face that she'd almost missed the moment. Her instinctive reaction had taken over, and she'd pressed the shutter button as a reflex rather than a decision. The end result was Andi's beautiful serene face—long dark eyelashes, glowing smooth skin, droplets of moisture from the milky waterfall spray clinging to her dark-blonde hair. *Magic.*

"Caitlin? Are you still there?" Andi's voice at the other end of the phone pulled her back to the present.

"Sorry, I couldn't hear you. Must be a bad line," Caitlin excused her lapse in concentration. "How's the painting going?"

"Pretty much on schedule." Andi hesitated. "The surf's been great. I've had a few distractions…"

"Lucky you," Caitlin said. "I was actually ringing to see if you'd received that information I sent?"

"I did. Thank you so much for contacting your friend. I was interested to read her paper on Vermeer's use of ultramarine in his paintings. I sent her an email asking a few questions. I hope that's okay?"

"Good, I'm glad it was useful. I think Florence would love to chat with you about her research at the Sorbonne. Now, I should let you get back to whatever…I don't want you standing around in a towel all night," Caitlin murmured.

"Err…yes." There was another slight pause before Andi spoke. "Caitlin?"

"Yes, Andi?"

"If it's not too much trouble, I wondered if you could send me a couple of pictures from our trip to Lorne, and maybe some from Sheoak Falls?"

"Of course, I can do that. Any in particular?" Caitlin smiled, as she again skimmed through the many pictures she had taken that day.

"The diffused light through the tree canopy was brilliant. I'll leave it to you… Just a few of the trees—maybe a couple of the waterfall?" Andi asked. "What about that one I took of *you* by the falls? The light was perfect in that shot."

Caitlin smirked. "Sure, I'll email them to you shortly."

"I am glad you called. Goodnight, Caitlin," Andi whispered.

Caitlin breathed a slow sigh of frustration. "Goodnight, Andi, and sleep tight."

Andi returned the phone to its cradle. "Ellie, what did you say to Caitlin? How come she knew I was wearing only a towel?"

Ellie leaned forward, grabbed the end of the towel and, in a flash, whisked it away from Andi's body. She held it out of Andi's reach. "A towel? What towel?"

Andi turned on her heels and walked towards the bathroom to retrieve her clothes. "Michelle Anderson, grow up."

"Andréa Rey, Caitlin's still interested," Ellie called after her.

Five minutes later, when Andi emerged in her Little Miss Chatterbox T-shirt and pink flannel shorts, Ellie grabbed her playfully in a bear hug.

"Aww…Aren't you cute? Are you still mad at me?" Ellie lifted Andi off the ground, twirled her around in a circle, and then deposited her onto the bed. "I bet she wouldn't be able to keep her hands off you in these." She tugged at Andi's shorts.

Andi pushed her away. "Behave, you *goof*."

Ellie feigned rejection and threw herself on the bed beside her friend. "It's too late for me to start now."

Andi laid her head on Ellie's shoulder, and they settled comfortably together on top of the sheets. It was only a matter of seconds before Koda jumped up and maneuvered in between them.

"This is nice," said Ellie. "Just like old times."

Andi rose up on one elbow to look into Ellie's wistful, hazel eyes. "It is, but we're not teenagers anymore, Ellie."

"I know." Ellie tightened her grip around Andi's waist. "You know I'll always love you, don't you? So whatever you decide about this Irish lass…you have my support."

"Yeah, I do, Ellie. I love you too…and thanks." Andi held on, enjoying the warmth of her friend's arms.

They had been inseparable through secondary school. One day, a month before she turned fourteen, Andi opened her locker to find Ellie had put a gay pride magnet inside the door with a note attached. *Rowing shed. After school. Ell.*

That was the first time she and Ellie kissed. Two weeks and over a hundred kisses later, they shared the happy news of their love with Andi's parents. Emmanuel and Lina had taken their adolescent outburst a lot better than Ellie's parents. A whole lot better.

"Are you asleep?" Ellie whispered in Andi's ear.

Andi turned to face her. "No." She gently pressed her lips to Ellie's, then pushed off the bed and jumped to her feet. "Come on, I'm too wired to sleep. How about we just chill out, curl up, and watch a movie? Have you seen the Nicole Conn movie, *Elena Undone*?" Andi rifled through her DVD drawer below the wall-mounted television.

"No, I haven't. They don't show movies like that in the hospital staffroom. I want some hot chocolate with marshmallows to go with it." Ellie pouted.

"Okay. You're such a *wuss*. You get the movie ready and make yourself comfortable, and I'll be right back."

Andi headed for the kitchen as Ellie called after her, "Don't forget the *marshmallows*."

The following evening, tired after painting, Andi went to the platform overlooking the beach. She caught sight of Ellie swimming just beyond the reef. She watched her move with strong, even strokes, her body gliding gracefully through the water.

Andi thought about that weekend when they were sixteen and they'd returned from the end-of-year school camp. Ellie's father picked them up, and on the drive home, they'd sat in the back seat of Doctor Anderson's Mercedes, Ellie holding on tightly to Andi's hand.

Andi shivered as she remembered Doctor Bob's cold, hard stare. When Andi glanced into the driver's mirror, he glared directly at her. She tried to free her hand, but Ellie would not let go. When they reached the farm, Ellie insisted on walking Andi to the front door. Out of sight, she pulled Andi towards her in an emotional embrace.

"Andi, we're flying to Fiji next week for holidays," Ellie said.

"I know. How lucky are you? All that sun and swimming, coconuts and mangoes." Andi wished she could go to Fiji. Her parents would never think of spending their hard-earned money on a family holiday. All their extra cash was ploughed straight back into the farm.

"We'll be gone for four weeks." Ellie's voice was a strained whisper. "Mum, Dad, and the twins are away in Daylesford tomorrow night. Can you come over? Stay the night?"

They would have the entire house to themselves. For the first time.

"Please, Andi." She lifted Andi's chin and pressed their lips together.

Surprised and breathless, Andi said, "Yes." This was what she wanted. The butterflies in her stomach turned into soaring birds.

As the Anderson's car moved down the long driveway, Andi stared, wide-eyed, at the trail of dust swirling behind it.

That weekend had been the first time they'd slept together.

As the sun set majestically behind her, the sky was reflected in the glassy, tranquil sea—a canvas of strong reds, oranges, and pinks. With the high concentration of salt particles suspended in the air over the ocean, the sunsets at Hakea were often particularly red. This evening the colours were brilliant.

"Andi," Ellie called from the beach, as she waved her arms. At the sound of her name, Andi stirred from her trance. She watched as Ellie walked towards the stairs, her tall, lean body graceful in motion.

A few minutes later, they stood together on the platform. Ellie rubbed at her arms vigorously to kickstart her circulation. "Might be spring, but the water is bloody cold without a wetsuit. I've been trying to get your attention for ages. Where were you? Daydreaming?"

"Just thinking. I saw you out there, bodysurfing. You're in good form." Andi handed Ellie her thermal sweatshirt. "Remember our last weekend together before you went to Melbourne for university? We didn't realise then, did we—that things would change so fast?"

Ellie stared at Andi and then pulled the garment over her head. She used her towel to dry her hair.

"I'd thought that because Melbourne was only two hours away, we would still see each other often," Andi said. "But once you started, you were so snowed under with lectures and coursework, you hardly had a chance to come home."

Ellie leaned towards Andi and rested her head against Andi's shoulder. "And you were busy at college during the week and were expected to help at the farm on the weekends." Ellie stepped back and looked across the water at the setting sun. "Realistically, even if you'd travelled to Melbourne more often, I really found that first year at med school the most demanding. I was just so tired all the time."

Andi nodded. "I think we both knew it wouldn't work…not that we didn't try."

"Yes, we tried," Ellie said, her eyes shimmered in the evening light. "Do you remember that time I snuck you into St. Mary's Hall for the weekend? If you hadn't screamed—"

"I beg your pardon. I did not scream." Andi tried to look indignant—but she probably failed.

Ellie laughed and nodded exaggeratedly. "Oh yes. You screamed. If you hadn't made so much noise, Sister Laura would never have barged into my room, afraid that a murder was taking place."

"Why on earth did your parents insist that you board at that particular hall of residence? It was positively archaic…full of old-fashioned rules."

Ellie slid her arm around Andi's waist. "Regrets?" she asked.

They stood together watching the light change over the ocean. "No regrets."

Andi looked down at her paint-splattered clothes. "Hey, I was wondering if last night's leftovers would do? I don't feel like cooking tonight, and I need to get rid of this paint on my arms with a hot shower."

"Look at you—you're a walking canvas." Ellie's laughter was warm, full of tenderness. She used her thumb to wipe at the smudge of paint on Andi's forehead. "Good idea. I'm happy with leftovers. It's a cool evening. Maybe we can light a fire and share a single malt?"

"Sounds perfect." Andi agreed.

In Andi's studio, the fire crackled in the log burner. She and Ellie stretched out at either end of the large sofa—snug and relaxed, with tapered glasses cupped in their hands to gently warm the whiskey.

Ellie reached for the bottle of eighteen-year-old Jameson. "Since when did you acquire a taste for *Irish* whiskey?" She poked Andi's ankle with her toe.

Andi looked over her glass into the fire. "That's the bottle of duty-free Ana gave me last Christmas."

"But maybe it isn't just your taste in whiskey that's changed?" Ellie read the description from the label. "On the palate—it has a note of fudge, toffee, hints of wood and leather, vanilla, and a gentle, sophisticatedly spiced finish." She giggled. "Really Andi, that description could just as easily be *Doctor* Caitlin Quinn."

Andi rolled her eyes and lifted her glass.

"Speaking of whom, have you heard from the ravishing Irish woman again?" Ellie asked.

"Not since the other night."

"What're you going to do about it? Can you resist her?"

Finishing her drink in one swallow, Andi sighed loudly. "Don't want to…"

"Don't want to what? Resist her or go there?"

She rested her head back and closed her eyes. "Resist her. Okay, *there* I've admitted it. I don't want to resist her. Let's face it, Ellie, Caitlin is sophisticated, intelligent, stunning, and funny."

Ellie snickered. "Let's not forget sexy, beautiful… I agree totally… And she probably has women falling all over her."

Andi frowned and poked her tongue out at Ellie. "Thanks for that. Exactly. So why would she want anything to do with me? Struggling artist, surfer, country bumpkin, nerd."

"Take a look in the mirror, honey. You already know why she likes you. You're beautiful, inside and out. Charming, creative, funny, and *hot*." She leaned forward. "Did I mention, fantastic snowboarder?"

"Ha, ha…Won't let me live that down will you?"

"Well, let's face it. If you hadn't been trying to impress Martha with that nose grab, you wouldn't have landed on your bum in front of all those people." Ellie snorted.

"Yes, well, the problem wasn't when I grabbed the nose of the board. It wasn't even the fall. It was the embarrassment of being carried off the mountain on a stretcher—in front of *everyone*."

"It was just a precaution. The paramedics have their instructions from the resorts. Everyone's afraid of being sued," Ellie said.

Andi got up from the sofa, extended her body out along the rug on the floor, and did a short set of yoga backstretches.

"Does it still cause you pain?"

"No, none at all. But you, my friend, can still be a pain in the *arse*. I try and keep up with my stretching every day."

Ellie yawned and extended her legs out along the full length of the sofa. "I could use a bit of that myself…and a body like yours."

Andi sat up and shot her a bemused smile. "Eh?"

Ellie laughed. "That didn't come out right. What I meant to say was I could use yoga and regular stretching. I spend too many hours on my feet. This paediatric surgery rotation is taking its toll." She rolled her shoulders and rubbed at her lower back. "Six more months, and I can finally take up that fellowship." Ellie poured a little more amber liquid into their glasses and handed one to Andi. "To us."

"To us." Her heart swelled with pride at Ellie's achievements, but at what price?

"Ellie?"

"Yes?"

"Don't you ever miss it?"

"Miss what?"

"Being in a relationship. You know, someone to come home to, share things with—curl up on the couch and watch old movies, discuss your problems—stuff like that?"

"Of course. But most days, I'm so tired, physically and emotionally that I'd never have much to offer anyone. It isn't always easy, but I've made my choices. Don't get me wrong, I enjoy the idea of a relationship. But if I take up a fellowship in Seattle, I'll be gone for two years. Who is going to put up with that?"

"I'll miss you." Andi cuddled into Ellie's side with a sigh.

"And I'll miss you. Seattle is a fantastic city, and Seattle Children's covers the widest spectrum of paediatric surgery. This is what I've always wanted to do,

Andi, what I've been working towards. Anyway, you can come over. It has a great art scene, so it is a wonderful place for artists to visit."

"Two years," repeated Andi. "Seems like a long time."

"You know, don't you, that I will probably eventually come home and work in Melbourne." She moved her hand to scratch Koda, who was lying across Andi's midriff. "Mum and Dad are here, and so are the twins."

"I can't imagine living anywhere else but here. But I'd love to travel, and if I have a chance, I will," Andi said.

"It's an exciting time for you right now, working towards your first solo exhibition. Bloody *fantastic.*" Ellie raised her glass in a toast. "This is what you've dreamed about, and it's happening. And if you want my advice—don't let *her* get away. I have a good feeling about Caitlin Quinn."

Chapter 13

Caitlin loved the view from the floor-to-ceiling corner windows of her living room. From her cross-legged position on the yoga mat, she looked out over the magnificently landscaped garden with its central water fountain. The sun was rising, bringing early light into the estate's formal, east-side garden. Through an open window, she could hear the wind move through the trees with a rustling whisper. English box and hebe hedges corralled flowering azalea and rhododendron. In parallel lines to the main building sat neat rows of purple lavender, white hydrangeas, and hosta.

She finished her session of Iyengar yoga asanas—a routine she and her mother had practiced since their visit to Pune, India. At that time, Orla Quinn was on a quest to improve her concentration and posture. The primary aim of Iyengar was to unite the body, mind, and spirit for health and wellbeing, but the added bonus for Caitlin was increased flexibility and sensual power. She'd always worked hard to keep her body and mind in tune. Now, however, restlessness inhabited her, and she yearned for more earthly pleasures. She rolled up the yoga mat and headed for the shower.

Caitlin had an easy day, with few pressing appointments on her calendar. She looked forward to accompanying Isabella to an illustration exhibition at the Royal Botanic Gardens, where they would view both watercolour paintings and pencil-and-ink drawings that depicted native and ornamental plants.

Then, maybe, if Isabella was up for it, there would be a short walk around the spring blooms and a light lunch at Jardin Tan. The French Indo-Chinese restaurant was located in the gardens. Dining there would round off their outing nicely.

Caitlin finished her second espresso and checked her phone. She'd picked it up three or four times already, tempted to call Andi. So far, she had resisted. So many questions flooded her mind. Had Ellie left? What was Andi doing? Should she ask her if she would like to attend the Women in Arts bash at the Emerson hotel, or should she just send her the tickets? She checked the time. It was still too early to call, and she shouldn't disturb her now. Maybe she would ring her tonight.

"The gardens are glorious this time of year," Isabella said, as she settled back into her chair. The fragrance of star jasmine and sweet, cut grass carried on the warm wind drifting across the river. The restaurant, Jardin Tan, was big and airy, with a patterned tiled floor and sturdy, wooden tables.

"What did you think of the exhibition?" asked Isabella.

Caitlin refilled her water glass. "One hundred and fifty entries; I think the Domain House Gallery does quite well to display such a large collection of works. Impressive."

"I noticed you had your favourites." Isabella pointed to the certificate of purchase in Caitlin's hand. "Heather's watercolours are of an international standard."

Caitlin nodded. "Yes, I love the way she's captured the perfection of the pincushion-like flowers at various stages of development. Beautiful colours."

"*Hakea laurina*. Have you seen the plants around Hakea? They are much more common in Western Australia, but, for some reason, they have always grown in that pocket of Victoria, hence the town's name."

"I have. At first, I thought they were a wattle, with those woody seed cases. I was lucky to see one in bloom. Those flower heads with their red and white styles are amazing. There is a magnificent specimen in Andi's garden."

"Andi?" She stared at Caitlin. "I gather you *have* been keeping in contact with the young artist."

Caitlin closed her eyes for a fleeting moment and pictured Andi's broad shoulders, narrow waist, and smooth olive skin. She remembered the surprising fullness of Andi's breasts pressed against her own and the warmth that radiated from her passionate smile. She inhaled deeply and steadied her breathing. She nodded slightly. "I talked to her on the phone once last week."

"Have you sent Andi the tickets to the dance?" Isabella asked.

Caitlin shook her head. "Not yet, but I will."

"Well, I am pleased to hear it. That will be a step in the right direction." Isabella smiled. Caitlin wished she were as sure as her grandaunt. It was totally inconvenient that her trip to Sydney overlapped with the night of the dance. There still was a chance that she wouldn't get back in time.

Isabella's eyes lit up as the waiter placed colourful plates of food on the table. "Lemongrass beef, banh mi with house-made terrine, and a fresh and light Asian-style salad, all made with produce from the café's kitchen garden. Enjoy your meal." He bowed gracefully, leaving them to relish their food.

"A feast," Isabella delighted, rubbing her hands together. "What a colourful spread."

At her grandaunt's obvious pleasure, Caitlin smiled. Isabella was as adventurous with food as Caitlin.

Isabella always seemed to bring out the best in her. Without judgment or undue interference—Isabella was a steadying influence. The fact that her grandaunt was a lesbian made it so much easier for Caitlin to talk openly about her personal life—much easier than talking to her mother.

After making certain Isabella was safely back home in the cottage, Caitlin parked the estate's Prius in the red-bricked stable garage at the rear of the property. She made her way to the house along the tiled pathway and entered through the back door of the main building. She climbed the stairs straight up to her first-floor office.

Currently, the small ground floor gallery was open to the public by appointment only. Caitlin, Kim, and their team were in the process of setting up a new relational database system. Once that part of their work was completed, they would begin the preparation of showcases, plinths, and labels, as well as the hanging of artworks in the main gallery. Caitlin turned on her computer to check her email and reached for the stack of snail-mail that had been delivered to her desk that morning.

Letters, bills, and invitations. "Ah…here it is." She opened the red-and-grey cardboard envelope stamped with the Victorian Women in Art's logo. These should be the tickets for the fundraiser—the dance to be held at the Emerson hotel. *Excellent.*

Each year, the estate purchased ten tickets. This year, Caitlin planned to keep one for herself, whether she made it back from her meeting in Sydney or not. She would post two to Andi's studio, and the rest were for the staff and interns.

Bringing her calendar onto the screen, she checked through tomorrow's schedule. Her job demanded a combination of artistic consciousness, business acumen, social skills, and practical abilities. She'd discovered that, to her surprise, it was much more demanding than her academic career, and so far, she was enjoying the challenge—very much.

Caitlin opened an email from Erica, reminding her about the Edge Gallery opening on Thursday evening. As Isabella's representative, she'd enjoy dressing up for the occasion. Maybe she would choose something bold and funky; she liked to mix it up.

Erica Hunt, the director, planned to introduce her to many of Melbourne's art elite, so it wouldn't hurt to look the part and feel confident.

Satisfied with her productive but exhausting day of painting, Andi was too tired to prepare a hot meal. Instead she settled for a bowl of diced pawpaw, strawberries, and coconut yoghurt. She lay on the couch with Koda nestled on top of her legs. Andi loved spending any time she could with Ellie, but now that Ellie had returned to Melbourne, she needed to concentrate on her painting and the exhibition.

Next week, she'd meet with Anthony Broadhurst, the director of the Watershed, to discuss her progress. She wanted to review dates and deadlines to clarify the gallery's and her own responsibilities.

Andi was painting feverishly again after her weekend off, and it was all very well to be painting, but there was so much more involved in having a solo exhibition. The hardest part was getting her head around the other tasks on her ever-growing list.

The document Anthony emailed, listing all the tasks she had to complete, overwhelmed her. There were so many things she needed to take into account; she wished she could focus on her art and leave the rest to someone else.

A surge of panic descended on Andi. Framing, packing, insurance for transportation, pricing, planning the placement of the works… It was never ending.

Koda licked her knuckles, her tongue rough like sandpaper, and brought Andi's attention to how tightly she'd been holding Koda's foot. Andi rubbed the paw and kissed the top of Koda's head. "I'm so sorry, darling. So sorry…" Koda purred loudly and settled back into position.

When the phone rang a few minutes later, Andi reached over to grab it. Disturbed again, Koda bit firmly into her finger, the first infraction forgiven and the second swiftly punished. "Ouch!"

"Andi?"

"Caitlin."

Caitlin's laughter travelled through the phone, seductive and irresistible. "I don't usually elicit such a response."

Andi closed her eyes, charmed by the cadence of her voice.

"Sorry about that. Koda just bit me. She was on my lap and wasn't pleased when I moved. Her teeth just found my little finger."

"Okay, poor Koda," she said in a mellow tone. "How are you, apart from the new teeth marks on your pinkie?"

Andi grinned, brushing her hand lovingly across the purring feline. "I've been working, but I've had a few distractions. The weather is warm. Surf's been good, and I've had company."

"Ellie?"

"Yes. She went home yesterday, so I got straight back to painting this morning. I've a meeting with the director next week, and I have to admit I'm feeling a bit swamped." She couldn't keep the anxiety out of her voice.

"I might be able to help. Tell me, what's worrying you?" Caitlin was calm and reassuring. "I hope you don't mind, but after you told me your exhibition was at the Watershed, I did a Google search and visited the website."

"Really? Thank you. I would appreciate your opinion."

"It's quite an impressive space. I love how the building is curved along the waterfront like the hull of an old sailing ship. I also like the director's attitude, the way he supports emerging artists. In addition to showing two new artists, they seem to have at least six major exhibitions every year."

Andi was impressed that Caitlin had taken time to research the Watershed.

"My meeting is with Anthony Broadhurst, the gallery owner and director."

"I've asked around. He seems to have a very good reputation," Caitlin said. Andi imagined that Caitlin would know the right people to ask. "You haven't told me about the application process; I gather you had to submit a CV and portfolio. When did you know your application was accepted?"

She felt Caitlin was genuinely interested, and Andi's confidence grew. "It was a surprise. I got an email from Anthony five months ago asking me if I was interested in submitting for an exhibition. I couldn't believe it. Of course, he wanted high-quality images and my resume. I was pretty astonished."

"So how did he know about you? You told me you'd not produced or exhibited for over a year."

"Anthony and his partner, Todd, were holidaying in Aireys Inlet. They're friends with Cynthia, and Todd was impressed with the same painting you saw and wanted to buy it. She wouldn't sell, but Anthony asked for my details."

"Just like I did. That's rare for a director. He must have been impressed."

"I don't know about that," replied Andi. "Todd's practice is in Geelong, and he'd already been my osteopath for over a year. We get on well, and I guess he put in a good word for me."

"Don't sell yourself short. There is no way someone like Anthony would take on an artist if he wasn't one hundred percent confident of their ability."

"Thanks. Be that as it may, I still have to produce another eight paintings by the first week of December," Andi said.

"I have every confidence in you. Remember, I've seen some of your pieces already. I know you'll be fine." Caitlin's voice was melodic and encouraging. *That* was the word. Andi was *encouraged* by Caitlin's support.

"Why the need for an osteopath? Did you fall off your surfboard and land on a wave?" Caitlin asked.

"That is so *not* funny. It was a ridiculous snowboarding incident. More embarrassment than injury, actually. I'm sticking to waves in the future."

"I'm very happy you weren't seriously injured. And it's wonderful to hear you laugh." Caitlin paused. "So, can I help you with anything else? I could make some time later in the week."

Andi could easily pour out her insecurities about her preparation for the exhibition, but pride and her need to keep their friendship as just that stopped her.

"No, I'm okay. I just need to keep working through the list. It will all get done eventually."

"Okay." Andi detected a hint of disappointment in Caitlin's voice, but she had to keep some distance between them for her own sanity.

"But my offer still stands," Caitlin said. "Let me know if you change your mind."

Though their conversation ended on a pleasant note, Andi hoped she hadn't sounded ungrateful or abrupt. *Am I protecting Caitlin or myself?*

Chapter 14

Caitlin entered the contemporary building of glass and stone and went straight to the cloakroom. She unloaded her cropped leather jacket and satchel with the attendant at the desk, which left her hands free to juggle champagne and canapés. She was there to represent Isabella and the estate at the Edge Gallery's latest show, *Women in Time*.

Although confident in her role, Caitlin took a deep breath as she entered the main exhibition room with some trepidation. Tonight, she would mingle with notables from Melbourne's art world, a sophisticated gathering, and she'd dressed suitably.

"I'm so glad you showed up." A woman's arms circled Caitlin's waist as a sultry voice purred, "*God*, you always manage to look so damn delectable, Caitlin Quinn."

"Erica." Caitlin gasped and gently prised Erica's arms from her waist. She turned to face the willowy, blonde gallery director. "It is always good to see you too."

"I don't know how you manage to pull it off—but you do. Impressively arty with the essence of smart." Erica stroked the fabric of Caitlin's sweater dress. "Cashmere?"

Caitlin shifted uncomfortably as Erica's gaze dropped from her form-fitting dress and black leggings to her suede three-quarter boots.

Erica whisked two glasses of champagne from a passing waiter's tray as she studied Caitlin; her intentions were boldly transmitted and positively lascivious. "I hope you'll stick around. You're not going to disappear after the obligatory half hour of mixing, are you? You've done that before, but there are a few people here tonight I'd like you to meet."

Caitlin scowled.

"Don't give me that look. You, of all people, understand the importance of networking in these circles." Erica's hand lightly clasped Caitlin's forearm. "Afterwards, we'll have a late supper together, as soon as I can get away."

Before Caitlin could reply, Erica's assistant waved from across the room.

"Excuse me, darling, I think Nicola is having a hard time with Councillor Norton. That old lech can't keep his hands to himself. I'd better rescue her. *Don't* disappear." Erica strode towards her assistant, and Caitlin made her way through to the main exhibition.

Using the catalogue, she soon found the piece the estate had loaned to the gallery for the show. It was a large oil painting that perfectly captured its subject—the innocence and spirit of Isabella O'Riorden, a young Red Cross nurse—surrounded by a group of Korean orphans. The portrait, painted by Maggie in 1952, showed Isabella, bright eyes staring directly ahead. Her slender figure and ivory complexion created a vast contrast to the horrors of war that were reflected in the stricken faces of the children.

"You don't have her hair, but you certainly share her beauty," Erica whispered. Her lips brushed Caitlin's ear.

Caitlin turned. "Thank you for the compliment." She raised her glass in a toast to Isabella. "She was a woman in love, and she still has that eternal fire burning inside her…after all these years."

"What was their story?" Erica asked. She looked up at the portrait.

Caitlin moved forward to stand beside her. "At the end of their war service, Isabella had to return to Ireland. Maggie came home to Australia. She carried the unfinished portrait of her lover home with her."

"Going to opposite corners of the world must have been heartbreaking."

"Yes, but Maggie was determined to reunite and, after less than a year, made the arduous six-week voyage to Ireland by ship with the finished painting." Caitlin gazed up at the canvas. "This was her trump card. Her chance to secure Isabella's love."

"It obviously worked. When did they come to Australia?"

"A few months later. It was tough on Isabella. She left her country, her home, and family."

Erica raised her champagne flute. "Let's drink to a remarkable woman."

"She is…indeed."

Isabella *was* a remarkable woman and had led an amazing life. Caitlin was proud of her grandaunt. She was exuberant and passionate—an inspiration to Caitlin.

"So, what happened next?" asked Erica.

Caitlin recounted the story of how Isabella and Maggie became part of the fifties' art movement in Melbourne. Local artists were rejecting international art trends in favour of a uniquely Australian artistic perspective. Their relationship withstood separation from family, immigration, red tape, and the pressures of living as a lesbian couple in Melbourne's high society.

Gently tugging Caitlin's arm, Erica directed her across the room. "Come on, I'd like you to meet the director of the Victorian College of the Arts. As one of our leading arts academics, she is definitely someone you should get to know."

Caitlin suppressed a yawn. It had been nearly an hour since Erica had left her with a group of university academics. She stood with the remaining stragglers and was relieved when Erica approached. She placed her arm around Caitlin's waist, rather possessively, and said, "I hope you don't mind, ladies and gentlemen, but I've finished my duties here tonight and was hoping to steal away this gorgeous creature for a quiet supper."

Caitlin acquiesced, and she and Erica stepped outside into the mild evening and made their way towards the car park.

Fifteen minutes later, she followed Erica through an unassuming, unmarked door and up a flight of wooden stairs. As they reached the top step, Erica turned to her and smiled flirtatiously. Erica looked extraordinarily good in her navy-pinstripe, double-breasted wool suit jacket and pants and her white button-down shirt. Caitlin gazed at her, momentarily disconcerted, then turned her attention to their host, who greeted them at the entrance of the Supper Club. The friendly but officious host recognised Erica as a regular patron and led them to what was arguably the best seat in the house; a corner table near a picture window overlooking Parliament House and Saint Patrick's Cathedral.

"Sparkling?" Erica asked, as she flipped through the leather-bound, encyclopaedic wine menu.

Caitlin nodded, leaned closer to Erica, and pointed to the Chandon cuvée.

Erica motioned to the barman and placed their order for a bottle of Tasmanian bubbly and a light meal. Caitlin knew from a previous visit that the Supper Club was a perfect venue for intimate conversation. It was devoid of background music, with an understated old world charm and inviting ambience.

"I haven't heard from you for weeks, Caitlin. Too busy?" Erica pouted her glossy lips, feigning disappointment—although you could never be sure with Erica.

"I have been busy. Some days are totally frantic, and I'm constantly behind time. And I am still finding my way around Melbourne."

Erica lightly placed her hand on Caitlin's thigh and stroked the fine fabric of her dress. Caitlin put her hand over Erica's, discreetly halting its progress.

"Erica," she murmured.

The waiter cleared his throat and set the platter of food and two plates on their table. "Enjoy your supper, ladies," he said.

"The food here is divine." Erica reached for the platter and skilfully sliced the croque monsieur into sections. She held out a crispy morsel to Caitlin. "Try this. It's probably the best ham and cheese toastie in town."

Caitlin bit into the velvety brown sandwich, careful not to burn her tongue on the gooey melted Gruyere cheese. "Oh, this is…so good." She licked her lips.

"It's equally satisfying to watch you eat it." Erica pushed the platter closer to her.

Caitlin drained the flute of luscious sparkling wine and relaxed back into the plush sofa.

"You seem distracted tonight, Caitlin," Erica said.

"Just tired. It's been a long week." She glanced up at Erica and gave her a lopsided grin. Caitlin told herself to get over it—whatever *it* was that drew her to Andi. She'd dug a trench in the sand that Caitlin was clearly not invited to cross. Erica, however, was beautiful and willing. Caitlin added, "But not too tired."

Under Erica's gaze, she picked over the platter of appetizers. Tuna ceviche infused with coriander and lime dressing. Crispy house tortillas. Stilton and pickled walnuts.

"That should fortify you," Erica smirked. "More sparkling?"

Caitlin nodded. "Why not." She dabbed at her mouth and then placed the napkin on the table. "One more, and I'll walk you back so I can pick up the car," Caitlin said. She had parked her car ten minutes away at Erica's apartment.

Erica smiled confidently. This was familiar territory. The last time they'd shared dinner in the city, they had ended up together in Erica's apartment—in Erica's bed. The memory was certainly not an unpleasant one. Caitlin was enjoying the evening—delicious food and excellent wine in the company of Erica—a highly intelligent and attentive woman.

It was a mild spring night, and the city hummed. Fairy lights glittered in the plane trees that lined Collins Street. At this hour, the Paris end of the street certainly earned its name, with its grand old buildings, prestigious restaurants, and high-end boutiques. As they stepped out of the Supper Club, Caitlin and Erica joined the well-dressed patrons leaving the Princess Theatre.

"By the look of things, the exhibition opening went as planned," Caitlin said.

Erica seemed pleased with the attendance and level of interest shown in their latest show.

"I think so. Max from *The Age* newspaper and a handful of other reporters were in attendance. I believe the exhibition will draw enough media attention to attract sponsors for our arts program."

"Isabella and the estate are proud to be part of the program, especially as it sponsors young, disadvantaged women artists."

"We're glad to have you on board." Erica smiled sweetly. "You're a native already. Are you enjoying our city?"

"Yes, I do love Melbourne. It lives up to its reputation for being one of the most liveable cities in the world." Suddenly, Erica lurched forward and pulled Caitlin to safety as a cyclist veered towards them.

"Damn. Maybe I spoke too soon. Thank you." She stared at the disappearing bike and shook her head. Close call. "Having said that, I also love getting down to the coast as often as I can."

Erica scoffed. "Not for me, I'm afraid. I'm a city girl—born and bred. Too much sand, mosquitoes, and open spaces…"

They came to a standstill outside Erica's sandstone apartment located in the historic nineteenth-century building, Treasury on Collins. Erica used her card to access the electronic security door, and Caitlin followed her into the vaulted entry foyer.

The space was empty, apart from the night doorman, who looked up and smiled discreetly before lowering his gaze to his book. As they approached the elevator door, Erica stood close and delicately brushed her glistening lips against Caitlin's cheek. "You *are* coming up for a nightcap, aren't you?"

The elevator door opened smoothly, and without further conversation, they both stepped through.

Chapter 15

"Come on, Andi. Move along. The taxi will be here any minute," Ellie shouted from the other side of the bathroom door. "You've been in there *forever*."

Five agonising minutes later, Andi turned the doorknob and reluctantly walked into Ellie's living room. A group of Ellie's friends had gathered, and they wolf-whistled in unison, filling the apartment with a high-pitched sound.

Andi had left her hair naturally windswept and tousled. It had taken her ages to decide what to wear to the dance, but she'd finally selected straight, black, tailored trousers and her favourite vintage black-and-white chequered jacket. Her charcoal silk shirt, pencil-thin red tie, and leather hi-top sneakers—shiny and black—completed what she hoped was an acceptable look.

"Wow. Andi, can you be my date?" asked Helen, the overzealous young theatre nurse who worked with Ellie.

Andi's cheeks burned, and she shoved her hands deep into her pockets.

"Oh, sweetie…if you blush like that, you'll have half the room eating out of your hands. You are simply *too* gorgeous," added Helen.

Andi tried to smile, but her nerves were on edge. She shook her head dismissively, and when she trembled, Ellie put a reassuring arm around her shoulders.

"You do look sensational," Ellie whispered softly, as she gave Andi a hug; then she turned to the group. "Helen, please stop the teasing. *Go*. And take the rest of these delinquents with you." Ellie shooed her friends out the door, allowing Andi some space. "Splendid. I think we're ready. The taxi should be here."

Andi rocked back and forth on her heels. Four hundred women at one dance. "Oh, crap," she said. How had Ellie talked her into this?

The tickets had arrived in the mail, with an accompanying note from Caitlin suggesting the event would be a perfect place for Andi to network with artists and other *arty* women. At the end of the note, in an informal scrawl, was a smiley symbol and the words—*could be a lot of fun too.*

Ellie jumped at the chance to use the second ticket. When Andi telephoned Caitlin to thank her for the generous gift, she'd been forwarded to her voicemail. The recorded message said that Caitlin was out of town on business. Discouraged, Andi had texted her and was even more reluctant to attend when the return message explained that Caitlin might not be back in time for the dance. Now that Ellie had finally persuaded her to go anyway, she'd be disappointed if Caitlin *didn't* make it to the dance.

"You are really on edge. What are you nervous about? Are you worried she will be there, or that she won't?" asked Ellie.

Andi wished she knew that herself. "I don't know." She shrugged noncommittally. "I'm…I just don't like large crowds. You know that," she said. Who was she kidding? She wanted to see Caitlin tonight. Andi hadn't thought of anything else since their last conversation.

Ellie laughed, "Yeah, sure." She pulled on her Burberry jacket. "Well, if she doesn't turn up, there will be…oh, let me see…just another four hundred or so lesbians at this charity bash. Just remember, if you don't go—and Caitlin does—she will be there with those four hundred other women instead of with you."

"Oh God," Andi groaned. "I haven't been out to a nightclub in ages. Maybe it *will* be fun. I actually feel like dancing." And maybe it will be good to hang out with some of the old crowd from Melbourne; burn off her agitation on the dance floor. She gave Ellie an admiring glance. "You look fantastic tonight, Ellie."

"Thanks, Andi *Pandi.* Dancing is the best way for you to work off all that nervous energy. Let's not forget all those women… I know, I'll shut up. I'm just trying to get you to chill. Come on, the taxi is here."

Friday night's seven thirty flight from Sydney was full of business commuters heading home for the weekend. Caitlin had chosen to leave her car in the car park at the airport and had taken only carry-on luggage, ensuring a quick getaway. It would have been near impossible to secure a taxi ride back to Kew on a Friday evening.

By the time she got to the estate, Caitlin buzzed with excitement. She bounded up the stairs to her apartment, tossed her briefcase and suitcase into the wardrobe, grabbed the outfit she'd pre-planned to wear, and headed for the shower. The thrill of expectation gave her a burst of energy. Caitlin managed to shower, dress, and head into South Yarra by ten o'clock.

Tonight, Caitlin would attend her first event at the Emerson hotel. She was ready to let loose and have a bit of fun. All the way home, she'd thought about Andi—in the plane, driving down the motorway, and especially now that she was nearly at the venue. Andi's texts during the week had been noncommittal, but she was confident Andi would be at the dance.

She thanked the parking fairy as she reversed the Roadster into a car space, directly in front of Prahran Market, two hundred metres from the hotel entrance. People spilled out of cafés and restaurants, and Caitlin hummed impatiently as she weaved and dodged through the noisy, jovial crowd.

"G'day love," called an inebriated man as he staggered towards Caitlin. "There's a party down in Greville Street. Want to join us?"

Shaking her head at the invitation, Caitlin walked on until she reached the steps of the hotel. Wide-eyed, she observed the sign over the entrance doorway.

That which we call sin in others, is experiment for us—Ralph Waldo Emerson

"Intriguing choice," Caitlin murmured. She flashed her ticket at the tux-suited doorman and made her entrance into the large, double-height, open lobby. She looked up at the curved staircase and contemplated the meaning of Emerson's words.

Tonight, Caitlin had every intention of enticing Andi to go home with her. And like the quotation implied, she would have to face the consequences of her actions.

She took the carpeted stairs two at a time to the central club level. She headed towards the pulsating, pounding music. The room reverberated, and she scanned the vast expanse of moving bodies and coloured flashing lights. "Be still my beating heart," she said and took a deep breath. With a stunningly crazy decor, a grain-wood dance floor, and a DJ booth, the setting would fire up any party.

She noticed that the room focused on excitable colours—deep reds, purples, and bright mahogany. What could you say about a club that boasted seating especially designed to be danced on? Caitlin walked past the perimeter seating, avoiding eye contact with the women who lounged near the entrance and who checked out the passers-by.

"Caitie," Kim greeted her with a booming voice and wide smile. "So glad you made it, sweetheart." She pulled Caitlin into a crushing hug. "I tried to save you a seat…but these women are throwing themselves at me." She winked and waved her hands excitedly in front of her ample chest.

Sharon playfully slapped her partner on the behind. "In your dreams…lover."

Kim and Sharon led Caitlin to their booth at mezzanine level, where the intimate lounge area and cocktail bar had a bird's-eye view of the DJ booth and the thumping dance floor below.

"What's your poison, Caitie?" Kim asked, heading for the bar.

"I'll have a cosmopolitan, please," Caitlin shouted, in an attempt to make herself heard. "Let me help you."

Kim held up her hand. "Stay right where you are. One cosmopolitan coming up. Your usual, Shaz?"

"Make it a double," Sharon said. She held down the hem of her hot-pink, pleated shift and edged closer along the bench seat towards Caitlin. She looked Caitlin over, from head to foot. "You look amazing. You've probably been running around all day. How do you manage?"

"Thanks, Sharon. Everyone looks fabulous." Caitlin smiled at the group of women seated at the booth. She turned back to Sharon. "It's been a long week, but I'm hoping to absorb some of the vitality from this crowd. I believe there is enough energy in this room to fuel the next trip to the moon."

Sharon nodded. "All the way there and back again, love," she said.

Kim sauntered back to their table. As she handed over the martini glass, she slyly motioned towards an attractive young woman who was ogling Caitlin. "I can see you're already causing a stir, Caitie. The way you're dressed tonight… oh my. You are either a femme fatale or the angel incarnate—I haven't decided which one yet." Kim bowed and collapsed beside Sharon.

"Agreed." Sharon giggled. "Only you could get away with indigo sailor trousers, shiny brass buttons, and that figure-hugging top. It shows a nice expanse of midriff. Chic and sexy," Sharon purred.

"I'm totally bowled over by these trousers. *Hello Sailor*. I've never seen anything like it before; I'm all at sea." Kim placed her hand just above her left breast. "Makes my heart race." She scanned Caitlin from top to bottom, her eyebrows arching mischievously. "And if I do say so…*damn*…those legs go on forever."

Sharon slapped Kim's hand. "Behave," she said.

"Don't worry my love, I only have eyes for you. But there *will* be others who don't have my willpower."

"Yes, too true… But I'll still be watching you."

Kim stood and placed her hands on her hips—head to one side. "To put it plain and simple, Sharon, our Irish lass here is dressed to seduce."

Caitlin shook her head at the comical banter between the two women. In a very short time, she had discovered that, to some Australians, *nothing* was sacred. But she had also learned that this fair dinkum joking and teasing was not personal. They enjoyed a great belly laugh, just like the Irish.

The luscious pink, slightly sweet, slightly sour cocktail slipped down effortlessly. Caitlin intended to drive home, so the sensible thing to do was go easy on the alcohol. Plus, she needed to have her wits about her if—when—she found Andi.

Caitlin grew restless. Where was Andi? Was she even here? It was time to find out. She excused herself and walked to the open balcony. The transparent glass rail allowed an unrestricted view of the crowded dance floor below. She tapped the railing with her hand. How would she find Andi in this multi-storied, *ridiculously* crowded venue?

She placed her now-empty glass on a passing waiter's tray and slowly scanned the room from the entrance and across the expansive dance floor. It seemed like an eternity before Andi finally came into view. Caitlin grinned. Without a second thought, she descended the stairs through the lounge bar and made her way down onto the dance floor. She blinked as her eyes adjusted to the intense flashing colours from the club lighting.

Caitlin recognised the dance remix, "I Found You" by UK band The Wanted. The room was pumping. The air was electric, and energy ricocheted and rebounded from every surface. Bodies moved, alone or together, vigorously and seductively in the high-octane atmosphere. Caitlin was exhilarated and edgy with nervous anticipation. She had no idea how Andi would react to her.

Through the haze, Caitlin noticed Ellie—her attention was clearly fixed on a woman wearing a super short emerald dress. Even though a small group of women danced around Andi, Caitlin could tell she was in her own world. Andi moved with a sensuous internal rhythm that was both graceful and alluring. Strong and so, so desirable. Caitlin needed to be closer.

She wove her way into the circle of dancers to stand directly behind Andi, who seemed unaware of Caitlin's presence. She gently trailed her fingers across the back of Andi's shoulders and encircled her waist as she breathed in the intoxicating mix of sandalwood and sunshine.

"Andi," Caitlin said with a longing sigh.

Andi's body tensed for a fleeting moment but offered no resistance. In rhythm with the music, their bodies moved together to the bouncing synths and the lengthy, high-pitched chorus. It was provocative and tempting, so seductive.

When the tempo of the music slowed, Andi whispered, "Caitlin."

"I'm so glad you're here." Caitlin slid her hands down to Andi's hips, hooked her fingers into the loops of her trousers, and drew her close. They danced effortlessly, curved together. The music pulsed like a heartbeat as the swell of her breasts pressed against Andi's back. As she turned in Caitlin's arms, Andi's gaze swept over her. Caitlin's body was on fire; pleasure sparked through her as Andi skimmed her fingertips lightly across her exposed skin, and she leaned in to place tender kisses along Caitlin's collarbone.

The song ended, and the DJ's gravelly voice boomed through the room. "Pace, pace. Pace yourselves… This is a change of pace for all you romantics out there. You can do it, ladies… Show us you're all a little 'Human' by Cristina Perri."

As the crowd on the dance floor stilled, Andi lowered her arms and began to walk away. Caitlin reached out and tugged lightly on Andi's wrist.

"Stay…*please*."

Caitlin entwined their fingers and gently placed Andi's hands onto her shoulders. Her hands moved to caress Andi's waist and trace the contours of her body. Andi gazed into Caitlin's stormy eyes. They were iridescent and flecked with every shade of blue.

Lulled by the singer's sultry voice, she rested her head against Caitlin's shoulder. Her lips brushed soft skin, and her hands moved lower in order to outline the sensuous curves of Caitlin's hips.

"Andi…" Caitlin moaned. "If you keep touching me like that…"

The song ended. Andi gasped as their bodies separated and the rush of air cooled the heat between them.

Dazed, Andi led Caitlin to the bar where Ellie and a group of her friends were leaning against the stone-grey counter.

Caitlin whispered, "I'll be right back. Don't go anywhere." She headed towards the restroom. Andi missed her already as she watched her walk away. A woman caught Caitlin's attention, and she stopped at the group of sophisticated women who sat at an amoeba-shaped communal table.

An attractive blonde rose to plant a kiss firmly on Caitlin's lips. Andi observed the interaction between the two women until the blonde looked openly at *her* with a calculating stare that turned into an inquisitive half smile. Caitlin glanced in Andi's direction and seemed to wink, but Andi couldn't be sure from such a distance. Caitlin continued on her way to the restroom. The striking blonde did not follow.

Ellie handed Andi a bottle of water. "I think you could use some rehydration," she said and nudged her shoulder. "That's not the kind of Irish dancing they do on *Riverdance*, is it?" She looked up towards the ceiling. "I thought the fire sprinklers were going to explode."

Andi held the cool bottle to her heated forehead. "She's gorgeous, and I'm a *goner*."

"Hmm… Right on both counts, my friend," Ellie said with a twinkle in her eye. "Are you coming back to Fitzroy tonight?"

Before Andi could answer, Caitlin suddenly appeared at her side. Ellie blinked in surprise. Andi looked from Ellie to Caitlin. "Caitlin, this is my friend, Ellie Anderson. You talked on the phone a few weeks ago."

"It's lovely to see you again, Doctor Anderson. I'm glad you could make it tonight."

Ellie tipped her head. "And it's a pleasure to see you too, *Doctor* Quinn. I believe I should thank you for my ticket."

Andi rolled her eyes. "Okay, you two."

"Can I get you a drink, Caitlin?" Ellie asked.

"Thanks, it was steamy on the dance floor. A sparkling mineral water would be grand," Caitlin said.

Ellie joined the drinks queue at the other end of the bar.

Caitlin moved closer and pressed against Andi—every muscle in Andi's body tensed with expectation.

"There's a blue Roadster outside with heated leather seats. Although I don't think we'll be needing them tonight." Caitlin met Andi's gaze, unblinking and fixed. "Come home with me," Caitlin murmured.

Andi swallowed hard and lowered her eyes. "I'd never turn down a ride in the Roadster." She was nervous and dizzy; her entire body tingled. Caitlin's hand rested in the small of her back, grounding her and spinning her out of control at the same time.

Ellie returned and handed Caitlin a green-glass bottle of Pellegrino.

"No, I won't be returning to Fitzroy tonight." Andi grinned and looked at Ellie's new…*friend*, who stood near the bar. "Looks like you have your hands full anyway."

Ellie planted a quick kiss on Andi's cheek. "Maybe. And maybe I'll see you both at the barbecue tomorrow night?"

Andi nodded. "I'll ring you."

"Enjoy your night," Ellie called.

Caitlin grabbed Andi by the hand, and they headed across the barroom floor, towards the staircase, and down to the cloakroom.

They stepped out onto the footpath, amid the noise and buzz of the one-in-the-morning crowd. As they approached the Roadster, Caitlin drew Andi against her, blue eyes half-lidded with desire. Andi trembled.

"I want you so much, I can't think," Caitlin said.

Her lips were soft, warm, and sweet. She glided her tongue along the edge of Andi's mouth, graceful and teasing, until Andi yielded and parted her lips.

A passing motorist leaned out of his car window, whistled, and hooted. They reluctantly drew apart.

"Time to go," Caitlin declared breathlessly, as she dashed to the driver's side.

Chapter 16

Andi realised they had reached their destination when Caitlin drove into a laneway and a set of wrought iron gates automatically opened. Two sandstone columns flanked the gates, and the tyres crunched on the gravel driveway. Caitlin brought the Roadster to a halt at the rear of a large, imposing building. Maybe this was one of those old Victorian mansions that had been converted into apartments.

"Andi," Caitlin said as she turned the key and the engine purred gently to a stop. Before Andi could unclasp her seatbelt, Caitlin's arm slid around her waist.

"Um…yes?" Andi closed her eyes.

"Are you okay? Do you feel alright about this?" Caitlin trailed her finger along Andi's jaw and tilted her face until her stormy, blue eyes met Andi's gaze directly. "You are so beautiful."

Andi could barely nod…barely breathe. Her stomach was in knots. "Yes," Andi said. Her voice was nothing more than a murmur.

"Thank God." She exhaled. She seemed to have been holding her breath. Her mouth pressed against Andi's trembling lips, at first gentle and unhurried. Caitlin's tongue teased her lips. She pressed harder, and their kiss deepened. Caitlin's mouth was warm and sweet and persistent—heat spread through Andi's body as she returned the kiss. Suddenly, Caitlin moved away and pulled the key from the ignition. No way. She wasn't going to let that kiss end. Andi grabbed Caitlin's wrist and pulled her back to capture her mouth again. Caitlin moaned into her mouth and ran her fingers along her inner thigh. Andi gasped at the trail of fire Caitlin's touch left in its wake.

"Upstairs." Caitlin's words were issued as a plea rather than a request. Andi looked at her leg, expecting Caitlin's fingers to have burnt through her trousers. She was aware only of her loudly beating heart and her desire for Caitlin's continued caress.

Caitlin opened the car door, stepped out, and collected her belongings from the rear seat. Andi followed, hands shoved deep in her pockets, and looked on as Caitlin swiped a card to disengage the electronic lock on the door.

She looked around. What was this place? She bit her lip, overwhelmed by the sudden urge to flee. Before she had time to process how impossible that would be, Caitlin clasped her hand and tugged her inside the building.

Light illuminated a large vestibule with dark linoleum flooring and stark white walls.

Caitlin led her up a stairway that brought them to the first level. They walked through solid oak doorways, past ornate plasterwork, and under high ceilings. Her leather shoes squeaked on the highly polished timber floorboards.

"Where are we?" Even though she whispered, Andi's voice echoed through the empty landing. At the end of the hallway, they stopped at another door. Caitlin pushed buttons on an access panel, and the door opened. It relocked behind them with a loud *clunk,* causing Andi to jump. Caitlin flicked on a series of switches that lit the stairs and the space above them. Andi looked up into a black, cast-iron, circular stairwell with polished wooden treads. Stairway to heaven?

A breathless whisper escaped Andi's lips. "Do you live *here*?"

Caitlin turned. Her hands came to rest on Andi's hips, and she pushed her up against the closed door. Andi played with the hem of Caitlin's blouse, and she trailed smoothly up to caress the swell of Caitlin's full breasts.

Caitlin kissed Andi, and her lips moved to Andi's ear. The path of her tongue left Andi giddy, light-headed. "Not quite," she whispered, and briefly gazed upwards. "Can you make it up the stairs?"

Caitlin skilfully popped several buttons on Andi's shirt with one hand, and her thumb brushed Andi's overheated skin. Andi's legs threatened to give way. She laid her forehead against Caitlin's and drew her body close.

"Maybe not," she sighed. The butterflies in her stomach mixed with a surge of pure desire.

Caitlin smiled. She took Andi's hand, squeezed it reassuringly, and led her up the spiral staircase.

Caitlin stepped onto the landing and turned to find that Andi had stopped two steps below her. She dropped her bag, jacket, and keys on the sideboard and pulled Andi up the last steps and into her arms. "*This* is where I live," she said.

Andi's jacket fell to the floor beside her. Caitlin walked her backwards, never losing contact. "This isn't the right time for a tour, but if you need it, the bathroom is here on our left." Caitlin leaned around the doorway and flicked on the light switch.

"Yes, I do. I mean, I would," Andi said, flustered.

Caitlin released her reluctantly. Andi looked startled, and she held her arms tight across her middle, as if to protect herself.

"There you go. Clean towels on the rack. When you finish, make your way through the magic wardrobe and into the bedroom." Caitlin pointed to the door on her right. "I promise you there's no witch on the other side." Caitlin wriggled her eyebrows.

Andi disappeared into the bathroom and closed the door. Caitlin made her way to the guest bedroom ensuite. Andi was clearly nervous, but Caitlin wondered why *she* was so anxious. This was what she'd wanted, wasn't it—Andi here, in her apartment? Caitlin put down her toothbrush and stared at herself in the mirror. *Stay calm, Caitlin.*

When she returned, Caitlin lowered the lights in the hallway and passed through the wardrobe into her bedroom. Andi wasn't there. She pulled the merino throw away from her platform bed. The room was ready, the bed adorned with smoky-grey Irish linen that softened the curved oak headboard. Where was Andi?

She walked through to the open-plan living area. "Andi," Caitlin called.

Andi stood near the kitchen sink, glass in hand, looking dishevelled and alluring, her silk shirt unbuttoned to reveal a hint of sheer black bra and that unbelievable golden, smooth midriff. Caitlin took a deep breath and exhaled slowly.

"I was thirsty… I hope you don't mind?" Andi held the glass aloft, perhaps as an apology for not being where Caitlin expected her.

She looked sexy and strong, in bare feet, wearing a shy grin. Caitlin approached and placed her hands on Andi's hips; her skin tingled. Her fingertips brushed Andi's bare stomach, and a shudder moved through Andi's body. Andi's muscles tensed under her touch, and Caitlin inhaled sharply.

"Are you okay?" Caitlin asked.

Andi nodded. "Are *you* okay?" Her fingers traced a line along the outside of Caitlin's sleeveless top and down her arms. Caitlin's breasts swelled in response, her nipples tender even against the soft material of her bra.

Caitlin lowered her hands to unfasten Andi's trouser buttons. When Andi pressed her mouth into the hollow of Caitlin's neck, it was *her* body that trembled. Andi tangled her fingers in Caitlin's wavy hair and gazed into her eyes.

"Bed now. *Please.*" Caitlin moaned.

Andi followed as Caitlin led her into the bedroom.

As Andi began to shed her clothes, Caitlin couldn't look away. Andi stepped out of her trousers and placed them neatly on the chair. She removed her shirt, folded it, and put it with her trousers. Andi approached her, clad in boxer shorts and bra, and Caitlin worked to unfasten the buttons on her own garments.

"Here let me…help you with that," Andi said and placed her hands over Caitlin's to ease the buttons through the fastenings, all the while edging her backwards, closer to the bed. Caitlin's flared trousers fell easily to the floor, and she sat down. Andi picked up the trousers, folded them neatly, and draped them over the chair.

Caitlin grinned. "Come here." Impatient, she pulled Andi onto the cool linen sheets. Andi balanced her weight above Caitlin as she released the clasp at the front of Caitlin's lacy bra with one hand. It fell away, and Andi moaned. Caitlin tossed it aside and pushed herself towards the head of the bed, taking Andi with her.

They quickly discarded their remaining clothing. When the heat of Andi's naked body pressed against hers, every muscle tingled. Andi's hands were like magic, and all of Caitlin's senses were on alert. Her body was the canvas, and Andi's fingers brushed over her skin, gentle, yet with a confidence Caitlin hadn't expected. She revelled in the luxurious sensations that flooded through her. Exquisite pleasure.

She tightened her arms around Andi's waist. They kissed, and Caitlin relished the lushness of Andi's mouth. The plains and valleys of Andi's sensual, lithe body fit with hers perfectly. She caressed along the silky contours of Andi's back and her gloriously muscled shoulders and lower to her gently curved hips.

Andi moved against her so lightly. Caitlin tightened her legs around Andi's hips to increase their connection. She was astonished that Andi's exquisitely delicate, feather-light caresses ignited her body so quickly.

Flooded with warmth, she arched her back as waves of pleasure pulsed through her body. "Andi," she whispered.

Andi met her gaze, her eyes heavy and unfocused. Seconds later, Andi's body tensed, her mouth opened, and she bit her bottom lip. With a shudder, Andi cried out. "Oh my *God.*"

Caitlin tightened her embrace and held Andi protectively as her rapid breathing slowly returned to a steady pace. With one hand anchored on Caitlin's hip, Andi gently rolled beside her. They lay side by side, arms and legs entwined.

A gentle breeze from the open window above the bed cooled their heated, damp skin. Caitlin traced her palm along Andi's body, exploring the curve of her hip and her finely muscled thigh. She laughed and pushed Andi onto her back.

"You are amazing," Caitlin said. She lowered her body between Andi's legs. "You're not tired, are you? Because I haven't even started."

Andi pushed her hand through Caitlin's hair. "No, I'm not tired."

"Well, let me see what I can do about that."

Caitlin stroked the back of her knees, and Andi squealed. "No tickling. I'm really sensitive. Please, anything else."

"*Anything*?" Caitlin raised her eyebrows, pursed her lips and blew a raspberry near Andi's belly button. "I do love a challenge." She moved further down the bed and gazed up at Andi. She kissed the slight flare of Andi's hip. "Your body is truly a work of art."

"Caitlin…I don't know if I can—" Andi whispered.

"Really?" Caitlin exhaled slowly and gently bit the inside of her thigh. Andi shuddered, and Caitlin laughed. "I'm sure I can change your mind. I've wanted to do this for so long. I've crossed the Atlantic…just to taste you."

"Help." Andi moaned. She twisted her hands through Caitlin's hair and held the back of her neck. Andi was so responsive to her touch. So receptive. Caitlin wanted to prolong their pleasure. She slowed until Andi lifted her hips and called her name. Caitlin increased her pressure, and within moments, Andi's body arched and shuddered.

When she eventually stilled, Caitlin slid up along Andi's glistening body and kissed her tenderly. "Are you okay?" Caitlin whispered.

Andi nodded, her eyes shimmering.

Then she surprised Caitlin by flipping her onto her back and kissing her thoroughly.

"My turn," she said.

Later, relaxed and heavy lidded—temporarily satisfied—Caitlin gazed at Andi sleeping. Her beautiful body gracefully curved towards Caitlin with one arm resting above the sheet, hand open. Her other arm curled with her fingers tucked under her chin. Her dark lashes fluttered in sleep. Caitlin's gaze was drawn to the gentle rise and fall of her breasts.

Asleep, she looked even younger. Andi shifted closer, as if seeking warmth, and Caitlin lifted her arm to allow Andi's head to rest against her shoulder. She pulled the sheet up to cover them both and closed her eyes.

She couldn't remember the last time she'd felt this comfortable falling asleep so close to a woman.

Chapter 17

Andi woke with a start. Fine rays of early morning light filtered through the shutters inside high arched windows. She rubbed the sleep from her eyes and watched dreamily as sunlight danced on the leaf motif of the feature wall beside the bed.

She looked at the tangled sheets that half covered her body, aware of Caitlin's hand resting lightly on her waist and the caress of soft breath on her shoulder. She sighed.

Andi thought she'd been dreaming, but the ache in her abdomen and thigh muscles was a pleasant confirmation. It was real. She turned onto her side, careful not to wake Caitlin. Andi stared in amazement—in sleep, Caitlin was even more beautiful, so serene. Her soft, pink lips curved up at the corners. Her chin cupped gently in the palm of her hand.

Andi carefully pulled back the sheet to admire the sensuous curves of Caitlin's body, the gentle hollow of her neck. Andi longed to reach out, to caress her perfect breasts. Her heart raced, as she remembered their hours of shared passion. Andi inched closer, her fingers trembling as she skimmed along the subtle wave from Caitlin's shoulder to her thigh. *Body surfing.*

There was nothing more beautiful than a woman's body. *This* woman's body. The way the light flowed over her, accentuating her details and dipping into the shadows…

A hand closed around Andi's wrist. Startled, she blinked as Caitlin met her gaze with sleepy blue eyes.

Andi laughed guiltily. Caught.

Caitlin whispered in a husky voice, "And a good morning to you." She tightened her grip on Andi's wrist and moved sensuously. Andi bit on her bottom lip as Caitlin lengthened her body in a long, languid stretch, like a panther stirring from sleep. Lost for words, she could only grin.

Caitlin released Andi and stifled a yawn. "How long have you been awake? What are you up to?" she asked, as she threaded her fingers through Andi's hair and pressed her lips tenderly against Andi's forehead.

"Would you believe *body surfing*?" she asked and nuzzled Caitlin's neck.

"Oh?" One eyebrow arched enquiringly. "Tell me more."

Caitlin stared at her with such intensity that Andi, suddenly shy, lowered her gaze.

In one swift movement, Caitlin rolled onto her back and pulled Andi on top of her.

Caitlin's nails lightly grazed her shoulder; her eyes sparkled playfully. "Better still…why don't you just show me?"

The enticing, mellow scents of vanilla and star anise combined with the pulsating steam to calm Andi's senses. She luxuriated under the cascading water from the rain showerhead. The heat soothed her aching muscles. It was like standing under a waterfall in a tropical jungle.

Andi recalled the overwhelming sensations. Caitlin everywhere. All at once. It was more than just the heart-pounding way her body responded to Caitlin's touch. It wasn't just the sexual energy between them—and there was plenty of that. When Caitlin had let down her guard, they had shared an emotional connection, a mutual tenderness and affection.

Andi wrapped herself in a soft, amazingly absorbent bath sheet. She stepped out of the bathroom and into the walk-in wardrobe to browse the rows of colour-organised garments on coat hangers and neatly folded on shelves. She stepped around a small overnight bag, searched for last night's discarded clothes, and realised they were in Caitlin's bedroom. Maybe she could borrow something of Caitlin's to wear? She didn't feel like putting on last night's clothes. Not yet.

Andi ran her hand along the first rack of elegant, classic pieces. Tailored linen, hemp, and light wool trousers, shirts, and jackets. She grinned at the couple of knee-length pencil skirts and a very sexy little black dress. Andi would definitely like to see Caitlin wearing that. The rack on the opposite wall held a range of more edgy clothes, from faded Levi's, plaid trousers, an emerald-green peacoat, and a cropped vintage biker jacket in the softest leather. She moved to the neat shelves of T-shirts, cardigans, and jumpers. There, something caught her eye. Draped over a stylish Japanese valet was a long, sage-green cashmere jumper. Andi held it against her face and inhaled, taking in the fragrance that had haunted her since meeting Caitlin. She'd found the small bottle of Tallulah Jane Aiyana perfume on a glass shelf in the chic, grey and white tiled bathroom. Rose, vanilla, and a hint of lemon. Warm, sexy, decisively feminine, earthy, and *so* Caitlin.

She shed the towel and pulled the feather-light, soft as down cashmere over her head. Caitlin was a few centimetres taller, so the V-neck jumper rested halfway between Andi's thighs and knees. Snug and comfortable, she caught sight of her reflection in the full-length mirror and ran her hand through her tousled hair. She sighed contentedly. It would do for now.

Andi was starving. It was time to explore and find something to eat.

In the kitchen, Andi opened the blind above the sink, and sunlight flooded the room. She scratched her head and stared at the cone-shaped Bugatti kettle until she found the switch. The handle had a clock and self-timer, and it flashed, asking her to set the temperature. *What the hell?*

Andi decided Caitlin was not the type to use teabags. She hunted through the rollout drawers for leaf tea and a teapot.

She placed her teacup and saucer carefully on a placemat at one end of the ash refectory table in the dining area and looked through a timber casement window at what looked like the formal entrance garden.

Inside a bluestone and wrought iron fence, the garden was lush and green, with neatly clipped box hedges forming geometric patterns parallel to a tessellated tiled path. On either side of the path were rows of coral maples, under planted with hydrangea and pinkish-white, oriental hellebores.

Bouncing bunyips…what is this place? Andi asked herself.

She grabbed a banana from the fruit bowl on the stone island bench and sat at the table to eat it and finish her tea. She gazed around the apartment. It was spacious, eclectically decorated, and stylishly furnished with a classic sectional sofa, two green Featherston contour chairs, and large, stainless steel arch floor lamps. The accompanying coffee table, sideboard, and media stand were sleek and contemporary. The vaulted ceiling had a combination of recessed and industrial pendant lamps. Elegant and chic—just like Caitlin.

Andi took her empty cup to the sink and poured a fresh cup of tea for Caitlin. She remembered Caitlin liked hers strong and black.

She placed the steaming teacup on Caitlin's bedside table, next to a small carriage clock. It was eight in the morning. Andi felt pretty good, considering she'd only had three hours sleep.

"Okay Caitlin Quinn, you gorgeous sleepyhead, I'll let you rest a little longer," Andi whispered as she made her way back to the living area.

She noticed a set of four framed photographs displayed in a row on the wall next to a flat-screen TV. While each picture shared the same viewpoint, they were clearly taken during different seasons. The first three showed a sapphire-blue sweeping ocean, majestic cliffs, and pastures of the deepest, most vivid green imaginable. The last was a winter scene, the green fields now snow-covered and the sea a stormy grey with billowing, dark clouds. These must be Caitlin's photographs. Caitlin certainly knew how to use that top-of-the-range Leica. The rugged cliffs looked a little like the Great Ocean Road, near the Port Campbell National Park. However, the green pastures and high peaks were unmistakably Ireland.

Andi paused briefly in the foyer. The bookcases that lined the walls were filled with art and history books, along with shelves dedicated to English literature—works by Shakespeare, Jane Austen, Homer, Virginia Woolf, and Browning. There were also Irish writers and poets—Edna O'Brien, Oscar Wilde, and George Bernard Shaw. From the look of Caitlin's book collection, she certainly was well read.

She wandered down the steps to the door that led into the first-floor rooms. Last night, she had walked with Caitlin on polished wooden floors, the chandeliers glistening above. She wanted to explore further.

Andi pressed the large, green knob on the wall, and the door slid open in a smooth motion. She stepped through, and the door slammed shut.

"Oh no! That was a smart move. How will I get back into the apartment?" she muttered.

She spied a bell beside the door with the word *Private* written below and breathed a sigh of relief. She wouldn't have to scale the outside of the building, wearing only the green jumper. But she would have to wake Caitlin.

Andi couldn't find a light switch. She walked carefully down the hallway, and her eyes adjusted to the semidarkness. She reached a left turn, finding herself on a wide landing facing the front of the house. Rays of coloured light danced through impressive stained glass windows. Andi peered over the ornate, curved-iron balustrade and saw a broad, sweeping staircase that descended elegantly into a spacious entrance foyer. She was gobsmacked. Was this where Caitlin's Aunt Isabella lived?

The walls on the landing were decorated with ornately framed oil paintings. A large portrait caught her eye, and she moved to stand in front of it. Painted in the late modernist style, it depicted a seated woman, perhaps in her sixties, wearing a mauve, flowing shirt and tailored, grey trousers. The use of bold brush strokes and exaggerated lines gave the woman a confident and larger-than-life disposition. She was striking and vaguely androgynous.

"That's my Maggie you're admiring." A woman's voice startled Andi. It was soft, with a hint of an Irish accent.

"Now would be a good time for the floor to open up and swallow me," Andi muttered. She turned and pulled nervously at the hem of the borrowed jumper.

A fine-boned, elegant woman stood just a few metres away, and before Andi could say a word, she held out her hand and said gently, "Hello, I'm Isabella, and you must be Andréa. I'm so happy to meet you, at last."

Andi accepted Isabella's hand and took a deep breath. "I'm happy to meet you too, Ms…"

Isabella looked directly at Andi with a bemused smile. "Isabella. Please, call me Isabella."

"It's nice to meet you, Isabella." Andi couldn't help but stare; Caitlin and her grandaunt shared the same deep blue eyes. Although Isabella's eyes were less intense, they were no less dynamic.

"I'm so sorry to be wandering around your home. I hope I'm not trespassing?"

Isabella shook her head. "No Andréa, you're not trespassing." She patted Andi's hand comfortingly. "This is Caitlin's home too, and you are welcome here." Isabella looked up at the life-size portrait of Maggie. "This was our home, when my Maggie was alive—but I now live in a cottage out the back. Near the rose garden. Speaking of Caitlin, where is my lovely grandniece?"

Andi shifted from one foot to the other. She was not dressed appropriately to be talking to anyone, especially not Caitlin's grandaunt. What was she thinking? Roaming around the mansion, half-dressed.

"She is sleeping," Andi said and remembered her embarrassing predicament. "I seem to have locked myself out of the apartment by mistake. I don't know the passcode…"

Isabella's face crinkled with laughter, and her eyes filled with mischief. "Oh, you did, *did* you? Lock yourself out? Well, let us see if we can remedy that situation."

"Remedy *what* situation?" asked Caitlin. They both turned towards her. Andi felt a rush of tenderness. Caitlin's hair was dishevelled, her skin flushed from sleep. She was the most beautiful sight, standing there in a lavender sleepshirt.

"Hi," Andi whispered. She looked down at her own attire. Her entire body felt flushed and overheated.

"Good morning." Caitlin smiled. She glanced at Andi's bare legs. Her voice was a slow caress, and Andi almost dissolved into a puddle.

Isabella coughed softly.

"Isabella, a very good morning to you. I see you two have met." Caitlin grinned.

Unlike Andi, Caitlin appeared at ease and totally composed.

It was surreal, the three of them standing there together. Andi and Caitlin were hardly dressed for the occasion. Andi rocked on the balls of her feet and glanced around the landing. It was safer to look anywhere other than at Caitlin.

Behind where Isabella stood was a vast room with parquetry floors, decorative high ceilings, and pendant lighting. So much space—large enough to be a ballroom.

"Andi?" At the sound of her name, Andi refocused. She felt light-headed, and her stomach rumbled loudly.

Isabella chuckled. "Caitlin, I think you need to feed our guest. I do believe Andi is in need of nourishment." As she turned away, her low-heeled, black pumps clapped on the shiny floorboards. "Enjoy your day, girls. I may see you both later. I'm off to my Saturday game of mahjong."

Caitlin put her arm around her grandaunt. "I'll walk you down…"

"You'll do no such thing," Isabella protested. "I'll use the lift. Thank you, dear. The car will be here soon to collect me. I just came up to put some mail on your desk." Isabella turned to face Andi. "Hopefully, we will have more time to talk next time I see you, Andréa. Now, I think you should persuade Caitlin to prepare you one of her special cheese omelettes. Simply delicious." She gave them a friendly wave. "Bye-bye."

Andi bid Isabella good morning as the small elevator door at the end of the hallway closed.

"Well, what do you think?" asked Caitlin. Her arms snaked around Andi's waist—which caused the jumper to rise dangerously up Andi's thighs.

"Oh, she is lovely. She has your eyes. I mean, you have her eyes," Andi rambled. "She is very sweet."

Caitlin tugged Andi's sleeve. "I mean are you ready for breakfast? But yes, she is very sweet." She grinned and smoothly moved her palm down the soft wool that Andi was acutely aware barely covered her bottom. "Thank you for the tea. That was very thoughtful."

Andi snuggled into the warmth of Caitlin's shoulder. "You're welcome."

Caitlin trailed her hand down Andi's arm and entwined their fingers together. "How did you sleep? Did you get any sleep?" Caitlin asked.

Andi nodded. "Enough." She looked at their joined hands.

"I had the best night I've had in ages." Caitlin squeezed her hand.

They walked back to the spiral staircase. Caitlin gave a graceful bow. "After you, *Andréa*. By the way, my cashmere looks so much better on you. Exceptional, in fact."

She swallowed. The look on Caitlin's face was shameless. Andi shook her head. "I don't think so." She pushed Caitlin gently forward. "Beauty first, you lead. I might get lost on the way…"

Caitlin took Andi's hand in hers. "I think we'll do this together…shall we?"

Caitlin sautéd thinly sliced onions in butter, along with chopped vine tomatoes. Andi swivelled on the bar stool at the kitchen island bench and watched her crack eggs with one hand. She separated the whites into a ceramic bowl and vigorously whisked until they were light and fluffy. She combined it with the yolks and poured the mixture over the tomatoes and onions.

Andi looked ravenous—and ravishing.

"Can I help?" she asked.

Caitlin pointed to the loaf on the breadboard. "Could you slice the sourdough and do the toast in five minutes? The grill is already on. She looked around and grinned at Andi. "The coffee machine is ready. Breakfast won't be long."

Andi read the label on the shiny, red coffee maker. "Francis Francis X1. I'm glad *it's* ready, because I wouldn't know what to do with it. I had enough trouble with the kettle."

"It's actually very simple. Insert the capsule, press the button…voila, a full-bodied espresso with spectacular créma."

"If that's all it takes, I think I can manage to press a few buttons," Andi said. She moved to stand behind Caitlin.

"Cheeky brat." Caitlin snapped the tea towel at Andi's thigh. "The chef is not on the menu…*yet*."

"Hey, that's not fair." Andi held Caitlin's wrist and grabbed the tea towel.

"Unhand the cook, or breakfast will burn." Caitlin sprinkled fresh herbs and grated cheese onto the egg mixture and placed the half-cooked omelette under the grill.

"Yum, I'm starving." Andi went to the other side of the bench and prepared the toast. "Who are you *really*?" she asked.

Caitlin grabbed the plates, cutlery, and serviettes and placed them on the bench. "What do you mean?"

Andi looked around and shrugged her shoulders. "I mean… Are you some kind of Irish royalty or something? This place is incredible. The art on the walls downstairs. I have a million questions."

Caitlin divided the omelette onto two plates, slid the toast into a rack, and went around the bench. She kissed Andi leisurely, taking time to enjoy the feel of Andi's body against hers. "How about we take all this to the table and start our breakfast before you faint away with hunger? Then you can ask me anything you like," Caitlin said.

"Sounds like a plan." Andi took a step back. "I might just go find my trousers."

Caitlin had pulled on a pair of loose-fitting yoga pants before she'd started cooking, but Andi was still dressed only in the soft jumper she'd borrowed from Caitlin's closet.

"You don't need them. No one else will join us for breakfast, I promise. My clothes look good on you. I'm sure we can find you something else later." She pulled out a chair.

Andi took her seat. She looked adorably sheepish, and Caitlin kissed the top of her head. "Now, eat. You need to keep your strength up," Caitlin said.

Andi slipped a forkful of omelette into her mouth. "Hmm…" She moaned.

Caitlin sipped her espresso and looked on while Andi took a bite of toast. When the melted butter slid off, she licked her lips.

"I'm sorry. I was so hungry." Andi dabbed at her mouth with a napkin.

"Don't apologise. I love that you enjoy my cooking." Caitlin lifted her fork. "Eating should be sensual and mindful, engaging all the senses." She reached for Andi's hand. "When I travelled in India, I saw people eat with their fingers. They delight in the sensual pleasures of eating. Sight, smell, sound, taste, and touch—they believe that using your hands gives you a tactile connection with your food." Caitlin dragged her hand across Andi's thigh, making her gasp. She pressed her palm into Andi's flesh just to hear her make that sound again. "And it's a sensuous experience watching you eat." Caitlin cleared her throat. "You had some questions for me?"

"Yes, if it's still okay?" Andi patted her stomach. She'd all but licked the plate clean. "Thank you, that *was* scrummy. I think my blood sugar level is back to normal."

"Well, I am delighted to hear that. Can't have you light-headed, can we?" Caitlin asked.

Andi fidgeted and twisted about on her chair. "I knew from Kinsale that your grandaunt was unique, but this place is mind-boggling. Tell me about Maggie."

"Maggie and Isabella met during the Korean War, at the army hospital in Seoul. They fell in love and were together for over fifty years."

"That's a long time." Andi smiled. "Isabella *is* Irish, right? How come she was in Seoul? I didn't know the Irish were involved in the Korean War."

Caitlin walked back to the table with her second cup of coffee. "Yes, you're right. She was serving with the joint forces, International Red Cross contingent. Isabella's ancestors are from the Dingle Peninsula... You've heard of it."

Andi looked over to the other side of the room and pointed in the direction of Caitlin's photographs. "Only from reading National Geographic magazine. Your photographs are incredible."

"Those were taken near Slea Head. Green rolling hills and long sandy beaches with cliffs and mountains towering over the ocean. The scenery is stunning, dramatic. I guess it is County Kerry's answer to your Great Ocean Road. From what I've read, Apollo Bay and the Twelve Apostles will remind me of home."

Andi returned from stacking their dishes in the sink. "Your parents live in Cork? And you too?"

Caitlin snared Andi's hand and pulled her onto her lap. She lifted Andi's chin so their eyes met, and a questioning gaze passed between them.

"That's correct. Our home is in Cork, but we've always spent holidays and many weekends on the Dingle coast. Our cottage is very close to a beautiful, secluded sandy beach with views of Dingle Bay, the ocean, and the mountains."

Caitlin lightly stroked the muscle above Andi's knee.

"Sounds...very beautiful." Andi's breath hitched as Caitlin's fingers brushed featherlike touches along her inner thigh under the jumper. "Caitlin..." Andi rested her face in the curve of Caitlin's neck and nipped with her teeth.

Caitlin gasped. "You *bit* me."

Andi kissed the corner of Caitlin's lips and whispered, "Serves you right, with this straying hand." She held onto Caitlin's roving fingers. "Caitlin?"

"Yes, Andi?" Caitlin murmured against Andi's moist lips.

"Do you have plans...for today?"

Caitlin moved her head back and grinned. "What do you think?" She manoeuvred her hand free from Andi's grasp and continued her exploration of Andi's flesh.

"I meant later. There's a barbecue at Ellie's this evening. You're invited..." Andi grabbed Caitlin's waist.

"I'd love to spend the rest of the day getting to know you better," Caitlin whispered, her hand lightly stroking Andi, her thumb finding Andi's centre. "And I will come...to the barbecue with you...Andi."

Andi breathed in sharply and sought Caitlin's mouth again. "Kiss me, Caitlin."

And Caitlin did, deeply.

Caitlin increased her pressure, growing more determined, luxuriating in the feel of Andi's arousal beneath her touch. Caitlin gently sucked her earlobe and murmured, "You are so beautiful…like this." Her heart thumped loudly inside her chest. "So open to me…"

Andi's muscles pulsed around her fingers, and her eyes grew wide. "*More… more, please…*" In release, she shuddered, and her body was molten honey in Caitlin's arms.

As Andi's breathing slowed, Caitlin held her tightly and looked into her eyes, drowning in liquid amber.

Chapter 18

Caitlin turned left into Yarra Boulevard, drove along Studley Park Road, and crossed the bridge over the broad, tree-lined Yarra River.

"Melbourne has such a spring in its step. It's so busy and alive. There's something happening on every corner; it's incredibly vibrant," Caitlin said as they passed a row of cafés and bars bustling with people in High Street.

"Spring Racing Carnival is one of the busiest times of the year. It *is* a world-class event. Thoroughbred racing and fashion," Andi said.

Caitlin turned to Andi and grinned. "I hear champagne flows through the streets at the race that stops the nation," she said. "Have you ever been to a Melbourne Cup?"

"Yes. One of our clients invited me to the Emirates marquee last year. I drank more than my share of champagne. The whole day was mind-blowing. It was a great experience, but I hate large crowds." Andi shrugged. "Once was enough for me."

They were stopped at a red light. Caitlin, unable to resist an opportunity to kiss, leaned towards Andi and was met halfway. The driver in the car behind sounded his horn, cutting the moment short.

She drove down Brunswick Street. It was a great area to hang out, with its mix of art galleries, cafés, and specialist shops only four kilometres from the centre of the city. Since her arrival in Melbourne, she often wiled away a few hours here, exploring the quirky boutiques, enjoying the gay-friendly atmosphere, and perusing the second-hand bookshops.

At their destination, Ellie's party in North Fitzroy, Caitlin reversed the car into a tight space and then turned to Andi.

"Hey." Caitlin lightly pressed Andi's forearm. "How are you doing?"

"*Hey*." Andi half smiled and wrinkled her eyebrows. "I guess we'd better do this. Ellie's parties are usually fun. She invites such an interesting mix of people. They're never boring," she rambled.

"Don't worry. There's not much that surprises me," she reassured Andi. Caitlin leaned forward, kissed her gently, and whispered in her ear, "Let's just enjoy our time together."

Andi reached into the backseat for the bottle of wine, and sixpack of ale. "Yes we'd better go into the party, before I throw you into the back seat." Andi laughed and glanced into the cramped space of the Roadster. "Maybe not."

They entered the brick terrace house to the sounds of loud music and laughter. Caitlin followed Andi down a long hallway. They passed a spiky-haired, leather-clad blonde and rooms scattered with an eclectic mix of women. Andi wasn't wrong.

"Andi, you made it," said one of the partygoers as she waved a bottle of beer precariously in front of her. "Oh, you haven't been home, have you? You're still wearing last night's clothes." The woman smirked.

"Actually, Helen, I'm about to fix that." Andi placed the drinks on the kitchen bench and whispered to Caitlin, "Ellie's in the garden, through there." She gestured to the rear of the house.

Beyond a narrow staircase, Caitlin spied Ellie through a set of open multifold doors that led to a Mediterranean-style courtyard garden.

"I'll be back in ten minutes. I need to nick upstairs and change," Andi said.

"Sure." Caitlin held on to Andi's forearm and whispered in her ear, "Are you sure you don't need help with that?"

Andi lifted one eyebrow. "I'll be fine. Maybe later." She turned to Helen. "Could you please show Caitlin where to get a drink and tell Ellie we made it. I won't be long." Andi bounded up the stairs.

"Of course, my pleasure," Helen said, as she led Caitlin towards the bar that was set up in a back corner of the living room.

Caitlin sipped her drink and scanned the crowd. She noticed Ellie beckoning her to come outside. "Thanks, Helen. I see Ellie out there. I'd better go and say hello." She made her way into the courtyard, aware that several women were gazing at her openly.

"Glad you could make it," Ellie said with a welcoming smile. She checked Caitlin out from head to toe. "Love your gear."

Caitlin had selected an outfit from the edgy end of her wardrobe. Red and black tartan pants, white cotton T-shirt, sable midcalf leather boots, and sleeveless black biker jacket. She pulled the red slouch beanie from her head and ruffled her hair.

"Thanks for the invitation, Ellie. It's really nice to be here."

A woman approached, and Caitlin recognised her as Ellie's date from the Emerson the night before, the woman in the emerald dress.

Ellie drew her friend close to her side. "Caitlin, I'd like you to meet Meagan. Meagan, this is Caitlin, Andi's friend."

Meagan took Caitlin's hand in a firm handshake. "Lovely to meet you. You were at the dance last night." Her dark eyebrows arched over piercing green eyes that appraised Caitlin with a casual, cool confidence.

"I was indeed. Good to see you again, Meagan."

"Meagan and many of the other women here tonight are colleagues from the hospital," Ellie said. "Meagan consults with me on some of my special cases."

"You're an M.D.?" Caitlin asked.

Meagan tipped her head towards Caitlin. "Psych consult."

"A psychiatrist?"

Ellie laughed, and she tightened her grip around Meagan's waist. "That's correct, Caitlin. She's a headshrinker, but you'll be safe with her while I duck inside for a minute."

"Caitlin, come and talk to me while I play chef," said Meagan. She moved towards the grill, and Caitlin followed. A colourful mix of kebabs were sizzling, popping, and smelling delicious.

"*Blast*, just in time. I would have been toast if they'd burnt," Meagan said.

"And you would've had a bunch of cranky, hungry women on your hands. What is it like to be a psychiatrist in a big hospital?"

Meagan chuckled, turned the vegetable kebabs, and basted them with marinade. "Busy. I'm part of the behavioural medicine unit that serves children and teens. And you? Ellie mentioned you are working in Melbourne?"

"Yes, I'm helping to set up a private art gallery, and in a couple of weeks, I'll present my first guest paper for the art history department at the University of Melbourne."

"You've got quite a lot on your plate, then. How do you like it here?" Meagan asked.

"I'm enjoying it very much. Better to be busy than to have idle hands." Caitlin lifted her glass of wine in a salute.

Meagan threw her head back and laughed. She picked up her glass to return the gesture. "For some reason, I doubt very much that those hands have been idle lately." She looked around. "Speaking of which, where is Andi?"

Caitlin bit her lip to stifle a grin.

Meagan nudged her lightly. "Here she comes now."

They watched as Andi descended the stairs. She wore slim-fitting denim jeans and a black T-shirt that accentuated her sculptured body. She stopped at the foot of the staircase to talk with two women Caitlin recognised from last night. They were part of Erica's crowd. Caitlin was surprised when one of the women looked directly at *her*, then whispered something to Andi.

"She always looks like sunshine, doesn't she? All golden and glowing," Meagan said with a grin.

"Ah ha, that she does." Caitlin cleared her throat and drained her glass of wine. Andi was simply stunning.

Andi moved to the bar, where she poured herself a drink and threw back the shot. Whiskey, perhaps.

A few minutes later, Andi made her way towards them, holding a half-empty bottle of beer. A crowd had gathered around the grill, all of them women with their plates already loaded with food.

Caitlin followed Andi to a small bench under a weeping cherry tree in the corner of the garden. It was good meeting Andi's friends, but after the intimate time they'd just shared, Caitlin wished they were alone together.

Andi's brow furrowed, and her back was unnaturally straight. Caitlin wanted to wrap her arms around her and pull her close. She wanted to take Andi home to bed and start all over again. She longed to touch Andi, breathe in her intoxicating scent, and see the unconcealed desire and longing in her eyes once again.

Caitlin tugged on the straps of Andi's red braces. She was startled and disappointed when Andi pulled away. What was wrong? Did Andi regret last night?

"Are you hungry?" Caitlin asked. Perhaps she just needed food.

"Not really."

"I recognise the two women you were talking to by the stairs. They were at the Emerson last night."

Andi turned to Caitlin. She narrowed her eyes. "Yes. They're interns at Edge Gallery. They work with Erica Hunt. I believe you know her."

Oh, so that's what this was about. Caitlin took a deep breath and spoke in what she hoped was a soothing voice. "I do. Erica is the director of the gallery. Isabella loaned her a painting for an exhibition a few weeks ago."

Andi glared at her. "I'm a bit confused, Caitlin. The interns, Jess and Sarah, have the impression that you and Erica are *seeing* each other."

"Seeing each other?" She rolled her shoulders back and matched Andi's gaze. "Seeing each other is a very broad statement."

Andi drained the rest of her bottle, turned abruptly, and headed inside.

Caitlin ran her hands through her hair, looked around, and sighed in frustration. What could she say?

Andi returned with two bottles of beer. She held one out to Caitlin, took a large swig of her own drink, and placed the empty bottle down on the bench with unnecessary force.

Caitlin placed her untouched bottle on the bench and wiped her damp hand on her trousers. "Erica and I *have* seen each other a few times. Our paths do cross a bit, professionally." Damn, whatever Caitlin said was bound to come out wrong.

Andi reached across Caitlin's lap to grab the full bottle. "If you're not going to drink that, I will."

"Don't you think you should slow down? You've hardly eaten a thing since this morning."

"I'm fine. I think I know how much I can drink." Her voice was raised and edged with frustration. Her hands were balled into fists.

Caitlin rolled her eyes. She reached for one of Andi's hands and gently stroked her fingers. "I was hoping you'd want to come back to Kew tonight. If you stay, we could go to the farmers' market tomorrow and have lunch at the Convent Bakery."

Andi shook her head and pulled her hand out of Caitlin's grasp. "No, I can't do that," she said. "I have to go home to Koda in the morning, and I'd rather leave from this side of town."

"That's not a problem. I can drive you back here in the morning," Caitlin said.

"I don't think that's a good idea, Caitlin." Andi stood and started to walk away. She stopped and turned back to Caitlin. "It looks like our paths have crossed too." She shoved her hands into her pockets.

Caitlin took a few deep breaths and forced herself to remain calm. "Do you want to talk about it now? We can go and sit in the car." She looked around them. "Just not here."

"No, I don't want to talk about it. I'm the one who has obviously got it wrong."

Caitlin stood. "No, Andi, you haven't got it wrong. But…"

Women spilled out into the courtyard, and it became uncomfortably crowded. Caitlin pulled Andi into a corner to avoid making a scene.

"But what?" Andi shrugged to release her arm.

Caitlin rubbed at her forehead. Was Andi jealous, or was she annoyed that she'd found out about Erica from two strangers? Caitlin had been the one to pursue Andi. What bad timing—they'd finally slept together, and *now* she learned about Erica. As far as Caitlin was concerned, her infrequent encounters with Erica were no reason for Andi to be so upset.

She was developing a headache. "I'm sorry you're upset. There is really nothing to be jealous about—"

"I never said I was jealous, Caitlin."

"Well, what then? Tell me what you're thinking."

"I'm pissed off. I discovered that you and Erica were sleeping together—after last night. It's how I found out. *God,* what was I thinking?"

"Last night was wonderful. I don't want to spoil that," Caitlin said. "Why can't we talk about it in the car? I can't do this here."

"What's there to talk about? You don't owe me an explanation. We had sex. It was great," she said bluntly.

It *was* great. Caitlin was exhausted from this whole ridiculous scene. "I should make my way home now. I'm sorry." She looked at Andi and hoped that she would ask her to stay. She didn't.

Disappointed, Caitlin pulled her into an embrace and said, "I *will* call you tomorrow."

Andi's rigid hug lacked warmth, and Caitlin gave up trying. She released her and stepped back.

"Enjoy the rest of the party, Andi." Caitlin leaned in to kiss her cheek. Andi looked distant and conflicted. If only Andi would ask her to stay.

Caitlin walked away, telling herself not to look back. She headed into the house, down the hall, and out the front door. She was thankful neither Ellie nor Meagan were anywhere to be seen. It would have been awkward to explain her sudden departure.

That the party hadn't gone well was an understatement. Caitlin drove home in a bit of a daze. When she arrived at the estate, she parked in the garage and, in her frustration, tried to slam the car door, but the soft-close mechanism prevented her from doing so. Instead, she yelled, "Damn!"

She walked the well-lit brick path to the house, replaying the evening's events over and over in her mind. How had something so incredible turned into something so horrible in such a short time?

At the rear of the building, the automatic door closed smoothly behind her. "*Fuck it,*" she yelled and dragged herself up the stairs to the first floor.

The confusion on Andi's face was etched in Caitlin's mind. She'd wanted to say more—to explain—but Andi wouldn't let her. Now she felt totally stuck and inept. She didn't mean to be evasive or make excuses. She knew she'd have to explain the situation with Erica eventually.

She hadn't even had time to process her own feelings about Andi and their night together.

Caitlin stepped into the stairwell that led to her apartment and pushed forcefully at the heavy door. It closed with a satisfying bang. "Finally. A door I *can* slam!"

What did Andi expect from her—that she'd been a nun prior to meeting her? So she hadn't told her about Erica, but she hadn't seen any reason to explain. And how could she expect to have a conversation like that at a party? It was totally the wrong place.

Caitlin reached the top step. The foyer was lined with bookcases, a small library that represented the last ten years of her life. She wished she could catalogue her emotions as easily as she could her book collection.

Since her relationship with Rachel had ended, she'd placed a high priority on her studies, research, and travel. She'd also been free to engage in a series of affairs. And that had suited her just fine. She enjoyed her independence and freedom. It wasn't that she went out of her way to avoid intimacy—it was just convenient to keep things at the *fun* stage, that initial foray when two people experienced a mutual attraction, enjoyed each other's company, and had sex. Uncertainty and unpredictability had always added to the excitement for Caitlin.

She'd connected with Andi almost immediately. They shared a love of nature, fitness, and art. Just being around her elicited a powerful physical response.

Her friend Kiera was a scientist. She would explain away the initial giddiness and arousal to the presence of dopamine. Was it the *chemical* that caused her heart to race when she was around Andi? Caitlin wanted more, *felt* more, than just carnal intimacy. But what was she willing to offer Andi?

Erica's bloody interns! Why they'd told Andi about Erica was beyond her comprehension. Gossip? Telling stories about their boss? Whatever the reason, now she had to deal with the fallout.

Assuming Andi ever gave her a chance to explain.

When Andi questioned her about Erica, she'd been unprepared—taken off guard. She should have responded directly and told Andi about her dalliance with Erica. It was time for Caitlin to acknowledge that there was a difference between her experiences with Andi and those with Erica.

She looked across at the dining chair. Memories of *their* morning flooded her senses. She kicked the skirting board below the kitchen bench.

Caitlin wanted to touch her, kiss her, hold her. She just wanted Andi.

Chapter 19

Andi rolled a thin layer of paint onto a canvas she'd prepared earlier. The cadmium red and raw sienna would give a transparent-toned ground, allowing light falling onto the canvas to radiate through the paint layers and to illuminate the entire surface.

She used a broad, flat brush with a long handle. It was perfect for covering the canvas with quick, dramatic strokes. Andi mopped the beads of sweat from her brow. Her body was taut and vibrated with emotion like the colours on the canvas.

In February 2009, Andi's first year in Hakea, a series of horrific bushfires across Victoria had left carnage and devastation in their wake.

Even though the coastal town had been spared, smoke had drifted along with the clouds and filled the air with the acrid smell of burning wood and dust. Andi's chest tightened as she recalled how the lives of so many had changed that day.

She used a palette knife to apply violet and neutral grey, in order to capture the rhythm of elongated clouds. To highlight the subtle manipulation of colour and tone, she cut in the ivory, black, and ultramarine shadows and used a thick, round brush with yellow ochre and flake white to create splatters.

A final layer of semitransparent vermillion over the entire surface created the desired effect of glowing heat. The sky was blood red and saffron with celestial, clear rays of luminous white. *Firestorm Sunset.*

Andi stepped back and examined the finished painting. It captured the fine lines between fascination and danger, beauty and horror, light and darkness. She was exhausted.

Her emotions matched the painting—a collage of experience and intensity. *Regret.* She'd behaved like a child. *Guilt.* Ellie and Meagan had tried to talk to her this morning, but she'd taken off. *Jealousy.* She didn't want to share Caitlin with

Erica. Or any other lover. *Passion.* Caitlin's naked body beneath hers. *Loss.* It was possible that she'd stuffed it up completely.

Andi yawned sleepily and set Koda down in front of her food bowl. It was Monday, and she'd slept in. Being at odds with Ellie, in addition to where she'd left things with Caitlin, was making her sick. On top of everything else, she was feeling sorry for herself.

Last night, she'd finally responded to Ellie's texts by sending a short reply.

I'm fine. Talk later in the week.

It wouldn't be as easy to appease Caitlin. She'd ignored her messages, but early this morning, she'd dealt with Caitlin's texts with monosyllabic replies.

Are you okay? You haven't returned my calls. Caitlin x

Fine.

I'm glad you are fine. But you still haven't returned my calls. Caitlin

Later.

Fine!

Andi looked at the painting she'd completed last night. *Firestorm Sunset* reflected everything she'd felt since leaving Melbourne yesterday. It was an outpouring of her current turmoil, mixed with the helplessness and anguish she had experienced on Black Saturday in 2009.

She carried her bowl of muesli and a cup of coffee to her desk, and dropped carelessly into her chair. What was she supposed to do now? Andi didn't want to phone Caitlin, because she was confused and couldn't bear the thought of saying the wrong thing and upsetting her more than she already had. Until she knew exactly how she felt and what to say, it was better for her to simply not talk.

Instead, she opened the messenger app on her phone and re-read Caitlin's texts for the twentieth time. The words hadn't changed, and she struggled to reconcile the simplicity of the texts with the complicated reactions of her body and the intensity of her feelings.

She slumped in the chair, head in her hands, and grabbed at her hair in frustration.

Thud.

Koda raced around in circles, and the frenetic movement mirrored her own state of mind.

A sharp knock on the door halted Koda in her tracks.

"Koda, I'm not in the mood for visitors," Andi said with a moan.

The knocking grew even more insistent. Obviously, whoever was there couldn't read her mind. Still wearing her pink shorty pajamas with the teddy bear motif, Andi dragged herself out of her chair.

She shrugged to herself. "I hope it's not the Seventh Day Adventists again." She cautiously opened the front door, prepared to tell the unsolicited visitors that she did *not* need saving, except, maybe, from herself.

As the door swung wide, Caitlin came into view. She stood at the entrance shaking her head. She visibly sucked in a deep breath and then let it out very slowly as she scanned Andi from the top of her head down to her sheepskin UGG boots. She brushed past her and into the house.

Andi was incapable of speech as Caitlin paced back and forth in the short distance between her and the workbench. Her flat-ankle boots sharply echoed Caitlin's anger on the timber floorboards, each step reverberating through the house.

"Caitlin. I didn't know you were…" Andi bit her lower lip and moved towards Caitlin. Koda meowed loudly.

A few metres from Andi, Caitlin stopped pacing. Her stormy expression made Andi shudder. Caitlin held up her hands. "No, please don't say anything." She pushed her hair roughly from her face and began to pace again.

Andi walked over to her desk and sat down heavily in the chair. "I was just going to email you…really," she stuttered.

Caitlin walked over to Andi. "*Really?* No, Andi, I need to say this first." She placed one hand on each arm of the swivel chair and turned Andi to look directly into her eyes.

Andi held her breath. Caitlin's eyes were dark—the colour of starless midnight.

She spoke slowly, enunciating each word succinctly. "You did not answer any of my calls."

Andi looked in every direction. Anywhere but Caitlin's face—which was flushed with anger.

Caitlin traced a finger along the line of Andi's jaw and turned her face to meet her gaze. "It was an intense weekend—for both of us." She sighed heavily, and her voice softened. "Andi, this is *so* new. We've had so much fun together over the last month. I've loved being with you." Crouching down so their eyes were on the same level, she said, "Do you understand why I've been angry?"

Andi chewed her lip. "I would have called you. I know I've been acting irrationally, but I feel…a little crazy." Tears formed at the corners of her eyes. She blinked, ducked under Caitlin's arm, and started towards the kitchen. "I need a glass of water."

She returned and placed two glasses on the coffee table. "I'm sorry if I made you worry and feel that you had to drive all the way here." She rubbed her temples to ward off her developing headache.

Caitlin sat in the chair across from Andi. "I just wanted to know you were okay." She pulled her seat closer and grasped Andi's hands.

"I'm sorry, Caitlin."

"It's not only your fault. I should have insisted that we talk on Saturday night." Caitlin drew her into a comforting embrace. "*I'm* sorry," she said and looked into Andi's eyes. "I want you to feel that you can ask me anything." She smiled reassuringly. "I would like us to be able to talk, no matter… I care about you and promise to answer you as truthfully as I can. I'm out of practice, but…" She raised her eyebrows. "*Not* out of practice telling the truth," Caitlin clarified. "I meant out of practice explaining my actions or reasons. But I will try. Is that okay?"

Andi nodded her head. "Yes."

"So." Caitlin sat straighter in her chair. "Do you want to start now? No avoidance tactics on my part."

Andi rolled her head from side to side, trying to ease the muscles in her neck, hoping to shift her headache.

"Yes."

Caitlin tilted her head to one side. "Do you have a sore neck?"

Andi squinted. The sunlight streaming into the room made her head pound even more.

"Do you need to take something? Can I get you an aspirin?" Caitlin asked.

"I took one a few minutes ago. It should start working soon," Andi said. "I'll be okay."

Caitlin ran a soothing hand through Andi's hair. It was almost enough to make her forget the conversation they needed to have. Almost. But not quite.

Andi sat up straight and frowned. "At Ellie's party, the couple who work at Edge seemed to think that you and Erica are in a relationship." She stared at Caitlin. "Are you?"

Caitlin gulped her water and put the glass down. "No, Andi, I'm not. I wouldn't be here with you if I were." She reached for Andi's hand. "Erica and I are *not* a couple. We move in the same circles and have spent time together. We shared a brief, physical relationship." Caitlin squeezed Andi's fingers. "I won't be going there from now on."

"Good. I guess that answers *that* question, doesn't it?" She looked fixedly at Caitlin. "Are you involved with anyone else?"

Caitlin shook her head. "No. I've preferred to keep things casual, and *one* at a time is enough."

Andi stretched out on the sofa, removed her boots, and propped her feet on a cushion. She hadn't been wrong about Erica. If only she'd given Caitlin the opportunity to explain on Saturday night, they could have avoided all this anxiety.

"If I hadn't been such an idiot, you would have had the chance to tell me. I'm sorry I didn't give you that chance."

"I'm here now, and we are talking." Caitlin leaned across and tugged Andi's pink teddy bear shorts. "Very cute, by the way. Adorable."

"But you rushed all the way here on a Monday morning. I'm sorry you had to do that."

"I didn't have to. I wanted to."

Andi started to sit up.

Caitlin placed her hand on Andi's shoulder. "Lie back and relax. *Stay.* At least till your headache lifts."

Andi leaned back into the sofa. Caitlin walked across the room and picked up the bag she'd thrown inside the door when she'd arrived. Andi angled her head on the pillow. Caitlin removed her lightweight denim jacket, and Andi loved the way her black jeans perfectly accentuated her long legs. Caitlin was beautiful and expressive. She was capable of switching from playful to passionate—persuasive to intense—within seconds. Through her insecurities, Andi had nearly blown it.

Caitlin approached the painting that leaned against the far wall. She studied the canvas, and then looked inquiringly back at Andi. "When did you do this?"

"Yesterday."

Caitlin evaluated the image for a few moments. "It's…breathtaking." She was silent for what seemed to be forever. Finally, she said, "You've captured the intensity and power. I can feel the heat and energy, yet there is also an ethereal, peaceful quality."

Andi closed her eyes. Caitlin could seemingly look through her painting and see the rawness and passion Andi felt.

"*A great fire burns within me, but no one stops to warm themselves at it, and passers-by only see a wisp of smoke.*"

"What is that?" Andi asked.

"It's a quote from Vincent van Gogh." She turned to Andi. "I love your painting."

"Thank you." Andi stared. She was just scratching the surface. There was so much to discover about Caitlin. Suddenly, it was vitally important that she had the opportunity to do that.

"I was so frustrated that you ran back here and wouldn't talk to me." Caitlin returned to sit in the chair across from the sofa.

"I know." Andi glanced at her painting. "I couldn't. Sometimes, I have to paint to express my feelings instead of using words."

"I think you've done that," she said.

Koda jumped up behind Caitlin to use the green material as a scratching post and startled her. "Crikey!" Caitlin sprang out of the chair. "Well, that will shorten my life." She sat back in her chair. "How's your headache?"

"Much better, the painkiller's working. I think it's time for me to hit the shower." Andi slowly pulled herself into an upright position.

"Has the headache *actually* gone?"

Andi smiled. She was so relieved that the tension between them had eased. "Yep, it has. I won't be long in the shower." She stood and Caitlin moved to her, pressing herself into Andi's side, tucking her thumbs into the waistband of her shorts.

Maybe not *all* the tension had gone.

Caitlin lowered her head to Andi's ear. "I thought I could keep you company in the shower. Help to relieve that tightness in your neck and shoulders. Make sure your headache doesn't return."

Caitlin held out her hand and led Andi to the shower. She knew they had a lot of things to negotiate. This was a beginning, and she was happy for Caitlin allowing it.

Chapter 20

As Andi secured the zip on her wetsuit, Caitlin indulged in their physical closeness and enjoyed the brush of Andi's hand against her neck. Andi moved carefully and lingered with her fingers lightly resting on Caitlin's cool skin. Tension and relaxation, movement and stillness. After so much worry, irritation, and frustration, their shower together that morning had been a sensual discovery.

Caitlin inhaled sharply at the memory of Andi's silken body, rivulets of water cascading down; her taut nipples pressed against Caitlin's overheated skin. She'd run her hand up and down the gentle arc of Andi's waist, tracing the swell of her hip. With her other hand, she'd braced against the cool green tiles for support. Andi's thumb had moved so slowly over Caitlin's sensitive flesh. Her legs weakening at Andi's touch, she'd shuddered as the first delicious burst of pleasure rolled through her body, and she'd melted into Andi's arms.

"Caitlin. Are you listening?"

At the sound of her name, she refocused on what Andi was saying.

"This is called a mini-mal. Best choice for a beginner, because it's easy to paddle," Andi said eagerly. "The waves are small today, so this is a perfect board for you to start with."

"I'm in your hands. You're the expert." Caitlin smiled and stretched out her arms. The dry wetsuit was stiff and restricted her movements.

"You look awesome in my spring suit. You fill out all the curves much better than I do." Andi's brown eyes gleamed. "Okay, I think we've practiced enough on the sand. Let's get out on the water."

"I don't know. I'm not sure I'll be able to stand up on this." Caitlin lifted up the eight-foot board. "This is much heavier than I thought it would be."

"Don't worry about that. Once you get it in the water, you won't notice the weight. We could have used a foam board for your first time out, but with your height, this will be easier for you to stand. You've already told me you're a strong swimmer." Andi looked to Caitlin for confirmation and waited until Caitlin nodded before she continued. "I'll be right there with you all the way. If you remember those few things I told you, everything will be good. You'll be a surfer chick in no time."

Andi glowed with joy. Her sparkle was contagious, and Caitlin, unable to contain her own happiness, laughed along with her.

Caitlin gathered her hair and pulled it through a scrunchie. "So, first I look on both sides. If anyone is on the wave before I take off, I stop paddling. You said, 'Don't drop off?'"

Andi giggled. "Don't drop *in*. You'll just annoy the other surfers if you do that." Andi adjusted her wetsuit, picked up her 60+ ultra-light, and stood before Caitlin. "Let's get this on you, and then we're set." She squeezed a liberal amount of the sunscreen on her fingertips and applied it to Caitlin's face.

"Okay. So you said to paddle wide?" Caitlin asked. "Keep my eyes on everything. Paddle out where *you* go, because you know where the rip current is? And if I do get caught in a rip, don't panic, go with it, not against it." Caitlin screwed up her nose as Andi covered it with white cream.

"You've got it. Now, let's surf."

Caitlin fastened the Velcro strap around her ankle and picked up the attached board. Andi gave her a thumbs up, and they made their way to the water.

Careful not to lose her footing on the slippery rocks, she eased her body off the rock shelf, onto her board, and into the surf.

Andi called out, "Remember, above all else, enjoy yourself."

Andi was a patient and encouraging instructor.

Caitlin took a deep breath and followed Andi. She shivered as the cold water trickled down her neck and seeped into the wetsuit.

After catching small waves for nearly an hour, belly down on the board, Caitlin was confident that she could stand up. The water swirled around her, the thunderous noise sometimes hissing and gushing. She clung to the board and looked up. The shore seemed miles away.

She knew Andi was close by, but she heard the distant cry of a seagull and felt momentarily alone. Her arms ached, and she shivered as the cold salt water rippled over her. Now or never.

Caitlin recalled Andi's instructions and picked a reference point on the shore. She rotated the board, pointed it to the beach, and let the power of the wave push her forward. As directed, she kept her body straight and as far back on the board as possible. She began to paddle. As a wave came up behind her, she went faster. Then, using a technique they'd practiced, she went from kneeling to standing in one swift movement.

Caitlin couldn't believe she was actually upright. Knees bent and arms loose, she was able to balance and ride the wave for at least twenty seconds before she was tossed into the ocean. The leash tugged sharply on her ankle. *Ouch.* Crikey, that was a new experience.

Caitlin surfaced and shielded her head with her arms in case the surfboard came back at her. She pulled herself back on again, rested for a moment, and then reached down to untangle the leash that had wound itself around her calf.

Andi moved over to her and placed one hand on the edge of Caitlin's board. "That was truly amazing," she said. "You did great."

Caitlin beamed. She couldn't contain her pleasure. "Hardly, but I suppose being a downhill skier helps."

"No doubt about it, you have good quad strength." Andi smiled mischievously. "You're a natural and the best looking *kook* I've ever seen."

"Mind you, it's been a good eight months since I was last on skis, and my muscles are a little out of shape." Caitlin frowned. "Kook?"

"It just means a beginner." Andi pointed to the shoreline. "This is probably a good time for us to finish, before we both end up with noodle arms."

Caitlin paddled after her. "Remind me to buy a dictionary of surf terms. Are you pulling my leg?"

"Don't know what you mean," Andi said with a cheeky grin.

Lying down, they rode the next wave in together and coasted slowly to the shore.

As they walked along the sand towards their gear, Andi tapped Caitlin on the shoulder. "Oh, by the way, I don't know why you think your quadriceps need work. From here they look pretty good."

Caitlin lowered her board onto the sand and shook her hair free. She looked across at Andi, and admired the way her wetsuit moulded to her frame. "Ah, I'm rather enjoying the view from here," she said.

"Yeah?" Andi smirked.

Caitlin's shoulder and arm muscles were strained from constant paddling. No wonder Andi's upper body was so well defined. Surfing was a lot more physically taxing than she'd realised.

Andi swiftly removed her wetsuit and wrapped herself in a towel. "It's easier if you take your suit off now while it's wet."

Caitlin reached for the back of her suit and struggled with the cord attached to her zip.

"Here, let me help. It's horrible getting your hair caught." Andi drew it down and turned Caitlin around. She grabbed the neoprene material at Caitlin's shoulders and peeled it halfway down her torso, imprisoning her arms to her side. "Got you." She grinned.

"Hey, that's not fair; I'm trapped." Caitlin sighed as Andi tightened her arms around her waist and gave her a teasing kiss at the corner of her mouth.

"That's the idea."

Her arms still held captive, Caitlin leaned down to capture Andi's mouth with her own. Andi's lips were soft—yielding. "You're salty," Caitlin murmured, as she drew a path with her tongue along Andi's neck.

"Hmm." Andi moaned. "I could get used to this."

Caitlin struggled and tried to free her arms, with no luck. Andi laughed and held on tight. Caitlin placed one leg between Andi's feet, hooked her ankle around Andi's, and toppled them both onto the sand. "Free at last," she cried, and brought her lips back to Andi, who giggled and squirmed beneath her. "And now, I've got *you*."

Andi tossed the wetsuits over the railing as they entered her studio through the back door. Surfing together this afternoon had left her surprisingly invigorated.

On the short drive back from the beach, they hadn't said much, as though afraid of breaking their fragile connection.

Andi threw the entire bag of wet clothes into the laundry sink. "Can I get you anything? A cold drink, something to eat, something hot?"

"What did you have in mind?" Caitlin asked.

Andi encircled Caitlin's waist and guided her into the kitchen, through the studio, and into the bedroom.

"I have a few suggestions," she said.

Caitlin's body, pressed against Andi's, pulsed with life, and the energy between them sizzled.

It was late afternoon, and Andi's northwest-facing bedroom had retained the warmth of the sun. She half closed the narrow cedar blinds to ensure their privacy.

Andi caressed Caitlin's shoulders and slowly lowered the thin straps of her midnight-blue swimsuit down her arms. She eased the fabric to Caitlin's hips and kissed the curve of Caitlin's neck, moving slowly until her lips rested in the hollow between her breasts.

Andi murmured softly against Caitlin's skin, "I love you here… So incredibly soft." She rolled her tongue over Caitlin's nipple, and Caitlin gasped.

"You taste of the sea. You're strong, so hot… *God*, you're so sexy." Andi nuzzled her, teasing her flesh with featherlike pressure, as she effortlessly pushed the swimsuit to the floor. Caitlin stepped to the side and brought her hands to the nape of Andi's neck to twirl the short strands of hair through her fingers, then pulled her in for a lingering kiss.

Caitlin lifted Andi's cropped white top over her head and tugged impatiently at her swimshorts. "Off," she pleaded.

Andi quickly discarded her shorts, and their naked bodies came together, still warm from the sun. Andi was light-headed, on edge, as her body came in contact with Caitlin's flushed skin. She yearned for more.

Without words and with mutual understanding, they moved smoothly onto the bed and into each other's arms.

Chapter 21

Dappled light across her body
Flawless and golden
Marbled by the trickling rays that dance across her skin
Enticing me, tempting me out of my comfort zone
Seductively captivating in her innocence.

This body, her body
Arranges itself against me, like it is home
Embraces me, welcomes me
I am gladly received into her everyday.

Cherished
There is nothing ordinary about her
Or about my own emerging in her presence
Intoxicating and dynamic
She is my bridge.

Caitlin carefully placed her iPhone back onto the nightstand. Andi had fallen asleep in her arms, and Caitlin had slipped in and out of wakefulness for the past hour. The words to the poem drifted into her consciousness, and she quickly typed them into her phone. In the cold light of day, she may question the sentimentality of her words. But now, with Andi in her arms, she was a soppy mess.

Caitlin thought about how Andi used art to convey her feelings. Her newest painting, *Firestorm Sunset,* was powerful, passionate, and revealing. Poetry was Caitlin's form of expression—her private reflective mechanism for personal grounding.

She settled back against the pillow and placed her arm once again around Andi.

Their afternoon of lovemaking had triggered a raft of emotions.

She enjoyed sex with Andi, very much, but that term, sex, wasn't adequate anymore. Caitlin had been involved with women who used the words *having sex* and *making love* interchangeably, blurring the lines. Sexual desire, for her, was the need for physical contact with another woman's body and for the pleasure that contact created. It was purely sensory and, for many years, it hadn't involved anything deeper. She hadn't let it. She'd chosen not to become entangled in her sexual partners' lives. With Erica, it was uncomplicated. Even though they shared professional interests—and there was the sex, of course—she'd never expected to be invited to Erica's parents' home for Sunday lunch.

There was no doubt that, from the first time she and Andi had met, she was strongly drawn to her—spontaneous desire.

She watched Andi asleep in her arms and listened to her steady breathing. As her dark eyelashes fluttered, Caitlin saw an unshielded innocence that made her feel strongly protective. In a short time, Andi had managed to bring out emotions that had long been dormant in Caitlin.

On Sunday, Caitlin had been frustrated and angry when she couldn't make contact with Andi. After a sleepless night, she'd met Kim at work early and explained that she needed to take care of some unfinished business. She'd driven to Hakea, not really sure of how she was going to approach Andi, but she'd had no option.

At first, Andi had been cautious and withdrawn. Not that Caitlin had given her much of a choice, storming into her home. After they'd both calmed down, they'd dealt with the Erica situation. Then she'd glimpsed Andi's new painting, and the intense feelings that she'd expressed on the canvas had stunned Caitlin. The artwork was exquisite.

Caitlin drew her lips across Andi's satiny smooth shoulder. Her feelings were changing, the smallest details each time they were together, clearly remembered. "You seem to be on my mind…a lot," she whispered. She closed her eyes. "I don't know where this is going, but I want to be on the journey."

"Are you going somewhere?" Andi asked, as her eyes flickered open. She snuggled in and pulled Caitlin tightly against her.

"Hello." Caitlin pressed her face into warm skin. "No, I'm not going anywhere."

"Good." Andi grinned, sleepily. "Have you been awake long? You must have been tired. Your drive from Melbourne this morning, your first surfing lesson." Her smile broadened. "Our workout."

"Not long, I slept for a while. No, I'm not tired." Caitlin tugged the sheet from Andi's body, straddled her hips and tickled her ribs. "The question is, did *you* get enough of a workout?"

"Okay, okay, I give up," Andi pleaded. Her stomach growled loudly. "Oops! We seem to have completely forgotten about lunch."

Caitlin dragged her hair across Andi's honey-soft breasts. "Poor baby, didn't you get enough to eat?"

"Stop, you are evil," said Andi as her stomach rumbled again. "I really am starving."

"I guess I could buy you dinner if you let me stay the night?" Caitlin had planned to stay. She hoped Andi was receptive to the idea. By the look on Andi's face, she was. "But I do have to be back in Melbourne by early afternoon. I have a meeting at three o'clock, and Kim covered for me today."

Andi looked towards the ceiling. "Thank you, Kim."

Andi attempted to get up, and Caitlin held her down gently. "Why don't you stay here so I can kiss you again?"

In answer, Andi lifted her head to meet her lips.

"Hmm," Andi murmured, and surrendered to Caitlin's searching mouth.

Andi's meal of whole wheat mushroom pasta with spinach, goat cheese, and pine nuts satisfied her hunger. She pushed away her plate and looked at Caitlin. The café was quiet, just a few locals sitting at the bar. Ambient music played soothingly in the background, serenading them as they sat at an isolated table near the flickering wood fire.

"You devoured your meal in no time. Feel better?" Caitlin asked. When Andi nodded, she added, "This is cosy."

The reflection of the firelight danced in Caitlin's eyes as she sipped her wine.

"What are you thinking about?" Andi asked.

"This wine brings back memories of home. The pink petals of spring blossoms falling softly onto green grass. The smoke and perfume of cherrywood fires on chilly evenings."

"Sounds wonderful." Andi held her gaze.

Caitlin smiled wistfully. "Springtime in Cork, when the gardens and trees around the university are filled with blossoms—this wine with its fruity undertones brings it all back."

"Are you homesick? I suppose spring here is a lot different from Cork."

"Different, but still very beautiful. Isabella's garden at Kew is full of flowers now. But yes, there are things about home I do miss. Cork has many cherry trees, and when they bloom, the perfume fills the air. As a child, I loved playing in the petals." Caitlin placed her glass on the table and looked directly at Andi. "Okay, enough reminiscing for now."

"I do have a question," Andi said and squinted. "I was wondering, have you ever been in a long-term relationship?"

"I have. Rachel and I met at university, and we were together for six years. It ended five years ago, while we were both doing our PhDs. Unfortunately, our studies got in the way."

"Five years? That's a long time ago."

"Time has gone quickly. Work, study, travel, etcetera, etcetera."

"So what happened to you and Rachel? I mean, why did it end?"

Caitlin shrugged her shoulders. "We drifted apart. I think that, if our love for each other had been strong enough, it would have survived the external pressures."

Andi filled her water glass and took a couple of large gulps. "What was she like?"

"Driven," Caitlin said. "Rachel was determined to be the best in her field. She was obsessed, and she achieved her dream. Rachel is now a top criminal barrister."

Caitlin reached for her glass. "After our relationship ended, my work took me to Italy, Paris, New York, and now Melbourne. I was never really in one place long enough to form any lasting attachments."

"So what does *this* mean?" Andi spread her arms wide. "Don't get me wrong, but it's important for me to clarify things in my mind." She gathered strength as she spoke. "Is *this* a short affair, something to fill in the time while you're in Australia?"

Caitlin looked down into her empty glass. "No, I mean..." She looked up, her gaze intense. "I guess I'm asking you to be patient with me. I do know I want to be with you, *now*."

Their legs touched under the small table and Andi reached across and squeezed Caitlin's knee.

"Can you manage that?" Caitlin asked.

Andi took her time to answer; she weighed up the alternatives carefully. Casting caution aside, she said, "Yes, I want to be with you, Caitlin. I don't know *where* you'll be in seven months, but—"

"Andi."

"No, please, I don't expect you to say anything else." *Or make promises you can't keep*, she thought. "I have an exhibition to work towards, and you have an enormous task ahead of you, setting up the gallery and all that goes with it." Andi smiled and maintained steady eye contact. "If I think of the alternative, this is what I want. To spend more time with you, however long we may have. So yes, I can."

Andi empathised with Caitlin's situation. She was thousands of miles from home. Her job, her friends, and her family were in Ireland.

"Andi, if we spend more time together... I mean if we're *dating*—God, do people even date these days? I mean that if neither of us is involved with anyone else, are you interested in the possibility of being," Caitlin raised her eyebrows, "exclusive?"

Andi coughed. "Exclusive?"

Caitlin tilted her head quizzically. "Yes, that's what I mean." She growled. "I know I will be inexplicably..." Caitlin swallowed. "I am tongue-tied." She took a deep breath, clasped her hands tightly together, and placed them on the table. "If I think of you touching anyone the way you touch me, kissing someone the way you kiss me, making love with *anyone* else... Jealous. I would be indescribably *jealous*."

Andi reached across the table and gently unclasped Caitlin's fingers. She met her gaze and smiled. "Exclusive? With *you*? I think I can handle that."

Wow. Andi knew she'd managed to hold it together. This was a big step, and it felt wonderful, but was she leaving herself wide open for hurt?

Caitlin could hear a phone ringing, but she was lying face down in her pillow and hoped the ringing would stop soon. *Really* soon. The pillow smelled of Andi, and she didn't want to move. She groaned. What if it was Isabella? She couldn't take a chance that something was wrong. Still lying face down, she reached for her mobile.

As she moved, her foot knocked into Koda, and small, sharp teeth latched onto her bare ankle. "Koda! I didn't mean to kick you, but could you let go of my foot, please? Pretty please?" She touched the screen and pulled the iPhone to her ear.

"Morning. This is Caitlin."

"Oh? I am sorry. I must have the wrong number. I'm looking for Andréa."

Oh, oh! Caitlin was now awake. Fully awake. She blinked and rubbed her eyes, then looked at the phone. She was holding Andi's phone. "Ahm, I am so sorry. This *is* Andi's, err, Andréa's phone."

"Then good morning to you. This is Lina Rey. May I speak to Andréa, please?" the woman said. She had a slight accent.

Lina Rey? This could be Andi's mother. Nice one, Caitlin. "I'm sorry, Andréa can't come to the phone. Can I have her call you back?" Caitlin asked. She pushed herself back against the headboard, and Koda settled between her feet.

"Caitlin?" Lina asked.

"Hello, that would be me."

"I know that name. My son, Luca, has mentioned a Caitlin," she said. "This is Andréa's mother."

"Good morning, Mrs. Rey. Andi won't be too long."

"Please, call me Lina. Caitlin, I know you have a house in Hakea. Luca told me how magnificent it is."

"Thank you, Lina. The house, Kinsale, belongs to my grandaunt Isabella, and I am fortunate to be able to use it." Caitlin pulled the sheet up to her chin. She was way too naked to be on the phone with Andi's mother.

"I understand. You are very lucky. Hakea is a beautiful place." Lina paused. "It's just after nine o'clock, still quite early. Have you and Andréa been out *running* this morning?"

Caitlin cleared her throat. "No, Andi and I are planning to have breakfast together."

A low chuckle came through the phone. "Is she making you one of those horrible-looking, green energy drinks?"

"I don't think so. At least I hope not." Caitlin laughed.

When Andi, clad in a towel, returned from her shower, Caitlin pointed to the phone. "It's your mother," she mouthed, exaggeratedly. Andi rolled her eyes.

"It's been a pleasure talking to you, Lina. Andi's here now," Caitlin said.

"Goodbye, Caitlin, I hope we meet soon."

"Yes, I hope so too. Goodbye, Lina." Caitlin handed Andi the phone and rested her head back against the wall. Andi settled on the bed next to her and nestled into her side. With a soft sigh, Caitlin closed her eyes and listened in as Andi chatted with her mother.

"Yes, Caitlin is here for breakfast." Andi held the towel to her body. "No, I have regular food. Yes, toast and fruit. And cereal." Caitlin squeezed Andi's knee. Andi slapped at her hand and shook her head. She coughed. "No, Mum, I haven't forgotten the party. How could I forget Dad's birthday?"

Caitlin heard Lina's muffled voice in the background. Andi turned to Caitlin and poked out her tongue. "Yes, I'm okay. It was just a cough, Mum." She prodded Caitlin's hand, and Caitlin reluctantly removed it from Andi's knee.

"I don't know. Maybe I will. I'll let you know." She shrugged her shoulders. "I'm really looking forward to spending time with everybody. Yes, I'll go make breakfast now. Yes, a proper one." Andi held up her hand in frustration. "Love you too, and love to Dad." Andi ended the call with a sigh of relief and placed her phone next to Caitlin's on the bedside table.

"I'm sorry, Andi. I picked up your phone by mistake. I thought it was mine," Caitlin said.

Andi laughed, then blew out a breath and pursed her lips. "Well, now you've talked to my mother. Did she give you the third degree?"

"Do you think she bought my story, that I was here for breakfast?" Caitlin asked. "Your mother seemed to already know who I was. She said Luc had mentioned me."

"I'm not surprised. My brother was quite taken with you." Andi nudged Caitlin. "Anyway, that's not entirely wrong; you are here for breakfast. But I don't think much gets past Mum. She's guessed something."

"Will that be a problem?"

"No, my mother is just inquisitive. She wants to know what's going on in my life. You would think she'd give me a break. I am thirty years old." Andi sounded miffed.

"You're still *her* baby," Caitlin said.

"Don't you start. Between my mother and Ana, I get plenty of advice from older women—oops, I didn't mean it like that."

"Older women, eh?" Caitlin moved closer and wriggled her fingers in a threatening manner.

"Stop," Andi pleaded. "Anyway, she asked me to invite you to the family gathering in Navigators in two weeks."

"Really? She asked you to ask me? What's the occasion? And who else has she asked you to invite?"

Andi smirked. "Only you, *exclusively.* It's Dad's birthday and an excuse for the annual spring gathering," she said. "Don't worry. It's just family, friends, neighbours, and ring-ins."

Caitlin tugged at the towel that was slipping off Andi's body. "So. Are you going to invite me as your guest? Am I your ring-in?"

"I haven't decided yet. You may not like the farm."

Caitlin tugged at the towel again, but Andi clung to it tightly while Caitlin attempted to lower it a few centimetres. "I rather like the idea of a trip to the country. What if I make you breakfast and promise to behave? Will that get me an invitation?"

"You behave? Err…sure. I'll make breakfast, though. I can at least cook you some toast."

The idea of breakfast was very appealing, but so was Andi. Caitlin inched closer and dragged the towel off her.

Caitlin let out a shaky breath and sighed softly.

Andi placed kisses all the way along her neck to her ear. "How about I start my breakfast right here?" she whispered, her voice low and raspy.

"Andi, you've exhausted me already… I won't be able to stand, let alone drive," Caitlin said.

Andi's skilful hands roamed Caitlin's back, while her mouth nibbled her earlobe. "I'm sure I can convince you otherwise. What better way to begin your day?"

Chapter 22

A large sheet of plywood, 2400 by 1200 mm, lay across Andi's work table. She chose a roller from her tray of artist's tools and applied washes of raw umber and crimson hues in sweeping columns to depict the trunks of myrtle beech, eucalyptus, and mountain ash. She began with the darker elements and shadow patterns, tilting the roller gradually with each stroke to vary their width. To add light and shade to the tree trunks, she applied ivory and silver-grey with quick strokes of a flat brush. Hints of raw sienna and red oxide represented the eucalyptus bark. Remembering the freshness of the rainforest and its dense, green canopy, she used a fan brush for the base layer of the lush vegetation—emerald green, yellow oxide, and brilliant green. Giant tree ferns, maidenhair ferns, and glorious, mossy trunks.

As the trees came to life, she thought of Caitlin on their first magical day together in the Otway Ranges—Caitlin standing beside her at the base of Sheoak Falls. The way sunlight picked up the highlights in her dark hair. The way the misty droplets of water made her eyes sparkle. Her radiant smile intensified Andi's pleasure. The temperate rainforest had always been an extraordinary place for Andi, but now it was overlaid with a sensual resonance.

Since their relationship status had changed over a week ago, Andi was hyperaware of everything. Especially Caitlin. The electricity that sparked between them. The way Caitlin's hands soothed one minute and drove her crazy the next. Caitlin's tender whispers, as she coaxed her to intense pleasure.

Andi felt her heartbeat quicken and pulled at her shirt collar.

She used a broad brush to create the dramatic cellular patterns of the rainforest canopy. She applied dots of colours with repetitive strokes in order to create vibrancy and visual richness. She left small slivers of the white background. The highlights showed the way sunlight threaded its way through the canopy of leaves and the umbrella-like trunks. Dappled light caressed the ancient forest floor.

"Finally, a car park." Andi pulled into the empty space, two blocks away from the university. She grabbed her satchel and jacket, ran towards Swanston Street, and entered the university campus past Edge Gallery. She jogged down a tree-lined pedestrian alley that teemed with students. Outside the Chemistry Block, she stopped to get her bearings and checked the map she'd printed off this morning. What building was she looking for? Arts? Old Arts?

The meeting at Bailey Graphics in South Melbourne had run overtime. She'd driven through the city in record time to get to Caitlin's lecture and slip in without being noticed. Now, she couldn't even find the building.

She wanted to surprise Caitlin. Hopefully, she wouldn't mind. They'd briefly spoken yesterday morning, and Caitlin had helped her compile a checklist for her exhibition preparation. At that stage, Andi hadn't known about the appointment in Melbourne.

Marcus Dedham, one of the senior staff members of the creative design team, explained that their client, Felicity Grant, had specifically requested Andi's presence at the meeting today. The appointment at Bailey Graphics was at one in the afternoon. If things had gone as planned, Andi had time to attend the meeting, make small talk with Ms. Grant, and then head to the university.

Not so! The meeting went longer than scheduled, and the attractive CEO of Grant Sports-Net, one of Bailey's principal clients, had put her on the spot by asking her to lunch.

Andi had tried to make excuses. If she went to lunch, she would never make it to the lecture on time. Felicity was appeased when Andi agreed to join her and Marcus for a drink.

Felicity paid her way too much attention, and Andi's patience was at its limit—she really wanted to leave.

Marcus came to her rescue at last. "Andi, I'm sure Felicity understands you need to be across town for another meeting." He turned to Felicity and said, "I do believe our table is ready."

"Andi, it's always a pleasure," Felicity said and held on to her hand a moment too long. "The designs are fabulous, and I look forward to seeing you again for the final presentation."

Andi had bowed out gracefully and hightailed from the hotel.

Now, she was finally at the university with only five minutes until the lecture was scheduled to start.

Melbourne University consisted of a dazzling number of buildings. Pathways led in every direction—stairways, wide expanses of lawn, pop-up cafés, and a conglomeration of different architectural styles—making navigation a nightmare. The Old Quadrangle, adjacent to the lecture theatre, was the most historic building on campus, thus making it the most popular destination for tourists and their cameras, which slowed her progress even more.

Andi ran along smooth cobblestones under vaulted cloisters, hoping she was going in the right direction. She was too proud to ask the students for help. They had their eyes glued to handheld devices and seemed oblivious to their surroundings. Exiting the Old Quad, she saw the imposing building diagonally across from her, clearly signed *Old Arts Building*.

Andi looked at her map again to follow her scrawled notes. She entered the north-facing entrance that faced Old Physics. This place had as many tangles and turns as Hogwarts.

"What is it with all these names?" Andi mumbled.

Through the open doors, she could see that the gothic revival exterior gave way to a thoroughly modernised interior. However, finding Lecture Theatre C was proving a challenge. In a mild state of panic, Andi traversed the second storey three times before she finally found it.

She made her way into the room and claimed an empty seat near the back wall. A small group of students was chatting together and continued to do so even when a tall, wiry woman, with a severe diagonal hairstyle walked to the front of the stage and tapped the microphone. Andi couldn't see Caitlin, and she started to panic again—was she in the wrong lecture theatre?

"May I have your attention please, ladies and gentlemen? My colleagues, today we are delighted to have you here for our latest edition of the Masters' Art Lecture Series. I am Professor Delores DeWitt." The woman spoke into the microphone, and it made a grating, screeching sound. Andi chuckled into her hand, as Professor DeWitt continued unaffected, "And I'm delighted to introduce our guest speaker, Doctor Caitlin Quinn from the University of Cork." She paused to glance at her notes. "We are very privileged to have Doctor Quinn, who will present her paper on Ireland's first foray into the Venice Biennale."

A woman wearing a charcoal-grey suit entered through a side door and Caitlin followed. Andi couldn't help her smile.

"Wow." Andi thought she'd whispered to herself, until the two women sitting in front of her turned to stare. There was a hush for a few seconds before a ripple of murmurs filled the theatre. Caitlin introduced herself to the audience. She declined the professor's offer of the microphone but, even where Andi sat at the back of the room, Caitlin's voice was loud and clear. People put down their phones, closed their laptops, and gave full attention to the speaker before them.

Andi was amazed as she listened and observed the professional side of Caitlin Quinn for the first time. She projected strength and confidence, and her demeanor commanded attention. Her paper explained how, in 1950, two women artists represented Ireland at the Venice Biennale.

Caitlin looked artsy, professional, and irresistible, all at the same time. She removed her double-breasted, green pea coat, draped it over the back of a chair, and shook out her dark, glossy hair until it brushed the top of her sleeveless, black shirt. Andi loved her red and black plaid trousers—they reminded her of the first day they'd met.

Caitlin talked about how Ireland's choice of Nano Reid and Norah McGuinness was controversial at the time—but how they were well received by the Italian public. The Italian president had bought one of McGuinness's paintings.

The students laughed as Caitlin apologised for the upside down slide on the overhead projector and she made a joke about her northern-hemisphere brain. She seemed to enjoy herself and had the audience in the palm of her hand. The accompanying slides illustrated the artworks. Caitlin pointed out that the art world was impressed, and the Italian art critic, Umberto Apollonio, praised both artists for their expressionist style.

Caitlin captivated Andi, not just the with way she looked and the way she made her feel, but also with the riveting story.

At the end of the presentation, it was clear from the enthusiastic response that Caitlin's paper was well received.

Andi remained at the back of the room while students surrounded Caitlin. She watched with fascination as Caitlin engaged with the eager group that hovered around her.

The crowd dispersed, and the woman sitting in front of Andi turned to her. "Great lecture, don't you think? Terrific speaker, eh?" The young woman, probably in her twenties, continued, "I love the Irish accent. Did you like it? The lecture I mean?"

"Yes, it was wonderful," Andi replied. She saw Caitlin's surprised expression followed by an incredulous smile—she had evidently just noticed her. Andi gave her a small, self-conscious wave.

The young woman turned to see Caitlin beckoning Andi to join her. "Hey, you know Doctor Quinn?"

"I do," Andi said.

The woman grinned. "Cool. Lucky you. Please tell her the lecture was awesome." She moved towards the exit.

"I will," Andi said as she headed towards the front of the room.

Caitlin grasped her hand. "What are you doing here? Where have you been, all dressed up?" Her eyes widened admiringly as she checked out Andi's tailored, ash-coloured hemp trousers and soft, chocolate corduroy shirt jacket. She gently touched the toe of her black leather boot to Andi's suede hi-tops. "Love the boots."

Andi ducked her head shyly. She blushed under Caitlin's admiring gaze.

"Caitlin, we're just about ready here. I've let Angie at Epocha know that there'll be ten of us," a voice called out to Caitlin, and they both turned.

Caitlin looked at Andi. "There could be eleven, Liz. Would that be a problem at all?"

Liz shook her head. "No, no problem, I'll tell them."

"Liz, this is Andi Rey. Andi is an artist currently working on her solo exhibition. Andi, this is Liz Jacobs, she's a curator at Edge Gallery."

Andi shook Liz's hand politely. "Nice to meet you." The curator, an elegant woman Andi guessed to be in her early fifties, observed her intently.

"A pleasure to meet you too." Liz glanced at her wristwatch. "And I look forward to learning more about you and your exhibition at dinner. Caitlin, I've told the others we'll meet at Hannah's bar first. So I'll take off now. Unless you'd like a ride to the restaurant?"

"I have the address here somewhere. We'll meet you there," Caitlin said.

"Wonderful." Liz Jacobs headed for the doorway and left them alone in the near empty room.

"Your lecture was excellent," Andi said. "It's an incredible story, inspirational too. I'd never heard about Nano Reid and Norah McGuinness."

"Thank you, I'm glad you liked it. Seeing you here gave me quite the surprise."

"Not an unpleasant one, I hope?"

Caitlin leaned in, nudged Andi playfully with her shoulder, and then pulled her into her arms. "Not at all. But I'd rather have you all to myself. Unfortunately, I am expected to join the group for dinner."

"Will Erica be there?" The words were out before Andi could stop herself. She wished she'd been able to keep that little jealousy demon from surfacing. "Sorry about that. I'm really glad I made it to your lecture, but I don't have to crash your dinner plans. I'll just head back home."

"No," stated Caitlin emphatically. "I mean, you should come. It's just a group of women from the gallery and the art department. Erica may be there, I don't know for sure." She looked directly at Andi. "Anyway, I want you with me. I've missed you. They're a friendly lot; you might have fun. Please?"

How could Andi possibly refuse? She answered to the affirmative with a kiss on Caitlin's cheek and was rewarded with a sexy smile.

They left the university grounds, and walked to Andi's car. She was relieved she'd asked her neighbour Molly to feed Koda and lock her in for the night. However, going to dinner with Caitlin's university friends had not been her plan. Especially since Erica might potentially be there. Andi brushed aside her insecurity. It would be good to meet Caitlin's friends and colleagues—wouldn't it?

Epocha Restaurant was in Montefiore House, an impressive Victorian terrace on the edge of the Central Business District. When Caitlin and Andi arrived, most of the women were upstairs at Hannah's bar enjoying predinner cocktails and grazing on a selection of appetizers. Their table on the first floor was at one end of the balcony, with views of Carlton Gardens and Melbourne Museum.

Caitlin sat back and picked up her drink—a dry gin martini. While she sipped her cocktail, her gaze was fixed on Andi, who was deeply engaged in conversation with Liz. Andi's head tilted to one side, exposing the gentle curve of her neck. Her long, dark lashes cast shadows across her cheek as she pursed her lips in concentration.

"Can't take your eyes off her, can you?" said a sharp voice from behind Caitlin. Erica leaned over her shoulder and lifted Caitlin's glass to her lips. "Hmmm. What are you drinking?"

"Good evening, Erica," Caitlin said. She rescued her drink and placed it on the table. "It's a Charlie Gibson, gin and vermouth." Caitlin shifted to allow Erica to pull a chair in beside her at the table.

"In that case, I'll stick to champagne." Erica looked across to Andi and back at Caitlin. "Not that I blame you, though. She is rather delicious."

Caitlin licked her lips, cleared her throat, and tucked a tendril of hair behind her ear as Erica scrutinised her.

"Oh my *Goddess,* Caitlin. If that look on your face is any indication, you already know that."

"Really, Erica, must you?" Caitlin asked.

"I haven't seen you like this before. It's precious. You're blushing, and on you, that's divine."

"I'm not."

"Oh, you are, darling," Erica said.

Andi looked up. Her gaze caught Caitlin's and her forehead wrinkled. The waiter announced that their table in the Green room was ready, and Caitlin breathed a sigh of relief. Erica stood to go but hesitated and leaned down to whisper in Caitlin's ear. "I'll miss our date nights, but by the look on *that* beautiful young woman's face, you have your hands full. Is that so, Caitlin?"

"Erica." Caitlin shook her head. "I owe you an explanation, don't I? I thought we could meet for coffee early next week? Is that okay?"

Erica nodded. "I can guess what's going on. But yes, coffee next week is fine. We are friends, after all. No promises, no regrets," Erica said wistfully as she moved to join the other women gathered at the base of the stairs.

Caitlin sat quietly. That had been easier than she'd anticipated.

Andi touched her shoulder. "Are you okay?" Her thumb stroked the back of Caitlin's neck.

Caitlin turned and looked into Andi's smoky, brown eyes. "Yes, I am. Thank you. How about you?"

"That was Erica?"

"Yes, that *was* Erica."

"Okay," Andi said.

Caitlin lifted her hand and gently stroked Andi's cheek. If she wasn't careful, she might just drown in the unguarded desire she saw in Andi's eyes.

"If you look at me like that, I won't be able to sit through dinner," she whispered.

Caitlin held on to the bottom of the ladder as Kim balanced near the top. "There you go Caitie, all done." Kim passed down the box that had been sitting high on a shelf above the door of Caitlin's office.

Caitlin lifted the lid and peered inside. "You are right again, Kim. Here it is." She grabbed the electronic tape measure and surveyed the other instruments stored in the cardboard box. "Spirit level, screwdriver set, roll of masking tape, pliers and fishing wire." Caitlin listed the contents as Kim made her way down the ladder. "And what were you planning to do with this little hoard?" Caitlin asked.

Kim shrugged rubbing the back of her neck sheepishly. "This is my emergency stash. At the museum, things were always going missing. So, when I first came here, I thought I should keep my own set of tools hidden in the office."

"Well, I'm glad you did, because I seem to have misplaced my measuring tape, and I promised I'd email the figures to the architect today."

The restoration was going to schedule. Caitlin was pleased that the work on the landing's pressed metal ceiling, almost the length of a cricket pitch, was due to begin next week. The 150-year-old metal panels had only suffered minor corrosion and could be saved.

Caitlin opened up a spreadsheet on her desktop computer and turned the screen towards Kim. "So, once Period Restorations does the ceiling, the electricians can reinstall the original Victorian chandeliers and wall lighting."

"The new halogen lights are going to complement the original lighting. I think it will look fabulous," said Kim.

"And the reduction in overall energy consumption fits with our goal of working sustainably," Caitlin said. They'd decided to retain the original period lighting for ambience but had added a modern lighting system for efficiency.

The door hinges squeaked, and Kim and Caitlin turned simultaneously towards the sound. Andi stood holding a tray laden with three steaming coffee mugs. Caitlin bit her lip to stifle a grin. The sight of her, leaning against the doorframe—golden tanned skin still flushed from her shower—filled Caitlin with a mixture of longing and contentment.

At the university, Caitlin had always maintained her professional decorum. But this morning, she was comfortable with the convergence of both her worlds. Personal and professional. This was her home too, and seeing Andi here in her office made Caitlin very happy.

"Andi," Caitlin said as she took the tray. She ushered her inside. Andi smiled and seemed to devour her with her appreciative gaze.

Kim stood with her mouth open.

Caitlin was amused to see her colleague, for once, stunned into silence. She turned back to Andi. "Good morning. I see you got my note," she said. "Did you find everything you needed for breakfast?" Caitlin placed the coffee mugs onto her desk. She gestured for Andi to sit in her chair.

"I helped myself to fruit and yoghurt, thanks," Andi said. She pushed her hands into the pockets of her faded jeans and moved behind the desk.

"Good." Caitlin smiled. "Kim, this is Andi. Andi, I'd like you to meet Kim."

Kim leaned across the desk and offered her hand. Her face was red as a beetroot. "A pleasure to meet you, Andi."

"Lovely to meet you, Kim," Andi said, as Kim continued to grasp her hand firmly.

"Kim is our registrar and curator, but I've discovered her talents are boundless."

Kim shook her head, let go of Andi's hand and sat down. "Caitie is being too kind. What she really means is that I can't resist meddling with everyone around here."

Caitlin choked. "I think you mean every *thing* around here."

Andi laughed. "I do recall Caitlin mentioning that you've come to the rescue with your ingenuity on many occasions," she said.

Kim's face flushed a deep crimson. "On the other hand, I've heard only a tiny bit about you. Our Caitie is a secretive one," Kim said.

Caitlin sat and stretched her legs under the desk, brushing against Andi's calf. "Kim and her partner Sharon were at the dance at the Emerson."

Kim placed her hands on her hips. "Well, it was noted that you made a very hurried exit Caitie—and we didn't even meet Andi."

Caitlin felt her own face colouring. "Yes, I do apologise Kim. It was a rather rushed getaway."

Andi spluttered.

Caitlin calmly sipped her coffee as Kim questioned Andi about her exhibition and just about every other aspect of her life—or so it seemed to Caitlin. Knowing how shy Andi could be, Caitlin was surprised how easily Kim drew her out.

Twenty minutes later, Kim rose to her feet. "It's been a real treat getting to know you, Andi. I'm sure we'll meet again." She bowed her head to Caitlin. "Now, I have a hundred things to do. I'll see you in the gallery, boss."

Caitlin nodded. "Give me about fifteen minutes. I won't be too long."

Kim closed the door behind her and Andi said, "Quite a colourful character. She'll keep you on the straight and narrow. She's a good sort though, isn't she, *Caitie*?"

Caitlin raised her eyebrow. Nobody but Kim had got away with calling her Caitie. She stretched her arms above her head. "I really needed that coffee. I was rather hoping you'd venture down here in my green cashmere jumper. Like the first time you stayed the night."

"I don't think Kim could have gone any more red in the face. She would have had a coronary," Andi said.

"Possibly. I can't argue with that, can I?" Caitlin grinned. "After last night's activities, that could have been my fate as well." She raised an eyebrow again.

Andi whirled around in the chair to face the floor-to-ceiling window. "You have an excellent view. All those colourful spring blooms. I don't think I'd ever get any work done sitting at this desk. I'd want to be out there in the garden."

Caitlin stood behind Andi's chair and rested her hands on her hips. "Why don't you go downstairs and explore?" She kissed the top of Andi's head. "I have an hour's work before we join Isabella." She turned Andi to face her. "Is that still okay? You said last night you'd have lunch with us today."

Andi wrapped her hand around Caitlin's neck. "I'd like that," she murmured and pulled Caitlin in for a kiss. "I don't want to outstay my welcome. I should head back after lunch."

"Keep kissing me like that, and neither of us will leave this office," Caitlin whispered softly, as she returned Andi's kiss.

A loud knocking sound emanating from the floor above caused them to draw apart. They looked at the ceiling and giggled.

"That will be Kim trying to get my attention. I guess it really is time for me to do some work," Caitlin conceded.

Chapter 23

Unlike the native bush garden and coastal vegetation at Kinsale, the estate garden was more in the style of Sissinghurst in Kent. Andi had discovered a lot about the garden from a recent television documentary. One day, she hoped to visit Vita Sackville-West and Harold Nicolson's property, but for now, she was more than happy to just be *here*.

Andi was overcome by the fragrance of wisteria that clung to latticework bordering the formal, structured garden. The vivacious, lilac-coloured petals contrasted with its grey, crusty gnarled branches. The sound of rippling water drew her along the pathway lined with English box hedges towards a tiered Victorian fountain. Her senses were flooded with the sound of birds chirping and the incredible beauty of spring. Near the fountain was a garden with clipped hedges, purple lavender, and white hydrangea. The rose garden, further down the path, was filled with a multitude of blooms—dark reds, burgundy, light pinks, pale peach, and orange. Andi thought of her mother, who loved roses. She would be totally overwhelmed by this display.

"Oh Mum, I wish you could see this."

She stood under a giant weeping elm. It must have been at least ten metres tall. The tree cast a light shade and intricate patterns across the tiled pathways with their neat cobblestone edges.

Beyond a row of fig, apple, and apricot trees sat a beautiful stone cottage with a wide covered veranda. Near a high stone fence lay a vegetable and herb garden tucked beside the brick garage.

Andi hadn't even walked two sides of the extensive garden before she heard Isabella call.

"Andréa. Come join me." She was on the veranda, pushing a small-wheeled trolley. "I have fresh lemonade. Come and sit with me in the shade."

Andi stepped onto the veranda and pulled out a chair for Isabella.

"Thank you, Andréa. That is such a lovely name, but if you prefer Andi, that's what I'll call you. Do you prefer Andi?"

Andi gently pushed Isabella's chair closer to the table until she was comfortably seated. "My mother calls me Andréa, especially when she wants to make a point. But I don't mind. I answer to either."

"Andi it is, then. Now, if you would be so kind, you can pour the lemonade. We have an abundance of lemons. You must ask Caitlin to pick some for you before you leave."

"I'd love some, thank you." Andi carefully filled the glasses and replaced the tapestry cover, which was weighted with tiny beads, on the pitcher.

"You can still smell the last of the flowering magnolias. I adore their perfume." Isabella's blue eyes crinkled with pleasure.

"Your garden is extraordinary. Actually, the whole estate is stunning, and you have a beautiful home," Andi said.

"Thank you, dear. The house belonged to Maggie's family, but I can take some of the credit for the garden. I've spent many, many hours here."

"It is a credit to both of you, then. I feel very lucky to be able to visit."

Isabella looked directly at her. Andi was captivated by the same intense blue of Caitlin's eyes—so compelling.

"You are a beautiful young woman. I can see why my niece is so taken with you." Andi blushed and looked down at her lemonade glass. "Shy and charming as well," added Isabella, making Andi even more self-conscious.

"Thank you."

"As far as visiting, you are welcome here anytime."

Andi nodded slightly in response and searched for something she could add to the conversation.

Before she could, Isabella said, "This is Caitlin's home as well. I love her with all my heart, and I'm glad to see her enjoying life."

Isabella was remarkable. She seemed vivacious, graceful, and sharp as a tack. Andi hoped she'd have the same grace and pluckiness when she reached Isabella's age.

"I haven't known Caitlin very long, but it's clear she admires you. She's lucky to have someone she loves and respects so much," Andi said.

Isabella placed a delicate hand on Andi's forearm. "You are very sweet. I look forward to getting to know you better," she said, then shifted her gaze to the other side of the garden. A wide, sparkling grin spread across her face.

Andi turned to identify the source of Isabella's happiness. Caitlin was striding across the lawn. Seductive, confident, and shining as she picked two flowers from the frangipani branch above her head. She twirled the flowers in her fingers before making her way to the veranda.

Watching Caitlin made Andi deliriously happy.

Caitlin kissed the top of her grandaunt's curly, grey hair and handed her a flower. " A flower for you," she said. She leaned over to Andi and tucked a flower behind her ear. "And one for you."

Caitlin sat down in a chair beside Andi. She took her hand, entwined their fingers together, and placed their joined hands in her lap. "I've obviously done something right in my life." She smiled, and her eyes danced with mischief. "Lunch with two of my favourite and most irresistible women."

Isabella released an unrestrained burst of laughter. "Well, darling, whoever said the Irish charm was a dying art was wrong." She looked lovingly at her grandniece. "Caitlin, would you collect the tray from the kitchen? The sandwiches are in the refrigerator, and the vegetable tart is in the warmer. I'm feeling rather peckish now."

Caitlin squeezed Andi's hand lightly. "Right, will do." She sprang out of her seat and stepped into the cottage.

"You've certainly put a spring in *her* step," chuckled Isabella.

After seeing Andi to her car and sharing a rather prolonged goodbye that involved a lot of kissing, Caitlin returned to the veranda.

She heard the familiar *ring* of a silver spoon as Isabella tapped the bone china teapot.

Caitlin sank back into her chair and watched Isabella stir the tea. She was entranced by the gentle back-and-forth movement of the teaspoon, transported back to the rituals at home and the afternoon tea parties hosted by her parents.

Pots of dark, aromatic teas, along with three-tiered plates of lemon and vanilla curd cake, buttermilk scones, soda bread, and delicate sandwiches. Her father would entertain his students and colleagues with stories. He was handsome in his rustic Donegal tweed jacket and matching houndstooth cap. Caitlin recalled the oaky smell of his small, root briar pipe.

"Are you all right, Caitlin? You seem lost in thought," said Isabella "What's on your mind?"

"Ma and Da. All those tea parties with students on the lawn terrace. The sound of you stirring the teapot brings it all back."

"Are you feeling homesick?" Isabella asked.

"A little. I only just realised it." Caitlin sighed. With her elbow rested on the table, she cupped her chin in one hand and stared out into the garden.

"When was the last time you spoke to your mother?"

"Two weeks ago. But we email regularly. Ma gives me news about the apartment and my tenants." Caitlin's gaze returned to Isabella. "I like to catch up with the gossip on campus."

"I talked to Orla last week." Isabella poured the tea for them both and passed the cup and saucer to Caitlin. "Your mother, as usual, has ten things going at once. Next week she's off to a librarian conference in Edinburgh. She was helping your father organise a dinner for the dean—I think they have an American writer staying at the house for the weekend. I'm flabbergasted by your mother's schedule and her boundless energy."

Caitlin laughed. She, too, admired her mother's limitless enthusiasm and zest for life. Her role as the main librarian responsible for the university's arts and humanities collection kept her fully occupied. How she managed the role of professor's wife and their joint social and community obligations was amazing.

"Orla has always been a busy bee. Frankly, I don't know *when* she found the time to have you," Isabella said with raised eyebrows in feigned astonishment.

"That's what a weekend of passion in Paris will do. They've never made a secret of their first trip to *La Rive Gauche*," Caitlin said. "I'm the mistake that resulted."

"You are the beautiful mistake that resulted." Isabella smiled. "I still remember your mother's letter about their first trip to the Left Bank. She was totally besotted with Patrick and Paris. You may have been unplanned, but they were enchanted by you. They doted on every minute detail of your progress. I have albums filled with photographs from the day you took your first breath, Caitlin Isabella Quinn," she stated dramatically, but not without affection. "Orla was never the stay-at-home, overly maternal type—but she's always loved you. And, well, you can do no wrong by Patrick. You've had your father wrapped around your little finger all your life."

"You are right, Isabella," Caitlin said. "I'm very lucky. Ma and Da have always shown belief in my career and me. They've been very supportive—without being imperious."

Two small blue and black birds perched on the end of the silver tea trolley.

"The naughty scoundrels. I think they're after the crumbs," Isabella laughed and waved her hands at the tiny thieves.

"Possibly after Marion's sultana scones, do you think?" Caitlin smiled. "What are they?"

"They're superb fairywrens. These lovely cobalt-blue birds are the males." Caitlin and Isabella watched as the birds flitted away to forage in the dirt under the decaying leaf matter. "They're actually more likely to eat worms and insects than sultanas. Beautiful little creatures, aren't they? We're lucky that the garden attracts so many birds."

They sat in companionable silence for a few minutes and listened to the sounds of the garden—the wind rustling through the elm tree foliage, the chattering of birds, and the delicate tinkling of a Japanese glass bell hanging in the red maple.

"I do wonder sometimes what it would have been like to have siblings. Maybe a younger sister who followed me around and borrowed my clothes. Or even a brother who tried to date the same girl and defended me against bullies," Caitlin said. "I was just expected to mix with the adult crowd."

Isabella's eyes brightened with sympathy. "I suppose there weren't many children around the campus when you were young."

"Yes, it wasn't like we lived in a village where there were a lot of other families. On campus, there were mainly teachers and students."

"Well, this coming weekend will be a change for you. You're expected at Andi's parents?" Isabella asked.

"Yes, I am." Caitlin rubbed the back of her neck.

"Are you worried?"

"A little. It will be the first time I meet Andi's family, apart from Luc. It's Andi's father's birthday and the farm's spring festival—all rolled into one." Caitlin shrugged her shoulders. "Well, there's nothing like jumping in with both feet."

"True. I can understand why you're anxious."

"It doesn't help me that Andi's previous girlfriend was from overseas. She suddenly up and left, and Andi's family had to pick up the pieces. I'm another foreigner, temporarily in the country."

"I see. Hopefully, you can just enjoy the weekend and her family won't make any judgments before knowing you. One step at a time."

"I hope that's the case."

Isabella patted Caitlin's hand. "More importantly, how do you feel? Andi is a beautiful young woman. She seems quite taken with you."

Caitlin struggled for the right words. She wasn't her usual coherent, logical self. "Andi's got me all tied in knots." Caitlin gazed at Isabella. "Not like my customary…"

"I think you're falling for her," Isabella said. When Caitlin didn't deny her words, she continued, "Caitlin, sometimes you just have to let go of control."

Caitlin had always been comfortable keeping within boundaries of her own making. Was she ready to let go? Why was she having doubts about the weekend? She'd enjoy the farm and Andi's family—wouldn't she? But was she getting too involved? Caitlin was definitely out of her comfort zone.

Chapter 24

Caitlin escaped the inevitable bumper-to-bumper rush-hour traffic by leaving for the farm by early afternoon on Thursday. In her last text, Andi had said she hoped to arrive around five thirty. Caitlin estimated it would take her about an hour and a half to reach Ballarat, where she intended to visit the art gallery. That should put her at the farm about thirty minutes after Andi. By arriving just after six o'clock, she would have Andi at her side when she met her parents for the first time.

After half an hour, she turned off the motorway, and the car's GPS indicated one hundred and twenty kilometres to her destination. She steered the Roadster into the sparse traffic and headed along the open country road.

The last few weeks had been incredible—a whirlwind. Caitlin, Kim, and their staff had worked a tight deadline in preparation for the installation of the large, upstairs gallery. The builders were finished, the lighting system had been installed, and the work on the parquet flooring was complete. The exhibition space and foyer looked outstanding. Next week, with the help of two extra casual staff, they would install the display cabinets and the freestanding sculptures and hang the paintings.

As she drove, Caitlin noticed the undulating flaxen wheat fields, small pockets of residential areas, and mature stands of trees bordering part of the scrubby state forest. So different from the green rolling hills and valleys near her home in Ireland. *Home.* Caitlin knew she would have to choose the right time to tell Andi her latest news. Would there ever be a *right* time?

She had worked all her academic life for a chance at this opportunity—Academic Promotions to Associate Professor. The presentation process from Senior Lecturer to Associate Professor would begin the first week in December in Cork. When she'd received the papers in the mail last week, her emotions had cascaded from elation and exhilaration to bewilderment and uncertainty. Caitlin talked at length to Kiera about her dilemma, torn between her career, family, and friends in Cork and her current life and job in Melbourne.

Andi. She couldn't even bear to throw into that mix her oh-so-new relationship with Andi. The intense attraction and their heart-thumping sexual intimacy had escalated—even though distance and commitments meant their time together had been severely curtailed.

Caitlin wished her interview could have been better timed. If Andi were free in December, she could have asked her to travel with her. It would have given her a chance to show Andi around her city and for them to visit the other Kinsale, on the southwest coast of Ireland. But Andi had reached a milestone in her own life—her first solo exhibition.

Caitlin checked the directions into Ballarat and drove towards the main street. She stopped at a red light and rested her head heavily on the steering wheel.

"*Dammit*, there is no easy answer," she muttered.

A few hours later, Caitlin pulled into a long driveway lined with tall, dark cypress trees. They stood like sentinels, and led her to a stone-walled courtyard. She stopped to check the nameplate to make sure she was on the right property.

"Casa de La Rosa. This is it."

The Rey villa was not what she had envisaged, and she chided herself for expecting an older, traditional homestead. The rectangular, white, cubic-style exterior of the villa was modern, contemporary—almost sleek. It formed a contrast between the green of the cultivated fields and today's deep-blue sky.

Caitlin parked near a grey Jeep Cherokee and opened the car door to a fragrant mix of orange blossom and eucalyptus. There was no sign of Andi's car in the front yard, and she was nervous at the prospect of meeting Andi's family on her own.

As she approached the burnished copper front door, she looked up at the slatted wooden veranda roof with wide overhanging eaves that cast a stripy pattern on the grey slate tiles at her feet.

The front garden was a mass of colour, swathes of purple iris, gladioli, granny's bonnets, and freesias. The vivid hues were fantastic. Caitlin stood in the shade of the veranda absorbing the beauty around her. Compared to the landscape she had just driven through, this was an unexpected oasis.

Suddenly, the front door was flung open. "Welcome, you must be Caitlin. I'm Lina, Andréa's mother." Lina greeted her with a warm, welcoming smile and a firm handshake. "Come in, come in."

Caitlin took a deep breath, feeling a little more at ease. Lina ushered Caitlin into the house and guided her through the foyer. They entered a double-height living room separated from the hall by a stylish, architectural, wood and glass divider. The exposed beams and the large recessed fireplace were complemented by the strong, clean lines of a sizeable open-plan kitchen and dining space. Large windows gave a view of an outdoor living room. Caitlin was drawn to the welcoming atmosphere and the fragrant smells that drifted from the kitchen.

Even though Andi had given Caitlin the option of driving to the farm on the day of the party, Caitlin had chosen to arrive earlier. Despite her conflicted feelings about becoming more deeply involved with Andi, she wanted to be part of the preparation and spend time with the family.

A tall, handsome man bounded across the lawn towards the courtyard doors. He directed a beaming smile at Caitlin, and she immediately saw a strong resemblance to Andi. This *must* be her father.

Home. Even though Andi had lived away from the farm for many years, Casa de La Rosa was her home. As the old Jeep chugged into Sugar Creek Road, the green rolling paddocks and tall line of trees was, as always, a welcoming sight. The temperate climate, fertile volcanic soils, and consistent rainfall of the region enabled the farm to grow crops year round. Andi never failed to be amazed by the abundance of their produce.

Even as a child, she'd loved the colour and patterns of the planted fields. Rows of green and purple kale; intense green of sweet-stem broccoli; the deep, rich red of radicchio. As she approached the hilltop near the farm gate, she could see the curved fields planted with iceberg, red oak lettuce, chicory, and an array of Asian greens. She wound down her window and inhaled the heavy, loamy earthiness of a freshly ploughed field.

Andi drove down the farm road past the circular planted, terraced herb and spice gardens, through the open gates and into the villa compound. Caitlin's car was parked near the open garages, and she pulled in alongside. Andi was more than half an hour late, but hopefully Caitlin hadn't arrived too long ago.

She grabbed her backpack, stood on the front veranda, and looked towards the twin dams at the bottom of the property. The setting sun spread a pinky-red glow upon the gently moving water, and the mature trees planted on their banks cast ghostly shadows into the surrounding fields.

The espaliered fruit trees on the old red-brick walls of the Casa compound were covered in sweet-smelling blossoms. The house garden, with its orange trees, roses, and freshly mown lawns, was the perfect setting for the coming weekend celebrations.

"Andréa," her mother called. "You are here at last. You're *almost* an hour late. Why didn't you ring?" Lina grabbed her youngest child in a tight embrace.

"Mum, you are squashing me," Andi said, as she tried to pry herself from her mother's arms.

Lina stepped back and noticed the state of Andi's clothes. "You're covered in mud! What on earth happened to you? Are you okay, Andréa?"

Andi laughed, and placed a finger on Lina's lips. "Shoo… One question at a time, please. It is great to see you too, Mum." As they talked, Andi surreptitiously searched for Caitlin.

"If you are looking for your Caitlin, she is not here. Anyway, why would you want her to see you like this?" Lina scolded her daughter and turned her in a circle to check the full damage.

"But where is she?"

Lina picked up Andi's bag and walked towards the enclosed glass breezeway that lead to the guest quarters.

"Caitlin is worried about you too. She tried to phone you every *ten* minutes, but it kept going to the answering service. I asked your father to take her for a walk around the garden before sunset. We thought it would keep her calm until you arrived."

Andi looked down at her muddy jeans and shirt. "I had no choice. The Jeep has been giving me trouble. I took the back road to save time, and then I ran over a branch that got stuck under the car." She pointed to her clothes. "And this is what happened."

Andi followed her mother into the guest suite and noticed Caitlin's overnight case and a shopping bag emblazoned with the Ballarat art gallery's logo, placed neatly on the side dresser.

Lina guided her daughter towards the bathroom. "I think it's a good idea for you to have a nice hot shower and change into some clothes with no mud," she said.

"I'm sorry I worried you, but there was no phone service along the back road. If I'd been stuck, I would have walked to one of the farmhouses. Anyway, I'm here now."

"Into the shower with you. I have to check the dinner. Just a simple meal tonight, Andréa. We have a big day of preparation tomorrow. Your father and Caitlin should be back soon." Lina tilted her head to one side and smiled. "Although, I must say, he seems very taken with your friend. He is probably questioning her intentions right now."

Andi rolled her eyes. "God, I hope not. Oh, I *really* hope he doesn't give her a hard time."

Lina pushed Andi into the bathroom. "Oh, my darling, *you* are so easily teased," she said and pulled the door closed behind her.

Andi stripped off her clothes and turned on the shower. Enjoying the steaming hot water, she thought about the weekend ahead. It was going to be interesting. How would Caitlin cope with her overprotective family and inquisitive friends and neighbours? Hopefully with patience and a sense of humour.

First, Caitlin had to survive tomorrow, a day of family Rey—preparing, cooking, and decorating. Andi reached for a large towel and rubbed herself dry, wrapped it around her body, secured it, and ran her hands through her hair to loosen any tangles.

"*Poor* Caitlin," Andi moaned.

"Why poor Caitlin?" A voice from the doorway startled Andi. "Well, aren't you a sight for sore eyes?"

Andi looked up into the mirror and saw Caitlin's reflection. She leaned nonchalantly against the doorframe. As Andi turned around, Caitlin entered the room and casually kicked the door closed with her boot.

Andi grinned. Caitlin stepped towards her and drew her into her arms. "Your mother explained what happened. I'm so glad you're here. I've missed you." Caitlin kissed Andi's bare shoulders and tugged at the towel until it fell to the ground.

Andi gasped as Caitlin pressed the length of their bodies together and her nipples pearled against the sheer fabric of Caitlin's T-shirt.

"I think you have me at a slight disadvantage here." Andi slipped her hands under the black material and dragged her fingers up Caitlin's waist and over her ribs to stroke the soft skin above her silky bra.

Caitlin buried her face in Andi's neck and skimmed over her damp skin with hungry lips.

Andi grazed her thumb along Caitlin's breast, and she trembled.

"I don't know about that," Caitlin murmured. Her tongue traced Andi's cheek, and as if seeking permission, she kissed the corner of her mouth. As Caitlin moved her hands along her back and down to caress her thighs, Andi captured Caitlin's mouth fully in a lingering kiss that left Andi weak at the knees.

"Andréa and Caitlin, dinner in five minutes," Lina's voice echoed from the hallway.

Caitlin pulled away as Andi reached for her towel. "Oh my goodness, I completely forgot where we were," Caitlin said, her cheeks flushed. "*God*, I've missed you."

Andi laughed and secured the towel once again around her torso. "I've missed you too." She ran her knuckles gently along Caitlin's pink skin. "Welcome to my family home. I think I'd better dress before my mother joins us in here."

Caitlin patted her face with a cool, damp cloth and rearranged her clothes. "I'll let them know you won't be long." She took a deep breath and smiled at Andi sweetly, then made her way through the doorway.

Caitlin lifted the wine to her lips, hiding her smile behind the glass. She sat back and observed Andi. She longed to feel Andi's lips against hers again—she could almost taste their sweetness.

As if reading her thoughts, Andi raised her eyebrows, rolled her eyes, and smiled at her. She was adorable, and Caitlin had been caught staring.

Andi sat between her parents, and it was clear that she was a beautiful combination of them both. Like her father, Emmanuel, she was agile, with the same sun-kissed olive skin, dark-blonde hair, long eyelashes, and brown eyes. Emmanuel's hair, greying at the temples, gave him a distinguished look. He was handsome and charming.

Lina Rey had a wiry, slender frame. Her dark, wavy hair was kept short and neatly styled. Andi was lucky to share her mother's high cheekbones, full lips, and classic straight nose.

Andi laughed easily as her father recounted a story about his grandson Manny's first time behind the wheel of the farm truck. Caitlin winked at Andi across the table, and Andi grinned shyly. Caitlin turned to meet Lina's intelligent hazel eyes, as she observed their interaction. She was sure nothing got past those shrewd eyes.

"Your kale and potato soup is lovely," Caitlin said. Lina had served their first course of finely chopped kale, spicy chorizo, and potato soup, with freshly baked cornbread and black olives.

"Caldo verde, I'm glad you enjoyed it. It is just a simple dish from the Douro region, where Emmanuel and I were born."

"As is this excellent wine you brought for us, Caitlin," Emmanuel added and held up the half-empty bottle of guru branco to refill their glasses.

"Is it made by the Portuguese woman you were telling me about?" Andi asked.

Caitlin nodded. "That's right, Sandra Tavares da Silva is the oenologist at Wine and Soul."

"It is a beautifully finished wine that will also go with our next dish," Lina said. She placed a platter on the table, piled high with baked fish on a bed of stewed tomatoes and capers. "Help yourself to the cod, please."

Andi skimmed Caitlin's shoulder as she put a large bowl of green salad in front of her. She drew back and whispered in Caitlin's ear, "Yes, help yourself, *please*."

"Andréa." Lina shook her head with an amused expression.

"Yes, Mother?" Andi asked.

"Please bring the pomegranate dressing from the refrigerator."

"Yes, Mum."

Emmanuel looked lovingly at his youngest daughter and then directly at Caitlin. "It is good to see our Andréa laughing and happy." He lifted his glass in a toast. "Let's drink, to family, new friends, and good food. *Saúde*."

They clinked their glasses together.

"*Sláinte mhaith*. Good health. Thank you so much for inviting me to your home," Caitlin said.

"We are delighted you could be here, and I look forward to introducing you to the rest of the family tomorrow." Lina raised her glass.

Caitlin placed her hand over Andi's mouth. "Quieten down, will you? How much wine *did* you have?" She couldn't help but smile as Andi giggled and wriggled beneath her.

Andi looked up impishly. "Only two glasses of white and a port after dinner—not much at all."

"It's payback time. You were deliberately taunting me in front of your parents," Caitlin said and held on to Andi's wrists lightly to stop her wandering hands. "I was trying to make a good impression, and you were not making it easy."

"I was. I did not." Andi shook her head from side to side. "Anyway, how could they not like you?"

"You did too. Whispering in my ear and playing with my leg under the table."

"I did not!"

"Did too. Whose hand *was* it on my knee then?" Caitlin scowled and narrowed her eyes. "You delinquent. How old are you?"

Andi grinned and struggled to free her hands. "There are, let me see, only nine years between us… That would make me thirty."

"You cheeky little brat—hey, it's only eight years."

"Don't worry," Andi squeaked. "I've always had a fantasy about seducing an older woman."

Caitlin opened her mouth and looked into Andi's sexy, brown eyes. She was speechless.

"I don't believe it. Caitlin Quinn at a loss for words."

Caitlin blinked and threaded her fingers through Andi's. She rolled onto her side, and they lay facing each other, centimetres apart, knees touching. Andi slid her leg across Caitlin's thigh and drew their bodies closer. She kissed her with an intensity that left Caitlin's heart beating powerfully in her chest. A sweet ripple of desire, and something she couldn't quite name, swept over her.

"Are you okay, *Caitlin*?"

Caitlin nodded and moved gently to roll Andi onto her back. She repositioned her body and lay above her. "Yes, I am." She sighed. The heat between them was like a tender caress. "I love…the way you say my name," Caitlin whispered. "You leave me breathless."

Chapter 25

Andi stirred at dawn to the sound of a rooster crowing, with the silky contours of Caitlin's body pressed against her. One protective arm lay across Andi's waist, and a hand curved just under her breast. She gently lifted Caitlin's arm and turned, careful not to wake her. She pressed her lips into Caitlin's shoulder to inhale the scent of her skin. She closed her eyes and once again fell into a blissful sleep.

When she woke an hour later, sunlight streamed through the east window, and a pair of intense, blue eyes gazed tenderly into hers. "You're awake," she croaked, lazily stretching out her limbs and nestling closer into Caitlin's warmth. "This is nice."

Caitlin's arms tightened around her. "You are a snuggler, aren't you?"

"Do you mind?" Andi murmured.

Caitlin ran her fingers through her hair, settled her right hand at the nape of Andi's neck, and then placed her lips tenderly against her hair. "I've never been one to cuddle, but I like this very much."

"Never? Not with anyone?"

"Not really. Rachel often worked on her writing late at night, and she wasn't really the type to stay hugging for too long, *especially* after the honeymoon period was over."

"Well, I guess we won't have a chance for that to happen," Andi blurted before she could stop herself, immediately feeling the tension in Caitlin's body. *I'm such an idiot.*

Caitlin pushed the pillow up against the headboard and pulled herself into a sitting position, covering her body with the cotton sheet. Andi did the same and sat staring at her hands. "I'm sorry, that wasn't fair."

Caitlin reached for her T-shirt and sleeping shorts and swung her legs off the bed. She dressed quickly, then went around to the other side, handing Andi her nightshirt. She walked across the room, pulled the thin cord, and drew open the curtains.

Across the green fields, the misty fog was lifting to reveal a bright blue sky. "It looks like it's going to be a beautiful morning." Caitlin turned, her arms wrapped around her chest protectively. "You promised me a run this morning. Do you feel up to it?"

Seeing the inner turmoil reflected on Caitlin's face, Andi was overcome by a sense of guilt. She wanted to go to her, wrap her arms around her, but Caitlin's cool look stopped her.

"Well, do you feel up to it?" Caitlin repeated.

Andi swallowed. "I do. Let's get changed. It's a great time to run along the tree line on the outer farm road. There are usually koalas in the messmate stringybarks in the morning."

"Messmate stringybarks? That sounds *so* very Australian. Mess-*mate*." Uncrossing her arms, she searched through her bag for her running gear.

Andi tied the drawstring of her shorts and pulled on a lightweight hooded top. "It's a type of eucalyptus the koalas love to eat. The messmate provides a corridor of treed areas linking patches of bush. The tree corridor means the koala are less likely to come down to the ground, so they are much safer."

"Aren't you a wealth of information this morning?" Caitlin pulled on her leggings and a pair of red shorts over the top. "I've never seen a real koala. It will be a first for me."

"You have a treat in store for you, then." Andi attempted to make eye contact. *She won't look me in the eye.*

"Won't you freeze in shorts?" Caitlin asked, tying her laces.

"I'm tough. I'll soon heat up when we run." She smiled shyly, pulling on her well-worn Adidas runners. Caitlin's sleek Swiss Cloudsters didn't escape her notice. "They're nice," Andi said.

Caitlin looked down at her black and white shoes and shrugged. "Cushioned landing and barefoot takeoff. I need something to help me keep up with you, don't I? Come on, then. Let's do it." She tugged on her running cap. "I'll be well and truly ready for coffee by the time we get back."

"Let's not forget breakfast. We can pick up some fresh eggs from the hen house, and I spotted a loaf of Mum's Portuguese bread she prepared last night."

Andi opened the glass sliding door and shivered as the crisp air touched her face. "Herbed potato frittata and freshly baked sweet bread. It is great to be home."

Andi set out fast; she needed to work off those uncertainty demons that kept surfacing. As she increased the pace, pushing her legs, she reminded herself that she was not supposed to let negative thoughts spoil their few days together. She knew she'd stepped into this with her eyes open. Caitlin had never made any promises, and now Andi had to deal with the choice she'd made. *No regrets. I would rather have what I have with her than nothing.*

As she ran, she chanted over and over, "Caitlin is not Martha. Caitlin is not Martha. Caitlin is not Martha."

She glanced back over her shoulder. Caitlin had an easy stride and natural fluid motion. Her slight height advantage and long legs forced Andi to work even harder to keep ahead. When she reached the top of the outer farm road, she slowed and checked her sports watch. They had run six kilometres at a good pace, and Caitlin kept up with her the whole time. Looking at how effortlessly she was breathing, she wondered if *she* was holding Caitlin back.

According to her parents, the previous week had brought significant rain, and the dirt roads were a little muddy but not sloppy enough to slow them down.

Caitlin stopped beside her, taking a long drink from the bottle she'd attached to her waistband. "You're setting a good pace."

Andi blinked in the bright sunlight. "Too fast for you?"

Caitlin shook her head, fastened the water bottle back in place, and danced about on her toes. Then, as if she was ready to take off, she lunged forward to stretch out her hamstrings. Andi admired her fitted jersey singlet and her graceful, lightly muscled arms glistening in the sunshine.

Caitlin arched one eyebrow at her, looking a little cocky and too confident. "I'm ready, when you are," Caitlin said, cool as a cucumber.

"How far do you want to run?" Andi asked. Better not overdo things. She's not used to this terrain.

"A few more k's, just don't take me too far, or we'll miss breakfast."

"Okay, no problem." Andi bent over to retie her shoelaces.

Caitlin started off down the embankment, then came to a stop and turned around. "Hey, Andi?" she called.

"Yeah?" Andi raised her head to catch the wicked grin.

"Did I ever mention I was part of track and field at UCC Athletics Club? Not that I'm competitive at all…" she sang out as she sprinted ahead at a cracking pace.

"Damn! Now she tells me." Andi shook her head. *Have mercy.* She would probably kill herself trying to catch up to her, but she was willing to give it a go.

By the time they made it back to the house, Andi was breathing heavily. She untied the top that was around her waist and used it to mop up the perspiration from her face and arms… No, actually, it was sweat. She looked down at her grey Nike sports bra that was drenched, and a little revealing. Caitlin, who had stopped in the shade of the veranda, was calmly sipping on her drink bottle, stretching her muscles.

"You made it." She laughed, sauntered over to Andi, untied the sweatshirt from her waist, and used it to mop Andi's brow. "I thought I'd have to run back and find you."

Andi bent over to ease her breathing and let her heart rate slow down. "God, I'm a wreck," she scowled. "What was that you said about *not* being competitive? You're ruthless, and you didn't even stop to look at the koalas."

"There will be a next time, won't there?" Caitlin leaned forward to lick Andi's heated skin in the hollow at the junction between her breasts. "Poor baby. Did I tire you out?"

"Good morning," said a crisp, clear voice from the open doorway.

"Ana." Andi turned. She embraced her sister and kissed her on both cheeks while holding her hooded top between them. "Sorry, I got a bit hot… I'm a bit sweaty. I need a shower."

Andi stepped back and looked at Ana. Her long, dark hair hung in a loose braid over her left shoulder, and her large, alert hazel eyes scrutinised the scene like a hawk. But her eyes softened as she checked Andi at arm's length.

She wriggled her nose. "Yes, you do," Ana said.

Andi grabbed Ana's hand and dragged her closer to Caitlin. "I'd like you to meet my sister, Ana—Annalise Thompson," she said. "This is my friend—"

"Caitlin. Pleased to meet you, Ana." Caitlin stepped forward and took the hand offered in a matching strong handshake.

“You too, Caitlin. It is always lovely to meet one of Andi’s friends.”

Caitlin fiddled with her cap, twirling it around on her finger. “If you don’t mind, I need a shower, so I’m going to head inside. I’ll feel a lot more comfortable once I’ve freshened up. Excuse me, please.”

Caitlin walked in the direction of their room, and before Andi could follow, Ana marched her towards the main entrance of the house. “Why don’t *you* grab a shower in the other bathroom? Breakfast is nearly ready, and we have a long list of things to get done today.”

Chapter 26

Tomorrow night, the Reys would celebrate Emmanuel's sixty-fifth birthday, along with the farm's annual spring gathering with their extended family, neighbours, and friends.

At breakfast, Caitlin was seated between Luc and Mick, Ana's husband, who reminded her of an Irish rugby player—tall, muscular, and broad shouldered, with thick, sandy hair and freckles. Ana and Andi were across from Caitlin, and Lina and Emmanuel sat at opposite ends of the long table.

Ana apparently took her role as project manager very seriously. Caitlin shook her head as Andi rolled her eyes, watching her older sister take charge. Their meal doubled as a planning meeting, and by the time the dishes were cleared, Ana handed each of them a neat, handwritten list of their tasks for that day.

Caitlin had been volunteered by Andi to help Lina, Emmanuel, and Ana in the kitchen. Despite Ana's occasional call-to-order—mostly directed at Luc—with a quick toss of her braid over her shoulder, the atmosphere was lighthearted and friendly. Andi bubbled with excitement, and Caitlin, happy to be included in the preparations, enjoyed the friendly banter.

An hour later, Caitlin stood at the kitchen table, lining dozens of flan tins with thin pastry.

"Maybe you wish you'd skipped this experience and arrived in time for the party?" Andi asked, her arms full of coloured lights.

Caitlin dusted the tip of Andi's nose with a dab of flour. "What, and miss learning to make your favourite dessert?" She leaned closer. "Your brother assures me that if I learn to make these properly, you will be brought to your knees when you sink your teeth into the flaky, buttery pastry and rich, creamy custard."

"Andréa, maybe we can find you an apron, and you can help Caitlin with the *pastéis de nata*?" Lina called while expertly platting bread dough at the other end of the bench.

"No thanks, Mum. I'm in the middle of helping Mick with the tree lights. Then I have to drive into town to pick up the order from the hotel. Also, Manny and I are supposed to connect outdoor speakers and check the music when he gets home from school." Andi laughed, brushing the flour off her nose onto Caitlin's shoulder. "The list Ana made for me is a mile long."

"Don't forget the tablecloths. Shirley said they would be ready for pick-up after lunch," Ana called as she wiped her hands on a tea towel, followed with a quick shake of a finger at Andi.

Andi bowed to her sister. "Your wish is my command. Don't be too hard on Caitlin. She may never want to come back here again," she pleaded, glancing at Caitlin apologetically. "I'm sorry," she mouthed before escaping through the back door.

Caitlin watched Lina separate farm fresh eggs skilfully with one hand, placing the orange yolks into a stainless steel bowl. Following the instructions from the well-worn, handwritten book of family recipes, Lina had carefully weighed and measured all the other ingredients.

"How do you keep the custard from separating?"

"It's the corn flour. You mix the milk with the corn flour until you have a smooth paste. When it's cooking, stir all the time until the mixture is just under boiling point. It must never boil." Lina smiled, beckoning her closer. "Come on. I will guide you, but to learn, it is best for you to do it."

Under Lina's gaze and careful instructions, she placed the cream and crème fraîche into a saucepan with the sugar, salt, cinnamon, and lemon zest. As the cream heated, she stirred gently to help the sugar dissolve. She removed the stick of cinnamon. Beside her, Lina beat the egg yolks and then added the corn flour mixture.

"Now, Caitlin, you can pour the warm cream onto this, constantly whisking. Then we put the mixture back into a clean pan and place it on a low heat. Remember, stir *all* the time." When the custard was a little thicker than double cream, Caitlin took the pan off the heat and poured the mixture into a glass bowl, as directed, and stirred in the vanilla extract.

"It looks so amazingly smooth."

Lina nodded, testing the custard consistency on the tip of a teaspoon. "We have to wait until it cools, then we can fill the pastry cases and bake them in the oven till the custard is puffed up and blackened in places." She smiled. "That's what makes it just like my mama's, the slightly burnt caramel top. It's an old family recipe."

After lunch, with Andi still away on her errands, Caitlin was surprised when Ana asked if she would accompany her on a walk. Not since her summer job in Kinsale, Ireland, harvesting cabbages and lettuces, had Caitlin experienced such a large-scale market garden. "This is really an extraordinary place. There are so many different fields," she said, as they stood outside the courtyard gates and looked over the 180-degree view of the planted crops before them.

"We produce more than fifty different vegetable and herb crops in a calendar year. Most are marketed through the organic growers network of shops and wholesalers. We also supply directly to individual restaurants and cafés." Ana talked and walked briskly, moving in a decisive manner.

Caitlin observed Andi's older sister. She had a genuine, grounded appearance. She spoke about her family business with confidence and pride, reminding Caitlin of a lioness looking out for her cubs. Although she hadn't yet met Andi's nephew and niece, she imagined that Ana would be a protective and fair mother.

"I recognise the logo on the farm gate. I've seen it at Birdie's store in Hakea."

"Yes, that's correct. Birdie stocks a range of our produce, including our micro greens. Andi designed that logo," Ana said, smiling proudly.

"She's never mentioned it."

"Although Andi doesn't work on the farm, she helps when she can. Her creative talent has been a real asset in marketing and expanding the business." Her tone was unassuming, but her gaze was intent, as if she was trying to gauge Caitlin's grasp of Andi's role in the family business.

They walked through the herb gardens, where the air was permeated with the smell of lemon verbena, chives, and the pungent odour of marigolds. The circular beds were crammed with a mix of colourful plants and flowers. "I don't recognise some of these. What is that?" she asked, pointing to a spiky, weed-like plant with large purple flowers.

"Great burdock," Ana said, reaching out quickly to warn Caitlin. "Careful, it belongs to the thistle family, and they have nasty burrs. This is Mum's experimental garden. Those plants, from left to right, are echinacea, comfrey, fenugreek, and globe artichoke." She shook her head, her long braid swinging along her back. "Some things I never thought would grow here, but there you go. My mother's magic touch."

After they'd walked for nearly half an hour, Ana led Caitlin to an enclosed garden near the seedling house. With red-bricked walls, it reminded Caitlin of the monastic gardens she had visited in Europe. The clever use of space and colour was presented here in an almost accidental manner. They sat at a heavy wooden table beneath the shade of an old quince tree. The orchard around them was filled with fruit and nut trees, some still in blossom, some with a profuse growth of new green leaves.

Underneath the branching quince tree, mixed beds of chamomile, poppies, fennel, and lavender attracted bees and other flying insects. Along a wall, the attached lattice was covered with an abundance of purple and red passionfruit.

Ana grabbed two bottles of mineral water from the fridge in one of the sheds and handed one to Caitlin, who accepted it gratefully. She removed her broad hat to wipe beads of perspiration from her forehead. "Thank you, it's quite warm. I'm not used to this heat."

Ana looked at her inquiringly. "Andi tells me you've been in Australia only five months?"

"Six months," Caitlin answered.

"And you're working in Melbourne for your family? Helping set up an art gallery?"

"Yes, that is correct. It's my grandaunt's home and art collection, and I'm here to help her as much as I can."

Ana nodded. "I understand. So is that the kind of work you do in Ireland?"

"No, I'm a lecturer at the University of Cork. I teach art history to postgraduate students and write academic field studies for graduate students visiting Ireland."

"Oh, so you and Andi have *art* in common." Ana stared at the sky thoughtfully before adding, "I've noticed the way Andi looks at you. She's quite taken with you."

Embarrassed by Ana's observation, Caitlin said, "Andi is unique. She is an extraordinarily gifted artist."

"Yes, she is. And she needs to concentrate on her exhibition." She turned and looked at Caitlin. "Don't you agree?"

Caitlin was taken aback by her direct manner, and she decided to adopt the same approach. "She does. Do you believe I'd be getting in the way? I would never do anything to jeopardise her hard work or her dreams."

"No, I'm sorry, Caitlin. I don't think you would *intentionally* hinder her creativity. If anything, you must be a wonderful influence, with your knowledge and experience."

"What are you worried about?" Caitlin asked the obvious question.

"If you return to Ireland in six months, where does that leave Andi? I'm wondering why you two got involved in the first place? Does Andi know how soon you need to go home?"

"Yes, of course. Andi has always known. Look, Ana, we connect on so many different levels. It was like that right from the start. The truth is that we could never have stayed away from each other. Sometimes, even though logic tells you no, you can't help yourself."

"Don't misunderstand me, Caitlin, I'm worried about my sister. But if that's the case, then you *both* could be heading for hurt."

Caitlin took a deep breath. "You don't need to apologise. As Andi's sister, I know you are trying to protect her."

When Andi arrived back at the farm, her six-year-old niece was beside herself with excitement; the minute she climbed out of the farm utility, Mia launched herself into Andi's arms. Andi steadied herself and lifted the little redhead up off the ground.

"Well, I'm really glad to see you too, poppet. Goodness, you've grown since I saw you last."

She pulled Andi's nose and rubbed her face on her cheek. "My name is Mia Thompson, and I am six. I'm not *poppet*."

Andi pretended to struggle under the slight weight of her niece. "But you're *my* poppet, Mia Thompson, and you're getting too big for me to carry around."

"Oh Andi, I'm not too heavy." Her hazel eyes lit up with excitement. "Your girlfriend, Caitlin, is making pavlova with Vovó," she said, using her word for her grandfather. "But I know a secret. I know a secret," Mia said in a high-pitched voice.

"And what would that be?" Andi asked, tousling her fiery red curls. "Tell me."

"Caitlin dropped an egg on the floor. *Splat!* But it didn't matter, really." Mia spoke even faster. "No one was mad at her. Mum said there were plenty of fresh eggs, but Caitlin looked sad." She grabbed Andi's hand, pulling her into the house. "Hey, Andi…"

"Yes, Mia?"

"Caitlin is very beautiful. But I heard Luc say to Papa that he thought she was *hot.* Is it because it's hot in the kitchen with all the cooking? I tried to help and opened the back door," she said innocently.

Andi laughed. *They've got that right.* "You're very helpful. Let's go inside and check if she's still hot, shall we?" Andi grinned as they walked, swinging their joined hands.

Caitlin looked up, her face beaming, as Andi and Mia entered the kitchen. She washed her hands and grabbed a tea towel.

"Are you still hot?" Mia asked Caitlin, who looked at Andi questioningly.

"Mia was worried that all the hard work in the kitchen has made you overheat?"

"Oh? Actually, we've just finished, and your father's put the last of the hazelnut meringues into the oven." Caitlin's cheeks were pink, flushed from the heat in the kitchen, no doubt. She was even more beautiful.

Emmanuel placed his arm around Caitlin's shoulder. "Caitlin is a natural, Andréa. She has been a big help to me. Twenty-four meringue layers is a lot of eggs and a lot of whisking."

"Thanks for letting me help," Caitlin said. "I've enjoyed learning your secrets. You don't mind making the desserts for your own birthday party?"

"Dad is one of the best pavlova makers in the whole Western District. He is often called on to make them for weddings and birthdays, aren't you Dad?"

"Once, not so much now. I don't always have the time." He smiled. "Thank you again, Caitlin, for all your help."

"My pleasure, really. It has been a lot of fun, and I've learned a great deal today."

"Mia," Ana called her daughter. "Tell your Papa we're ready to go home."

Mia reluctantly let go of Andi's hand. Reaching for Caitlin's, she placed it into Andi's, smiling impishly. Her green-and-white checked school uniform and flash of red hair quickly disappeared out the back door.

"She's a whirlwind," said Andi affectionately.

Ana kissed her mother and gathered her belongings, sending a goodbye nod towards her father, Caitlin, and Andi. "Well, have a good rest tonight, everyone. I'll see you bright and early tomorrow morning. We got a lot done today with the extra pair of hands. Thank you." She smiled at Caitlin, who waved goodbye, before Ana's attention was taken by her shrieking daughter, who was being chased indoors by her brother, Manny.

As Manny entered the kitchen, his gangly frame came to a screeching halt. Seeing Caitlin for the first time, he ran his hands through his curly dark hair and gaped.

"Manny, where are your manners? Say hello to Caitlin, Andi's friend."

Caitlin stepped towards him, holding out her hand. "Hi Manny, I've been looking forward to meeting you."

He blushed and wiped his sweaty palm on his jeans before accepting Caitlin's handshake. "Nice to meet you, Caitlin."

Ana stifled a yawn. "Come on, children, we need to have dinner and get to bed. Tomorrow, is going to be a big day."

That evening, Emmanuel fired up the outdoor wood oven, and they shared homemade pizza and a glass of red wine. Caitlin excused herself to attend to emails and phone calls in their room, while Andi sat with her parents on the enclosed patio overlooking the rectangular swimming pool.

Emmanuel stretched out his long frame on a wicker chaise lounge, glass of port in one hand, while Andi sat beside her mother on the matching outdoor sofa. Lina took her hand, stroking it gently. "You look very well, darling, fit and healthy, and happy, too."

"I feel pretty good. The work for the exhibition is going well, and I've had enough graphic design commissions to keep me going."

Emmanuel raised a thick dark eyebrow. "Caitlin certainly seems very impressed with your paintings, Andréa. I would love to see them before the exhibition."

"I'd like that too, Dad. Maybe you and Mum can come and visit me soon?"

Lina nodded in agreement, but Andi sensed there was something else on her mind.

"Are you okay, Mum?"

"Andréa, how are things going with Caitlin? I can see that you both get on very well together. She's a lovely girl."

"We do and she is. But you do know, don't you, that Caitlin's home is in Ireland? She is only here for another six months," Andi said, trying to keep her despair hidden. "We enjoy each other's company… I don't know what more I can say," she added despondently. Her mood had darkened.

"Have you told her how you feel?" Lina asked quietly.

"What do you mean?" She looked everywhere except at her mother.

"That you're in love with her, querida."

Andi shook her head, denying her mother's insight and her words. "No Mama, I don't want to go *there*."

What her mouth spoke and her mind thought were two separate things. The way she responded to Caitlin, and the way Caitlin responded to her, was intense and so confusing. "No, I'm not going there," she repeated. Lowering her voice, she added, "We both have so many things going on, and she's leaving. I just can't." Andi stood up and walked over to her father to wish him goodnight. "Not long now, Papa, and you'll be a year older."

"Goodnight, my darling. Sleep well."

She bent down to kiss her mother and murmured, "Don't worry, Mama. I'll be okay." At the door, she stopped to look back at her parents who were now together on the sofa, holding hands. "See you both in the morning. I love you."

"We love you too, Andréa." Lina sighed, as Emmanuel blew Andi a kiss goodnight.

In the kitchen, Andi rinsed out her empty teacup and walked towards their room. Hoping to shake the negative thoughts and sadness from her body, she stood in the glazed breezeway between the central living space and the guest wing and stared up into the night, where millions of stars illuminated the country sky. Her eyes caught a streak of light that flashed across the heavens. Could a shooting star really fulfil someone's wish? If so, she knew what her wish would be.

Chapter 27

Caitlin woke to the loud, rippling crackle of a kookaburra's call. She glanced at her phone; it was five in the morning. Groggy from sleep, she lay there for a few minutes. She really didn't want to get up, but she knew that the longer she stayed, the stronger her urge would be to use the bathroom.

She edged quietly out of bed and tiptoed across the tiled floor. Her MacBook was on the dresser. *How did it get there?*

The last thing Caitlin remembered was reading the Cork University email notifying her about the date of her interview. Andi must have removed the laptop from the bed when she'd found her asleep. Caitlin rubbed at her forehead. Had she closed the email? *Maybe not.* Would Andi have seen it? *Hopefully not.*

Two hours later, having barely exchanged a good morning between them, Caitlin and Andi were hurried out of bed. It was going to be another hectic day, but Caitlin enjoyed the busy, frenzied activity of the Rey family.

At three o'clock in the afternoon, Ana announced that most of the work was done and they were free to take a rest so they'd be refreshed to entertain their guests that evening.

Caitlin would have liked to spend some quiet time alone with Andi. She'd hoped to tell her about the upcoming interview back home and was disappointed when Andi declared she had unfinished business in town. Not given the choice to accompany her, Caitlin chose to spend the time reading by the swimming pool.

It was now just after six in the evening, and a group of the Reys' close friends had arrived with platters and coolers of food to help feed the eighty-or-so invited guests.

Ana conducted the early arrivers with precision. Tonight, her long dark hair sat loose around her shoulders. She was elegant and chic in an off-the-shoulder, black jumpsuit made from a fluid fabric that subtly showed off her striking figure.

Luc set up the bar in the open-sided marquee near the swimming pool. With his cheeky grin and easy banter, he charmed the early imbibers.

Eclectic, dinner party music streamed through the outdoor speakers. The melodies blended with the sounds of guests greeting each other, laughter, and children squealing. It was a balmy night; the fragrance of flowers, the smoky-spicy aroma of roasting barbecue, and the sweet smell of saffron-infused paella cooking on the charcoal burner filled the air.

Caitlin savoured her glass of petit verdot, with its luscious mix of mouth-filling fruit flavours, as she scanned the crowd in search of Andi. She'd seemed quieter than usual, even a little preoccupied, all day. It was a big family weekend, and as the youngest sibling, perhaps she felt there was a lot to live up to.

Luc, who had abandoned his bar duties, had his arm around the shoulders of a tanned woman with tightly cropped blonde hair. She must be the new girlfriend Andi had mentioned.

Caitlin turned around at the sound of *that* unmistakably infectious, laughter. Andi stood with a glass of wine in one hand, her other hand resting on her hip as she conversed with an older man dressed in a black suit and clerical collar.

"She looks scrummy, doesn't she?" a voice behind her said. "That flirty-fit flare dress is, well…flirty. I think she's even managed to charm Father Bob, the cranky old bugger. It's been ages since I've seen Andi wearing a dress."

"Ellie. It's the first time for me." She had *never* seen Andi in a dress before, and she couldn't stop looking at her. She was irresistible. The lime, cotton-silk, sleeveless dress with cutaway shoulders showed an alluring amount of golden, silky skin. Her black, chunky ankle boots accentuated her toned legs. The combination gave her a girly, yet gritty look. Caitlin felt the colour rise in her cheeks. Ellie had caught her looking. *Am I drooling?*

"I think you agree with her," Ellie said. She looked Caitlin up and down. "And obviously, she agrees with you."

"It is nice to see you again. Andi will be so glad you could get the time off work," Caitlin said drily.

"It took some manoeuvring and schmoozing, but I would've hated to miss the party." Ellie gasped as a small pair of arms circled her thigh. "Mia!"

"Ellie, *Ellie* did you meet Andi's girlfriend?" Mia's voice bubbled with excitement. "She has a really funny way of talking. Mummy said Caitlin is from I-land."

Ellie crouched down so she was eye to eye with Mia. "I have met Caitlin. She has a lovely way of talking, don't you think? Caitlin is from Ireland. How are you, munchkin?"

"*Island*," she shouted and ran away. "I'll find Andi and tell her you're here."

"Well, that's one excited little girl," Ellie said and raised her bottle of ale to Caitlin. "So, out of the mouths of babes, as they say. Andi's girlfriend?"

She cleared her throat. "Hmm. Mia is a darling girl." Caitlin watched as the whirling dervish, dressed in a moss-green dress—her red curls springing as she ran—was lost in the crowd.

Ellie looked around her and waved to a couple across the lawn. "Looks like the regulars are here. Have you met many people yet?"

Caitlin nodded. "I haven't done too badly, but please don't ask me to recall every name. Lina introduced me to some friends from the Country Women's Association. I won't forget Doris and Estelle."

"The expert scone makers?" Ellie laughed, and her eyebrows furrowed. "They are, you know. They're first and second medal winners in the Country Show every year."

"I now have Estelle's recipe." Caitlin patted her forehead with her finger. "I've also met Michael, the winemaker responsible for this yummy wine." She raised her glass. "The mayor, the librarian, the owners of Organic Wholefoods, and two staff from the Ballarat art gallery."

Caitlin couldn't believe the diversity of guests. This group of friends and neighbours were, undoubtedly, the Reys' extended family, and the party hummed with comradeship and celebration. The guests were plied with delicacies of Portugal—Emmanuel and Lina's homeland—and of the country they *now* called home.

Andi approached, appearing at ease with a toddler on her hip and Mia by her side.

"Caitlin, this is Bruce," Mia said. She slipped her hand into Caitlin's. "Andi said we have exhausted her *out*, and it's nearly time to eat, so the children can be put to bed."

Caitlin winked at Andi. "Well, that's an idea. Hello, Bruce. And who do you belong to?" The beautiful, rosy-skinned child looked more like a cherub than a Bruce. He giggled and reached for Caitlin's hair.

"Oh, no you don't, Bruce." Andi caught his hand and blew a raspberry on his cheek, making him squeal. "I think it's time I returned you to your mother. Come on, Mia. Help me find Rosie. I'd rather Bruce was with her before he needs a nappy change."

As Andi and the children moved away, Ellie called out, "You're a natural. I can see you with a couple of your own one day." She nudged Caitlin with her elbow. "Sorry, I'm just teasing. Really. Would you like another drink?"

"Why not?" Caitlin smiled and drained her glass. "Andi seems at ease around children. They obviously love her." The family-oriented, nurturing side of Andi appealed to Caitlin just as much as her strongly independent self.

"I need to dance off that dessert. That is the best meringue I've ever tasted. Come on." Caitlin grabbed Andi's hand and led her towards the paved courtyard, where people were dancing under the strings of coloured lights.

Andi rested her hands lightly on Caitlin's hips. "I don't think you have to worry about a bit of meringue." She glanced downwards at Caitlin's statuesque form in her wide-leg chocolate-coloured trousers. "You look amazing and, by far, the sexiest woman at the party." Andi sighed and moved her hand to the split back of Caitlin's lace-up, plum-hued vest.

"Need a room, girls?" Luc gave his younger sister a friendly jab as he and his girlfriend, Penn, danced alongside them. "Ellie may need to resuscitate Estelle and Doris if you keep dancing like that." He grinned wickedly and swirled his partner away.

"I could say the same about you, Luc," called Andi. "I'm so glad he's happy," she said to Caitlin.

As the music changed to a Cesaria Evora song, Caitlin took Andi's hand and turned her around in a loop to the quick, quick, slow rhythm of the salsa beat. She draped an arm across Andi's shoulder to draw her closer.

"They look good together. I talked to Penn earlier about her job as editor of *Living Sustainably*," said Caitlin. "She's very focused and passionate about her work."

"They do seem a good fit. It's been a long time since I've seen him show so much interest in someone."

"Looks like Ellie's found a dance partner too. Isn't that Laura, the curator at the Ballarat art gallery?"

Andi looked at her friend and smiled. "She does look like she's having fun. Except Laura is straight."

"Oh, why *doesn't* Ellie have a girlfriend? I thought Meagan would be here tonight."

Andi shook her head. "Meagan and Ellie prefer a casual arrangement. Medicine is Ellie's vocation. She doesn't do relationships."

"She's not carrying a torch for you, *still*, is she?" Caitlin pulled back and asked earnestly.

The question surprised her. "That was a long time ago. Carrying a torch... is a *very* broad statement," Andi said. Caitlin's eyes widened, and Andi knew she remembered. She'd used the same words when Andi had asked about her relationship with Erica. "Ellie wants to save the world," Andi continued. "But maybe she hasn't met the right woman yet."

"Maybe not. I guess that's the only answer I'm going to get," Caitlin murmured.

Lina rested her head against Emmanuel's chest as they danced together. Her parents were such romantics. Andi hoped, someday, she would share a special bond with someone.

"It's been a successful night. Even Ana is enjoying herself." Andi gestured towards her sister, who swayed in the arms of her husband.

Caitlin pulled Andi closer.

"This is a little different than the last time we danced," Andi said.

"And look where it has got us." Caitlin kissed Andi's forehead.

Andi recalled the evening at the Emerson and their first night together. The stakes were a lot higher now. So much more at risk and *so* much more to lose.

Chapter 28

"So what did you think of your first koala sighting?" Andi asked. They'd walked in silence for the last half kilometre. They entered the farm gate and ambled down the driveway. Andi stopped and crouched to retie her shoelace. "You were very lucky the mama koala had her joey out of her pouch and clinging to her back."

"Adorable aren't they? Seriously, how cute was that? Although, she did have a stern look on her face, giving us a warning." Caitlin took a deep breath of clear country air. "I'm so glad we decided to walk today, so I could bring my camera. That baby was no bigger than my hand. I got some great shots."

"I'm glad we did too. After last night's party and the clean-up this morning, I'm not up to facing your competitive self. How come you never mentioned before that you competed in track and field at university?"

Caitlin grinned and leaned forward to ruffle Andi's hair. "It never came up, and you've never asked." She playfully pinched Andi's arm. "Anyway, it was a long time ago."

"Were you part of the boxing team as well?" Andi rubbed her arm, feigning injury. She stood up, and they continued their walk towards the house.

"Stop it, you." Caitlin wrinkled her brow and snapped a few photos of Andi. "Actually, I did finish first in the flat four hundred and third in the eight hundred hurdles."

"That figures. I had no chance at all." Andi shook her head, poked her tongue out, and pointed at Caitlin's camera. "Please, no more."

"Are you cranky?" Caitlin pulled a face in an attempt to cheer her up.

"No, just tired."

It was after two in the afternoon when they arrived back. They entered their room, and Andi threw herself across the bed onto her stomach. After the bustle and chaos of the last two days, the house was strangely quiet. Caitlin opened the curtains wide, and the bright afternoon sun poured into the room.

Andi rolled over and raised her hand in front of her eyes. "Not fair. I hardly got any sleep last night, and you woke me at nine this morning."

"Oh, poor baby. It's this bracing, clear, country air, and we had to help with the cleanup."

"I guess so." Andi rolled over onto her back. "If you don't mind, I'll close my eyes for twenty minutes."

"I don't think your parents are home." Caitlin peered out into the garden. No sign of anyone. "I remember your mother mentioned the borrowed trestle tables had to be returned to the church hall." She sat on the end of the bed and reached over to run her fingers lightly across Andi's shoulders.

"Aren't you even a little tired?" Andi asked.

"No, I'm not. Just a wee bit restless. It's a beautiful day outside." She brightened. "I know what will make you feel better."

"Me? What did you have in mind?" Andi muttered drowsily from underneath the pillow she'd pulled over her head.

"A swim."

"Now?"

"Why not?"

Andi dragged herself into an upright position. "You often do that, you know."

"What?"

"That. Answer a question with a question."

"Do I?" Caitlin teased.

"Okay, let's go for a swim. But not in the swimming pool. It will be shady and cool near the dam at this time of day. You haven't been down there yet, and I can show you my hideaway."

Caitlin jumped to her feet. "Hideaway? You have me intrigued. Come on then, let's go."

The twin dams at the lower end of the property came as a surprise. Caitlin had expected a muddy pool of water filled with dead branches and reeds. Instead, the dam must have been spring fed—the water sparkled and was a welcoming sight on such a hot afternoon. "This is incredible; the water doesn't look at all murky. You have a jetty *and* a boathouse?"

Andi placed their towels and a small icebox near the wide wooden jetty. "We do," she said. The red boathouse lay on narrow posts and appeared suspended above the water. A bench and two timber chairs sat under an overhang, making it a great place to rest.

"Nice hideaway."

"Well, it didn't always look *this* good," Andi said. "It was originally just a lean-to. I used to escape here with something to read or my sketchbook. I loved drawing the trunks of these gum trees and ferns." She pointed towards the fence line of the property and the bank of forest beyond. "Luc built the shed and jetty ten years ago. We're lucky he wanted to practise his carpentry skills."

"We are indeed," Caitlin said, glancing around at the peaceful bush surroundings.

"The dam is dredged every year to clear it of unwanted creatures, and the water is tested for algae and toxins. But try not to swallow any water, and watch out for nibblers in the shallow parts," Andi warned.

"Nibblers? Maybe I'll just lie up here on the jetty and get some sun." Caitlin raised her eyebrows. She pulled the T-shirt over her head and removed her jeans. Wearing mini-board shorts and a bikini top, she dropped into a chair.

Andi threw off her denim shirt and stood in her sports bra and cut-off shorts, revealing a tantalising expanse of skin. Caitlin hummed quietly.

"Oh no you don't." Andi grabbed Caitlin's hand and hauled her to her feet. "This was your idea in the first place. You're not scared of a little yabbie or turtle, are you?" Still holding onto her, she walked Caitlin along the sloping path through the ferns, reeds, and grasses towards the dam.

Caitlin didn't want Andi to think she was a wimp, but the squishy sludge underfoot was disconcerting. "Oh hell…here goes." She glanced around, checked for nasty creatures, and waded straight in.

They were waist deep when Andi stopped, placed her hands on Caitlin's shoulders, and said, "In Australia, please don't *ever* dive into dams, creeks, or rivers, unless you can see right to the bottom. Even then—never head first."

"I won't. I can still picture that deeply disturbing drowning scene in *Japanese Story.*"

"Did I warn you about the eels?" Andi asked, quickly changing the subject.

Caitlin moved back towards the water's edge.

Andi grabbed Caitlin's shoulder. "Got ya. Sorry, I am just teasing. Eels have never been a problem here, and, anyway, they don't bite. Much."

"Well, thanks for the warning." Caitlin believed Andi, but would definitely stay alert.

Caitlin was overheated, and luckily, the water was refreshingly cold. She pushed off and turned over to float on her back. She moved cautiously on the surface of the water. "I think it'll be a quick swim anyway. Turtles and eels are bad enough as swimming companions, but what on earth is a yabbie? And how big is it?"

Andi opened her arms wide, then slowly drew her hands together till they almost met. "It's a tiny, freshwater crayfish. About five to ten centimetres long." She laughed. "Are you chicken?"

Caitlin flapped her arms, made clucking sounds, and splashed water onto Andi's face.

"*Jeez*, Caitlin." Andi groaned and wiped the water from her eyes.

"What? What did I do?"

Andi stared at Caitlin, then swam vigorously to the far side of the dam.

For whatever reason, Andi appeared to be in the grumps today. Caitlin had suggested the swim to improve her mood, but so far, it had not worked.

Caitlin carefully stepped out of the water and hastily wrapped herself in her towel. Despite her surroundings and the eventful weekend, the promotions interview was on her mind. Caitlin *really* needed to talk to Andi about it soon. She sighed and stretched out in the shade.

Andi emerged from the dam and towelled herself dry. She opened the doors of the boat shed, went inside, and brought out a cushion. "Would you like this?"

Caitlin shook her head.

Andi sat next to Caitlin, the cushion beneath her and her back propped against a pillar.

Caitlin lifted her head and peered through the gap between the timber doors. "Whose boat is that?" she asked.

"Luc's. She's a ten-foot-long, flat-bottomed skiff. Hand built." Caitlin twitched as Andi's cool fingers traced the inside of her calf. "I'll show you in a minute, but first let's have a drink. I'm thirsty," Andi said.

Andi reached into the cooler and pulled out two bottles of homemade lemonade and a container of fresh fruit.

"This is a lovely spot for a picnic. A great place to read or just watch the birds. I could sit here for hours." Caitlin accepted a bunch of pinkish-red grapes from Andi. "It isn't grape season, is it?"

"These are our homegrown red globes. It's too early for the seedless ones, so watch the pips."

As Caitlin bit into the firm skin of the round fruit, juice trickled down her chin and neck. "Yum, they are sweet and juicy." Before Caitlin could reach for her towel, Andi leaned across and slurped the juice from her neck. "Andi," Caitlin gasped.

"I don't seem to be able to stop myself," Andi said. She settled back and finished her lemonade in one gulp.

"So, who else have you brought here?"

"What do you mean?" Andi tilted her head and gazed across the water. "People come here all the time."

Caitlin grabbed Andi's hand that was still on her knee. "I mean your girlfriends. Do you bring them to your hideaway oasis to seduce them?" She raised an eyebrow.

Andi coughed and nearly choked on a piece of orange. "No." She removed her hand from Caitlin's grasp and rubbed her neck. She was blushing. "No, I don't. Years ago, Ellie and I spent time here after school. Martha didn't come to the farm very much. It wasn't her thing, I guess." She coughed again.

"Nobody else?" Caitlin raised her eyebrows inquiringly. She drew gentle circles on Andi's back. "What *did* you get up to in the boat shed?"

Andi was too slow to take the hint, and Caitlin wasn't prepared to wait any longer. She sprang to her feet, pulled Andi up with her, and ushered her inside. Most of the space was taken up with fishing gear, a small blow-up dinghy, a pile of rubberised air mattresses, paddles, and Luc's boat. "Why don't you show me what you got up to in here?"

"Okay." Andi pushed the double doors closed behind her and secured the rope latch.

A stream of sunlight poured through overhead skylights, illuminating the wooden boat.

Caitlin ran her hand over the smooth lines of the skiff, where plank edges were butted together smoothly, seam to seam. "She's beautiful."

Andi stared at Caitlin from the doorway. "Yes, she is."

Caitlin licked her lips and returned Andi's steady gaze. Desire flashed across Andi's face. But there was something else. An edge of anger? Frustration? Whatever it was, Caitlin couldn't ignore it any longer. "What's going on?" she asked.

Andi flinched at the sound of Caitlin's voice. The turbulent emotions that she'd tried to control surfaced. Her body was on fire, and her heart pounded in her chest.

She didn't want to explain. Not now, when she was vulnerable and angry. The protective boundaries she'd kept in place for the last two months were crumbling.

Andi hadn't intended to read the email on Friday night when she'd found Caitlin asleep with her MacBook half closed beside her on the bed. She'd carried the laptop to the dresser and opened the screen to shut down the computer. And there it was. She shouldn't have looked, but she couldn't help herself—*Academic Promotions to Associate Professor.*

Caitlin's interview in Cork was scheduled for the first week in December. Andi had stared at the words, trying to comprehend all that they implied. She'd closed the screen.

The atmosphere in the shed was hot and dusty. Caitlin moved towards her; Andi stepped backwards and held her hand up in defence.

"Andi, are you okay? What's going on?"

As if she doesn't know, Andi swore to herself. Was it too much to expect Caitlin to tell *her* what was going on?

Caitlin stopped her movement forward and looked at Andi with the same hungry passion and confusion that surged through her. She wanted to touch Caitlin, hoping the physical contact would quieten the doubt and uncertainty that had her half crazed. Was it possible to be angry and aroused at the same time? Andi needed to take control.

Andi's eyes were hooded and dark with passion. The muscles in her neck and shoulders were clearly visible as she lifted two inflated mattresses into the boat and placed them between the bench seats. She shook out a large towel and threw it across the rubber surface.

"I want you." Andi abruptly pulled Caitlin into her arms. She pressed her lips to Caitlin's.

The intensity of her kiss ignited Caitlin's desire. Andi raised Caitlin's arms to remove her top, and the heat of her hands seemed to scorch Caitlin's skin. She offered no resistance when Andi grabbed the waistband of her shorts and pushed them down and away. Caitlin stood naked beneath the skylight.

Andi tore off her own clothes and dropped them in a heap, reached for Caitlin, and lowered her into the boat. The rubber mattresses squeaked under the weight of their bodies.

Andi's kiss was urgent and all consuming.

At the taste of Andi's desperation, lust shot through Caitlin in hot, shimmering waves. Andi's body, pressed into her, was taut and glistened with perspiration.

She gripped Caitlin's shoulders and began to move rhythmically against Caitlin's thigh. She grazed Caitlin's shoulder with her teeth. She was wet with arousal, but when she moaned, Caitlin sensed her frustration, urged her onto her back, and shifted over her to take control.

"Tell me. What do you want?" Caitlin urged.

"You," she pleaded. "I want *you*."

Caitlin slid her body across Andi's hot, slick skin. Andi grabbed Caitlin's hand and placed it between her own thighs. She arched her back. Caitlin held Andi firmly against her and pressed her fingers deeper. Caitlin wanted to take her time. Andi smelled incredible—of sun-drenched green grass and something primitive and earthy. She wanted to give Andi pleasure—to take it slowly.

"You are amazing." Caitlin stroked Andi with one hand and cupped her breast with the other. "Beautiful." She kissed the soft flesh, then circled Andi's nipple with her tongue and drew it into her mouth.

"Yes. Please." Andi's body tensed. She was close. Her breathing was ragged; there was no holding her back. Within seconds, Andi shuddered and cried out, "Caitlin."

Andi's eyelashes fluttered. Her brown eyes were teary. Caitlin embraced her protectively and held her while her body calmed.

Andi's urgent need tugged at Caitlin's heart. "I love you, Andi," she said. Andi's heart beat strongly against her breast. "I love you," she repeated in a whisper. She couldn't hold it back any longer. Caitlin stared at Andi, whose face was unreadable. Maybe she'd said the wrong thing—but how could she not express what she knew to be true?

Without warning, Andi rolled over, away from Caitlin, and lifted herself out of the boat.

Caitlin gasped. Andi stood with her back towards her and pulled on her shorts and top. She turned back and handed Caitlin her clothes.

"No. Caitlin—don't say that." She let out an anguished cry and wiped angrily at the tears that spilled down her cheeks.

"Please…Andi, don't be so upset." Caitlin struggled to dress in the limited space of the boat.

"*No*, it's not fair. I've played by the rules. *Your* rules. You said *this* is temporary." Andi pushed her hands through her hair. "You said you were in Australia for only twelve months… I mean eight months. *God*, whatever. I've never asked you for more, Caitlin. You are not allowed to say that."

"I'm sorry, Andi. I can't help—"

"When were you going to tell me about the interview, *Professor* Quinn?" Andi's face was twisted in pain. "I shouldn't have read your email, but you left your computer on."

A cold shiver ran down Caitlin's spine. "You do know," she said quietly. "I've been trying to tell you. Oh, hell, I just didn't know how. It is only an interview." Caitlin looked at Andi in desperation. She wanted her to understand how confused she felt. She wished she'd told her as soon as she'd found out.

"Only an interview? Isn't this what you've been working towards your whole career?" Andi's voice was tremulous as she struggled to speak. "Academic tenure and prestige."

"Yes, but that was before…" Caitlin dropped her head into her hands. Hot tears rolled down her face.

The doors creaked when Andi opened them, and a gust of wind blew dead leaves across the timber floor.

"It's your dream, Caitlin. I would never want to stand in your way," Andi said without turning back to face her. "But you don't play fair." She walked out of the boat shed and out of sight.

Caitlin sat in the boat and stared out at the long shadows reflected across the rippling water. She gripped the sides of the wooden planks and let her tears fall. The intensity and surprise of Andi's outburst left her unable to follow. She was utterly deflated.

Chapter 29

When Caitlin finally made her way back to the house, she was exhausted and emotionally wrung out. The Reys' car was parked near the garage, making it impossible to avoid Andi's parents. Caitlin had no idea where Andi was or if she'd shared any of what had happened with her parents. She took a deep breath and pushed open the front door.

Lina sat at the kitchen table, leafing through a magazine. As Caitlin approached, Lina lifted her head and removed her reading glasses. "Caitlin. How was your swim?"

Caitlin pushed her sunglasses up and hoped her eyes were not as puffy and red as they felt. "Good, thank you, Lina. Although I'm not used to swimming in a dam. I was a bit worried that something would attach itself to my toe."

Lina laughed. "Yes, for me, I prefer the swimming pool. At least you can see all the way to the bottom." She got up to refill her cup. "Would you like a cup of coffee?"

Caitlin shook her head. "I might have a quick shower and pack. I should get on the road before dark." Although Caitlin tried to keep a distance, it became impossible as Lina walked towards her with open arms. She allowed herself to be held, and another round of tears threatened to fall. "I've had a wonderful time. Thank you again for inviting me to share in the celebrations."

"It's been our pleasure to have you here. We will see you again soon?" Her embrace tightened before she released Caitlin, and she held her at arm's length. Lina's face was filled with concern. "I can see many things, Caitlin. I've watched you and Andréa this weekend, and I know from how my daughter speaks of you that there is something special going on."

Caitlin started to speak but stopped as Lina held up her hand.

"I also know that your family and job are in Ireland. I am not saying I understand everything you are struggling with, but I know a little about having to make difficult choices—about being in a foreign country away from your family and feeling torn between following your heart and staying with what is familiar." Lina spoke with compassion. "It is not an easy time for you or Andréa."

"Where is Andi?" Caitlin asked. Although thankful for Lina's kindness, she was embarrassed. Lina obviously knew about their argument at the dam.

"In your room. I think she is packing," Lina replied. "Caitlin, can I just say one more thing?"

"Of course."

"My Andréa wears her feelings so close to the surface, and when she is frightened or angry, she finds it very hard to talk. She closes up like a clamshell. She's always been like this. Even as a child."

"Lina, I hope you know I would never hurt Andi intentionally. She's come to mean a great deal to me in this short time. I do have things to sort out, decisions to make, and I have to return home to do that." Caitlin rubbed her brow in frustration. "I just don't know how to make her understand…" She looked at Lina for help.

Lina hugged her once more, wordlessly giving her the acceptance and support she needed.

"Talk to her. Never part in anger or silence. You must tell her—let her know what's going on in here." She tapped Caitlin on the head affectionately. "And here…" She pointed to Caitlin's chest.

It was clear Lina didn't know the entire story. Caitlin had done just that. She'd said those *three words,* and look where it got her.

She stood outside the bedroom door. Her mouth was dry, and her hand trembled as she reached for the doorknob.

"Andi?" she called and walked into the room.

Andi removed her headphones and let them hang around her neck. She spun around in the desk chair to face Caitlin. "Hi."

"Hi." Caitlin sat down at the edge of the bed and stared at the floor before lifting her gaze to Andi. "You're already packed?"

Andi tapped her leg nervously on the floorboards and pushed angrily on her left knee to still her restlessness. "Yes," she said. "You wanted to leave before sunset. I thought I'd head back at the same time. I'd like to get home before dark." The anguish on Caitlin's face was clear, but Andi desperately needed to keep her own responses controlled.

"Will you be okay to drive back? Your Jeep gave you some trouble on the drive here." Caitlin looked down at her hands and played with her silver thumb ring.

"I'll be okay. Mick checked it over this morning. No leaks or anything. The tree branch didn't do any damage." Andi stood up and took a tentative step towards Caitlin.

Caitlin met Andi's gaze. "That's good, then." She reached for Andi's hand, and although she didn't mean to, Andi flinched.

Caitlin rubbed Andi's knuckles with her thumb. She looked tired and drained.

"I am glad you could come this weekend," Andi said, gripping Caitlin's hands firmly.

"I loved meeting your family and all those lovely, funny people at the party."

She recalled Doris Hargreaves cornering Caitlin in the kitchen. She had written her scone recipe on a scrap of paper, insisting it was so much better than Estelle's.

"You were definitely a hit with the ladies. Especially Mia." Andi smiled.

"She's gorgeous. A little firecracker," Caitlin said. She turned Andi's palm upwards and stroked it slowly. "The kids loved watching you swing the bat at the piñata with the blindfold around your eyes."

"Kept them out of mischief for a while."

"Do you want to have your own, one day?" Caitlin asked.

"A child?" Andi asked. "I haven't thought about it a lot, but maybe, someday."

They both fell silent. Neither seemed to know where to take the conversation.

Andi removed her hands from Caitlin's grasp and buried them deep in her pockets. "I know you need to go back for the interview," Andi said, eventually. She kicked distractedly at the chair leg. "In the next few weeks, I have to complete the paintings for the exhibition, organise framing and labels, and work through that list you helped me compile." She attempted a grin.

"I remember," Caitlin mumbled.

She wanted to pull her close. Bury her face in the warmth of Caitlin's shoulder and hold her tight. For now, though, that wasn't an option. She'd raised a protective wall around herself—and needed Caitlin to keep a distance.

"You said you have a busy time at the estate and another guest lecture to prepare, so I think we should focus on our own stuff—for the time being." Andi did her best to ignore Caitlin's pained expression. "I'm just suggesting we should give each other time to think about what we want."

"I know you're right, Andi. You and I have a lot to do in the next few weeks," she agreed.

"I'm not saying we shouldn't keep in touch, but I need a bit of space." The words came out of her mouth, then she realised what she'd said. Was this the right decision? How would she handle being away from Caitlin?

Andi sat quietly in the desk chair while Caitlin grabbed her overnight bag and packed her belongings. She lifted the small bag onto her shoulder and looked around the room, as if considering her options. She moved towards the door, then stopped and turned around. "Andi," she said.

"Yes?" She gazed at Caitlin.

"It is just an interview."

"I know."

In her heart, Andi knew how she felt about Caitlin. But the fear and uncertainty was paralysing, rendering her incapable of seeing a positive outcome.

Chapter 30

On Wednesday, Andi spent the whole day hiking in the Otway forest, through scrubby ironbark, stringybark, and gnarly eucalyptus trees. Ever since she'd parted company with Caitlin, Andi had been intensely frustrated and restless. She desperately needed the physicality of the outdoors to work off her chaotic energy. It took all her strength to push Caitlin to the back of her mind, and even though rationally she had to do it—it hurt like hell.

The track undulated steeply, with occasional breathtaking glimpses of the sea and sky through the vegetation. She'd chosen a challenging route, and the uncovered parts of her legs were grazed and scratched. Andi wiped roughly at a small trickle of blood that ran from a scrape just below her knee and into the top of her hiking boot. At least it was the same colour as her socks.

Many of the eucalyptus trees stood over thirty metres tall, with trunks two metres in diameter. The towering sentinels were simply magnificent. Andi noted the colours of the peeling bark, the sticky browns and reds of the gum veins. The air was a mix of the salty sea and the damp, earthy, penetrating smells of the forest. The light through the tree canopy was heavenly. For her next painting, Andi aimed to capture the energy and rays of the afternoon sunshine hitting the solid, unbroken line of giant tree trunks.

It was dark by the time she returned home, and Koda was waiting impatiently for her dinner. Although exhausted, scratched, and filthy, Andi penciled ideas in her drawing book for the painting she would tackle the next day.

She rose early after a restless night. With those magnificent trees fresh in her mind, she placed two 1520mm high by 900mm wide pieces of prepared board against the wall. After a rough sketch with a thirty-five millimetre flat brush, Andi set about covering the white space with forceful scrubbing brush strokes. Her movements were broad and fast, fevered. She worked on both canvases together, side by side.

The act of painting was so seductive—the application of the paint upon the wooden board and the mood her chosen colours evoked. Andi was in turmoil, and she painted frenetically and aggressively, more so than usual.

Once the boards were covered with heavy outline strokes, she rubbed them back with a piece of a sea sponge. She built the lighter verticals of the trunks using a broad, freestyle brush with white paint running through scarlet, raw sienna, Indian yellow, and a touch of ultramarine blue. For the seeping sticky gum and shaded areas, she used crimson, blue, and grey.

Andi's style reflected her love of strong colours. The Fauves, who used pure, brilliant colour directly from the tubes onto the canvas without using a palette for blending, had influenced her style. Andi laughed and looked at her exposed, paint-splattered arms and legs. She certainly resembled the Fauves, or wild beasts, today.

She ran a line of white along the sunlit side to define a tree. She was careful not to overbrush, regularly cleaning the roller and thick bristles before picking up more paint. With a soft brush loaded with a few colours, she repeated her movement. Up, turn, and down to create the peeling bark. Up, turn, and down to darken one side of the tree and lighten the other. Finally, capturing the character of each tree with subtle pinks and vibrant earth colours.

Andi pushed away from the wall where the two canvases now sat. She'd achieved what she wanted—a long, unbroken line of tree trunks. This was her representation of the majestic giants. *Diptych: Luminous Gums.*

"Oh, for Christ's sake!" Caitlin grabbed the bookshelf to save herself from falling off the ladder.

"Goodness, Caitie, let me help you." Kim steadied the ladder until Caitlin was safely back on the ground. "Why on earth were you at the top of the ladder without asking for help? Safety comes first, always."

She nodded sheepishly. "I'm sorry, Kim. I know. I was stupid." Caitlin dropped into the seat at her desk and leaned her head back against the chair. "That's all I'd need—to break a limb."

"Exactly." Kim flicked her fringe off her forehead with her index finger in an exasperated manner. "Then where would we be, eh?" From across the desk, she patted Caitlin gently on the hand. "Do you want to talk about it?"

Caitlin rubbed her eyes. She hadn't slept well for the last few nights and, needing the distraction, had worked extra long hours. So far, she'd avoided Isabella, but Caitlin wouldn't be able to hide from her grandaunt much longer.

"Do you want to get out of here for a while?" Caitlin asked. She grabbed her wallet out of the top drawer of her desk. "Come on, Jonesy. Lunch is on me."

Kim pumped her hands in the air and straightened her blue and white striped shirt over her ample hips. "Okay, now you're talking. Ooo…there's a new Vietnamese café in Victoria Street. It'll only take us twenty minutes to get there. We'll be there in a flash." Leaning towards Caitlin, she added in a conspiratorial tone, "I won't tell the boss if you don't."

They sat at a corner table, away from the other late afternoon diners. She'd let Kim place the order, and an array of dishes lined the table: chicken fried with chilli, basil and snake beans, spicy salmon, green onion and sesame tartare on glutinous rice.

Caitlin used her chopsticks to grab a piece of crispy crêpe bulging with shrimp, bean sprouts, fresh herbs, and lettuce. She dunked it into a tangy sauce before popping it into her mouth. "Yum."

"Yes, yum. I will need an afternoon nap in Isabella's garden." Kim rubbed her stomach.

Caitlin sipped her weak black tea. "This is the first real food I've had in days. Mind you, I did overeat last weekend. Andi's family created an incredible feast."

"So how *did* last weekend go? It was the first time meeting the family, right?" Caitlin nodded, and Kim continued, "I feel like you've avoided talking about it, Caitie. You haven't said much of anything since you got back."

Caitlin shrugged and piled the empty dishes into a neat stack. "The whole weekend was intense. They're a close family. Loving and protective—especially Andi's older sister, Ana."

"Did you get the works thrown at you? Interrogation? Questions? Did you have to state your intentions?" Kim teased but looked serious.

"They are just looking out for Andi, like families should. Her mother, Lina, is understanding and kind. Shrewd and perceptive too." She placed her cup down on the table and moved her shoulders around to ease the tension in her neck. "I hadn't told Andi about travelling back to Ireland in December for the interview."

"Oh. Didn't you know about it over a week ago?"

"I was trying to find the right time to tell her, but she inadvertently read the email on my computer. I feel so guilty—so stressed and miserable for not telling her. But when would have been the right time?" Caitlin dropped her head into her hands. "I got carried away… I told her…*damn* it, Kim, I couldn't help it." Caitlin looked up at her colleague beseechingly.

"You told her how you feel?" Kim hit the nail on the head.

"Uh-huh, I told her how I feel." Caitlin realised this was the first time she and Kim had talked about personal matters. "Is this all right? Here I am, blurting out my woes."

Kim looked at Caitlin across the table. "We are friends. You're upset, and I am here to listen." Kim pushed her plate aside. "What did Andi say?"

"She totally freaked out and told me she needs space." Caitlin frowned.

"Oh, that's bad. So what now?"

"I need to respect her wishes. I haven't much choice, have I? I've made no decision about my future yet, and there are so many things to consider. I can't talk to my Mum and Dad about such an important subject over the telephone."

Kim nodded understandingly. "What else are you thinking?" she asked. "Surely you must be excited about the interview and the prospect of a promotion?"

"Yes, it is a fantastic opportunity—there's no denying it. I have worked towards this for a long time, and now it is within my grasp."

Kim's face lit up. "That's perfect then, Caitlin. It sounds fantastic." She gave her a searching look. "But obviously there is more to the story. How about you and Andi? I guess it depends on what *you* decide to do. I, for one, would love it if you stayed longer. Is it even a possibility?"

"I don't know, Kim. I can't take the promotion *and* stay here. I know it sounds totally ridiculous, but it's like there's an invisible thread that draws me to her, connecting us. When she's near me, my body needs physical contact, craves intimacy—even her eyes on me are a caress." Caitlin rubbed the back of her neck. "Do I sound like a lovesick teenager?"

Kim shook her head and then nodded. "Yes. *Phew!* That night at the Emerson, when we were watching you two dance…" Kim's face flushed. "I said to Sharon, if we had an electricity blackout now, those two would light up the whole dance floor."

Caitlin sighed. How could she forget that night? It was the first time she'd held Andi in her arms.

It had been a relief to share her feelings with Kim that afternoon, and now she was trying to wear herself out. Caitlin's feet pounded the winding track along the river at Yarra Bend Park. Although her body was tiring, her mind still raced ahead.

She followed the sealed course, taking in the views of the Melbourne skyline and people leisurely walking their dogs, enjoying the parkland. The sound of wattlebirds and bell miners in the trees mingled with the whooshing of rowing skulls gliding on the water. Despite the serenity of her surroundings, she was strung out. Nervous, uncertain, and filled with longing, she found it hard for logic to prevail over her desires. How had things become so complicated?

Until now, Caitlin had kept things simple. Her mantra was study hard, work hard, play hard. Although there were no set rules for her casual relationships, there were still rules. Rules made it easier and safer for everyone.

Obviously, she had changed. Caitlin had broken one of her own rules. She had deluded herself into believing she could have a casual relationship with Andi. Their connection had been immediate, and even after their first weekend together, it was never going to be *just* about sex.

On the cliff-top, the first day they'd met, Andréa Rey had saved her lens cap and captured her attention. In a short time, Andi had ignited her passion. Caitlin wanted everything—she wanted it all.

Caitlin propped her body against the Roadster door. She slowed her breathing and stretched out her tired, overworked muscles. Now physically exhausted, she hoped tonight she might be able to still her mind enough to sleep.

Chapter 31

"What the hell were you doing, going out when the sea is treacherous?" Ellie growled. She used a towel to apply firm pressure to the nasty gash above Andi's knee. A steady flow of blood trickled down Andi's left leg and onto the wooden deck where she sat.

Andi had somehow managed the short drive home—despite being groggy and disoriented. She was surprised and relieved when she saw Ellie's car parked in her driveway.

Ellie appeared on the porch as Andi parked the Jeep and helped her out of the car and onto the deck. The shocked expression on her face said it all. Ellie sat her down on a bench and carefully assisted her with removing the ripped wetsuit.

"Did you make contact with the rocks anyplace else?" She scanned the rest of Andi's body, expeditiously checking for injuries.

"A scrape under my ribs, and my shoulder's sore." She winced as Ellie applied even more pressure to the wound on her thigh. "My ribs, here on the left side… damn…" she inclined her head to indicate where it hurt and cringed as Ellie lifted the rash vest.

"Take in a slow, deep breath."

"*Ouch*," Andi cried, as Ellie examined her chest and rib cage.

"Tender?" Ellie continued to explore. "Badly bruised—hopefully nothing worse." She shook her head. "What about these?" She pointed to the scrapes on Andi's right calf and ankle.

"Just scratches, nothing serious." She leaned back against the wooden post as a wave of nausea engulfed her.

"What about this one below your knee? It doesn't look new. You didn't do this today."

"No, that happened a few days ago."

Ellie rolled her eyes. “Are you light-headed? Nauseous?” She looked closer to examine Andi’s pupils. “Since you’re going to need stitches anyway, I’m taking you to the Medical Centre. You need to be fully checked.” She shook her head in disbelief. “What on earth were you trying to do? Get yourself *killed*?”

Andi’s thigh throbbed, and she felt like someone had landed a punch to her ribs below her left breast. She’d behaved like an idiot, surfing Bells Beach when the water was unsafe. She’d taken a stupid risk, pushed her body to its limits, and now suffered the consequences.

“You know better, Andi. You’re usually so careful. You know to respect the water,” Ellie said. She sounded exasperated.

Ellie was right. Andi knew that when the winds were strong and blowing on the surface of the water, the waves could be huge and powerful enough to throw even an experienced surfer onto the rocks.

“I was stupid, Ellie. I thought I could handle it. Guess I learned my lesson, huh?” Andi felt sick at the sight of blood, especially her own. She looked away from the once-white beach towel that was now soaked red.

“Okay, I need you to keep your hand on here. Keep the pressure up. We’ll get you inside, cleaned up, and dressed. Then, I’ll drive you to the clinic in town.”

“Do I have to? Is it that bad? Can’t you hold it together with a butterfly strip thingy? The bleeding seems to be easing.”

Ellie shook her head. “No, that won’t do. Unless you want me to get my kit out of the car and sew you up on your workbench? It could make an interesting piece of installation art.” She squinted her eyes and studied Andi. “If you don’t have it stitched, it will take twice as long to heal. It could open up again the minute you move around.” She rubbed her thumb affectionately over Andi’s forehead. “Since I’m not carrying any anaesthetic, you’d have to bite on a piece of bark.”

“Haha, you’re so funny.”

“Stop being a baby, then. Anyway, I’m not going to be held responsible for scarring your beautiful thigh. Come on, let me give you a hand up.”

She allowed Ellie to help her to her feet and wrap a clean towel around her.

Two hours later, they were back home. Andi’s leg was propped up on the armrest of her sofa. The local anaesthetic was wearing off, and Andi felt completely drained of energy. She slumped back on a pile of cushions. Koda licked her hair from where she sat on the back of the sofa.

Ellie handed her a glass of water and two painkillers. "This should help. You're lucky there was no arterial bleed. So, the twenty stitches on your thigh shouldn't incapacitate you for too long, but the contusions on your shoulder and ribs will restrict your movement. You're going to be very sore for a few days—but you're damn lucky, Andi."

"I know," Andi said. With a shaky hand, she pushed her hair out of her eyes. "I was totally irresponsible today. I just wasn't thinking clearly."

"What's going on? I haven't seen you like this before. Is it something to do with your exhibition?" Andi shook her head. "Then what is it? *Caitlin?*" Ellie looked at her questioningly.

"She leaves for Ireland in just over a week," Andi said despondently.

Ellie raised her eyebrows and placed her hands on her hips. "So what did you imagine? You'd kill yourself, and she'd have to cancel her trip?"

"No. Of course not."

"You told me she's going to Ireland for her interview. Caitlin hasn't said she's not coming back, has she?" Ellie asked.

"No, she's supposed to be gone for two weeks."

"Okay, so that part hasn't changed. But what is going on in your head? Something is triggering this self-destructive behaviour." Ellie sat down across from Andi and waited. "Spill it."

"I haven't seen her since the weekend at the farm. I miss her. I really tried to keep this thing between us light and easygoing. Just tried to have a good time and enjoy her company." Andi sighed and attempted to shift her leg into a more comfortable position. She grew more miserable by the second. "I always knew she would return to Ireland after her twelve months were up, and I made the decision that I could handle it. It's not like I was *dragged* screaming into her arms. It was my choice."

"But?"

"I talked myself into thinking that I could have a casual relationship with her. I like her a lot, and now I'm scared out of my wits."

"What are you afraid of, Andi?"

"I may not get the chance to see her before she leaves. I'm scared of how I feel about her. It wasn't meant to become so hard..." Her eyes welled up with tears; her head was fuzzy. "As if I could help loving her."

Ellie knelt on the floor in front of the sofa and pulled Andi into her arms. "It's okay, let it go." Ellie gently held her, taking care not to make contact with her injured leg or shoulder. "Have you told Caitlin how you feel?"

"No. She told me she loved me," Andi mumbled softly. She sniffed, and buried her head in Ellie's shoulder.

"I didn't catch that. What did you say?"

Andi rubbed her eyes. "She told me she loved me."

"Oh, Andi, that's good, isn't it?" Ellie exclaimed. "How come you're only telling me this now? How did you respond?"

"I *totally* went hysterical, got mad, ran away, and then pretended that nothing had changed." She shrugged her shoulders. "I told her I needed space." Andi pulled herself into an upright position and winced as her injured leg dragged on the sofa. "*God*, I am such an idiot."

"Come on, Andi. Caitlin's told you she loves you. That does change things, doesn't it? Think about how Caitlin must feel. She must be a mess." Ellie gently helped Andi lower her leg to the ground. "I think you should call Caitlin tomorrow. You're too tired now. Those Panadeine Forte will make you drowsy, and you should sleep."

Andi ran her hands through her hair and scrubbed at her eyes.

"Come on. It's time you were in bed. You're totally wiped out. Excuse the pun." She smiled. "I'm going to sleep on the couch tonight, so I don't hit your leg by accident. That way I won't be far away if you need me."

Andi *was* exhausted. She stood shakily and leaned her weight against Ellie as they walked to her bedroom. Her last memory that evening, before she drifted into sleep, was blue. Blue swirling ocean, and Caitlin's deep blue eyes.

Caitlin had texted Andi every day. She'd emailed her with photographs of their weekend together at the farm. Andi had responded in a courteous, friendly manner. Caitlin didn't want polite and friendly. She missed the passionate and humorous conversations they'd shared. She missed their physical intimacy. She missed Andi.

She understood that Andi's controlled, guarded responses were her way of coping. But she couldn't imagine leaving Australia—even temporarily—without seeing her again.

Isabella had requested her company for an early dinner. She glanced at her watch; it was time to go. She'd decided to ring Andi later that evening and ask if they could meet during the week. If Andi did not give her a definite answer, she would drive down to Hakea in the morning.

Caitlin leaned over the kitchen bench, a whiskey glass in one hand. She sipped the pot-stilled single malt and watched Isabella plate the desert and prepare the coffee.

"I say we make ourselves comfortable by the wood fire," Isabella said. "It's a cosy place for us to chat."

Caitlin stole a sliver of sweetly sour fruit from one of the bowls of caramelised, buttery dessert on the counter.

"Babka's Bakery is a Melbourne gem," Isabella claimed. "It produces the stickiest, loveliest apple tarte Tatin I've ever tasted. You really shouldn't have, Caitlin; this will go directly to my hips." Isabella laughed, adding an extra dollop of cream to her serve.

"I was in Fitzroy with Kim and some of her friends from the museum. I knew it was your favourite. I couldn't resist."

"Oh well, a small piece won't do me any harm. But I will need a good strong cup of coffee to wash it down." She looked up cheekily and grinned. "I'd better not fudge my Zumba class at the senior citizen's this week."

Caitlin laughed. She added another log to the fire before sitting back in the armchair across from Isabella.

"You're looking tired. You've been working too hard, Caitlin."

"I'll be away for two whole weeks, and Kim has enough on her plate. We've been trying to get ahead."

"The other two girls you employed are an incredible help, aren't they? Especially Jane. She's a lovely young woman."

Caitlin agreed. Her team had been working well together, and they'd finished installing the artworks.

"When I return, it will be just two weeks before Christmas. Can you believe how time flies? If all goes well, we'll be ready to open Bella Gallery to the public in late January—right on schedule."

"Marvellous. You've done a fantastic job, darling."

"It's been truly a great team to work with, Isabella."

Caitlin's phone vibrated where she'd placed it on the mahogany sideboard. They both turned towards it.

"Caitlin, that's your phone. Do you want to answer it?"

"Do you mind? I wasn't expecting a call tonight, but I'd better see who it is."

"Please, go ahead."

Caitlin picked it up and moved into the hallway. She didn't recognise the number.

"Hi Caitlin, this is Ellie Anderson. I hope I haven't disturbed you?"

Caitlin was surprised to hear Ellie's voice. "It's okay, Ellie. How are you? Is there something wrong?"

"I'm fine." Ellie hesitated. "Look, I didn't want to worry you, but…"

"What's going on? Is it Andi?"

After another pause, Ellie replied, "She's asleep now, but she will be pissed off if she knew I was calling you."

"For goodness sake, Ellie. What is wrong? You *are* starting to worry me."

"Andi had an accident while surfing today. She suffered a deep laceration to her left quadricep. Badly bruised ribs and shoulder." Ellie rattled off the information.

"What on earth happened?" Caitlin could hear the hysteria in her own voice, and Ellie apparently heard it too.

"Calm down, Caitlin. It happened at Bells Beach. She came off her board in rough conditions, but she's been to the clinic for a full checkup."

"Damn. How is she really?" Caitlin paced up and down the hallway. She looked at her watch. It was just after nine thirty. Was she able to drive down to Hakea tonight? How many drinks did she have with dinner?

"She did require twenty stitches in her thigh. Though there shouldn't be any permanent damage to the muscle or function."

Caitlin refocused while Ellie shared the rest of the details.

"It's more her mental state I'm worried about," Ellie said.

Although Caitlin wanted to immediately drive to the coast, Ellie convinced her that Andi was now sedated and sound asleep. It would be better if Caitlin arrived in the morning.

They ended the call with Caitlin partly relieved that Ellie would be with Andi overnight, but she wouldn't be satisfied until she saw Andi herself. She took a few deep breaths before returning to the living room.

"Caitlin, dear, you're white as a sheet. What's happened?"

"It's Andi. She's suffered a nasty gash to her thigh and bruising to her shoulder and ribs while surfing. Ellie assures me she's going to be okay. But I want to see her myself." Caitlin's hand trembled as she lifted her empty glass. "I need another drop. Do you mind?"

"Of course not, dear. I only take it for medicinal purposes myself. Please, go ahead and pour yourself a large one."

She refilled her glass and, with a deep sigh, lowered herself into her chair.

Isabella wanted every detail. "It is fortunate that her friend is a doctor and was on the scene." Isabella patted her hand. "I'm glad you've decided to drive down there in the morning, Caitlin. I know you won't rest until you've seen her for yourself."

Caitlin hugged Isabella, stepped out into the night, and made her way across the courtyard. The air was clear and cool. She gazed up at the stars and whispered. "Thank you." From what Ellie had told her about the conditions that day, Andi could have been much more seriously injured.

Chapter 32

Andi was confused, disoriented, and bruised, as though she'd spent the night in a tumble dryer. She focused on the murmur of distant voices. It was highly unlikely that Ellie was watching morning television or talking to herself. Who else was in the house?

"Who is it, Koda?" she asked, stroking silky beige fur. Koda meowed softly and nuzzled Andi's neck. Koda had stayed close to Andi all night.

"What time is it?" Andi drowsily rubbed her eyes and checked her phone. "Ten thirty!" Her eyes slowly adjusted to the bright light coming in through the blinds. She lifted the sheet and examined the nasty bruises and stitches on her upper left thigh. She groaned. "No wonder I can hardly move."

A noise in the hallway had distracted the young cat, and she'd jumped off the bed. "Hey, where are you going?" Andi asked Koda. She took a deep breath and winced at the pain and tightness below her breasts. Her ribs… Had Ellie said they were broken? She couldn't remember. Andi turned her head slowly towards the door. "Koda?"

The door opened, and Andi dragged herself into a half-seated position, struggling to cover her naked body with the sheet. "Ellie?"

"Andi." Strangely, Ellie sounded a lot like Caitlin.

She automatically pulled the sheet up around her shoulders.

"Caitlin?" Was it really Caitlin? Or was she delirious, and her muddled brain was playing tricks on her? Ellie had given her two more tablets sometime during the night. Maybe it was a side effect of the codeine? The apparition—who looked like Caitlin but couldn't possibly *be* Caitlin—knelt beside the bed.

"Hello, you," Caitlin said in a whisper, and her warm breath tickled Andi's face. Her brow was drawn together, and her index finger trembled as she traced a scratch below Andi's chin.

Andi was not hallucinating. She leaned across to grab her T-shirt from the pillow beside her and flinched as she tried to pull it on.

Caitlin gazed at her chest and inhaled sharply as she helped ease the shirt over Andi's head. Andi couldn't see her ribs. She didn't know what they looked like this morning—but they hurt like hell.

Caitlin soothed the material down Andi's back and sat down beside her. Her touch sent a wave of goose bumps along Andi's arms.

"When did you get here? Where's Ellie?" Andi's mouth was dry.

"About half an hour ago. You were asleep, and I didn't want to wake you." Caitlin inched closer. "Ellie's gone to pick up bread and milk for breakfast." Caitlin's hand hovered near the sheet. "Can I see your leg?" she asked.

"It's okay, really. It probably looks much worse than it is." Andi pulled the sheet up to reveal her thigh. There was bruising below her knee and the semicircle of stitches. The area around the wound was a nasty shade of crimson and dark-blue, and was swollen.

"Oh Andi. Baby, that looks so painful."

"No really, it's not too bad." She tried to smile. "Out of the two of us, I'm the one that got off lightly. You should see the shark." Andi smirked.

Caitlin looked puzzled, then frowned. "That is not funny. This isn't a joke. You could have been more seriously hurt. And you were alone… What if you were struck unconscious on the rocks…or you got tangled in your board ropes or…" Tears spilled down Caitlin's cheeks.

Andi drew her into her arms. "I'm sorry, Caitlin," she mumbled. She curled up against her, and Caitlin tightened her hold around her. Andi flinched.

"Oh, I'm so sorry." Caitlin tried to move, but Andi held on.

"I'm okay, Caitlin. Or I will be. I just have some bruises and scrapes." They held each other silently for a few moments. "I don't want to move, but if I don't get up and use the bathroom, I'll have an accident." She grinned weakly.

"Okay. I'll help you."

"I can manage." Andi carefully lowered her injured leg to the rug and pulled the T-shirt down. She struggled to stand upright—still light-headed. She lurched forward, and Caitlin circled her waist protectively with her arm.

"I'll help you," Caitlin repeated.

She closed her eyes briefly and then allowed herself to lean into Caitlin, grateful for her strength and comforting warmth. When they reached the bathroom, Andi pushed Caitlin out of the room. She may need help to walk, but she could use the toilet by herself, thank you very much. She wanted a shower but settled on a one-handed sponge bath, which was adequate for now.

After, Andi settled into a chair at the dining table.

"Coffee?" Ellie, who'd arrived home from her shopping trip, asked.

"Yes, please." She relaxed as Ellie and Caitlin took over her kitchen. Ellie toasted bagels and made coffee, while Caitlin sautéed tomatoes, onions, and parsley for their scrambled eggs. They worked in tandem alongside each other, as if they had done it a hundred times before.

"Okay, we're nearly ready." Ellie placed a plate, piled high with split-toasted bagels, on the table in front of Andi. "Do you want marmalade with your bagel?"

She nodded. "I was too queasy to eat anything last night. But I'm starving now."

"Probably better if you put something solid in your stomach while you're taking codeine," Ellie said.

Caitlin served the eggs onto three plates, carried them to the table, and sat down beside Andi. "Have you started on the arnica I brought you?" she asked.

"I have, thanks." Andi smiled and reached for the marmalade.

"Marmalade?" Caitlin shook her head in disbelief. "You're one of the few people I know who enjoys jam with their eggs." She looked at Andi affectionately.

"What?" she asked. "It's an awesome combination, isn't it, Ellie?"

"It's the best, Caitlin. You should give it a try. Especially with Ana's orange marmalade." Ellie passed the salt and pepper to Andi. "Caitlin's right. Arnica will help. It stimulates the healing process by clearing and cleaning the tissue of unwanted debris. But remember to rest, ice, compress, and elevate," she said, gesturing with her fork. "I need to head back into Melbourne after breakfast." She winked at Caitlin. "Andi, you need a cold compress on the worst of your bruises; and keep your leg elevated. It will lessen the amount of bleeding under the skin. You'll heal much faster."

"Thanks, Ellie. I'll be okay." She turned to Caitlin. "You must have a million things to do before you leave next week?"

Caitlin shook her head. "I've already organised to be here. Andi. I'm staying."

By the way Caitlin stared at her, Andi had little chance, if any, of persuading her to leave.

"At least till tomorrow. Longer if you need me," Caitlin added emphatically.

Ellie and Caitlin shared a subtle, knowing look. She was tired and sore—still a little fuzzy—but not enough to miss their nonverbal communication. It dawned on her that Ellie must have phoned Caitlin. How else did she know? And why was Ellie leaving already? She was supposed to stay tonight.

"There you go. It's all settled," Ellie said, lifting a forkful of scrambled eggs to her mouth. "This is tasty, Caitlin. Andi, you can't drive for a few days, so accept help when it is offered."

Andi nodded. "Okay, okay. Thank you, to both of you. I really appreciate all your help." She looked from one to the other and rolled her eyes. "You two are quite the team." She yawned. "I will take your advice, Ellie, and take it easy for the rest of the day."

The next morning, Caitlin curled into Andi's uninjured side. "Are you sure this is okay? I'm not hurting you, am I? It's hard not to touch you in the wrong places."

"No, you're not hurting me." Andi's voice was soft, her eyes heavy lidded. "I'm okay, Caitlin."

"Are you in much pain? I could move, give you more space so you can stretch out?"

"Shhh…I'm fine." Andi placed a finger over her lips. "This is precisely where I want to be."

Andi nuzzled into Caitlin's shoulder. "Your hair smells of vanilla and cinnamon. I adore these lovely wavy strands." She twisted a lock of dark hair between her fingers. "It's soft and feminine, but kind of messy and tousled. It gives you a wild, bad-girl look."

Caitlin smiled. "Bad girl?" She lifted herself onto one elbow and turned to look into Andi's coffee-coloured eyes. "I've missed you."

"Yeah, bad girl." Andi giggled. "When you look at me like that, your eyes sparkle—a deeper blue than any ocean pool. I've missed you too."

They lay still with the sounds of morning drifting through the open window. The rustle of gum leaves in the coastal breeze, the warbling of magpies, and distant waves breaking on the rocks, all mingled with Koda's soft snoring at the end of the bed.

"Andi, you can't run away this time. We have things to discuss, don't you think?" Caitlin turned to brush her lips along Andi's collarbone and then gently rested her chin between Andi's sweetly curved breasts.

"I know. We do. Now?"

She moved her hand to Andi's forehead. When she felt Andi tense, she caressed her furrowed brow. "Is that okay?"

"Uh-huh."

"I want to understand what's going on in here." Caitlin tapped the side of Andi's head. "We need to talk about what's happened and what you *think* is happening. You really scared me. You can talk to me if you're frightened, embarrassed, or angry." Although Caitlin had a sense of what was going on, she wanted Andi to put it into her own words.

"I want that too."

When they eventually got out of bed, Caitlin helped Andi rig a waterproof cover for her thigh, and she was able to take a shower.

She smiled as Andi appeared, looking refreshed in loose cargo shorts and ribbed tank.

"Feel better?"

"Much better, thanks."

"You look it," Caitlin said. She poured peppermint tea and handed a cup to Andi, who sat huddled in one corner of the sofa with her leg propped up on a cushion.

Caitlin sank into a chair across from Andi, keeping some distance between them. Two artworks she'd not seen before leaned against the wall.

"Your new paintings are incredible. I love the rawness of the towering cliffs in the smaller painting. It is such a powerful image. Like stone monoliths soaring against the blue horizon."

"Thank you. One of my favourite subjects."

Andi had captured the red and yellow ochre clay pigments in harsh horizontal strokes, in stark contrast to the smooth golden sand below and the bright blue, cloudless sky above.

Caitlin placed her cup down on the table in front of her. "Don't you think you've been a bit reckless lately? You don't come across as someone who would take unnecessary risks."

Andi rested her head against the back of the sofa. Slowly, she opened her brown eyes and glanced at Caitlin quickly before staring up at the ceiling. "I guess. With the exhibition approaching, I've been feeling pressured." Suddenly, she leaned forward, startling Caitlin. Her eyes were wide, and she pulled at her hair. "I just made a bad decision. The sea was rougher than I expected. I *hate* that I haven't seen you for nearly three weeks—even if it was my call. I hate that you're going away in just a few days. What if you don't want to come back?"

Caitlin remained calm despite Andi's outburst. "Andi, I'm only going for two weeks. I won't miss the exhibition opening. We can keep in touch regularly on FaceTime or Skype. Or text?" Caitlin struggled to dispel Andi's fears, because the future was unclear for her as well. "I feel horrible about not being here to help you with the exhibition. You have so much to do. I wish I could be here. It's really bad timing."

Andi didn't reply, so Caitlin attempted to draw her out. "Tell me about your paintings. What did you feel when you did this one?" She gestured towards the smaller canvas.

Andi rubbed her thigh. "I wanted to present the cliff rising out of the smooth sand and the even, flat plain of the intense blue sky. It's terror and beauty all at once. Simultaneously." She hesitated. "Sometimes, I feel like that, like something is impossible, and my doubts multiply."

"Is that how you feel about us?"

Andi ran her hands through her hair and fidgeted restlessly. "Yes."

"Please, don't be unsure of how I feel about you."

Andi half smiled and said, "I know you've been working towards this promotion for a long time. It's important to you." She glanced out the window, where a strong wind was lashing tree branches against the deck. "So, what else will you be doing in Cork? I don't suppose you'll be surfing?"

Caitlin shrugged halfheartedly at Andi's side-step. "Funny you should mention that. I am hoping to visit the other Kinsale. There's a famous surf beach at Garretstown very close to where Isabella grew up. My parents have a cottage nearby, so I may just do that."

"But you've only had one lesson!" exclaimed Andi, she rolled her eyes. "And it will be winter."

"Okay, then, maybe not." She winked. "You'd love Kinsale. It's an old fishing port with a beautiful rugged coastline. It has winding little streets with cafés and restaurants. I'd like to take you there someday." Caitlin moved to the sofa and lifted Andi's injured leg onto her lap. She thought carefully about what she wanted to say next and took a deep breath. "Do you ever think of going to Europe again? Or living away from here, even for a short time? Could you see yourself travelling?" *With me?* She imagined them exploring galleries and museums together in London and Italy. Andi could have her own studio and paint.

Andi yawned and reached for Caitlin—her beautiful hands framed Caitlin's face. She kissed her slowly, gently.

"You're tired," Caitlin whispered.

Andi nodded. "Caitlin?" she asked, her breath warm and sweet against Caitlin's lips.

"Hmm?"

"I would. I could travel…*anywhere, with you.*"

Caitlin sighed and gazed into Andi's drowsy eyes. She drew her close, and they sat quietly until Andi's breathing had slowed. She'd fallen sleep. Caitlin caressed the darkening bruise on Andi's cheek and kissed her hair. She took her hand and entwined their fingers together.

Her hands are sun-kissed and strong
Capable, creative—artist's hands
Veins subtly visible; a roadmap to her heart
I look down at our connection
I am the silent cartographer
Longing to unravel the mysteries concealed in her hands.

Chapter 33

The clouds cleared and gave way to open spaces and rolling hills of green grasses. Caitlin leaned forward and stared out at the glorious patchwork of colour, the wide harbour and meandering river—the town's familiar landscape that welcomed her home. Minutes later the Airbus tyres squealed at touchdown, and she momentarily tensed then sighed in relief as the plane slowed on the runway. The aircraft rolled towards the terminal, and the captain began his welcome speech. It wouldn't be long now before they finally disembarked.

"Welcome home, Doctor Quinn," the officer said as he handed Caitlin her passport.

She smiled tiredly and passed through immigration control—the last official step of her long journey. After the insufferably long flight from Singapore to London, Caitlin was grateful for the four-hour stopover at Heathrow. She'd taken advantage of the business-class lounge to shower and change into fresh clothes.

Suitcase and bags in tow, she made her way into the Cork Airport Arrivals Hall and scanned the afternoon crowd for her mother.

"Caitlin, Caitlin." Orla Quinn wrapped her arms around her daughter and hugged her tight. Finally, she let go to hold her at arm's length. "Let me get a good look at you, darling." She carefully scrutinised her daughter. "Oh, you're a sight for sore eyes. I don't know how you do it, but you manage to look marvellous even after travelling for thirty hours."

"Thanks, Ma. It's wonderful to see you. You look sensational yourself." Caitlin embraced her mother and kissed her cheek. "I love your hair shorter. It suits you."

Orla patted her new hairstyle and smiled at Caitlin's compliment.

"It's not *too* wet or too cold, just some good old-fashioned Cork drizzle. But after the Australian weather, you will feel it."

Caitlin shrugged into the loose-fitting knitted coat her mother had brought for her. "Thank you for taking time off to collect me. Really, Ma, I could have grabbed a taxi."

"As if. I haven't seen you for nearly seven months. There was not a chance. If your father wasn't entertaining some foreign guests this afternoon, he would be here himself." Orla lifted the smaller bag, and they headed for the exit, towards the short-term car park. "I would've had to bring the Rover if he'd come along." She pointed to the shiny, sage-green, vintage Jaguar XK. "I thought you'd like to be picked up in your own car."

Caitlin fastened the coat buttons and pulled the collar up around her neck. The air was damp and cold, but at least a little sun peeped through the clouds. She stroked the bonnet of her car. "I'm happy to see you, Lois. Thanks, Ma," she said and crammed her luggage into the small rear boot.

"Aren't you tired? Are you okay to drive?"

Caitlin slid into the driver's seat. "I'm fine. I've missed driving her." She sat behind the wheel and adjusted the seat. "One thing hasn't changed—you haven't got any taller."

"Cheeky devil, *you* haven't changed." Orla laughed and slid into the low passenger seat. Caitlin grinned, turned the key, and the classic car purred as a Jaguar should.

"Welcome home, darling." Orla held onto the wooden dashboard as the car zoomed forward.

Caitlin took the short walk from her parents' home along the river. No matter how many times she approached the Glucksman Gallery over the footbridge, she had a sense of entering a special place. The upper floors of the timber-clad building seemed to float above the river that ran beside it. Its permanent collection housed 350 works of contemporary Irish art. Wouldn't it be grand to show Andi around *this* gallery?

Caitlin followed the pathway to the lower grounds, and as she entered the Fresco Bistro, a familiar voice called, "There you are." Kiera enveloped Caitlin in a crushing hug and, in her excitement, lifted her off the ground. "You're all healthy and glowing from the Aussie sunshine."

"Kiera, I'm glad to see you. It's nice that you've missed me so damn much." Caitlin chuckled at her friend's exuberance. "But please put me down." She gripped Kiera's forearm. "You look fighting fit. Still swimming twenty laps a day?"

Kiera grinned and her grey eyes sparkled. "Come hail, rain, or shine—every day."

She steered Caitlin around a rowdy, unfamiliar group standing at the bar.

"Come on, girl, we have a table at the back. Your old friends will be surprised as hell and very happy to fix their eyes on you." Kiera sidestepped to avoid an inebriated colleague. "I'm *damned* happy to see you." She squeezed Caitlin's shoulder. "You chose to arrive back home just in time."

The venue was hosting the university alumni end-of-year party, and it hummed with faculty and staff already getting into the holiday spirit.

They moved through the bistro. Its sliding doors opened towards the west, overlooking parkland between the river and the limestone escarpment. The dining terrace provided views of the picturesque, gothic college buildings. Caitlin sighed as she glimpsed the pink, evening light reflected on the River Lee.

At the table, she was greeted with peals of laughter from her familiar group. Oddly, she felt awkward standing there, waiting to join her friends. It was absurd to feel unsure of her place among this circle of colleagues and friends. After all, they were very much a part of her social life; at least the life she'd led before Australia, prior to Andi.

She'd spent last night with her parents, catching up on family news. Once she'd climbed into the four-poster bed in her childhood room and snuggled into the cotton sheets and mohair throw, Caitlin sent Andi a text to let her know she'd arrived safely. When the return text appeared, Caitlin stared at the screen that lit up with Andi's smiling image.

She'd fallen asleep, lulled by the memories of Andi in her arms, the smell of her skin, and the taste of her on her lips.

"Well, look who's here. Caitlin Quinn."

The sound of her name brought her back to the present. "Sally, lovely to see you." Caitlin hugged her friend. "Huge congratulations to you and Liam. What's the name of your little girl?"

"That would be Maeve Kathy O'Reilly, and she's almost two months old." Sally put her hands on her hips and shook her head. "Let me tell you, Caitlin, at four in the morning, her impersonation of Sinéad O'Connor is enough to drive us barmy."

The old crowd of friends welcomed Caitlin in a blur of hugs, kisses, and compliments. In danger of being completely overwhelmed by the attention, she was relieved ten minutes later to take a seat beside Kiera.

"Are you okay? You look a bit stunned, like a deer in headlights. I guess it is a bit much, seeing everyone all at once." Kiera handed her a Murphy's. "Here, get your mouth around this, Caitlin."

Caitlin rolled her eyes. "Thanks, I've missed it. We do get it in Melbourne, but not on draft. It's not the same in a tin." She lifted her glass to Kiera and then took a large gulp. "Yes, old friend, I am fine. Really. Don't give me too many of these though, or you'll be carrying me home." Caitlin licked the creamy-malt-caramel foam from her top lip.

Good intentions aside, Caitlin had a couple before she headed to the bar, requested a large glass of water, and drained it empty.

"This is a surprise."

Startled by a smooth voice, Caitlin turned around. "Rachel," she said. "This *is* a surprise."

Rachel circled Caitlin's waist with her arms. "I heard about your promotion. It's an unexpected pleasure to see you here tonight. Congratulations are in order."

"News travels fast." Caitlin took a step backwards out of Rachel's grasp as she clarified, "*Possible* promotion. You should know better, counsellor. Supposition only."

"Touché." Rachel laughed and flicked the fringe of her stylishly cut brown hair from her face. She leaned closer. "It is excellent to see you back again. I must say, Australia agrees with you." She examined Caitlin from head to toe. "Though, you must be relieved to be coming home." She smirked. "Can't be much Down Under to challenge you as an art historian?"

"On the contrary. It has been most inspiring. The art and cultural scene in Melbourne is vibrant, very much alive. It's an exciting place to live and work. I've learned so much about Australia's art movements from Isabella. I'm only *just* beginning to learn about indigenous art."

"Surely it can't compete with the richness and history of European art?" Rachel waved her glass of champagne in front of Caitlin to emphasise her point.

"What about Sidney Nolan, Namatjira, Albert Tucker? Just to name a few. As far as international recognition, surely you've heard about the contemporary Aboriginal artist, Lena Nyadbi? Her work is painted on the rooftop of the Musée du quai Branly, in Paris. Not only does Australia have one of the most exciting art cultures now, there is *also* evidence of aboriginal art that dates back at least thirty thousand years."

Rachel bowed her head and grinned sheepishly. "Wow, you've presented a very strong defence. Hmm, and there's something different about you. I can't quite put my finger on it." She tilted her head and tapped her index finger on her chin. "You're more relaxed, and I'd say you've got that just—"

"There you are, darling." A beautiful, mocha-skinned woman put her arm around Rachel's shoulder and held on.

Caitlin breathed a sigh of relief. Saved.

"Hi, Selina." Rachel placed her hand possessively on Selina's forearm. "Caitlin, this is Selina Davis from Washington. She is currently working at UCC as a sessional lecturer in classics and archaeology."

Caitlin accepted Selina's delicate outstretched hand. "Pleasure to meet you." That explained why Rachel was here tonight.

Selina's gaze travelled from Caitlin to Rachel and back again, curiously. She was striking, with glossy, black hair swept back with a silver clip. Her body curved into Rachel's side, a perfect fit.

"Do you work at UCC? I haven't had the good fortune of seeing you around here," Selina said.

"She's been in Melbourne, on sabbatical, but Caitlin's a UCC girl from way back. She's flown in to present for her Academic Promotions to Associate Professor."

"Ahh," Selina acknowledged. "Congratulations, Caitlin. Which department?"

"Arts." Caitlin smiled. They would be in the same department. "Actually, I work in the College of Arts, Celtic Studies, and Social Sciences."

"Okay. We should run into each other, then."

"We may indeed," Caitlin said.

Rachel shifted from one foot to the other in the restless way Caitlin recognised. She looked self-assured and sleek in a tailored, grey power suit, but she still loved to be the centre of attention.

Caitlin promised Rachel she'd try harder to keep in touch. They hugged briefly and made their polite goodbyes before Caitlin wound her way back to her table.

"Here you are. I thought you'd been kidnapped." Kiera indicated towards the bar. "I couldn't help notice you talking to Rachel. How'd you go, then?"

"Actually, okay," she said, breathing a sigh of relief. "God, it seems like a lifetime since we were together."

"Is it hard to see her?" Kiera tilted her head. "With her new girlfriend?"

"No, not at all. I'm very glad. She seems happy. It's not entirely a surprise. Ma ran into her last month, and she mentioned that Rachel was seeing someone." Although, she hadn't divulged that Rachel's new girlfriend and Caitlin shared similar academic backgrounds.

Kiera placed her hand on Caitlin's forearm. "Speaking of girlfriends, how's Andi after the surfing accident? She's a wild one, isn't she?"

"Ah, that she is," Caitlin said. "She's on the mend, luckily. She has heaps to do before her exhibition opens."

"And you're not there to hold her hand."

Caitlin shook her head. "She doesn't need me to hold her hand."

"But surely Andi's worried about the impending interview and what it means for the two of you?"

Suddenly, a heavy hand rested on Caitlin's shoulder.

"Lass, how's it feel to be back in civilisation?" A bushy, grey-bearded giant descended upon her and stooped low to kiss her cheek.

"Bobby, you brute. Take it easy on Caitlin," Kiera growled at the Scotsman who was clad in a tartan kilt. "You'll give her beard rash."

"Grrr…bollocks." He grinned and parked himself down on the bench beside Caitlin. "Seriously, Caitlin, it is good to see you. When do you start back here?"

Caitlin shook her head and smiled at Robert Murdock, the Scottish art history professor.

"I'm just visiting, Bobby." She glanced at his hairy knees. "Love the skirt."

He chuckled. "What're you complaining about? At least I've got the legs for it. Anyway, I heard about your advancement. It'll be a walk in the park, Caitlin. You so deserve this."

It was incredible to see everyone again, but the attention, constant questions, and assumptions were truly exhausting. The walls were closing in on her.

Kiera tapped her on the leg. As if reading her mind, she said, "I don't know about you, Caitlin, but I'm ready to flee this coop. I promised Emma that we'd meet her at Loafers. Let's get there and have a few. Then you can tell me what's really going on. Are you up for it? It is your first full day back home, and you're probably *jet-lagged*."

"No. I mean yes, I'd like that. Lead on." Caitlin gathered her jacket and purse and followed Kiera towards the exit.

As they left the building, Caitlin put her arm through Kiera's. "Thanks, pal."

"What for?" Kiera asked.

"Getting us out of there."

Kiera chuckled. "Don't thank me yet, darling. After a few more drinks, we'll have you dancing on the tables and singing karaoke. And let's not forget, you haven't answered my question."

Chapter 34

Astronomical twilight was surreal, the time when most of the warm colours in the sky faded, to be replaced by cool purples and deeper blues. Andi walked along her beach at twilight. Pale oranges and pinks still touched the clouds, and the rocky outcrops were silhouetted against the ambient sky. The glow of the setting sun had dimmed, and a faint band of zodiacal light stretched up from the horizon, illuminating the sky.

Uncertain of what lay ahead, Andi was pensive, but she couldn't be sad. The sky was flecked with striking silvery-white clouds, and the first of the visible stars sparkled. It was tranquil, calming, and beautiful. The deep rock pools at the edge of the sand rippled with the tremor of the incoming tide. Andi crouched down beside a pool fringed with seaweed. Mesmerised by the colours—turquoise, ultramarine, and the intense blue and green—she moved her fingers through the glistening seawater.

It was early morning in Ireland, the day of Caitlin's interview. Even though it was hard to imagine that Caitlin wouldn't be totally prepared, Andi thought she'd detected the hint of nervousness in Caitlin's voice when they'd spoken an hour ago.

While Caitlin talked, Andi had closed her eyes, enjoying the cadence, the rhythmical flow of her lilting Irish accent. Her voice was like the soothing sounds of the approaching waves, gently lapping at the edges of the dark sand.

In her studio, Andi stood before her canvas with single-mindedness and pure determination. Passion flowed through her veins. She worked quickly to harness that intensity, and used her brushes and paints to communicate the fervour, yearning, and hope that was transforming her life. More than anything, she wanted to express her love through this painting. She hadn't been able to say the words out loud but couldn't stop her emotions from pouring onto the canvas. Like one of her favourite artists, Georgia O'Keeffe, she'd found she could say things with colour and shape that she could not express in words.

Andi held the tiny container of ground pigment, the precious material that she'd picked up in Lorne three months earlier. The natural lapis lazuli had a historic importance for its jewel-like brilliance and had been used by many artists over time for its intensity and lightfast properties.

Andi had purchased lapis lazuli pigment from a reliable supplier, who promised that it was a very high grade. It would be quickly absorbed into the paint medium and enhance the brushstrokes, adding a luminosity and radiance to her painting. She hoped he was right.

Brilliance was the final painting in the series, and the most significant. With this piece completed, she would have to turn her attention to the business part of preparing for the exhibition. She wasn't looking forward to that stage.

She loaded the brush with paint and worked the bristles from side to side in a gliding motion. She mixed in a touch of white so the colour maintained its radiant purity and chromatic strength, even in the dark shades. Andi combined the pure lapis pigment with deep-blue paint, applying it smoothly to the canvas. She was back there, on the beach at twilight, immersed in the pool of seawater and its intense colour and energy.

This painting was for Caitlin. A reflection of her brilliance, her sparkle, and the light she'd brought into Andi's life.

When Andi's phone rang, she'd immediately thought of Caitlin, but quickly dismissed the idea; it would be two in the morning in Ireland. Instead, she was surprised to hear from Caitlin's assistant.

"Hi, Andi. This is Kim Jones. I met you at Caitie's office in Kew a while back."

"Hi, Kim. Of course, I remember you."

"So, you're probably wondering why I'm calling? I hope I haven't got you at the wrong time?" Kim asked.

"It's all good. You're a pleasant distraction. I'm sitting at my desk, thinking about all the things I have to do this week, and I don't know where to start."

Kim chuckled. "Ah-ha, I am ringing at the right time. With Caitlin away, Isabella and I decided that you may need some help." She paused. "Now, I can come down with the work van any day this week and help you transport the paintings to the Watershed. What day would suit you, Andi?"

"I was going to hire a van, Kim. How did you even know?"

"Well, a little Irish birdie whispered to me that you might need help in this particular area."

"Little birdie?" Andi smiled to herself.

"That's right, she did. Is there anything else you'd like me to do, because I'm yours for an entire day."

The friendly, flirtatious sound in Kim's voice made Andi grin. "Thank you, that's so kind of you to offer. All the paintings are ready. The smaller works are back from the framers, and Anthony Broadhurst has arranged to receive the entire collection early this week." Andi had a sudden thought. "While you're here, it would be great if you could check the hanging fixtures on a couple of the heavier paintings. I'm just not sure if they are adequate."

Andi was relieved. Isabella and Kim's offer was most generous, and with it, some of her tension eased.

"Oh, very good point," Kim agreed. "We can't have them falling off the wall, can we? I'll make sure my toolbox is in the van. How about this Tuesday morning? I can be at yours by nine thirty?"

Andi glanced at her calendar. "That would be fantastic. I will need to double-check with Anthony, but if I get the go-ahead, I'll text you."

"I'm writing it in my diary right this very minute. I'll make a note to toss two painting crates into the van, then we'll be sure to get those precious paintings of yours to the gallery, safe and sound."

"Okay, wonderful. Let me send you the directions. Thank you so much, Kim. I'll make sure I have coffee and breakfast ready for you when you arrive."

"I'd never say no to coffee, but don't trouble over the food. Sharon never lets me leave the house without eating breakfast."

"Okay, coffee it is."

"We're missing our Caitie and her Irish ways here. She's a bright spark in our day." Kim gave a discreet cough. "Although, I am getting some work done for a change—without the distraction."

"Distraction?"

Kim sounded amused. "Oh, she's a hell of a distraction, as you'd know, Andi. I caught her up a ladder the other day—"

"What, is she not allowed to climb a ladder?" Andi asked.

"Ah, not if it's to steal my toolbox."

They continued their playful exchange. Andi now understood a little more of the camaraderie that Caitlin and Kim so obviously shared.

Caitlin climbed the cherry wood staircase and placed her suitcase on the luggage bench. She was delighted that Mrs O'Brien had already turned down the bed and prepared the room for Caitlin's overnight stay. Downstairs, the antique wood stove was alight, and the house was toasty warm. A fresh loaf of soda bread, a platter of cheese, and a bowl of fruit sat on the kitchen bench near a small blue vase of wildflowers.

The 1890's white-painted, stone-faced house, set in tranquil woodland, overlooked the dramatic coastline, with a gently sloped, sandy beach a short walk away. The house was a mere fifteen minutes drive from the town. Kinsale was a mecca for sailing and water sports during the summer months.

Caitlin planned to avoid Kinsale's galleries, craft shops, and restaurants on this visit. She looked forward to some quiet solitude to process everything that had happened over the last few months.

A light sea mist was moving into shore. Caitlin reached for her Cotswold coat and pulled it on over her grey turtleneck jumper and wool trousers. The coat's heavy lining and hood would keep her dry as she walked the rolling green hills behind the property.

The letter arrived yesterday, by special delivery, to her parents' home. Caitlin read and re-read the few lines that had the power to make her dreams come true and, depending on her decision, change her life forever.

It is with pleasure that we confirm, Doctor Caitlin Isabella Quinn… the tenured faculty position, Associate Professor of Art History…

Caitlin clambered down to the shore and surveyed the sheltered cove, bordered by a curved, pink granite rockshelf. The sea shimmered in the last of the evening light, the closing of the day in Kinsale—the beginning of *Andi's* day in Hakea. So true, that day and night meet transiently at twilight and dawn. Caitlin felt connected to Andi, even though they were thousands of physical miles apart. She imagined standing in this spot with her.

As a child, Caitlin had explored secret caves that were exposed by low tides. She'd swum in the icy blue water, collected seashells, and searched for treasures in the rockpools. This was a magical place, and sharing it with the woman she loved would be perfect. *Someday.*

Caitlin reached into her trouser pocket for the folded piece of paper—Andi's email. Although she had read it earlier, now in this enchanted place, she allowed herself to re-read the last part of the email that had moved her to tears.

Through colour and brushstroke, I paint the emotions that lie within my heart. Paint is the sensuous medium I use to craft your elements—luscious, extravagant, unpretentious, delicate, and tender. Your emotional depth applied in fervent marks. Gestures made to the rhythms of the earth, the ocean tide, patterns in the sand, and rays of light.
My passion is a soft sable brush dipped in rich crimson. I celebrate surface texture, flirt with hues, and explore your beauty in vibrant, cascading washes.
I am seduced into your landscape through the layers of ethereal hues and explosions of colour. Dazzled by your brilliance. Andi XX.

The beauty of Andi's prose astonished Caitlin. She realised that even though those *three words* were not put in black and white, it was clear that *this* was her declaration of love. A strong gust of wind threatened to tear the piece of paper from her hands, and Caitlin held on firmly. She replaced the note safely into her pocket and headed back towards the house—her fingers wrapped tightly around the page.

Chapter 35

It was a balmy summer evening, and the cafés, restaurants, and bars around the Watershed Gallery buzzed with activity. Andi paced the terrace overlooking Corio Bay, with yachts, fishing boats, and cruisers bobbing around in the calm water. Her palms were clammy. She glanced at her watch for the hundredth time.

Although everything was as ready as it could be, it didn't stop the churning in her stomach. Kim had been absolutely fantastic, helping her transport the paintings. She'd been a huge morale booster, her encouragement and cheerfulness giving Andi a much-needed shot of confidence.

Anthony's staff worked tirelessly, and in two days, they'd installed the exhibition, fixed the labels, and finalised the lighting. The catalogues were amazing, thanks to Bailey Graphics.

The Watershed's catering staff stood at attention, ready to greet the guests.

Luc had arrived at the studio in the early afternoon and insisted on driving Andi to the gallery.

"Crikey," he'd exclaimed when he saw the billboard above the entrance. He read aloud,

"Where The Light Plays—A Solo Exhibition by Andréa Rey, December 13 - January 23."

Luc placed his arm around her shoulders. "I'm so happy for you, Sis. This is absolutely *awesome.* We are all so proud of you."

"Thanks, Luc."

Although her work had been part of group shows before, this was Andi's first solo exhibition, and she'd worked damn hard to make it possible.

"Here, darling. Maybe this will help." Anthony's partner, Todd, placed a champagne flute in Andi's hand. "Liquid courage," he grinned. "How are you doing?"

She greeted Todd with a smile. "I'd be lying if I said I wasn't nervous." Andi lifted the glass to her lips and took a long swallow. "Thanks for this."

Todd grabbed her free hand and gently twirled her around in a circle. He gave a long, slow whistle of appreciation. "You look fabulous. I'm a bit envious of these." He pointed to Andi's grey-cropped, linen, pinstripe trousers. "Mind you, I haven't the curves to carry that vaguely butch, unmistakably femme thing you're able to pull off." He raised his eyebrows in mock disgust.

Andi pulled nervously at her collar. She hoped her outfit was formal enough for the occasion. She'd chosen a classic fitted white shirt and a long-sleeved short jacket with an asymmetric hemline and a single fastening press-stud—a feminine nod to the latest tailored trend. Sleek, minimalist, and aesthetic.

"Yep, you really have that fifties-chic-style thing happening and with *these* boots, you are ready to kick arse." Todd gestured to Andi's comfortably worn-in ankle boots with pointed toes and two silver buckles.

"So, what do you say? Let's not keep your fans waiting any longer." He gave her a quick, reassuring hug. "Your family's just arrived, and I spotted Ellie with them. The reporter from *Geelong Arts*, Jason Travis, wants to grab a few photographs and a quick interview before everyone else gets here."

Andi pulled her hands out of her pockets, ran them through her hair, and reluctantly followed Todd. Maybe, if she clicked the heels of her boots together three times, she'd end up in Oz, or even better—home.

She scanned the room for Caitlin and frowned when she didn't see her. Todd hadn't mentioned seeing Caitlin either. When would she get there? Would she get there at all?

At the far end of the gallery, Ana and her parents chatted with Anthony. He had one hand on her mother's forearm and rubbed his bottom lip to give emphasis to his story. Lina looked elegant in a simple black dress and heels, an outfit she reserved for special occasions. Her family seemed remarkably unfazed by the unfamiliar surroundings. Andi grinned and thought how well they presented as a group.

They stood in front of one of Andi's favourites, *Sun Rays.* She'd used thin washes of muted tones under thicker, shorter strokes of solid colour. The canvas portrayed a grey morning sky over a field of sunflowers in full bloom, illuminated by the orange sun rising over the family farm.

Andi walked the perimeter of the room. Even though the outside of the building curved gently like a ship's hull, the inside space was rectangular. Using a series of floating walls, Andi and the exhibition team had determined how viewers would enter the space and in what order they would view the paintings. Adorning the wall directly opposite the entrance was *Come to Light*, loaned by the Black-Tern Gallery. The thirty-four other works were displayed so visitors could experience different stages in light reaction during the course of a day, from sunrise to sunset, and in distinct climatic conditions. Chosen to create visual syncopation, some paintings were grouped together, while some were displayed singly.

A light tap to the shoulder caught her attention, and she turned to see who it was. Mazy, from Bailey Graphics, took Andi's hand and gushed, "Andi, I had no idea. You are so talented. It makes sense. You have an incredible mastery of colour, evident in your designs, and I've always been envious of that."

"That's kind of you, Maz." She allowed herself to be pulled into the circle of work colleagues. "I'm glad you could all be here tonight. It means a lot." She gestured to the refreshment table, staffed by two attentive waiters. "Make sure you grab some champagne and yummy food."

Five minutes later, Andi was whisked away by Anthony, who insisted on introducing her to some of the crème-de-la-crème of Geelong's business owners and art collectors before leading her to the magazine reporter for her short interview.

"You lead the viewer's eyes into the landscape. It's clear these works are quite intimate," said the reporter.

"Yes, some of them are," Andi replied. She looked down at her feet and thought of Caitlin. "It has been an incredible journey and a significant challenge." She thanked him, shook his hand, and was grateful when he took his leave.

As the gallery filled, Andi felt an enormous sense of relief. Comments were positive and flattering. She was in a surreal space. All the excitement and attention made her light-headed. It was like an out-of-body experience.

"Finally, the star of the show. How are you doing? It's amazing seeing your works displayed professionally," Ellie said, as she pulled her into a quick hug.

"Thanks, Ell. Anthony's staff did a great job."

"Definitely. Have you noticed that there are red dots on over half the paintings," she whispered in Andi's ear. "You must be ecstatic." Ellie stepped back as two unknown guests approached them and stood quietly beside Andi. "I think that's my cue. I'll catch up with you soon." Ellie waved and headed towards Ana and the children.

Andi swallowed the lump in her throat and smiled. The fashionably chic pair introduced themselves as Anthony's friends from Sydney—Catherine and Alister Paulson. They congratulated Andi on the exhibition. "*Brilliance* drew our eye as soon as we walked in. Catherine was immediately captivated," said Alister. "We were devastated to know it is not for sale."

"Ah, but..." Catherine sighed. "I also have my eye on *Nocturne.*"

Catherine gestured towards the painting, one of Andi's moodier pieces, that depicted Gull Rock—the large weathered limestone formation on Hakea Beach—veiled in moonlight.

"We were very fortunate to spend a weekend near Hakea last year, and we strolled along the beach at night. You've captured that haunting, surreal atmosphere just like I remember." She smiled. "Your painting is exquisite, Andi."

Andi felt the colour rise in her cheeks. "Thank you. I'm glad you like it."

"Catherine, in saying that, darling, it seems you've made up your mind. I think it's time to secure that piece of magic for ourselves," Alister said. They expressed their gratitude and hastened away to finalise their purchase.

It was unreal to step back and observe how people reacted to her work. While she experienced a sense of satisfaction, it was tempered by vulnerability. As if for the first time, she realised that at the end of the exhibition, her paintings would be scattered, travelling to new homes, with owners who liked them enough to spend a substantial amount of money to secure them.

The clacking of shoes on the wooden floorboards, the hum of voices, the tinkling of glasses, and the strains of classical music quieted to a hush, and Andi instinctively knew *Caitlin* had arrived. She bit her lip, and her heart pounded. She gathered courage, and when she turned around, her gaze fell upon Caitlin. The force of her longing left her breathless.

Caitlin stared at *Brilliance* with her head tilted to one side. She withdrew a single sheet of paper from her purse and unfolded it.

Bewitched, Andi was unable to move. Caitlin's figure-hugging, deep-indigo cocktail dress showed off her gorgeous body. Its simple lines draped softly over her thighs and ended a few centimetres above her knees. The scooped bodice showed off her graceful neck and just enough cleavage to make Andi inhale sharply.

Caitlin's face was serene as she returned the piece of paper to her purse and continued to study the painting. A stylishly dressed woman, accompanied by an equally striking gentleman, approached Caitlin and chatted with her in a familiar way.

Then, as if drawn towards Andi's gaze, Caitlin turned, and their eyes met for the first time in nearly three long weeks.

Caitlin could barely stand upright when Andi whispered in her ear, "You look amazing, and even though you are absolutely stunning in this dress, I can't wait to help you *out* of it." Her knees grew weak from the warmth of Andi's fingers pressed lightly into the small of her back.

Her father cleared his throat loudly.

As Andi stepped back, Caitlin reached for her arm and secured it around her waist. Caitlin glanced from her father to Andi.

Andi's face was flushed, she looked bewildered. "Caitlin, um," she said quietly.

"Andi, I'd like to introduce you to Patrick and Orla Quinn, my parents," Caitlin said.

Andi's body tensed, and she attempted to pull away.

Caitlin placed her hand on Andi's to, again, anchor it firmly to her waist. "Ma, Da, this is Andréa Rey."

"It's a delight to meet you, Andréa, and to be part of your special day." Orla stepped forward to shake Andi's hand, and Caitlin reluctantly relinquished her hold.

Caitlin was amused when her mother continued to hold onto Andi's hand and gazed at her intently.

Patrick Quinn came forward and offered his hand.

Andi looked flustered and gazed at Caitlin's parents.

"Caitlin didn't prepare us for such a magnificent show. This is a very impressive exhibition. You are a talented and beautiful young woman," Patrick said.

"Thank you so much, Mr. Quinn," Andi stammered. "This is a huge surprise."

"Please, call me Patrick." He grinned and winked at Caitlin over Andi's shoulder. "It is now clear to me why Caitlin is so smitten."

Caitlin rolled her eyes and shook her head. Her father, the ever-charming English professor, was correct. Caitlin was definitely smitten.

Andi looked from Orla to Patrick, from Patrick to Orla, and from Orla to Caitlin. "I had no idea. This is a huge surprise," she said. "Did I say that already? I'm so happy to meet you both. I can see where Caitlin gets her incredible—"

"Charm?" Caitlin squeezed Andi's hand.

"Err, I was going to say *good looks,* but yes, that too; it definitely runs in the family," said Andi sweetly.

"Thank you, Andi, but I've just had the pleasure of meeting your family, and I have to return the compliment," Orla said. Her blue-grey eyes sparkled.

Isabella and Kim approached them. Isabella's arm was linked through Kim's, and they looked like a pair of naughty schoolgirls.

Isabella surveyed the small gathering. "What a lovely family group," she said. She hugged Andi tightly and kissed her on both cheeks. "Congratulations on the first of what will be, I am sure, many successful shows. Well done, darling."

"Congratulations, Andi. What a fabulous exhibition." Kim blushed. "Absolutely amazing."

"Thanks, Kim." Andi grinned.

Kim turned her attention to Caitlin and her parents. "Wasn't this a tremendous surprise? You must be over the moon—"

Caitlin raised her eyebrows to get Kim's attention. Kim hesitated, turned to Andi, and said, "I mean, you must be over the moon to meet Caitie's parents."

Andi gave Caitlin a bemused smile. "Oh. I am very surprised."

Caitlin reached for Andi's hand, and laced their fingers together. She fixed a guilty smile towards Kim and her family. "I wonder if you'd excuse us for just a few minutes, please?" She winked at Kim, whose already pink face grew an even brighter shade of red. "Andi and I have a few matters to discuss."

Andi shrugged shyly and allowed Caitlin to drag her away through the side exit and into the darkness along the waterfront. Caitlin tugged Andi into her arms and pressed her back against the wooden handrail that ran along the pier.

Andi buried her face in Caitlin's shoulder, and as her lips caressed her skin, they both sighed.

"Your parents?" Andi mumbled. "I mean, you never mentioned it. Did you tell me they were visiting Australia?"

"It was a last-minute decision. They wanted to spend Christmas with Isabella, among other things," Caitlin said.

Andi ran her tongue over her lower lip nervously.

Caitlin tightened her embrace around Andi and caressed the nape of her neck with her fingertips. "I've missed you. I really have to kiss you. Now."

"I've missed you too," Andi whispered.

"You feel amazing… You are amazing. I can't believe we have to wait. Do we?" Caitlin grazed her teeth along Andi's ear, then moved her mouth to Andi's lips and kissed her hungrily. She ran her hands along Andi's waist and down over the fitted pinstriped trousers, enjoying the closeness and overwhelming sensation of their bodies pressed together.

Caitlin leaned back to look into Andi's eyes. "The exhibition is everything and even more than I thought it would be. Your paintings are so incredibly passionate and powerful. You take my breath away." She nibbled Andi's ear. "Am I rambling? *Brilliance* is… I'm speechless for how your words and your painting affect me," whispered Caitlin. "Thank you for that email."

"I was afraid you wouldn't come back. I needed you to know how I feel." She took a deep breath and lowered her head. "I love you, Caitlin."

Caitlin lifted Andi's chin with one finger. "I love you too, baby." She looked into her eyes. "I *did* have a return ticket."

"Until June," Andi murmured.

Caitlin shivered, even though Andi's hands stroked her skin and left a trail of fire wherever they touched. "I need to ask you something—"

"I need to tell you something," Andi said in the same moment.

At the sound of a door shutting with a loud thud, Caitlin groaned, and they drew apart.

Ellie walked towards them. "Here you are. We've been looking for both of you. I thought you may have run off together or snuck into one of the storerooms." Her eyes sparkled with mischief in the darkness.

"Believe me, if I had a choice, we'd be there…" Andi sighed.

"Down, tiger, plenty of time for that later." Ellie grinned. "I am sorry to interrupt you, but it's speech time." She bowed towards the entrance. "Anthony is ready and waiting."

As they moved into the glow of the security light, Ellie cleared her throat and tugged the corner of Andi's shirt where it had come loose from her trousers.

"You may want to tidy up a bit," Ellie suggested. "How do you think you'll last? You still have speeches and dinner at Tides to get through."

"We'll be okay. Andi will be *okay*. This is her big night," Caitlin said and tightened her arm around Andi's shoulder.

Andi straightened her dishevelled clothes, looked up helplessly at Caitlin, attempted to rearrange her hair, and grabbed Caitlin's hand. "Let's do it," she said.

After Anthony's welcoming toast, the guests sipped vintage champagne. The private dining room at Tides Restaurant, perched at the end of the pier on Eastern Beach, gave the impression of being at sea. They enjoyed the moonlit views over the waterfront. The table settings of silver cutlery and crisp, white linen were impressive and suitably elegant for the post exhibition gathering.

Andi sat at one end of the table, with Caitlin on one side and Ellie on the other. Caitlin's hand under the tablecloth rested on her knee, occasionally moving against the taut material of her trousers. She gasped when Caitlin's fingertips pressed lightly along the inner seam.

"Did you say something?" Ellie asked.

Andi loosened the top button of her shirt and moved uncomfortably in the chair. She reached for Caitlin's hand and held it still.

"No," she squeaked. "The champagne went down the wrong way." She glanced at Caitlin, who ignored her and continued to innocently chat to Ana and Mick.

"How did you persuade Mia to leave with her brother?" Caitlin asked.

"Oh, it wasn't easy." Ana smiled, and pursed her lips. "She didn't want to leave her Aunty Andi. We promised if she went with Manny to our friends' place tonight, we'd take her to the zoo in the school holidays."

"So bribery does work." Caitlin laughed and arched an eyebrow.

"As a last resort, every time." Mick grinned. He nodded to Andi. "It's not surprising, when you painted the murals on the potting shed, that you would one day turn it into a successful career." He lifted his glass and said, "Congratulations, Andi."

"I love those murals of farm animals and so do the children," Ana said. "This exhibition is a huge achievement. Anthony mentioned that two-thirds of the artwork has already sold."

"Thanks, Ana. It's been quite a day." Andi stared at Caitlin. "One full of surprises. Who would have thought that I'd meet Caitlin's parents today?"

"Who would have thought?" Caitlin smirked.

"It's wonderful that your parents could travel over with you," Ana said.

"Yes, yes it is. My parents love Australia, and this was an excellent opportunity to visit Isabella and for us to spend Christmas together."

Andi waited for more information, but Caitlin was silent on the subject.

After finishing her meal, Andi sat back in the plush chair and listened to snippets of conversation from around the table. It had been a big day, emotionally and physically, but she was keyed up and restless.

Caitlin put down her fork and squeezed her hand. "You must be tired?"

Andi shook her head. "It may take awhile for me to wind down tonight. I am a little wired."

"Don't you worry. Once I get you to myself… I have a feeling I can take care of that. I know just how to help you unwind." Caitlin wiggled her eyebrows, making Andi squirm in her chair.

"You *do* know that Isabella asked Mum and Dad to stay overnight at Kinsale, don't you?"

Caitlin nodded. "Yes, it's all been arranged. Isabella, Ma and Da, and your parents are staying at Kinsale for the night." She leaned in to whisper in Andi's ear. "That way, I can have you all to myself at your place."

"Well, that's good planning. How did you get everyone to agree to that?"

"I told them we needed to talk."

"To talk?" Andi giggled. "Seriously? I can think of a lot of other things I'd rather do to you… I mean with you." Andi leaned closer to Caitlin. "You keep saying that. Do you want to talk now?"

"Not now. Let's wait till we're alone."

"You've been touching me under the table all night. All I want to do is get you home. You look so incredibly sexy in that dress. But I mean it. I *really* want you out of it."

Caitlin caught her breath, as Andi slid her hand under the hem.

Chapter 36

The sensation of Andi's hand on her thigh drove Caitlin to distraction. Slow, circular, torturous movements. The half-hour drive to Hakea seemed to take forever. Caitlin didn't want a speeding ticket, but the Roadster raced along the highway, almost by itself. At least, that was her excuse.

Stopped at a red light, Andi traced her fingers lightly over her bare skin, just above her hemline.

"Driving is hard enough, Andi. If you do that when we're moving, I'm going to send us right off the road," Caitlin pleaded.

"Sorry," Andi said. She withdrew her hand and placed it in her lap. "What did you want to talk to me about?"

"Ah, not while I'm driving." Caitlin shook her head as she reached across for her hand, kissed the inside of Andi's wrist, and put it back on her knee. She held it firmly in place. "You can leave it here, but you have to keep still." When she told Andi her news, she wanted to look her in the eyes and see her reaction. As the lights changed to green, Caitlin gunned the engine, but it wasn't long before Andi caressed her thigh with her thumb once again. "Keep still," she said.

Andi folded her hands tightly across her chest. "It is an automatic reaction. I can't help myself." She sighed. "There's a short cut coming up. Take the next turn left, and I'll keep a watch out for kangaroos."

"Please do that. You need a distraction. I don't." Caitlin steered the Roadster onto the side road and switched to high beam.

"Kangaroos *shouldn't* be on the road now. It's worse at dusk, but we still need to be careful," Andi said, peering into the night. "We'll be home in about ten minutes."

"Good."

The moment Caitlin pulled to a stop in her driveway, Andi raced around to the driver's side to open the door. She tapped a finger on the roof of the car.

Caitlin grabbed items from the back seat and removed the key from the ignition. As she stepped out of the car, Andi grabbed her wrist and dragged her up the stairs. With her free hand, she hastily unlocked the front door.

"Where's Koda? I can hear her," Caitlin said. There was a faint meowing sound coming from the other side of the door.

"She's inside. If I'm home late, my neighbour feeds her and locks her in at dusk." She opened the door, and the beige fur ball attempted to run through Andi's legs. "No, you don't. Koda, get back inside." She gently pushed Koda indoors, without letting go of Caitlin's hand.

They entered the studio, and the door slammed behind them. Andi reached for the light switch. Caitlin stood behind her and tugged at the tail of her jacket. The December night was warm and, through the open windows, the fragrance of lemon-scented gum filled the air.

"That perfume is intoxicating." Caitlin inhaled deeply and drew her close. "And so are you. My head is spinning, and my heart is racing." Caitlin pressed her breasts hard against Andi's back.

"It's warm in here." Andi turned in the circle of Caitlin's arms.

With her thumb, Caitlin wiped the moisture that glistened on Andi's forehead. "There are too many layers of clothes between you and me. I need your skin on mine," Caitlin murmured.

She pushed Andi's jacket off her shoulders and onto the back of the nearest chair. Caitlin reached for the pearl buttons and steadily worked her way down—deftly unbuttoning the white shirt to reveal Andi's golden skin.

Caitlin stilled as Andi's gaze—molten brown and filled with longing—swept over her body. She pressed her mouth gently into Caitlin's neck and slid her knowing hands over Caitlin's bare shoulders and under her hair.

"If we have things to talk about, Caitlin, I'm not sure *this* is the way to go about it." Andi moved her hands smoothly down the curve of her back until they rested on her hips. "And *you're* driving me crazy." Andi slid her palms under the dress, her fingertips grazing the silky material underneath.

"Oh no you don't." Caitlin pushed Andi's shirt off her shoulders and held her in place with the tightly stretched fabric. Andi was defenceless against Caitlin's lips. "We'll have time later." Caitlin trailed her tongue from Andi's neck to her ear. "Still want to talk?" she teased.

Caitlin pulled Andi's shirt from her body, followed by her bra. They both landed in a heap on the floor. She wound her fingers through Andi's hair, pulled her close, and kissed her. It was a kiss of want and surrender. She was lost in the silken feel of Andi's tongue, its sensual caress. Caitlin trembled, her entire body begging for more contact.

Andi settled her thigh between Caitlin's legs and rocked gently against her. Her breasts and midriff slid against the lustrous, indigo fabric of her dress. She moaned.

Andi's expression was inviting. Her smile curved seductively. "It's time you lost the dress."

Andi awoke to the high-pitched whistle of the kettle coming to the boil and an empty space in the bed. She yawned and stretched her arms above her head. "A cup of tea would be nice."

Right on cue, Caitlin entered her bedroom, balancing two teacups and a plate.

"Good morning. Room service…and I like the outfit," Andi said. Caitlin wore Andi's old Rip Curl T-shirt and nothing else.

"Good morning. I thought you could use some sustenance." Caitlin placed a steaming cup of tea on Andi's bedside table, along with a plate laden with toast. "How are you feeling?" Caitlin asked in a husky voice and placed a featherlight kiss against her forehead.

"Hmm." Andi stretched her body, luxuriating in the afterglow of an incredible night. She glanced over at the bedside clock. It was eight in the morning. "I am tired and a bit achy." She smiled.

Caitlin purred contentedly and climbed into bed beside Andi. "But that's not what I mean, Andi. Yesterday was a huge day for you. How do you feel?"

"Oh yeah, I had to make a speech in front of a hundred people. It was my worst nightmare."

Caitlin turned to her. "You did really well. I'm so impressed." She leaned forward and kissed Andi lightly on the lips. "The fact that the regional gallery has acquired one of your paintings for its permanent collection is a great honour. You should be proud of yourself."

"Let's just wait to see the newspaper reviews. It might be a different story then."

"Andi." Caitlin grabbed her pillow and bopped Andi over the head with it. "You're an eejit. Stop being daft. The exhibition was a sellout." She threatened Andi with the pillow raised above her head. "So, are you going to share the toast and honey?"

"Three weeks away, and you've come back sounding even more Irish." Andi nudged Caitlin with her foot. She felt a sudden stab of pain and winced. "Ouch." She pulled back the cotton sheet and rubbed the scar just above her knee. "Anyway, we have three weeks to make up for."

Caitlin traced the slightly raised, pink scar. "Is this still tender?"

"No, not really. It just needs a bit longer for the tissue to heal. I'll probably always have a small scar to remind me to be more careful."

Caitlin trailed her fingers playfully along Andi's shoulders. "I'm glad the bruises have disappeared. I'd hate anything else to mark this perfectly gorgeous skin."

Caitlin gently bit and sucked on the tender flesh of her neck, and Andi nearly choked on her toast. Caitlin laughed wickedly. "Unless it's from me. Consider yourself marked." She rested her head on Andi's stomach.

"Marked? Is that some kind of ancient Irish thing?" Andi asked.

Caitlin nibbled her flesh and moved down the bed. "Not that I can recall. But hey, let's call it a new, *Caitlin* thing."

"You have the endurance of a marathon runner. You've exhausted me. Considering you are the older—"

Caitlin silenced Andi with her hand over her mouth. She leaned up on her elbow. "Cheeky brat. I have plenty of stamina. Get used to it, darling, I have every intention of keeping *you* active."

"Is that a challenge? I love a challenge. I'm up for it." Andi grabbed Caitlin's hand. "Caitlin?"

"Hmm?" Caitlin pulled herself back up the bed and sat beside her.

"When you have to return home to Ireland in June—"

Caitlin interrupted, "Andi, I wanted to ask you—"

Andi held up her hand. "I need to say this, please?"

Caitlin clenched the sheet and waited for Andi to continue.

"I do love you, Caitlin," she said. "You make me feel positive and strong and that *anything* is possible. You make me want to experience everything—new places, new cultures." She leaned over and wiped the tear that slid down Caitlin's face. "I can paint anywhere. I know how important reaching this point in your career is to you, Professor Quinn." Andi swallowed. She hoped she wasn't making an entire fool of herself.

Caitlin shook her head. Tears continued to run down her face, and she wiped them with the corner of the sheet. "No, I mean yes. I love you too."

Andi was confused. "Then why can't I?"

Caitlin placed a finger under her chin and tilted her head until their eyes met. "You can, but you don't have to, Andi. I'm not accepting the promotion."

Andi was sure she'd misheard. "I don't understand. This is what you want, isn't it? What about your parents? They must be so proud of you." It suddenly dawned on Andi what Caitlin was saying. She opened her mouth and then closed it again.

Caitlin smiled. "That's why they're here, Andi. They wanted to meet *you*. I've discussed everything with them, and they support my decision."

"What decision?"

"My decision to stay in Australia."

Andi was speechless.

Caitlin took her hand, and stroked her fingers with her thumb. "I loved my job at UCC, but when I was back home, I realised I've changed. I want something different now. My involvement with Isabella and the gallery has been a tremendous challenge for me. I love it, and I'm passionate about making it a success. This is my future, Andi. I hope you'll be a part of it." She held Andi's gaze. "Part of my future."

Andi nodded slowly, still finding it hard to believe.

Caitlin prodded her in the ribs. "Is this okay, Andi? You're not going to be the professor's wife after all."

She giggled. "So, you'll be the artist's muse then?" She stared at Caitlin. "I thought yesterday was the biggest day of my life, but you've totally blown me away." Andi couldn't stop grinning. "Are you really staying?" She snuggled into Caitlin's arms. "It's still early, and I'm totally exhausted. I must be dreaming. Let me get this right. You actually are staying?" She smothered a yawn.

"Have you got a problem with that?"

Andi rolled her eyes. "One day, I'll get you to answer my questions directly."

"Really?"

"If I'm lucky, yeah." Andi yawned. "I'm so happy, and I'm so tired."

Caitlin took Andi's face in her hands and kissed her slowly. They settled into each other's arms and, eventually, drifted into a peaceful sleep.

Chapter 37

Caitlin dragged a piece of driftwood through the wet sand. In an enclosed shape of a heart, she marked out

C.Q. loves A.R. 4ever

She threw the stick aside, shielded her eyes from the sun, and watched as Andi emerged from the surf. Her skin glistened in the sunshine. Droplets of water trickled down Andi's neck and disappeared into the hollow between her breasts at the top of the orange one-piece swimsuit.

Andi stood with her hands on her hips, head tilted to one side, and gave Caitlin a puzzled look. She walked towards and then around her, following the lines Caitlin had drawn in the sand.

"Forever?" She grinned, wrapped her arms around Caitlin's waist, and pulled their bodies together.

"And beyond." Caitlin gasped as her sun-warmed body was pressed into Andi's cool wet skin.

"*Coo-ee!*" A long, high-pitched call carried through the air. Caitlin looked up towards the house, and Andi followed her gaze.

Their parents and Isabella stood in a row at the glass balustrade of Kinsale's sun deck.

"*Lunch*," shouted Caitlin's father, as he beckoned them from above.

Caitlin and Andi stood in the sand, arms around each other, and waved back.

"I guess it is time we joined them." Andi combed her fingers through her hair and then reached down to grab her towel.

"I don't think I'll ever get tired of seeing you like this."

"Hmmm?"

She took Andi's hand. "So heart-stoppingly beautiful and golden. Achingly desirable."

Caitlin sighed as they gazed into each other's eyes.

After lunch prepared by Orla, Andi sat between Isabella and Lina at the long outdoor table on the deck.

"So, Paddy, you're going to visit Emmanuel and Lina's farm," Isabella said, swatting at a flying insect. "*Dash*, it's the fly season again."

Caitlin's father pushed the thick mop of grey hair from his eyes. "To be sure. We've been invited to spend a day or two on the property. It's a grand way to learn more about the area and the agricultural methods practised here." He grinned at Lina and Emmanuel.

Orla put down her knitting, stood up, and stretched. "I'm looking forward to seeing a bit of the Victorian countryside. Navigators—what a quaint name."

"Caitlin mentioned koalas on your property, Lina. I'd love to see them for myself," Patrick said.

Orla laughed and nudged her husband. "It'll be a pleasant change, indeed, for you to have your head out of a book. Won't it, Paddy?" She raised an eyebrow. Andi inclined her head to one side and smiled discreetly behind her hand as she recognised that familiar Caitlin quirk.

"That it will, my love. That it will." Patrick nudged Orla back.

Andi had been nervous about spending time with Caitlin's parents, but they were engaging and affable, and she felt comfortable with them. Caitlin, too, appeared relaxed as she sat back and watched them entertain and charm Andi's parents.

"I don't come to Kinsale as often as I used to, but I couldn't miss your show." Isabella reached for Andi's hand and held it firmly. "I was deeply moved by the exhibition. The level of talent represented in your body of work is impressive." She sipped her tea and patted the chair beside her. "Lina, come sit. You must be very proud of your daughter."

Andi was touched by Isabella's unexpected compliments. She looked up and met Caitlin's gaze. Her mouth turned up in a knowing smile, making the heat rise in Andi's face.

"Oh, we are delighted," Lina said. "It is a joy to see Andi achieve such a wonderful response to her paintings. Andi has always loved to draw and paint. She is a great artist, just like her grandfather. We are blessed."

"Isabella, your house is, how can I say it...*maravilhoso*." Andi's father stood up and moved to lean over the balustrade to enjoy the panoramic view of the ocean and the surf beach below. He turned around to face them. "It is marvellous!"

"Thank you, Emmanuel. I've had wonderful times here, for many years, in fact." Isabella lifted her hand to shade her eyes from the bright sunlight.

Caitlin sprang to her feet and adjusted the automatic sunblind to give Isabella more shelter.

"You are a darling, Caitlin." Isabella relaxed back in her chair. "I do enjoy the tranquility and peace of my garden in Kew and my cottage filled with trinkets and treasures."

"But this place is special, no? You named it after your birthplace in Ireland," Lina said.

Isabella spread her arms wide to encompass the house and grounds of Kinsale. "Yes, this was a very special place for Maggie and me. I was born near the sea at Kinsale, and this property fed my longing and restless spirit. I will always cherish the times we shared here together and my memories of Maggie...here. Nothing will change that. Now, Kinsale is for others to enjoy." She winked at Andi. "Something tells me Caitlin will be in Hakea a lot more often."

Andi acknowledged Isabella with a smile and then turned as her mother spoke to Orla. "It is a difficult time when your child moves away. I do ask myself how I'd feel in similar circumstances."

"Yes, we will miss her terribly." Orla gazed at Caitlin with such affection that Andi let out a deep sigh.

Caitlin leaned forward and squeezed her mother's hand. "I love you, Ma," she whispered.

"All Patrick and I want is for Caitlin to be happy and settled." Orla kissed Caitlin's forehead.

Lina nodded as if she understood completely. "Yes, that is the same for us, for our children and grandchildren." She closed her eyes briefly. "It was difficult for my parents when Emmanuel and I left Portugal and settled in Australia. It was painful for us to leave our families and friends."

"It did come as a shock when Caitlin told us that she was turning down the promotion." Patrick looked affectionately at Caitlin. "But priorities change, and we understand she is passionate about her work with Isabella and the direction it is leading her. She has our blessing."

"I hope I haven't made things harder for you, Caitlin. I didn't want to unfairly influence your decision to stay in Australia," Isabella said.

Orla looked across to Andi. "I do believe she has another, very important, reason for staying, Izzy." She patted Isabella's hand. "Caitlin has always made her own decisions. Haven't you, darling?" Orla looked from her daughter to her aunt. "Anyway, dear one, you didn't tell Caitlin about your plans until *after* she'd turned down the Associate Professorship."

Andi and Caitlin barely had a moment to talk about the news Caitlin had shared with her, yesterday. Isabella planned to gift the Kew estate, the collection, *and* Bella Gallery to Caitlin. It was a huge responsibility, but Isabella had set up a trust for her and had clearly worked out the details meticulously. The trust assured that Isabella and Maggie's legacy would be fulfilled, and Caitlin would get all the support she needed.

Andi moved into the empty chair beside Caitlin, placed her hand on her knee, and gave it a gentle reassuring squeeze.

Chapter 38

Caitlin grasped her phone in one hand, swung her legs out of bed, and pulled a T-shirt over her head. She lowered her gaze to the caller ID. "Is that you, Kiera?" she asked quietly.

"Good morning, Caitlin. I mean good evening to you. Why are you whispering? Did I get you at a bad time? What time is it?"

"Er, seven in the evening." She gently closed the bedroom door behind her and climbed the stairs to the living room. "Hi, Kiera." She glanced at her reflection in the balcony window and threw herself into an armchair. "Sorry about that. I didn't want to wake Andi."

"You were in bed that early?" After a few seconds, Kiera chuckled and said, "Ahh. Say no more."

"It's been a huge few days. We've only been able to snatch a couple of hours alone here and there," Caitlin said. "Andi's asleep."

"To be sure, Caitlin. I received your text about Andi's show. I'm so happy it was a success."

"It was, Kiera. In fact, it was an overwhelming success. I'm immensely proud of her."

"That is so sweet, girl. I'm sure you are."

Caitlin stared out at the early evening light, across the dark, blue ocean. "So what has *you* up so early?"

"You know me. I'm an early riser. Em and I are heading to London. Spending Christmas with her family and a week visiting friends. I just wanted to wish you and Andi the best for the holiday season, and I have some exciting news."

Caitlin crossed her fingers. "Did you get it?"

"Yes," Kiera said. "My grant was approved, and I will be attending the conference in Queensland this coming July."

"That's fantastic, Kiera."

"Can you handle a couple of visitors for a week or so?" She laughed. "That way we get to meet your girl and see where you'll be living for the near future, at least."

"Yes," Caitlin said. "Definitely."

She'd agonised about telling Kiera about her permanent move to Australia. At first, and understandably, her friend was shocked and saddened by the news. They'd talked for hours and finally Kiera had said, "You've obviously found your missing link. As they say, sometimes in the waves of change, we find our true direction." Kiera had promised Caitlin she would visit her in Australia. Caitlin was thrilled she was going to see Kiera in July.

She'd just ended the call and put her phone down when Andi called out to Caitlin and walked towards her, dishevelled and adorable in shorts and a tank top. She blinked at Caitlin in confusion, rubbed her eyes, and smiled.

"I couldn't find you." Andi arched her back, rolled her head from side to side, and stifled a yawn.

Caitlin beckoned Andi over and pulled her onto her lap. "I was on the phone. I didn't want to wake you."

"Everything okay?" Andi wrapped her hands around Caitlin's neck.

Caitlin nodded, placed her hands lightly on Andi's shoulders, and stroked the silk of her singlet. "Everything's perfect."

"Perfect?" Andi grinned.

"Yeah, perfect." Caitlin tugged at Andi's top. "So, did you get enough sleep? Are you rested enough?"

"I am. I love going to sleep with you."

"Me too. I love going to sleep with you, waking up with you, feeling you close to me," Caitlin said. Loving Andi made her happy. She was exhilarated and contented at the same time. "I love you, Andi." She pulled Andi closer. They kissed deeply, and Caitlin was propelled into a rolling wave of emotion.

"Your parents are cool. I really enjoyed spending time with them. They seemed genuinely interested in my art and asked a lot of questions," Andi said. "It was crazy having both sets of parents here at the same time." She paused at the top of the stairs before she followed Caitlin.

"Beyond belief. But it was incredible, wasn't it?" They reached the entrance of Caitlin's bedroom, and she stepped aside to let Andi through. "Ma and Da are looking forward to visiting Navigators." She raised her eyebrows. "I would like to be a fly on the wall for that event. It will do my parents a world of good to spend time on the farm after swanning about at the writer's festival in Daylesford."

"Uh-huh." Andi was distracted by the sensation of Caitlin's lips on her neck.

"I just don't seem to be able to get enough of you," Caitlin whispered and swiftly pulled Andi's shirt over her head. She placed her hands to the top of Andi's shorts, pushed them down, and tugged them away. "In my bed, on the couch, in the chair, or the cantilevered shower… I want you everywhere." Caitlin trailed her fingers down Andi's neck and shoulder. She stopped, quickly pulled her T-shirt over her head and threw it across the room before lowering her mouth to Andi's breast.

Andi gasped. "I can feel you in my heart, on my skin, inside me…"

Caitlin exhaled, pushed Andi onto the bed, and they landed on the mattress with a gentle thud. The delicious warmth of Caitlin's body, pressed against her, was almost too much to bear.

"Let me see how long I can keep you feeling that way."

Their legs tangled together, and she tightened her grip around Caitlin's shoulders as her body responded powerfully.

Caitlin hugged the light sweater close to her body. Just before ten, at Andi's insistence, they'd strolled down to the beach. A patch of sea mist hung around the slight hollow where the creek meandered gently until it met the sand. There was a chill in the air, and the first stars of the night were just visible in a clear, moonless sky.

She threaded her arm around Andi's waist, inhaled tangy salt air, and listened to waves breaking gently onto the shore. A light breeze tickled the back of her neck as she gathered Andi close against her side.

"It'll be totally dark soon. *Why* are we here? Was there something wrong with the comfort of my bed?" Caitlin asked.

"It's a beautiful night for a walk on the beach." She leaned against Caitlin and whispered in her ear, "Where's your sense of adventure?" She tossed the torch she'd carried and caught it in midair.

Caitlin had to agree. It was a grand night to be out under the stars. There was a sense of promise in the air. Whenever she looked at Andi, she was overcome with gratitude, desire, and protectiveness. This was what she wanted… Andi in her life. Andi in her future.

"Hey, Caitlin?"

"Hmm?" Caitlin swallowed the sudden lump in her throat.

"You okay? You have a faraway look in your eyes."

"Just thinking," she said. "I'm right here, Andi." Caitlin squeezed her waist. "Does Koda like car travel?"

Andi looked at her with amused interest.

"You'll want her with you wherever you are, won't you?" Caitlin asked.

Andi stopped and turned to look at her fully. "What are you saying?"

Caitlin tucked her arms to her sides and curled her bare toes into the sand. "I'd like for us to spend as much time together as possible. I know it will take some negotiating. I don't mind if we're at your place, or Kinsale… We're spoiled for choice." She rambled. "The apartment in Kew is big enough for us all, and you could have your own studio—"

"Shhh," Andi whispered. She caressed Caitlin's face with her fingers and kissed the corner of her mouth. "Yes."

"Yes?"

Andi kissed her again, this time on her lips. "Yes. Just, yes. You do realise that Koda will run riot searching for mice. Are you sure you'll cope?"

"There hasn't been a house cat at the estate since Maggie's beloved Greyson passed away. The mouse population needs to be relocated." She kissed the top of Andi's hair. "And yes, I'll cope."

"There is a lot to think about, isn't there?"

Caitlin stared up at the sky. "There is, but it's exciting, because we're planning our future together, wherever it is."

Andi threw the blanket she'd been carrying onto the rockshelf beside a shallow pool, pulling Caitlin down to sit beside her.

"Why are we here, again?" Caitlin asked and shifted her body into a better position on the hard rock ledge.

Andi grinned. "We're here because you asked me about *Brilliance,* and there's something special about the painting I'd like to share with you."

"Tell me."

"I'd rather show you," Andi said. She turned towards the limestone reef and beyond to the gentle ocean swell. "Just let your eyes adjust to the darkness."

The wind had completely dropped. They sat close, thighs touching. Caitlin could hear the quickening pulse of her own heartbeat and the rhythm of Andi's steady breathing with the gentle rise and fall of her chest.

Andi entwined their fingers and placed their hands in her lap. Caitlin watched in awe as the red, pink, and yellow of twilight emerged and then faded within minutes. As the heavens around them darkened, a faint glow appeared on the horizon, and the rock pools glistened. They reflected the remaining light and danced with shadows—interlocking hues of turquoise and indigo.

Hypnotised by the spectacle, Caitlin murmured, "*Brilliance*." The vision emerging before them was almost too beautiful. "You captured it perfectly. It's unbelievable, Andi, the magical way you worked the lapis lazuli. The beautiful precious blue, the luminosity, and the subtle variety of colours, the light and shade in your composition."

Caitlin turned to look at Andi, whose eyes sparkled with desire in the last slivers of light.

Andi pulled Caitlin into her arms. "You inspired *Brilliance*. You inspired me to achieve so much more than I ever thought possible." Her voice was strong and steady. "My life has changed with you in it. With you, there will always be light at the edge of the darkness. You are where the light plays."

"And I'm supposed to be the poet." Caitlin sighed. She leaned back and met Andi's gaze. "You think?"

Andi gently poked her in the ribs.

Her heart filled with love, she grabbed Andi in a playful embrace, and they rolled onto the cool sand and landed in a breathless heap of tangled limbs. Andi began to giggle, and soon they both were convulsed with laughter.

Caitlin crushed her mouth to Andi's, and their lips fused in a hot, searing, passionate kiss.

About C. Fonseca

As a small child, C. Fonseca had imaginary friends. She told these friends stories, and her family set them places at the dinner table. When she grew up, she lost the imaginary friends, but she continued writing stories and poetry.

She was an executive chef for many years until a car accident stopped her in her tracks and forced her to change direction and become a tech geek. She is now known in her community as the "help-desk".

She lives by the sea with her Kiwi partner of fifteen years and their beloved Burmese cat. She is an expressionist landscape painter and can often be found at a cliff-top platform overlooking the Southern Ocean, daydreaming, plotting, and planning her creative adventures.

CONNECT WITH C. FONSECA:

Facebook: www.facebook.com/cfonseca1au
E-Mail: cfonseca1au@gmail.com

Other Books from Ylva Publishing

www.ylva-publishing.com

Rewriting the Ending

hp tune

ISBN: 978-3-95533-503-8
Length: 286 pages (10,7000 words)

A chance meeting in an airport lounge and a shared flight itinerary leaves Juliet and Mia connected. But how do you stay connected when you've only known each other for twenty four hours, are destined for different continents, and each of you have a past to reconcile?

Stowe Away

Blythe Rippon

ISBN: 978-3-95533-523-6
Length: 279 pages (97,500 words)

Brilliant, awkward Samantha Latham couldn't wait to leave rural Stowe for an illustrious career in medicine. But when an unexpected call from a hospital forces Sam to move back home to care for her ailing mother, a life of boredom and isolation seems imminent—until a charming restaurant owner named Maria inspires Sam to rethink everything she knows about Stowe, success, and above all, love.

Collide-O-Scope

(Norfolk Coast Investigation Story – Book #1)

Andrea Bramhall

ISBN: 978-3-95533-573-1
Length: 370 pages (90,000 words)

One unidentified dead body. One tiny fishing village. Forty residents and everyone's a suspect. Where do you start? Newly promoted Detective Sergeant Kate Brannon and Kings Lynn's CID have to answer that question and more as they untangle the web of lies wrapped around the tiny village of Brandale Stiathe Harbour to capture the killer of Connie Wells.

Times of Our Lives

Jane Waterton

ISBN: 978-3-95533-417-8
Length: 244 pages (60,500 words)

For the residents of OWL's Haven, Australia's first exclusively lesbian retirement community, life is about not being afraid to take chances. Together, Meg, Allie and their spirited group of friends share their lives, hopes and dreams, proving that whatever the setbacks, hearts that love are always young.

Coming from Ylva Publishing

Welcome to the Wallops

Gill McKnight

The villages of High Wallop and Lesser Wallop have graced either end of the Wallop valley since medieval times. And competition between the two has never ceased since, especially over the famous Cheese and Beer festival.

As head Judge of Show, Jane Swallow has always struggled to keep peace, friendship, and equanimity within the community she loves, but this year everything is wrong. Her father has just been released from prison and is on his way to Lesser Wallop with the rest of her travelling family and their caravans.

Her job is on the line, and her ex-girlfriend from a million years ago has just moved in next door.

Her life is going down the drain unless she can pull off some sort of miracle.

Flinging It

G Benson

Frazer, head midwife at a hospital in Perth, Australia, is trying to make her corner of the world a little better by starting up a programme for at-risk parents. Not everyone is excited about her ideas. Surrounded by red tape, she finally has to team up with Cora, a social worker who is married to Frazer's boss.

Cora is starting to think her marriage is beyond saving, even if she wants to. Feeling smothered by a domineering spouse, she grabs hold of the programme and the distraction Frazer offers with both hands. Soon the two women get a little too close and find themselves in a situation they never dreamed themselves capable of: an affair.

As the two fall deeper, both are torn between their taboo romance and their morals. But walking away from each other may not be as simple as they thought.

Where the Light Plays

ISBN: 978-3-95533-421-5

Also available as e-book.

Published by Ylva Publishing, legal entity of Ylva Verlag, e.Kfr.

Ylva Verlag, e.Kfr.
Owner: Astrid Ohletz
Am Kirschgarten 2
65830 Kriftel
Germany

www.ylva-publishing.com

First edition: 2016

Credits
Edited by Jove Belle and CK King
Cover Design by Streetlight Graphics

www.ingramcontent.com/pod-product-compliance
Lightning Source LLC
Chambersburg PA
CBHW030938260626
47169CB00002B/529